HELL SHALL MAKE YOU FEAR AGAIN

Jack Finn

For Roxana, my inspiration for all things great and small.

"Hell is empty, and all the devils are here."

WILLIAM SHAKESPEARE, THE TEMPEST

FOREWORD

For millennia, empires have spread across the globe and vanquished civilizations that existed since antiquity. As the victors destroyed the knowledge and cultures of the conquered, they relegated the lore and beliefs of these people to a thing of myth and superstition.

Four hundred thousand years of human history, imbued with the fear and awareness of the horrors that exist in the dark places of our world, was consigned to the flames by armies, conquistadors, settlers, explorers, and missionaries. They believed that the subjugation of the land and its people meant they were the unchallenged masters of their new domains.

However, creatures feared from the first epoch of man still lurk in hidden places, long forgotten but eager to remind us why we should fear the darkness, the shadows, and what comes in the night.

You will not find any Final Girls (or boys) in this book. No priests holding crucifixes and extolling, "The power of Christ compels you," well...at least not successfully.

The stories contained herein are the tales of those who, in their arrogance, greed, or ignorance, traversed lines best never crossed. They stepped off the sunlit path and found the world beyond dark, malevolent, and unforgiving.

As I now sit back and read the pages to come, I recall a quote from Edgar Allen Poe, "*my original soul seemed, at once, to take its flight from my body; and a more than fiendish malevolence, gin-nurtured, thrilled every fiber of my frame.*"

Enjoy the ride.

Heed the warnings.

Sleep tight.

But leave a light on...just to be safe.

All the best,

Jack

CONTENTS

Title Page
Dedication
Epigraph
Foreword
They Come When You Sleep   1
Bee is for Boy   11
Three Girls Swinging in a Tree   41
The Children of Cahokia   49
The Hunters   78
The Feast of Angels   97
Among the Wolves   124
The Eater is Coming   144
The Heart of the Island   158
No Man's Land   185
Wilson   203
The Last Reaping   260
The Vineyard   282
Their Roots Run Deep: October 1404   308
Their Roots Run Deep: October 1604   322

The Tall Man's Disciple	338
Vesuvian's Day	350
By the Light of Day	371
About The Author	391
Books By This Author	393

THEY COME WHEN YOU SLEEP

Katerina turned her head to hide her tears in the straw-filled pillow as she clutched her favorite doll, Sarah, close to her chest. She always tried to be brave for her parents and older sister when they hid in the cellar. The cellar was cold and damp, and she missed her soft bed and warm blankets.

"Hey now, kitty Kat, what's wrong?" Her father sat on the edge of the bed and ran a gentle hand over her hair.

"I'm fine," Katerina sniffed, holding back the tears.

"Well, what about Sarah? Is she ok?" He poked softly at the small raggedy doll.

"Sarah is scared," she rolled over to look at her father's kind face. "She's afraid the bad things are going to get her."

"No, kitty Kat, we're safe in the cellar. There's nothing to worry about."

"How long do we have to keep sleeping in the cellar?"

"Only until it is safe to sleep upstairs in our beds again.

But tomorrow, we can go for a walk in the woods together," he ran his fingers through his dark hair, a habit he had when he felt stressed or worried.

"What if they get into the house?" her eyes suddenly wide with fear.

"If they get into the house, Sergio and Andrew are upstairs; they won't let anything hurt you."

"But Sergio is just a gardener, and Andrew is an old man."

"They are good men; they will protect us," he smiled down at her reassuringly.

"Papa," Katerina sat up with a concerned look. "I forgot my flower up in my bedroom."

"It will be ok," He gently eased her back onto the small bed. "When Sergio comes to check on us, I will ask him to bring it to you."

"You won't forget?"

"I won't forget. I promise."

"Oh, sweetie, there's nothing to be afraid of. Why don't you try and get some sleep."

"Because they always come when you sleep, Papa."

Elena sat on the stairs and watched her husband in the dim candlelight of the cellar as he tried to calm their youngest daughter. Viktor was a good man, a good husband, and a good father. She smiled as she watched him; he looked just as young and handsome as the day they had met so many years ago. A lifetime ago, it seemed, as they sat hiding amongst the shelves of winter preserves and trunks of old clothes in the manor house's cellar.

Beside her sat her eldest daughter, Petia, staring gloomily at the earthen floor.

"What's on your mind?" Elena nudged the brooding teen playfully with her elbow.

"I was just thinking about Tatiana," Petia tried to give a weak smile, but her eyes filled with tears.

"Oh, Petty, that won't happen to you." She ran a hand soothingly across the girl's back.

"Mama, she was my best friend, and now she's gone. She had so many hopes and dreams, and those monsters took her while she slept. No last words. No final thoughts. She went to sleep, and they ended all that she was. Do you remember when Papa brought down that deer last month, and we shared it with Tati's family? How happy she was that night."

"I remember. She was a wonderful girl."

"It's not fair what happened." A tear ran down Petia's cheek.

"No, dear, it's not."

"I want to sleep in my bed. I want to go to sleep and not worry that those monsters will take me while I sleep. Or someone that I love," she ran her thumb over the carved wooden ring on her finger, turning it to see the etched rose in the candlelight.

"You're worried about Tomas." Elena smiled at her daughter and hugged her close.

"I just want a life with him, like you and Papa have."

"You'll have that, Petia. You and Tomas will have a long life together."

"Why is the world like this? Why are there monsters like that?" Petia searched his mother's dark eyes pleadingly.

"Just like we hunt the beasts in the woods, the monsters hunt us."

"But we hunt the deer to eat; they hunt us for sport."

"That is why they are monsters."

"How is Katerina?" Elena looked searchingly into her husband's eyes; the strength she found there always calmed her.

"She's resting, but she refuses to go to sleep." He wrapped his arms around Elena and hugged her.

"Do you blame her?" Elena pressed her head against his chest and held him close; he smelled like elderberry flowers.

"No, of course not. How is Petia holding up?"

"She's still upset over Tatiana and worried about Tomas."

"These are dark, sorrowful times," Viktor kissed his beloved's forehead. "So much death, so much loss. We need to bring the girls someplace beautiful and peaceful. Do you remember that lake in Iskar Gorge?"

"The one with the waterfall," despite all her worry, the memory made Elena smile against his firm chest, feeling safe in his arms. "How can I ever forget our time there?"

"Let's go back there. Take the children to swim in that lake under the moonlight."

"We'll have to wear clothes this time." She pressed her face into his chest and squeezed him tightly.

A knock on the cellar door rang out, followed by another long knock and four in quick succession. Elena turned in alarm, and Petia stood up from her perch on the stairs and stared at the door.

"Papa?" Katerina sat up in alarm.

"It's ok, everyone. Calm down. That is our knock code; it's just Sergio," Viktor looked at each of them assuredly. "Let me go see what he wants."

Viktor climbed the aged stairs and unbolted the thick wooden door. He cracked it open and saw Sergio's dark eyes and bearded face peering at him.

"Mr. Viktor, I'm sorry to disturb you," his deep Spanish-accented voice came across in a hushed tone. "Andrew has seen movement in the garden."

"Thank you for informing me," Viktor's countenance visibly showed his worry.

"You have been very good to me and my family. If it's them, we will do all we can to protect you."

"I know you will," a wordless exchange of respect passed between the two men.

"Good luck, Mr. Viktor. May God protect you."

"I think I'll leave God with you, Sergio. Take care of yourself and Andrew," Viktor closed and bolted the door.

He tried to fix his face into a mask of calm as he walked down the stairs to his family.

"Viktor, what did he want?" Elena spoke the words that all of them were thinking.

"It's fine; it was just Sergio wanting to…." The sounds of a loud crashing noise upstairs cut off his words.

They all stared at the ceiling as a cacophony of noise rang from the floor above them. Breaking glass and banging sounds, followed by a second loud crash.

"They're through the outside door!" gasped Elena as gunshots echoed from the upstairs rooms.

"Girls, I need you to hide." Viktor tried to keep the calm in his voice. "Kat, get behind the shelves; Petia hides in the herb storage under the bed."

Katerina leaped out of bed and ran to the shelving holding the preserves. The space between the shelving and walls was narrow and dark; she hesitated momentarily, thinking of the spiders and creepy crawling things that could be hiding in a place like that. But a banging at the cellar door urged her forward. She wriggled her small body into the tight space until wholly concealed.

"It's all going to be ok, kitty Kat. I need you to be brave and not make a sound no matter what happens. Your mother and I love you very much," Viktor reassured her as she leaned several old, dusty rugs against the side of the shelves to conceal the small opening.

Elena was helping Petia move the bed to access the trap door when the cellar door smashed inwards, sending shards of broken wood tumbling down the stairs.

The sound of a mechanism releasing echoed in the darkness, followed by a feeling of something swooshing through the air and a thwacking sound.

"Mama," Petia said softly and stood straight up, a wooden bolt protruding through her heart and chest.

Elena screamed as her daughter's eyes rolled upwards in her head, and she fell lifelessly onto the bed.

From her hiding place behind the shelves, Katerina peered through a crack and saw dark-cloaked men in hoods running down the stairs, followed by a wild-eyed priest holding a gleaming silver crucifix aloft. Spittle flew from the priest's lips as he screamed verses in Latin she did not understand.

She watched as her father flew across the room and tackled a man struggling to reload a crossbow in the narrow space. Her father's strong arms wrapped tight around the man as he sunk his elongated canines into the man's neck. The man screamed and kicked his legs as another hooded man plunged a wooden stake through her father's back, and his body went limp.

Two men rushed towards her mother, but she quickly batted both men aside, and they landed in crumpled heaps on the floor. She snarled at the priest and flashed her two sharp fangs at him. The priest retreated in terror and raised the silver crucifix. Katerina saw her mother laugh and smack the silver cross from the priest's outstretched hand. Crossbows releasing their bolts sounded from the top of the stairs, and two wooded shafts flew out of the darkness and embedded themselves in her mother's chest. She reached one last time for the priest and then collapsed to the floor.

"Father Grigori, help me," cried the man her father had bitten as he reached out towards the priest.

"He's been bitten, kill him," the priest ordered dispassionately.

"No, please," the man pleaded as one of the hooded figures stepped forward and thrust a wooden stake into the man's chest, silencing him.

The priest surveyed the room as the hooded men carried their dead and wounded up the stairs. He kicked at her mother's corpse and loudly proclaimed, "The Lord's will has been done!"

Katerina shook with terror and held her mouth closed tight, fearing that she would make a sound and give herself away. She watched as the hooded men sunk gleaming silver hooks into her family and dragged them up the stairs like pieces of meat. One of her father's black shoes came loose and tumbled down the stairs to land on the floor.

She stayed hidden behind the shelves for a long time, trembling and crying. Only when she heard the hoot of a barn owl outside did she feel it was nighttime and safe to go out. Katerina pushed aside the rugs and wriggled out from behind the shelves. She was covered in dust and cobwebs but did not attempt to brush herself off.

Bending down, she picked up her father's shoe and walked up the cellar stairs and through the shattered remnants of the door. Sergio lay dead in a pool of blood in the house's foyer, his body riddled with bullet holes. His eyes stared sightlessly at the ceiling, and she knelt, gently ran her hand over his face, and closed them so he could rest peacefully.

She found kind, old Andrew hanging from the staircase, his hands bound behind his back and a tight noose around his neck. Katerina tried not to look up at his face, choosing instead to remember him as she saw him every evening when she awoke with his wide grin and boisterous laugh.

The house felt strange to her, lacking in the warmth and laughter that used to fill its halls. She walked to her room and retrieved the small flower pot from the window. It was a night-blooming cereus, and its white flower reflected the bright moonlight. She smiled down at the little flower, remembering the day her father had given it to her. With a sad sigh, she placed the little flower pot in the opening of her father's shoe. She cradled it in her arm and left her room and all its happy memories for the last time.

The night air was cool upon her face as she walked outside. A burnt smell filled her nostrils, and she looked sadly at the three scorch marks on the lawn where the sun had turned her family's bodies to ash. The very place they had all laughed and danced together under the moonlight only a week before. Then her back went rigid, and a shiver of fear ran down her spine as she realized she was not alone in the front yard.

A dark figure stood by the scorch marks with his back to her; the shadows cast by the moonlight had hidden him from sight until her eyes adjusted to the night. Katerina watched as the figure stooped down and laid a single red rose on one of the darkened patches of grass. He cocked his head to the side, sticking his fingers into the scorched grass. Then the figure stood up and stared down into his hand.

Katerina walked silently up behind him and saw that he held a small wooden ring, a rose finely etched on its surface. He sensed her presence and turned, his handsome face a mask of alarm that quickly gave way to relief.

"Katerina, you're alive," the man breathed deeply as if he had been holding his breath. "I feared the worst."

"Tomas," the little girl collapsed into the man, finally letting herself give in to her grief. "I hid when the monsters came."

"You're safe now; I won't let anything happen to you."

"I'm sorry about Petia," her chest heaved with great sobs, the tears streaming down her face. "She loved you so much."

"I loved her too. She was my little rose petal," he looked down at the wooden ring in his palm as a tear slowly escaped his eye.

"I am going to miss them so much."

"I am too. Every moment of every day."

"Will the monsters find us?" She looked up into his face, the streaks of tears on her cheeks glittering in the moonlight.

"No, Katerina, the monsters won't find us," he looked down at her and then over at the three scorched patches of grass. "Because we are going to find them first."

BEE IS FOR BOY

James Harris felt the satisfying crunch against the soft skin of his palms as he slapped his hands together. He blew the crumpled body of the bee out his son's bedroom windows and slid it shut with the urgency of a man trying to seal the space off from a deadly contagion. Holding his hand up to the daylight, he searched his palms for the pinprick mark of a bee sting.

No holes. No redness. No swelling.

James had not realized he was holding his breath until he exhaled deeply and let his hands fall to his sides. He hated spring and the swarms of bees that danced among the flowers. It made him feel emasculated to carry an EpiPen with him everywhere. He swore he could always spot the bemused look on people's faces as their eyes trailed to the back pocket of his jeans, the slim auto-injector filled with epinephrine, and the dawning knowledge that the burley, six foot-five former high school football star could be felled by his body's allergic reaction to a sting from a bee, a thumbnail-sized insect. Time and again, his wife told him it was all in his imagination, but he knew the people in town snickered behind his back about his allergy.

After their son, Jaime, was born, James brought the child to an allergist who confirmed that the child had inherited his father's allergy to bee stings. James was devastated by the news until the doctor assured him that Jaime's bee allergy scored much lower on the allergen scale. While James had a life-threatening Class Six bee allergy, Jaime only scored on the high end of Class Three and was unlikely to manifest anything more than moderate swelling around a sting.

"I assure you, these things are very common," the doctor explained to James. "Parents do not just pass along their physical characteristics to their children. While it is true that parents can pass along an allergy, physical infirmity, or even mental health issues through their DNA, they also pass along such wonderful things as musical talent, academic aptitude, and artistic abilities. Believe me, James, as Jaime grows, you will see that you have passed along to him far more than just your allergy."

Jaime was now thirteen, and aside from a few swollen bites over the years, the boy's allergy left him relatively unscathed. James looked around his son's bedroom, the walls covered with posters of Marvel Universe characters, and frowned at the unmade bed.

Where had the boy gotten off to? James knew being a long-haul trucker for Stan R's Rolling Rigs did not leave him much father-son time, but the kid was always up for a ride to Home Depot with his old man.

James looked down at his hand as he left the room and noticed a small, black filament sticking to his thumb's side. One of the unfortunate bee's legs had dislodged when he crushed it. He wiped his hand clean on his blue jeans with a look of disgust and closed the door behind him.

◆ ◆ ◆

Thursday

Jaime sat in the back seat of his father's Ford pickup truck and tapped on the side of the small cardboard box in his lap. He could hear the creature's exoskeleton rubbing against the cardboard walls as a slender green leg tentatively touched one of the box's air holes.

"That's the first time I have ever seen a praying mantis for sale at Home Depot," Jamie's father's dark eyes glanced up to look at him in the truck's rearview mirror. "I've seen them selling ladybugs to eat the aphids but never a praying mantis."

"Yeah, it's so cool," Jaime peered through the air hole into the darkened box. He could see the long slender silhouette of the mantis with its small triangular head.

"Hey, if your mom asks, just tell her it eats lettuce and stuff like that," his father smiled and winked at him in the rearview. "Let's just keep it between us that it eats bugs. Your mother doesn't need to know that there's a dangerous predator in the house. Ok, kiddo?"

"Ok, Dad," Jaime replied without taking his eyes off the box.

Jaime reached out and lightly touched the slender, spiked raptorial foreleg that protruded from the air hole; a wicked smile crossing his face.

The praying mantis crawled up the stick, the only ornament in its new home in the old Folgers instant coffee jar. Its triangular head rotated upward to study the patch of window screening covering the jar's opening and affixed in place by a rubber band, its antennas twitching.

Jaime sat at his desk watching the mantis as he quickly thumbed through his dog-eared copy of *The Bees in Your Backyard: A Guide to North America's Bees*. It had been a birthday gift from his mother three years ago. He remembered how his father rolled his eyes and shook his head as Jaime held up the gleaming white with the picture of a giant yellow and black honey bee emblazed across the cover.

"Bees are amazing and fascinating creatures," his mother had cajoled her husband. "It will be good for him to see they are more than flying stingers."

"Bees are just mosquitos on steroids. They are vermin. Monsanto would do us a favor to eradicate both from the earth," James Harris folded his arms across his chest.

"Well, if there were no bees, there would BEE no fruits, vegetables, chocolate, coffee, or nuts," Jaime's mother playfully poked at his father, trying to turn his sour mood around.

"I love it," Jaime's eyes lit up excitedly as he leafed through the book's colorful pages.

Jaime did love the book. It was his favorite birthday gift that year. He loved it more than the video games, the comic books, Marvel action figures, and certainly more than the Thor pajamas from his grandparents.

Most ten-year-old boys would have groaned at such an educational gift, but not Jaime. He loved it because it told him everything he needed to know about bees- his arch-nemesis.

Earlier that summer, Jaime had made two important discoveries, both because of his father. When the elder Harris switched the family's cell phone plan from Verizon to T-Mobile, a free subscription to Disney+ and its treasure trove of movie properties was an added perk.

Jaime sat up in his room, watching hours of Marvel superhero movies. He loved the superpowers, the battles, and the eye-popping special effects. But most of all, Jaime loved the villains. Thor, Ironman, Spiderman, Captain America, and all the rest of the Avengers seemed boring and lame to the ten-year-old. However, Jaime reveled in the cackling Green Goblin, the scheming plans of Loki, and the raw power of Thanos. He spent his weekly allowance buying comic books at the local Walgreens and hanging their posters on his walls.

Villians had a plan, cool weapons, and almost always had a score to settle with someone. To Jaime's immense disappointment, every movie ended the same way, with the heroes ganging up on the villain to win the day. Lame. Boring. Why shouldn't Loki rule Asgard? Why can't Thanos be all-powerful?

Jaime's second discovery that summer was that his bee allergy was not a myth. He was sitting cross-legged in the grass, waiting for his turn to rotate into the soccer game at the Bight Summer Day Camp his parents had sent him to, when he felt a sharp pain on his upper lip. He frantically swatted at his face, crushing a black and yellow bee across his mouth and cheek.

His sudden cry of pain was loud enough to stop the soccer game and bring the camp counselors and children alike running over to where he lay sprawled on the grass. As if sobbing uncontrollably in front of the other campers was not embarrassing enough, his top lip reddened and swelled to the size of a golf ball at the site of the bee sting.

As one of the camp counselors led him off to the nurse's office, Jaime could hear the laughing and joking starting to ripple through the assembled children.

"I hope you're ok Jaim-Bee," called a large red-haired boy, followed by a chorus of laughter from the other children.

Jaime could hear one of the counselors scolding the boy, but he also heard several children giggling as they referred to him as "Bee Boy."

As Jaime lay on a cot in the nurse's office, waiting for his mother to pick him up, a zip-lock bag filled with ice pressed against his lip, the two discoveries gelled in his mind. He envisioned himself as cunning as Loki, as ruthless as the Green Goblin, and as powerful as Thanos as he waged war on his arch nemesis, the bees.

After begging his parents not to send him back to summer camp after the embarrassing episode, Jaime began his war of extermination on the bee kingdom. Armed with a rolled-up newspaper, he stalked his mother's flowerbed and garden, swatting hapless bees from the air and stomping them underneath his sneakers.

Jaime's mother stormed out of the house and took the newspaper from him. She scolded him that none of her tomato plants would fruit if he kept up this behavior. However, when his father came home that night and witnessed the bee carnage on the walkway, he nodded to his son and told him it was a good start, just be careful not to get himself stung again. Jaime smiled with delight at his father's praise, even though it made his swollen lip ache terribly.

"I was just like you as a kid," Jaime's father stared at his son for a long moment, eyeing the child curiously.

Later that summer, his mother's birthday gift of *The Bees in Your Backyard* became the battle plan for his war on bees. The book said dandelions were an essential first food of spring for bees, so Jaime stomped every dandelion he could find. He stalked the woods behind his house with his super soaker filled with white vinegar from the kitchen and gleefully sprayed a beehive nestled in the branches of a pine tree after reading that vinegar was lethal to bees.

Jaime slipped a six-pack of Pepsi from his father's stash in his sleek, black Peterbilt Model 389 semi-truck. He discovered the sodas a week earlier when he spied the corner of the blue soda box peeking out from behind the red and white Make America Great Again flag hanging over the bed in the back of the truck's sleeper cab. When he lifted the flag, Jaime found three cases of

Pepsi stacked on the over-the-bed shelf alongside a box of Hershey bars, a gallon of Clorox bleach, a bottle of Nailite acetone, and some Walmart dish towels.

Jaime poured all six sodas into an old white bucket behind the house after discovering in the book that unattended sodas posed a hazard to bees. They would mistake the sugary scent for a blossoming flower, swoop in, and drown.

The morning after he set the Pepsi trap, Jaime rushed outside and was delighted to find five bees floating in the dark liquid. The trap worked so well that he began to keep track in a black-and-white notebook of his daily tally, reaching a kill count as high as nine in a single day before his father discovered the bucket and poured it out, mistaking it for dirty water. After that, Jaime moved his trap into the woods with a fresh six-pack of Pepsi and enjoyed even high rates of daily bee mortality. He especially liked when a bee would still be wriggling its legs, trying to free itself from a sugary demise, and he would continuously dunk it under the dark waters with a stick until it floated motionless.

By the time he was thirteen, Jaime had honed himself into a supervillain that he had imagined bee mothers had warned their children about at bedtime. When he swatted a bee near the house, he liked to think these were bee superheroes sent to defeat him but failed and died.

Jaime still made his Pepsi traps, which he named Sweet Death. He also added new variants to his arsenal, including one that lored in specifically yellow jackets with meat and drowned them in soapy water that he called Meat Death.

When he spotted the boxes of praying mantis' by the checkout counter at Home Depot, a plan that would make Loki proud caressed the corners of his mind. Now, he could feel the mantis' bulbous eyes staring at him from within the jar as he turned the book's pages. Jaime found what he sought with a triumphant laugh and tapped the picture on the page. The image took up a full half-page of the book, showing a large, green praying mantis clutching a bee in its raptorial forelegs.

Jaime looked from the picture to the mantis in the jar, a malicious smile crossing his face. The arch villain now had a monster to unleash upon the bees.

◆ ◆ ◆

Friday

For most of the day at school, Jaime sat thinking about how to employ the mantis that weekend. Last weekend, he spotted a bee nest forming on an oak tree in the woods. The worker bees were still building the honeycomb structure, and he fantasized about the mantis tearing its way through the thin walls of the nest to get at the plump queen.

The nascent hive nestled in the crook where a low-hanging branch met the old oak's trunk, ideally located for the morning sun to heat the nest and the shade to keep it from overheating in the afternoon. Jaime had contemplated taking it out with the vinegar in the super soaker on the spot but decided to let the worker bees toil away for another week. He had read that it takes up to fourteen days for a new nest to become fully populated, so he felt another week would make it ripe for conquest.

He envisioned the mantis descending upon the hive like an insectoid Godzilla emerging from the waters of Tokyo Bay to lay waste to the city. Jaime mulled over the problem of the mantis in his mind. The bees provided an easy and ample food source, but the mantis had wings and could fly off once released. He thought about clipping the mantis' wings with a nail clipper, but in the end, he decided to tie a kite string around the insect and affix the other end to the ground. Just enough line to reach the hive, so the mantis would have to go for the bees to feed. Jaime supposed the string would inhibit the mantis from successfully evading a crow that saw the long insect as a quick and satisfying meal; however, if Loki or the Green Goblin never scraped a plan because of the risks, then neither would he.

So all day at school, Jaime occupied his thoughts with his self-ascribed cunning plan. He had a few friends at school, more acquaintances than friends, just some other boys he sat with at lunch and chatted with about movies, video games, and school gossip. However, he never shared his plans with them.

School rarely held Jaime's attention for long, though his grades were consistently above average, and this day was the same. The only exception was Mr. Kriaris' sociology class, which focused the afternoon discussion on the phenomenon of serial killers in society. On most days, Mr. Kriaris seemed as bored by discussions of social change and the impact of human behavior on society as the rest of the class. However, the ordinarily sedate teacher seemed electrified by the recent storm of media coverage of the hunt for the "Sixty-Six Strangler," a serial killer responsible for the murder of at least thirty-two homeless people along the stretch of highway between Chicago, Illinois, and Santa Monaca, California.

"Serial killers often start their careers by torturing or killing small animals," the rail-thin teacher tapped a cigarette-stained finger on the laptop's keyboard and the PowerPoint projected onto the screen at the front of the darkened classroom toggled through a series of grim-faced mugshots.

"They choose animals because they are weak and vulnerable," Mr. Kriaris continued as a picture of a handsome, smiling, dark-haired man appeared on the screen. "Ted Bundy was known to derive pleasure from torturing cats and dogs. I suspect that once the Sixty-Six Strangler is apprehended, similar details will emerge about him."

"Or her," Seol-Hyun raised her hand and added from the back of the room.

"Or her," Mr. Kriaris nodded and smiled at the correction, apparently thrilled with the rare class participation in a lesson.

Jaime was disappointed his teacher arrived at such a simplistic solution. He had spent hours dissecting live bees, watching them slowly suffocate in enclosed jars, starve on glue traps, or react when sprayed with various chemicals. While Jaime admittedly enjoyed it, he did not think it was fair to say he did it for pleasure. He did this to hone his knowledge of his foe. *"If you know the enemy and know yourself, you need not fear the result of a hundred battles."* That was straight out of the mouth of the Chinese tactician Sun Tzu from the sixth century BC.

Jaime imagined it was the same for serial killers; they did these things to increase their understanding, not for pleasure. Whatever his motivation, the Sixty-Six Strangler was abducting and killing homeless people, so Jaime thought it would be logical for the killer to start with animals to perfect his craft and lessen the chance of making a mistake that could get them caught.

Jaime attributed this to a need for more critical thinking to reverse a dumbing down of people that started with fairy tales and continued in every movie, book, and television show. The bad guys are cruel and evil, and the good guys are pure and innocent.

Many people were troubled by the growth of homelessness in America; he had heard his father go on endlessly about the topic. Jaime felt he was one of the few people cerebral enough to consider that, whether misguided or not, the Sixty-Six Strangler was one of the few people doing something about the growing homelessness epidemic. However, society ascribed serial killers as the bad guys, just like in movies, so their only conceivable motivation was to do evil.

Jaime imagined raising his hand and pointing out this flaw in society, and since this is a sociology class, is that not what we should be discussing? He would rest his case with the profound statement, "What if Loki wanted to rule Asgard because he thought Odin was doing a pretty crappy job of it, and Thor only stopped him so he could look like the hero and bang a harem of valkyries? History is written by the victors, after all."

Jaime envisioned the class staring at him with awestruck faces and Mr. Kriaris nodding thoughtfully at his revelation and keen observation.

It occurred to Jaime that serial killers were no different than supervillains, and he imagined a classroom full of bees looking at his grinning picture on a screen and shrinking back in terror. The thought made him smile.

A crumpled-up paper ball bounced off the side of his face and landed on his desk, jolting him from his daydream.

"What are you smiling about Jaim-Bee?" a blonde-haired kid with the buzz cut smirked at him from the next row of desks. "You gay for Ted Bundy?"

Jaime glanced over at Scott McNulty; the boy had been there that day on the soccer field when he got his bee sting and was singlehandedly responsible for spreading the nickname around the school. Behind Scott, Jenna Wilson, a gangly blonde girl with large blue eyes, snickered and laughed.

"Freakin' weirdo," the voice of T.J. Edwards, a new student whose family moved to town from Sierra Leone only two weeks ago, whispered in a thick West African accent.

Jaime swatted the ball of paper from his desk and stared at the projection screen at the front of the room as Mr. Kriaris droned on; his smile was gone. He imagined what it would be like to have Scott McNulty suffocating in one of his jars, eyes bulging and face reddening as he gasped for air. Jamie pictured Jenna Wilson struggling to stay afloat in a life-size version of Sweet Death, blonde hair matted to her face as her limbs desperately sought purchase.

He glanced sidelong at Scott and Jenna, who continued to whisper and snicker. How easy it would be to become their supervillain. The comic book of his origin story would start on that soccer field with their mocking laughter. It would cover the years of name-calling and shoves in the hall juxtaposed with Jaime mastering the ways of revenge and end with these two teenaged Ken and Barbies covered in dirt out in the woods.

Maybe one day.

◆ ◆ ◆

Saturday

Jaime carefully cradled the jar containing the mantis as he walked up the dirt path from the subdivision into the woods. Ultimately, tying the kite string around the mantis proved easier than he expected. The insect proved very docile as he held it in his hand and affixed the line around its upper body, just below its raptorial forelegs, to not interfere with the mantis' ability to extend its wings. He winced when he tied the string tight and heard a subtle crack in the insect's exoskeleton; however, the mantis seemed still functioning normally.

Kelly Burns, a small dark-haired girl in a flowery pink dress, casually swung an old blonde ragdoll as she exited the woods in front of Jaime. Her eyes immediately went to the jar in his hand, and he reflectively covered it.

"What's that, Jaime?" the ten-year-old girl craned her neck to glimpse the jar.

"It's nothing," Jaime covered it with his hand as he walked past her.

"Aw, come on, Jaime, let me see," disappointment crossed her young face, and then it lit up with joy as an idea struck her mind. "I can take you to something cool in the woods if you show me."

"What is it?" Jaime was annoyed at how interested his voice sounded.

A broad smile crossed Kelly's face, "Show me the jar first."

"Fine," Jaime moved his hand, and Kelly peered at the jar. He saw the questioning look on her face, "it's a praying mantis; they eat other bugs."

"But why is a string tied to it?" she tapped on the glass jar, and the insect turned its triangular head to study her.

"So it doesn't fly away," Jaime tried to mimic his father's look when telling his son something he thought was obvious.

The young girl contemplated his words momentarily and nodded, apparently content with the answer.

"So what is it you wanted to show me?" Jaime covered the jar back up with his hand.

"C'mon, I'll show you," Kelly turned back toward the woods. "It's so cool."

Jaime followed her into the woods, watching her doll's blond yarn-like hair bob up and down with each step. Walking behind her, he was reminded of sitting on the couch and watching the movie *My Girl* with his mother one afternoon. In the film, a young boy, played by a spectacled Macaulay Culkin, stumbles across a bee's nest while walking in the woods and is repeatedly stung until he ultimately dies of anaphylactic shock. Jaime imagined bringing Kelly to the old oak tree and throwing her little doll over by the branch with the bee hive and then striking the nest with a thrown rock when she went to retrieve it. If the bees stung her repeatedly and she died, the whole town would recognize the value of his bee-killing expertise. However, he quickly dismissed the notion after surmising that Kelly would likely survive the bee encounter since she did not have any bee allergy that he knew of, and tell her parents and get him in trouble.

"There it is," Kelly turned to him, beaming as she pointed at a small patch of grass between two trees a few feet from the dirt path. "Isn't it cool?"

Jaime squinted his eyes, staring at the area between the trees but saw nothing of note. He looked at her questioningly, and she rolled her eyes and threw her arms up in the air in exasperation.

"C'mon," she walked off the path toward the two trees and glanced down at her doll. "I would never have found it; Mrs. Beasley told me where to look."

"Who's Mrs. Beasley?" Jaime glanced down at the jar to check on the mantis, and the insect seemed unfazed by the jostling as its spiky legs clung to the branch inside.

"Mrs. Beasley," Kelly held the doll out. "She was my grandmother's; she tells me all kinds of things."

Jaime stared at the cloth doll; the eyes, nose, and mouth were sewn from faded black string, and she wore an equally faded red and white checkered dress. The graying, once-white cloth of her arms and legs ended in non-descript round ends without any discernable hands or feet. "Your grandmother tells you things?"

"No, silly," Kelly pursed her lips in annoyance. "Mrs. Beasley tells me things. Here it is, see." She pointed down to the patch of grass between the trees.

Jaime stared at a perfect circle three feet wide, ringed by a perimeter of white mushrooms with plump rounded caps atop thick stems. The grass inside the ring was an even darker shade of green than the grass outside.

"Very cool," Jaime eyed the circle. "Something must have died between the trees; I bet it was a raccoon or maybe a fox."

"No," the look of exasperation had returned to Kelly's young face. "It's a fairy ring. Mrs. Beasley told me the forest spirits put the mushrooms there so they had a place to sit after they got tired of dancing inside the circle."

"I don't think Mrs. Beasley knows what she is talking about," Jaime reached down to pluck one of the mushrooms. "I'm pretty sure these grow on dead things."

"Don't do that," Kelly's voice was shrill and panicked as she grabbed his hand. When he looked at her, the young girl's eyes were wide and full of fear. She spoke in a low, hushed tone. "You never mess with a fairy ring. It's a sacred place. If you disturb it, you'll anger the forest spirits."

"I'm sick of these baby games," Jaime yanked his hand out of her grasp. "I have more important things to do."

Jaime turned and left her standing there as he headed back toward the path and the old oak tree. He looked back to ensure she was not following him and saw she was still there, looking down at the ring of mushrooms. However, how she held the old doll made it appear that the doll's faded black eyes were watching him over her shoulder as he walked away.

Jaime had perfectly judged the distance between the beehive and the heavy branch on the ground; he was sure of it. He praised himself for his ingenuity, there was just enough kite string for the mantis to reach the bees' nest, and with the other end tied to the branch, the insect would have no choice but to attack the hive.

Behind him, the audible buzz of the bees filled the air with a steady thrumming, like an idling motor. There was a lot more activity around the nest than he expected. The bees seemed agitated by his presence close to the oak tree, and Jaime smiled as he took that as a clear sign the queen was inside.

He should have kept an eye on the beehive as he tied the kite string, but he was too busy picturing the mantis grasping the queen in its spiked forelegs. The pain in the back of his neck had been as sharp as it was sudden; he lost his balance and fell backward as he swatted the bee and felt its body crunch against the skin just above his collar. His foot had toppled over the jar, and he watched the mantis fly off into the sky. Jaime's eyes widened in horror as the loose end of the string fluttered behind the mantis as the insect climbed toward the tree's upper branches. He leaped and tried to catch the kite string, but his fingers only grasped air as the mantis flew out of reach. He cursed as he realized the bee had stung him before he could tie the end of the line to the fallen branch.

He paced angrily around the clearing, eyes fixed upon the length of string that dangled down from the mantis perch high up in the tree. The mantis would come down, and when it did, Jaime would grab the line and secure it to the branch. He would wait all afternoon if necessary.

However, the number of bees flying around the hive steadily increased, and Jaime swatted at them to keep them away as he backed further and further out of the clearing. Anger and frustration surged through Jaime's body at his foiled plan, stoked further by the burning pain of the bee sting on his neck. A bee landed on his pants leg, and only the thickness of his jeans saved him from another sting as he mashed the bug with his hand.

It was only a matter of time before another one of the angry insects landed a lucky sting, but another idea returned as he turned from the clearing and headed back down the path. He would throw Kelly and her ugly doll into the clearing; with this many bees as agitated as they were, she might be stung hundreds of times. He knew enough bee stings could be fatal, even for someone without an allergy.

"It takes approximately nine stings per pound of a person's weight for bee venom to be fatal," Jaime's thoughts raced as he stalked down the path.

As small and skinny as Kelly was, this could work. He would throw her back in again if she managed to leave the clearing. As long as no one heard her screaming, Jaime felt confident she would be stung enough times to die. Then it would be open season on bees; he smiled at the plan.

The smile quickly faded from Jaime's face as the path wound around the bend, and he saw the two trees with their odd patch of grass. Kelly was gone. He searched further up the trail and in the woods, but the child was nowhere to be found.

Jaime screamed in frustration. Everything had gone wrong. Then his eyes glanced down to the ring of mushrooms that circled the grass between the trees.

"Her precious fairy ring," Jaime imitated the girl's voice as a wicked smile crossed his lips.

He raised one foot, brought it down on the first mushroom, and reveled in the squishing feeling of the fungus beneath his sneaker. Jaime squashed another and then another, stomping his feet up and down on the mushroom until it appeared like he was dancing wildly on the little circle of mushrooms. He roared with laughter as he crushed the mushrooms, and in his madness, Jaime thought he detected an answering howl of wind among the trees.

Sweat poured from his brow and down his back when he finished. Jaime laughed and smiled from ear to ear as he surveyed the devastation he had wrought on the circle of mushrooms. Not a single stem stood; all that remained of Kelly's fairy ring were chunky smears of white and brown amidst the dark green grass.

"That felt good," Jaime panted from the exertion. "That felt very good."

A strong, cold wind blew through the woods, and the branches of the two trees beside the defiled fairy ring creaked dangerously. Jaime breathed deeply, trying to fill his lungs as the adrenaline of his chaotic dance of destruction among the mushrooms ebbed. However, the air stung his lungs, and his breath became a hacking cough that left his mouth tasting bitter and ashy.

Jaime tried spitting several times to get the taste from his mouth, but it did nothing to alleviate the acrid flavor on his tongue. His mouth tasted like he had been gnawing on a charred piece of wood. He sniffed the air, but it smelled fresh and clean, with no hint of smoke or fire.

The bee sting on his neck began to throb, and he reflexively raised a hand to the inflamed area. He grimaced and frowned at the feel of the golf ball-sized lump forming behind his head. Spitting another bitter-tasting wad of saliva onto the ground, Jaime started toward his house to get some hydrocortisone cream for the sting and maybe grab another of his father's Pepsi sodas to wash the terrible taste from his mouth.

Jaime lay in his bed, glowering at the ceiling. He slid his hand behind his head and poked the swollen bee bite on his neck. The skin was tender to the touch, but Jaime pressed on it until the pain almost brought tears to his eyes. He gritted his teeth at the pain, letting it feed his anger.

"Stupid," Jaime closed his hand into a fist so hard his fingernails dug into his palm. "Stupid, stupid mistake."

The mantis was gone, and the bees had won the day. The thought infuriated him. Tomorrow he would fill his super soaker with lighter fluid, douse the nest, and roast the queen bee inside. The idea made him smile; he envisioned the queen hearing the popping sound of the worker bees exploding as they were immolated by the flames eating their way through the hive walls to her resting place.

Jaime laughed out loud, a malicious sound filled with scorn, as he pictured Kelly's distraught cries at finding her fairy ring destroyed. "Mrs. Beasley didn't tell you about that, eh?"

His laugh turned into a cough, and he winced at the return of the acrid taste in his mouth. It had subsided some since he got home, but he could not wholly get the bitter taste from his mouth; even the pizza he had for dinner tasted ashy. He eyed the half-full cup of Coca-Cola, his mother's beverage of choice, on his nightstand but dismissed the thought of taking a sip when he saw the dark liquid had gone flat.

To make matters worse, his father caught him sneaking into the sleeper cab of the Peterbilt to grab a Pepsi and was furious. His father grabbed Jaime's arm so hard that he cried out in pain as he pulled him out of the truck's cab. Jaime had gotten in trouble with his father before but never saw his father's face so red and contorted with anger.

"This truck is my space," spittle flew from his father's mouth as he screamed. "You have a whole goddamn house and yard to play in, but you keep your ass out of my truck. Do you understand me?"

Jaime almost wet his pants as his father shouted the last four words just inches from his face, and all he could do was nod in response.

He loved his father; at least, he thought he did. However, Jaime often fantasized about his father becoming the Sixty-Six Strangler's next victim, his dark eyes bulging from his blue face as the killer choked him. He pictured being interviewed by all the news outlets about the loss of his father and the sympathetic look on CNN's Erin Burnett's face as he told her about the GoFundMe page he had created. Jaime bet he could get at least a half million dollars, maybe even more.

The back of his neck throbbed, and Jaime's countenance darkened as he imagined Scotty McNulty approaching him in the hallway and pressing the bee sting like a button as the other kids laughed.

If the Sixty-Six Strangler got his dad, he might take the Peterbilt and drive it straight through the schoolyard. He drifted to sleep, imagining the terror on their faces as the big, black semi truck barreled through the schoolyard — thumping their bodies against the grill and crunching their bones under the giant wheels.

❖ ❖ ❖

Sunday

Jaime awoke pleased to find the throbbing in his neck and the bitter taste in his mouth gone. He looked up at the poster of Loki above his bed and blinked. The poster of Loki, played by actor Tom Hiddleston with his long, black hair, shining armor, and red flowing cape staring down at Asgard, looked incredibly huge. It looked billboard-sized, and he noticed Loki's red cape was now a dull black.

He looked around the room, and everything seemed to have grown impossibly large overnight. Jaime tried to rub the sleep from his eyes and froze. His arm looked long and dark, with long straight hairs sticking straight out. Not looked, his arm was long and dark, narrowing to a skinny point that ended in a claw. Jaime's stomach sank, not just a claw but the thin tarsal claw bees used to grip and taste. He raised his other arm and saw a matching appendage.

Jaime's head swam as he looked down at his body, the segmented body of a bee. Six legs protruded from the round middle segment of a body covered in yellow and black hair. He saw the four pairs of wax-producing glands in his lower abdomen section, and then he leaned further forward and groaned. No stinger. That meant this was in the body of a common drone bee, not even a worker.

"This is the lamest dream ever," Jaime shook his head and ran one tarsal claw over the pointed mandible of his mouth. "Yep, definitely a drone bee."

Jaime rolled over and stood on his six legs surveying the vast field of white that it took him a moment to realize was his pillow. He flexed the muscles in his back and was pleased to feel his wings flap in response.

"Well, if I can't sting someone in my dream, I might as well enjoy a little flying," Jaime took a running leap off the pillow.

The cold feel of fear surged through his body as he plummeted the cavernous drop from his pillow to the bedroom floor. He worked his back muscles feverishly, trying to get his fluttering wings to engage. Jaime's bee body had fallen half the distance to the floor before the wings proved some lift, slowing his descent and then soaring up into the sky.

The initial sensation of flying left him feeling dizzy and nauseous as his eyes adjusted to the rollercoaster view of his room swooning before him. However, Jaime was quickly buzzing about the room with skill in no time. Posters and furniture zoomed past his eyes, and he reveled at the ability to land on the wall and upside down on the ceiling.

His antenna twitched, and he felt a surge of pheromones release within his body as he sensed nectar nearby. A sensation he took for a bee's version of hunger filled his body, and he swooped down from the ceiling toward the source of the nectar.

Jaime felt the air brush against the hair on his body as his antennae guided him toward the the nectar. His mind struggled to process the messages the bee's antennae collected and sent to his brain as the room flew by in a rush.

His flight suddenly stopped as he splashed into a dark, viscous liquid. The bee's six legs moved frantically as its wings dampened. Jaime felt panic rise as he struggled to keep the dark sea from rushing into his mouth. The messages his antennae sent to his brain seemed to be misfiring in confusion or overload; he was unsure.

"*Wake up, wake up, wake up,*" the words echoed in his

mind like a mantra as he tried to rouse himself from this nightmare.

Jaime bumped into a transparent wall, and his eyes caught sight of a man with long, dark hair staring down at him. He struggled with recognition momentarily and then realized it was the Loki poster on his wall. His legs paddled below him, trying to keep the insect body afloat.

With growing horror, Jaime realized that his antenna had guided him into the half-drunk glass of Coca-Cola by his bedside. The thought almost made him laugh, trapped in a Sweet Deathtrap.

"Wake up, wake up, wake up."

The legs desperately tread water and moved the little body around the glass like a boat in a small lake. Every time Jaime saw the scowling face of Loki, he knew he had circumnavigated the cup again. His attempts to move his wings again proved futile as the dark, sticky liquid held them close to his body. Inexplicably, the legs on the right side of his body seemed to be tiring faster than those on the left, so he began to list to one side and struggled to keep his mouth from submerging.

"Wake up, wake up, wake up."

Something splashed in the water to his left, and Jaime struggled to turn the bee's body to look. Had the bee had eyelids, they would have opened wide in surprise at the thick white rope that descended into the glass. With the last bit of energy he could muster, Jaime willed the six paddling legs to propel him through the liquid to the rope.

When he reached it, he sank his tarsal claws into

the soft white rope and lay still, his energy wholly expended. Jaime had no idea how he would muster the strength to climb the rope to escape the glass of soda.

"Wake up, wake up, wake up," his voice screamed inside his head. "*I don't like this anymore.*"

Then Jaime heard another voice in his head, a girl's voice that he somehow knew was that of the doll, Mrs. Beasley. It spoke to him in a sing-song tune, "*You never mess with a fairy ring. It's a sacred place. If you disturb it, you'll anger the forest spirits.*" The voice trailed off in laughter that chilled his soul.

Suddenly, Jaime's bee body hoisted high out of the water and into the air as the rope took flight. The rope yanked his small body so severely that he feared his tarsal claws would rip from his limbs. He fluttered chaotically through the air as the line bucked and swayed.

The rope dipped suddenly downward, and he saw bright daylight streaming through his open bedroom window.

"*Wake up. Wake up. Wake up,*" Jaime's voice whimpered inside his head.

The rope struck the white wooden window sill, and Jaime's body came to a crashing stop. He felt two of the tarsal claws on his left side separate from his body, and one of his wings bent with a loud crack.

Jaime freed his remaining tarsal claws from the rope, and he lay on his side, trying to assess the damage to his body. Remarkably, he felt no pain from the damaged limbs; however, he was sure the wing was broken.

A cool wind blew in from the window, and he felt his antennae twitch. Maybe sunlight would rouse him from the dream? Remind his mind that it's time to wake up. Then the doll's words echoed in his head, and he wondered for the first time, could this be real? Some punishment from the forest for his transgression against it?

Jaime refused to believe this could really be happening to him; he pushed his body forward toward the sunlight. It was time to wake up.

A long, dark shadow fell across his body, and he turned his head to find the source. He stared up into the triangular head of the mantis, its raptorial claws rubbing together in a gesture that reminded him of a man rubbing his hands together before a big meal. Jaime's eyes trailed down the long, green body of the mantis to the string that remained tied around its waist.

Jaime could have laughed if he was not so tired and scared; the loose end of the kite rope had saved him from the soda. Was it a coincidence, or did the mantis intentionally pull him from the drink? He did not know but suspected it was the latter.

The creature moved slowly toward him, and something about the look in its insectoid eyes told Jaime that the mantis knew he was more than a common drone bee. Jaime knew what came next, the grasping raptorial claws, dismemberment, and decapitation. He hoped the mantis started with decapitation so that this nightmare could end. Jaime hoped he would wake up; he was not so sure anymore.

The mantis took another step forward, and Jaime thought it was toying with him, prolonging the anticipation of the kill.

"I should have left you to die in that box at Home Depot," Jaime thought as the mantis took another step. "You'd be dead and discarded in the dumpster by now."

The mantis stopped and swiveled its head toward the open window as a shadow blocked the daylight. Jaime watched incredulously as a large, black crow swooped down onto the ledge, the bird's weight cracking the mantis's exoskeleton as it landed on the giant insect. The bird stared at the broken body of the bee curiously with jet black eyes, cocking its head quizzically. Then almost as quickly as it landed, the crow was flying off again, the white line affixed to the mantis body fluttering after it.

Jaime lay there in the sunlight, broken and exhausted. After a time, he tried his wings and found that even with the damaged wing, he could manage a short burst of flight. Though where he would go and what he would do was a mystery to him.

He heard a voice calling his name in the distance and realized it was his father coming down the hall to his room. Hope sprang into the darkness of Jaime's mind as he watched his father enter the room. His father was looking for him. Jaime tried to call out, but no sound emanated from his bee mouth.

A plan formed in Jaime's mind; he could spell something out like that spider in *Charlotte's Web*. Jaime just needed to get his father's attention. As his father passed by the window, Jaime mustered all his strength into his failing wings and leaped into the air.

James Harris felt the satisfying crunch against the soft

skin of his palms as he slapped his hands together. He blew the crumpled body of the bee out his son's bedroom windows and slid it shut with the urgency of a man trying to seal the space off from a deadly contagion. Holding his hand up to the daylight, he searched his palms for the pinprick mark of a bee sting.

No holes. No redness. No swelling.

◆ ◆ ◆

Police Searching For Missing California Boy Make Grim Discovery.

By Anna Levinson, CNN

Updated 9:57 PM EST, Thu January 12, 2023

Police searching for Jaime Harris, who disappeared from his home last Sunday, made a gruesome discovery in the sleeper cab of a semi-truck parked on the family property.

Blood evidence recovered from the 2020 Peterbilt Model 389 semi-truck has been linked to two victims of the Sixty-Six Strangler. Police executing a search warrant of the premises also recovered bleach and acetone, key ingredients in homemade chloroform, from the vehicle. Police Chief Andrew Platt also revealed that specific food and drink were located in the vehicle that matched previously undisclosed evidence discovered in the stomach contents of all the Sixty-Six Strangler victims.

Police took James Harris, the owner of the vehicle and father of the missing boy, into custody late last night on suspicion of murder...

THREE GIRLS SWINGING IN A TREE

The Ancient One strode through the forest, his large root-like feet sinking deep into the fresh New England snow. His green eyes were deep-set in his tree stump-like head, and leaf-covered branches extended upwards and outwards from his head like hair. As he walked past, he stretched two large branch-like arms to touch the trees. Never ceasing dark green vines slithered around his body and limbs like snakes.

A smile crossed his ancient face as his fingertips brushed the trees, and he heard them murmur in greeting; he remembered the mother tree of these old oaks when she was just a tiny sapling pushing through the acorn shell. He reached the tall maple tree he had sought out, his green eyes taking in the snow-covered orb hanging from one of the branches.

With slow, methodical movements, he reached up and gently brushed the snow from the orb, revealing the beehive beneath, careful not to dislodge it from the branch. He listened to the gentle thrum of the buzzing bees inside their winter home and breathed warm breath on the hive to give it added heat.

The smile faded from his face as a ripple of anger and outrage rippled through the forest. He felt it on the wind, through the trees, and up from the earth. There was something amiss in the woods, in his forest.

"*Three girls are swinging in a tree,*" the large black crow landed on his shoulder and cawed softly into his ear. "*The birch along the road to the town, three girls are swinging in the tree.*"

The crow continuously hopped to avoid tangling in the constantly shifting vines that traversed the Ancient One's body. Satisfied the beehive was sufficiently warm, the Ancient One turned his green eyes to the crow and nodded his head. The bird took flight in the direction of the tree, and the girls as the Ancient One followed steadily behind, the roots at the end of his long legs throwing up snow with every long stride.

"*Three girls swinging in a tree,*" he heard the words whispered by the trees as he passed through the forest.

"*Three girls swinging in a tree,*" the wind howled among the branches.

He knew the birch tree the crow spoke of; it stood

high upon the hill overlooking the town. The tree was tall and majestic, and you could see the whole countryside from its strong limbs. His eyes flickered to watch the crow swooping down from the sky to land among the birch's branches. The mid-day winter sun caused small rivers of melted snow to run down the birch's egg-shaped leaves and drip from their triangular tips and serrated edges.

"Three girls swinging in a tree."

The three girls were swinging in the tree by ropes tied to a thick, low-hanging branch, their shoeless feet gliding above the trampled snow at the base of the tree. The Ancient One's green eyes scanned the ropes that looped over their necks, which hung at unnatural angles.

He stood under the three hanging girls; they were teens just entering the first years of womanhood. No snow had accumulated on their white linen bonnets or plain grey dresses, so he knew the Puritans could not have hung them more than a few hours ago. The Ancient One looked sadly into their young faces, the terror of their final moments robbing them of the look of serenity that so many possess as they pass from this world. Their faces were pale and bloodless as their tongues lolled from frozen gaping mouths. A spot of dried blood stained the bonnet and crusted on the forehead of one of the girls. He observed the rock at the base of the tree; the dried red blood and black hairs on the stone stood in sharp contrast to the white snow.

The crow walked curiously along the branch, picking at the ropes that suspended the girls in the air. The Ancient One leaned down to study the white piece of paper nailed to the birch tree, wincing at the scent of hate and malice still lingering on the page. He could read the language the men with the tall, wide-brimmed felt hats, dark, dour clothing, and strange buckled shoes spoke, and his eyes scanned the words.

"...Witch..."

"....attested to by Abigail Cooper, Constance Beamsley, and the widow Mary Thomas...."

"...Witch...

"...judged by Minister Gideon Nash...."

"...Witch..."

"...carried out by Sheriff Nathan Pratt..."

"...Witch..."

"...witnessed by Goodman Newell, Caleb Morey, Isaiah Jones, Blacksmith...."

"...Witch...Witch...Witch..."

He turned his sad green eyes toward the girls and reached his long arms up to the broken bodies. His branch-like hands closed around the ropes tethering them to the tree and broke each like a piece of fine string. The Ancient One cradled the dead girls in his arms with a tenderness that the wicked men in the town had denied them in life.

The crow flew alongside him as he carried them through the forest and down to the river, where he washed away the crusted blood of their wounds and the dried tracks of tears on their cheeks. He discarded the hateful nooses that squeezed their neck and replaced their drab clothing with a winter vine of red berries and silver-green leaves that he wrapped around their bodies.

The Ancient One carried the girls to a peaceful meadow where he often sat and watched the birds glide through the sky. With his strong hands, he dug through the snow and frozen ground until he had cleared a hole large enough for him to lay the girls side by side gently. He placed them face up so that the sun would always shine upon their face.

The crow watched the Ancient One place the middle girl's hands into the hands of the girls on either side of her so that they would never be parted. The Ancient One knelt and sunk his hands deep into the snow until he reached the earth below. In a tongue rarely heard in the world, he sang a song of loss, sorrow, and renewal that echoed through the trees and on the winter wind as he freed the girls' spirits of their broken bodies and joined them with the earth.

With gentle movements of his hand, he covered the girls up with earth; the crow cocked its head and watched as the rich, dark dirt hid their pale faces from the world. The Ancient One smoothed snow over the earthen mound and smiled at the thought that this meadow would be lush with grass and colorful wildflowers in the spring. The crow rested among the branches of his head as the Ancient One sat beside the burial mound and told the girls of all they would see in their meadow. The deer would come to visit them as they grazed in this field, as would the floating butterflies and hardworking bees. The forest's creatures would rest beside them under the sun in the meadow and tell them all the tales of the world. The trees would sing them to sleep at night as the wind blew among their branches.

The sun was hanging low in the sky when the Ancient One left the meadow and returned to the birch tree. The trees rustled and murmured as he passed, his rooted-feet stalking purposefully through the snow.

His hand closed around the hateful note nailed to the tree and crushed it into a ball. The crow perched up on the tree branches as the Ancient One knelt and scooped handfuls of dirt and snow around the crumpled paper. His ancient gnarled fingers collected all the earth that had soaked up the blood, tears, and excrement that left the girls' bodies in those last moments of life and continued to pack it around the paper until he had shaped it into the rough shape of a person.

The Ancient One stuck long fingers into the shape

of the head, creating two sunken eyes sockets. He picked up the bloodied rock and picked off the strands of long dark hair, depositing them on the head. Cupping the stone in his hand, he breathed deeply on it until it felt warm in his hand, then he sank the rock into the snow and earthen chest and patted closed the hole.

Satisfied with his work, he sat down on a large rock and stretched out his long legs. He rested his arms on his knees and placed his chin on his hands as he watched the last embers of sunlight disappear into the night. The moon rose slowly into the sky as he heard the distant church bell of the town toll.

He sat in his quiet vigil as the moon's journey across the sky moved his creation from the shadow of the birch into the full moonlight. The Ancient One watched as the earth and snow coalesced into the form of a person. The empty eye sockets filled with coal-dark blackness, and the few black strands of hair grew into a thick head of long, wild hair that ran down to cover the creature's pale-skinned back and chest. It rose onto long spindly legs and curved black claws sprouted from elongated fingers and toes. The creature's body writhed into the form of a thin, bony woman with sharp, jutting elbows and knees. Desiccated breasts hung down the woman's chest, swaying in the moonlight. Her snow-white face opened into a wide mouth as her black tongue flicked over jagged teeth. She sniffed the air, smelling the scents on the wind.

Her body moved in a shambling, jerking motion as she walked towards the Ancient One, her clawed hand clenching and unclenching. The woman's head sat at an odd angle as if her neck was malformed or had once been broken. The scent of ancient rot and decay reached the crow's nostrils, flitting nervously among the branches as the Ancient One rose from the rock. The woman looked up at him, her empty black eye sockets meeting his green-eyed gaze.

He raised his long arm and pointed toward the town. Her head turned slowly to see the smoke rising from the homes of the sleeping New England town. Snow crunched beneath her bare feet as she turned wordlessly away from the Ancient One. He watched her ungainly stride as she moved down the road to the town.

The crow cawed and landed on his shoulder as the Ancient One listened to the rasping voice of the woman as she ceaselessly began to recite her mantra.

"....attested to by Abigail Cooper, Constance Beamsley, and the widow Mary Thomas...judged by Minister Gideon Nash ...carried out by Sheriff Nathan Pratt...witnessed by Goodman Newell, Caleb Morey, Isaiah Jones, Blacksmith...."

THE CHILDREN OF CAHOKIA

The late fall wind blew off the waters of the distant the Great River, the Misi-ziibi, and chilled the night air as the nine warriors stood solemnly in a wide circle around the shaman. They watched him with hard, distrusting eyes as a young Chippewa boy handed the shaman a stone bowl filled with a brew of macerated leaves and vines. The dancing light of the campfire illuminated the faces of the warriors, each wearing the hide or feathers of a sacred animal of the nations.

The feathers of crows, eagles, and owls fluttered slightly in the breeze as they hung from the buckskin shirts and pants of three of the warriors. The skulls of crows dangled from the braid of one of the warriors, and a necklace of eagle claws adorned the chest of another.

In contrast, the owl warrior wore a headdress shaped like the giant head of a barn owl, with two glittering dark eyes and a sharp curved beak perched atop his head. In the shadows of the firelight, he resembled one of the great owl gods of legend.

Other warriors in the circle wore the hide of a bear, wolf, or bison with the sacred creatures' head atop their own and its teeth hanging from necklaces and the fringes of their clothes. Two warriors wore the hide of a deer and an elk, with tall antlers casting long shadows on the ground.

From the east, a warrior wore a buckskin shirt with turtle shells affixed along down the chest and across the shoulders. Under different circumstances, these warriors would likely face each other in battle as the fortunes of their Native American nations ebbed and flowed. Many had already fought in skirmishes between each other's nations. However, tonight they stood as uneasy allies, eyeing the shaman suspiciously.

The shaman stood and raised the clay bowl in one hand towards the dark heavens of the night sky, firelight glinting off the copper bands he wore around his ankles and wrists. In his other hand, he shook a ceremonial mace; leather straps holding bird skulls and feathers dangled from the smooth, round wooden head. The skulls clicked together, sounding like ghostly crickets as he shook his hand. He wore the ancient beak of a large bird over his nose held on by leather straps tied behind his head.

He stood nearly nine feet tall, a giant among the assembled warriors but diminutive by the standards of his people. The shaman felt the distrust of the warriors, even though they joined for a common purpose. His people, the First Born, the Mound Builders, were their ancient enemies. Even now, nearly two hundred years since the nations allied together and threw down the ancient stronghold of Cahokia, eradicating all but the memory of his people, there was still a fear of his vanquished race.

The shaman wore his buckskin shirt u tied at the chest; the cold air felt good against his skin as he drank the bitter brew. His body swayed to the earth's heartbeat, causing his long, gray-streaked braid to pendulum across his back. As he felt the potion course through his veins, he nodded to the Chippewa boy, and the youth began to feed bundles of sage into the fire. The flames greedily consumed the dried leaves and filled the night air with the acrid smell of the burning herb.

He closed his dark eyes, shutting out the world around him as he let his inner sight travel to the spirit world. Geometric shapes flashed through his mind, and a floating sensation surrounded his body. Slowly the feeling changed from floating to falling; his heart beat rapidly in his chest as he plummeted through the darkness. His mind reeled at terrifying thought of his body striking the ground and shattering like a fragile seashell clawed at his mind.

Then he was soaring. The darkness cleared, and after momentary disorientation, he realized he was seeing out the eyes of a great bird, an eagle by the talons he saw beneath the body. Trees and ground passed beneath him in the night, his eyes detecting the movement of nocturnal creatures in the brush below. The eagle soared over the agricultural fields and darkened huts of the small villages that supplied the walled city of Cahokia. The bird came to land on the high wooden fortification that protected the Cahokia, its sharp talons digging into the ancient wood. The rows of wooden homes and open plazas were devoid of people, only the occasional stray dog slinked through the shadows.

The shaman looked toward the massive four-terraced platform mound rising over one hundred feet in the city's center. Hundreds of torches burned atop, and his heart sank with the memories of this night. The eagle retook flight, its strong wings propelling the mighty bird high above the titanic mound.

Atop the massive mound, the warriors of Cahokia stood in three concentric circles from the outer edge of the plateau. Each held a spear in one hand and a torch aloft in the other, the fires glinting off the copper arm rings of the warriors like stars in the night sky.

Other warriors led dozens of captives, several feet shorter than the towering Cahokians, in a procession that wound up the terraced mound. The shaman knew from the captives' long dark hair and lithe bodies that these were mostly women seized from the nations by the Cahokians. The steady thumping of the ceremonial drums mingled with the terrified cries of the captives as they were led toward the center of the mound, where the desiccated corpse of a male Cahokian lay.

The man, He Who Raises the Earth, lay atop a bed of thousands of white marine shell disc beads. He was the ancient god of the Cahokians, having come to them from the sea after the great cataclysms and taught them crafts, skills, and magic. Even in death, he remained their most significant source of power.

With the eagle's keen sight, the shaman scanned the dozens of Cahokia holy men dancing around the bed of shell beads, raising their long copper and bone knives in the ceremonial calling to He Who Raises the Earth. He spotted the young man he sought in the throes of the reverent dance and recognized his younger self.

The shaman pleaded with the eagle to turn away from the plateau to spare him from reliving the terrible deeds of that night, but the eagle held fast. An anguished wail escaped the shaman's throat that emanated from the eagle's mouth like a mournful cry as the scene below unfolded.

The terrified screams of the captives as the warriors led them forward. The chanting of the Cahokians as the shamans sacrificed the prisoners to He Who Raises the Earth, coating the skeletal body and seashells with waves of dark red blood. The primal frenzy of the Cahokians as the procession continued until there were no more to sacrifice.

Silence descended upon the plateau as the eagle drifted on the night wind. The high shaman, coated in blood and gore from the night's work, beckoned four tall warriors to come forward. The men wore long black robes covering all except their heads and hands. The robes trailed the ground as they crossed the plateau and stepped over the bodies of the sacrificed.

The high shaman led them to the four stone tablets and directed the men to lie down. The eagle stared down into the stoic faces of the four men as they lay, their dark eyes looking skyward.

The ceremonial drums continued to beat as the high shaman walked to the first man and raised a sword, crafted from the bone of a bison, over the man's head. The acute hearing of the eagle could pick out the chants of the high shaman to He Who Raises the Earth among the mingled voices of the ceremony.

The man did not flinch as the high shaman brought the white blade down and sliced the man's head from his body. With slight adjustments, the high shaman brought the sword down twice more, separating the man's hands from his body. Two Cahokian women placed the head and hands reverently in a basket. They followed behind the high shaman as he repeated the process on the other three warriors. Each accepting his end without sound or movements.

The shaman saw his younger self step forward with three others, each carrying a basket they set down beside the headless warriors. The high shaman returned to stand beside the first warrior, his hands circling the air over the body as he swayed and chanted.

Reaching into the basket, he withdrew the black-clawed skeletal paws of a bear and placed them against the corpse's bloody wrists. The high shaman withdrew the skull and jawbone of an elk from the basket and set it atop the decapitated neck. The creature's antlers branched outwards from the head, and the impenetrable blackness of the eye sockets seemed impervious to the hundreds of burning fires on the plateau.

The eagle circled the plateau as the high shaman adorned each of the warriors' corpses with the skeletal accouterments. The only sound the incessant beating of the ceremonial drums as the shamans began to dance around the bodies of the slain Cahokians.

Then the high shaman chanted, calling on He Who Raises the Earth to place his hand upon the warriors. The encircled warriors joined their voices to the chant, stomping their feet in rhythm with the drums.

The eagle swooped lower as all the drumming and chanting suddenly stopped. The shaman watched through the eagle's eyes as the first warrior slowly sat up. The creature's skeletal claws clenched and unclenched, then it slowly turned its elk skull to watch as its three companions slowly rose.

As the Cahokians shouted praise and thanks to He Who Raises the Earth, the first warrior stared upward and fixed the bottomless darkness of his eyes upon the eagle. Blackness engulfed the shaman's vision, and the sensation of falling resumed. His mind screamed, certain he would plummet to the earth.

Then he blinked back against the brightness as the feeling of soaring through the air returned, and daylight filled his vision. He was once again within the body of a bird, and with a sidelong glance, he saw the sleek black wings of a crow had replaced the mighty wings of the eagle.

The crow cawed as it circled high above an island the shaman recognized as the Powhatan island of Cuscarawaoke, which the pale invaders now settled and called Rawranoke, after the white beads made there as ornaments and currency for the Algonquian nation.

The homes of the invaders looked deserted, with their hearth fires extinguished and their fields long untended. The crow turned westward and flew across the expanse of water separating the island from the mainland. Swooping low along the coast, the bird cawed, calling the shaman's attention to the dozens of abandoned boats that dotted the coastline. Several small wooden boats had washed up on the sandy shores, while others lay smashed against the rocks or drifted aimlessly in the surf.

The crow landed on a footpath that led away from the beach. Through the bird's dark eyes, the shaman could see scores of footprints, the stiff leather footfalls of the invaders, had passed this way, crushing the soft grass.

The shaman's vision swam in a dizzying lurch as the crow took flight, and the ground rapidly disappeared below them. The crow flew northwesterly, covering hundreds of miles as it soared across the bright blue sky. Thousands of acres of forested land streamed beneath them as the bird followed the trail made by the travelers.

When they finally caught up to them, the crow circled in a wide arc and flew low over the heads of the men and women traveling in a silent procession. The shaman could see they wore clothes common to the English invaders but looked ragged and worn. As they ambled forward, their eyes stared straight ahead, vacant and unseeing.

The crow craned its neck, and the shaman's heart sank as a terrible fear rose in his gullet. The last two hundred years had not been kind, washing away all traces of the past and leaving only fields of green grass. However, there could be no mistaking the four-terraced platform mound that rose up before them.

The invaders were being summoned to Cahokia.

◆ ◆ ◆

The shaman fell to his knees and wretched, coughing up bile in thick, hacking wads. He felt the eyes of the warriors upon him, judging their ancient enemy for his weakness.

"What did your vision show you?" the warrior dressed in the bear skin eyed him.

"It," the shaman slowly rose to his feet. "It is worse than I had feared."

"Did you see the Wendigoes?" the Bear pressed him further. "Are they truly all here?"

"I believe they are," the shaman nodded.

"Why would the Wendigoes gather here?" the Elk shook his head. "They have plagued our people for generations, but never more than one has been seen at a time."

"They gather here because it is the place of their creation," the shaman looked at him with deep remorse.

"Their creation?" the Crow stared at him with hard eyes, and the Turtle spat at the ground before the shaman's feet.

"Yes, the Wendigoes are the children of Cahokia,"

the shaman steeled himself for their anger as dark murmurs rippled through the gathered warriors.

"Anasazi," the Wolf spoke his people's word for their ancient enemies as he glared at the shaman. "All from Cahokia are our enemies."

"Why would Cahokia create such monsters?" the Eagle gave the shaman a baleful look.

"It was pride and folly," the shaman met the gaze of each of the warriors. He deserved their hatred for his role in the dark deeds of that night. "Cahokia was defeated. Its empire had fallen, overpowered by the nations. Cahokia created the Wendigoes to punish the nations in the bitterness of defeat. To forever haunt the nations with an echo of Cahokia, a curse upon the victors."

"Our elders tell the tales of those days," the Bear looked at the warriors and then turned to the shaman. "They say the nations came to the people of Cahokia with peace in their hearts, but Cahokia made war upon them."

"This is true," the shaman nodded. "The nations came to us seeking to live side by side in peace. Our elders saw the potential for trade between our peoples and prosperity. But they grew fearful when they beheld the multitudes that came with you. The First Born live long lives, many times longer than your people. However, our children were few. The elders feared that you would swallow the empire up and pour over the walls of Cahokia."

"And we did," the Elk let the pride in his words show on his face, and the other warriors nodded in agreement.

"But only after Cahokia attacked the nations," the Turtle looked at the shaman. "You reaped what you sowed. And still, you unleashed the Wendigoes on us. To kill our people and steal our children in the night."

The Bear raised his hand to call for silence, and all eyes turned toward him. "Our elders have sent us to end the terror of the Wendigoes, and the shaman has led us to the gathering of these vile children of Cahokia, as he promised the nations."

"The blood of our ancestors calls out for vengeance, and they shall receive it, my brothers," the Bear met the eyes of each of the warriors with a steady gaze. "But first, the Wendigoes will die upon our spears and arrows, so I wish to hear what the shaman saw in his vision."

The shaman nodded to the Bear and then addressed the assembled warriors. "The Wendigoes gather atop the Great Mound of Cahokia. However, they are not alone; they have called nearly a hundred of the pale invaders from Rawranoke to them."

"The Wendigoes are allied with the English?" the Turtle looked shocked and alarmed.

"We will gather more warriors," the Wolf nodded. "We will shed the blood of the invaders alongside the Wendigoes."

"No," the shaman's rebuke came out sharply. "The invaders must not be harmed."

"They are both our enemies," the Bison narrowed his eyes. "Why fight one enemy and leave another to fight another day?"

"The Great Mound at Cahokia is a place of power and sacrifice," the shaman threw the last bundle of sage onto the fire, causing it to flare and send burning embers floating into the night sky. "It is the resting place of He Who Raises the Earth, who your people call Krowatowan, and he demands blood in return for his power and favor. I believe the Wendigos called the invaders there to sacrifice them."

"Let them shed the blood of the English," the Turtle spat on the ground. "I will not cry for their dead."

"No, their blood on the Great Mound of Cahokia is what the Wendigoes seek," the Bear stared into the flames.

"So we must protect the pale ones and kill the Wendigoes?" the Deer shook his head.

"That is correct," the shaman nodded. "Whatever their dark purpose, the Wendigoes need the blood of the invaders to invoke the power of He Who Raises the Earth. We cannot let that happen."

The Turtle swore and kicked at the dirt as uncertain murmurs spread among the warriors.

"How can we stop them?" the Bison looked to the shaman. "How do we kill the Wendigoes?"

"Your weapons alone will not harm the Wendigoes. They know this, which will give us the element of surprise," the shaman pointed to the dying fire. "We will coat our weapons in the ash of the sage leaves. The sage will make our weapons deadly to the Wendigo."

◆ ◆ ◆

"I am brave. I can fight with the Wendigoes," the Chippewa boy gripped a deer bone knife and looked up at the tall shaman.

"Yes, you are fearless," the shaman smiled at the boy. "But you are also very fast; if we fail, we need you to warn the nations."

The boy opened his mouth to protest, but the shaman placed a hand on the boy's shoulder. His shoulders slumped in resignation, and the boy looked down at his feet. He did not look up again until the shaman and warriors headed into the darkness.

◆ ◆ ◆

The shaman gripped his spear tightly as he ran alongside the warriors, his long strides compensating for the speed of the younger men. The faint light of the crescent moon did little to light their way, but it also hid them more easily from the eyes of the enemy.

The villages surrounding Cahokia had long ago turned to dust, leaving only a vast flat expanse leading up to the four terraces of the Great Mound. The men could see fires burning atop the Great Mound, causing the high plateau to glow orange against the night sky.

The moon was at its nightly peak as they reached the base of the Great Mound. The Elk silently pointed at the well-trodden grass on the winding path up to the plateau, indicating that many feet had passed this way recently.

The Bear led their ascent up the path of the Great Mound; he clutched two ash-covered war hatchets in his hands. Behind him striding side by side, were the Bison, Wolf, and Elk, each carrying long iron-tipped spears. The Eagle, Crow, and Owl followed four paces behind them; arrows nocked in half-drawn bows. The Turtle and Deer strode alongside the shaman in the last rank, armed with their ash-coated spears.

The cool night air blew the scent of burning fires down to them as they ascended the first two plateaus. As they quickly moved up the path, the steady beat of a drum reached their ears, growing ever louder as they climbed higher.

Memories of ascending the heights of the Great Mound in the days of Cahokia's greatness flooded back to the shaman and filled him with nostalgia, mingled with the feeling of growing dread as they neared the plateau.

As the warriors passed the third terrace and neared cresting the plateau, the Bear signaled for them to stop. Lowering himself to the ground, he quietly slid forward to peer over the lip of the table. The warrior's dark bearskin masked him against the darkness as he crawled forward.

Bum-bum-bum

The shaman knew the Wendigoes were using the drum to awaken the beating heart of Krowatowan. He had witnessed many ceremonies when the high shaman had done the same.

"Aim for the drummer first," the shaman whispered to the warriors, and the three bowmen gave him quick nods of acknowledgment.

When the Bear returned, he signaled for the warriors to gather around him as he drew shapes in the dark earth with the tip of his war hatchet. In the dim moonlight, the shaman could see the Bear made four lines, two side by side, separated from the second set by a hand span.

"English," the Bear pointed to the four lines. Then he made a round mark at the head of each pair of lines. "Wendigo"

The Bear made another two round marks behind the first set of circles. "Wendigo," he pointed to the first. "Wendigo drummer," the Bear indicated the second.

The shaman studied the markings and tapped the symbols for the Wendigoes standing before the English. "They will slice through the invaders like stalks of corn. We must not let that happen; their blood will summon the power of He Who Raises the Earth."

The Turtle muttered something, but the Bear silenced him with a stern look.

"We are ready," the Bison looked to the Bear, who nodded in return.

The shaman and the nine warriors resumed their formation, crouching low and gripping their weapons with determined fingers. The Bear looked back at them, then raised his war hatchets and charged onto the plateau.

As the small band crested the lip of the table, the shaman blinked from the sudden brightness of the fires burning on the plateau. Several large campfires, stacked high with dried wood, spat forth flames reaching high into the night sky. The English invaders stood transfixed in four straight lines, their heads thrown back as if staring blankly at the starry night, revealing their bare throats to the Wendigoes.

As the Bear described, two tall Wendigoes stood at the forefront of the English. Black eyes sockets peered out of the bone-white elk skulls atop tall dark-robed bodies. The Wendigoes bore long, sharp deer bone knives in each skeletal hand.

Another Wendigo beat ceaselessly on a large drum, his claw-like hands rising and falling in a tireless rhythm. Standing beside the drummer, a fourth Wendigo turned his elk skull head toward the newcomers.

"More offerings for He Who Raises the Earth," the creature's voice was a deep throaty hiss that chilled the shaman's blood, and he raised two axes carved from the gleaming white hip bones of a bison.

The Wendigo dipped its antlered head in a nod to its two companions, and the creatures stepped forward and sliced their knives across the first rank of English throats. The shaman saw the three pale men and a dark-haired woman pitch forward, the gurgling of their opened throats the only sound they made as they hit the ground, spilling their lifeblood into the earth. The next sets of English stood unmoving as the Wendigoes advanced on them.

The Bear charged at the leader, followed closely by the Bison, Wolf, and Elk. The Turtle and the Deer let fly their spears at the Wendigoes wading into the helpless English, but the creatures easily batted aside the long shafts.

The bowmen let loose their arrows and quickly nocked another as the Turtle and Deer drew their knives and charged at the Wendigoes. Two arrows sailed harmlessly into the darkness, but the third caught the Wendigo drummer in the shoulder. The creature fell backward with a cry of shock and pain, a terrifying noise of a pitch so shrill the shaman winced painfully at the sound.

The Wendigoes had cut halfway through the ranks of the English before the Turtle and Deer could halt their advance. The creatures warily dodged the warriors' ash-coated blades as their long limbs lashed out to keep their attackers from getting too close.

The Bear leaped at the Wendigo leader, screaming a ferocious battle cry as he sailed through the air and swung his war hatchets at the creature's head. The Wendigo moved incredibly fast for a creature its size, sidestepping the Bear's flying charge and swinging one of its bison bone axes at the warrior.

One of the Bear's hatchets sheared off the upper half of the Wendigo's right antler, but his moment of victory turned into a strangled cry of pain as the creature's axe cleaved his right leg from his body just above the knee. He landed hard against the ground, moaning as blood poured from his severed stump.

The Deer, too, had fallen, stabbed through the eye by the Wendigo he fought. The bowman had turned their attention to his killer, and three arrows now protruded from the Wendigo's torso as he resumed his assault upon the helpless English.

The shaman crouched, holding his spear, looking

for an avenue of attack. The cacophony and chaos of battle terrified him as it always had, and he watched in horror as the English fell like scythed wheat beneath the Wendigo blades. He could feel the rumbling of power pulsing through the plateau as He Who Raises the Earth became satiated with the blood of the fallen and sacrificed.

The Turtle had scored several strikes against his opponent, who hissed and gnashed his teeth at the warrior. The creature lashed out with a killing blow that glanced off one of the turtle shells affixed to the warrior's shirt and struck him alongside the head. The warrior crumpled to the ground, momentarily dazed, as the Wendigo slashed through the throats of the next two English men.

With the Bear out of the fight, the Bison, Wolf, and Elk advanced on the Wendigo leader, forcing him backward with thrusts of their ash-covered spears. The creature seemed incapable of finding an avenue to launch an offensive in the face of three skilled opponents until a spear sailed from the darkness behind him and buried itself deep in the Wolf's chest. The warrior fell back, dead before he struck the ground, as the wounded Wendigo drummer emerged from the blackness holding a second spear.

Taking advantage of his attackers' sudden loss, the Wendigo leader leapt forward and thrust his axe's blade into the Elk's throat. The warrior's head snapped backward, sending his antlered headdress tumbling to the ground. As the Wendigo freed his blade, blood geysered from the horrific wound as the Elk slumped to his knees.

The Bison thrust his spear forward and sank the tip deep into the Wendigo's hip. The creature roared in pain, bringing his axe down on the warrior's head, hewing his skull in half.

The drummer let loose his second spear, and the shaman watched as it sailed across the killing ground to impale the Eagle just as the warrior prepared to nock another arrow. The Eagle collapsed with a grunt and then lay still. Beside him, the Owl, his ash-covered arrows expended, drew his deer bone knife, and charged at the drummer. The creature roared a challenge in response, the feral sound of his call echoing above the din of battle as he barreled forward to meet the Owl.

The shaman watched as the two figures closed the distance between them. The Owl, the white and brown feathers adorning his shirt and pants fluttering in the night, reared his arm to strike with his knife as the Wendigo lowered his elk skull like a charging bull. As the two figures met, a bone-crunching crack resounded as the Wendigo drove the white bone of his skull up into the Owl's jaw. The Owl's head snapped backward, and his knife slipped from his lifeless fingers as he staggered back and then crumpled to the blood-soaked ground.

The urge to charge forward with his spear and defend the fallen warrior was squelched within the shaman by an overwhelming fear that rooted him in place. He could barely muster the courage to move more than a step forward, and he caught the disapproving glance from the Crow as the warrior continued to launch arrows in a futile attempt to stop the Wendigo from slaughtering the helpless English. The creature had a half dozen arrows protruding from its chest and shoulders but continued on its relentless path of carnage.

The shaman watched helplessly as the Wendigo drummer bent over and grasped the Owl in its skeletal claws. The warrior offered no resistance as the Wendigo lifted his limp body above its head. The creature's empty black eye sockets looked directly at the shaman mockingly, the blackness so complete not even the fires reflected there. The aged Cahokian detected an insatiable malevolence within the depths of those dark holes as the Wendigo slammed the Owl upon its upraised knee. The Owl's body bent at an impossible angle and shattered like a dry twig.

A triumphant cry drew the shaman's gaze away from the grizzly scene as the Crow pumped a fist into the air. The warrior's arrow sat shaft deep within its intended target's empty eye socket. The feathered shaft had finally stopped the Wendigo's bloody swath through the English as the creature's rigid body fell backward like a toppled tree. Only six English men remained standing, swaying in the winds like stalks of corn, oblivious to the sacrifice of their fellow colonists.

Across the battlefield, the other Wendigo closed on the last two pairs of English invaders, three men and a woman with strands of blonde hair that hung like broken spider webs from beneath her dirty, white linen cap. The Wendigo's knife dripped with blood as it prepared to land a killing blow across the woman's throat.

The Wendigo ground its teeth together and gave a guttural growl as it stumbled, its right leg buckling as the Turtle drove his knife hilt deep into its knee. With a cry of rage and pain, the creature stabbed its gory knife into the top of Turtle's head with such force that it snapped the deer bone blade off in the warrior's skull. The Turtle sprawled lifeless, like a starfish on a sandy beach, as blood poured down his dark hair.

The creature raised its skeletal hands and limped toward the English, intent on finishing the task with its long, black claws. A movement caught its eye, and it turned its head a moment before the Crow's last arrow sank deep into its eye socket and cracked through the back of its skull. The Wendigo's injured knee buckled as it spun from the killing blow, and the towering form fell dead across the body of the Turtle.

The Crow smiled as he watched the second

Wendigo fall by his hand, confident his ancestors guided his hand this terrible night. The shaman's shouted warning snapped him out of his reverie, and he turned to see the Wendigo drummer almost upon him. Dropping his bow, he reached for the knife in his belt.

His fingers closed around the familiar wooden handle just as the Wendigo plunged its deer bone knife deep into his chest. The Crow felt his hands slacken and the air whoosh from his mortally wounded chest. The Wendigo blew foul-smelling air into his face as it breathed, and the Crow had the impression the creature was gloating. The Crow's eyes ran to the arrow that had slid deep into the Wendigo's shoulder, and he recognized his feathered shaft.

The Crow had slain two Wendigoes and wounded a third; his ancestors would welcome him into the afterlife with pride on their faces. A wide smile crossed the Crow's face, and he gave a hacking laugh that dotted the Wendigo's white elk skull with flecks of red blood. This act of defiance enraged the beast, who twisted the knife buried in the warrior's chest; however, the Crow had already passed safely into his ancestors' arms.

With white-knuckled fear, the shaman gripped the spear and held it before him, trying to keep the Wendigoes at bay. A hoarse laughter emanated from deep within the Wendigo's skull as it backed away and slapped a hand across its shoulder, snapping the shaft of the Crow's arrow.

The shaman watched with sinking dread as the remaining two Wendigoes glided toward the remaining English. They dispatched them effortlessly, the drummer with slashes of his knife and the leader with brutal hacks of his bison bone axe. The blonde woman was the last to fall as the axe separated her head from her body in a geyser of red blood.

A feeling of despair overcame the shaman as he surveyed the carnage. The nine brave warriors lay dead and broken among the bodies of the sacrificed invaders. Two of the Wendigoes lay slain, but in his heart, the shaman knew he had failed to prevent the offering necessary for the Wendigoes to call upon the power of Krowatowan. For whatever dark purpose the Wendigoes had gathered here this night, the shaman's efforts to stop them proved futile.

Blood dripped in thick rivulets from the Wendigoes' weapons as they came to stand in front of him. Dark eye sockets stared at him, and the cold grip of fear clenched about his heart. In desperation, the shaman lunged with his spear, its ash-covered point still unblemished from battle. A mark of his cowardice this night. The lunge was weak, but he felt the blade sink deep into the thigh of the Wendigo drummer.

The Wendigo snorted in pain and batted the spear from the shaman's hands as it sank to a knee. The weapon barely made a sound as it fell to the soft earth. The leader looked silently from the shaman to the kneeling Wendigo, its gleaming skull with its fathomless black eye sockets turned to the shaman as it raised its bison bone axe.

Blood dripped from the sharpened bone blade, and the shaman shrank back from the deadly blow. The Wendigo swung the axe down in a wide arc, the force of the swing generating enough wind to blow the shaman's hair back from his face as it sliced through the air. The axe cleaved into the neck of the kneeling Wendigo, and the creature's elk skull tumbled from its shoulders to land at the shaman's feet.

The shaman stared down at the antlered skull in shock and disbelief. Before him, the Wendigo dropped the axe and reached both arms upward to the night sky. The sleeves of the robe slid back to reveal the pocked and blackened skin of arms that once belonged to the Cahokia warrior but now ended in skeletal bear claws.

"He Who Raises the Earth," the antlered skull hissed, invoking the slumbering god. "Accept our sacrifice and grant us our revenge!"

The plateau hummed with power, and the ground tremored with the ancient god's wrath. The bodies of the three fallen Wendigoes began to shake violently and then exploded into thousands of tiny black specks.

The shaman thought they were pieces of dark ash until he heard the humming buzz as the specks began to swirl.

In disgust, the shaman realized the three Wendigo corpses had transformed into swirling columns of flies. The flies rose like three dark pillars and merged into a teaming mass above the plateau. The buzz of the insects drowned out all other sounds of the night as the shaman watched the black cloud writhe above them.

"I don't understand," the shaman looked into the dark eyes sockets of the Wendigo and shook his head.

"There is a story among the Kumeyaay people," the Wendigo's voice was a hiss that sounded like it rose from a deep well. "In a time of famine, their god came to them and asked them to choose between living forever, living for a short time more and then dying, or dying forever."

"The people could not decide; they debated amongst themselves. Then a fly came among them and whispered in their ear to choose to die forever. And so they did. Thus, the fly became a messenger of death with the power to sway men's minds."

The shaman looked into the white bone of the Wendigo's face with inscrutable confusion.

"He Who Raises the Earth," the Wendigo hissed. "Has granted us that power. Pick up the spear."

The shaman hesitated, unsure of the creature's

intention.

"Pick up the spear!"

Feeling his guts liquefy with fear, the shaman quickly retrieved the spear and held its ash-covered tip toward the Wendigo. The feel of the strong wood of the spear shaft in his hand gave the shaman a shred of courage.

"We were wrong to create you," the shaman used all his will to keep the tremble from his voice. "Cahokia was defeated; we should have gone quietly into the night or learned to leave peacefully with the nations."

"The nations usurped the lands of He Who Raises the Earth," the Wendigo stepped forward until the tip of the spear pressed deep into its dark robe. "They have earned his wrath."

The shaman watched transfixed as the Wendigo stepped forward, impaling itself on the spear. He struggled to keep the spear from slipping from his grip as the Wendigo continued moving toward him, grunting as the spear burst forth from its back.

With a clawed hand, the Wendigo grasped the shaman's deerskin shirt. The shaman struggled to pull back from the Wendigo, but the creature held him firmly. It extended one long clawed finger on its free hand and pressed it against the shaman's chest.

"You have betrayed our god," the Wendigo thrust

the clawed finger into the shaman's chest, twisting and turning it as the shaman screamed. "Know this before you die. His flies will whisper in the ear of the invaders for generations to come. They will tell them to hate the nations and hunt them until they have no rest. They will tell them to kill the nations wherever they find them and to defile the lands so that the nations will know no joy from what they stole from Cahokia."

The Wendigo exploded in a whoosh of air, becoming a cascading torrent of buzzing flies. The shaman collapsed, gasping, his hands clawing at the gaping hole in his chest. Above him, the new flies joined with the swarm above the plateau.

As the shaman felt his heart fail, he watched the swarm disperse in all directions, carrying their vile message to every corner of the land. A single tear slipped from the shaman's eye and ran down the side of his face at what the hatred and bitterness of Cahokia had wrought. He felt shame and horror at the curse Cahokia had brought to the land and the ruination of all its people.

THE HUNTERS

Reed gripped the Mossberg shotgun as he quickly moved through the brush. A cruel smile crossed his lips as he heard the nearby whimpering and snarling that signaled he had caught a wolf in his trap. He quickened his pace; hunting wolves was illegal in Washington State, and Reed did not need one of those forest rangers coming down from a Cascade Mountain trail and hearing the creature stirring up a ruckus.

The forest opened into a clearing, and Reed could see the wolf nipping at its hind leg, bent at an unnatural angle, held fast in the steel jaws of his trap. He unzipped his red flannel jacket, letting some of the body heat from his quick trek through the forest escape into the cool fall air. A red-tinged moon, a blood moon, illuminated the clearing as he crossed to his prey.

"Aww shit," Reed noticed with disappointment that it was a young wolf; the small pelt would net him little more than beer money for the weekend.

The injured wolf glowered at him with pain-filled eyes and snarled as he approached. Reed could tell the trap had broken its leg, and a jagged white shard of bone protruded through the wolf's bloody fur.

"Quit your noisemaking," Reed raised the shotgun and squeezed the trigger. The gun roared as it propelled the slug into the young wolf's chest, jarring its body so violently that it tore free of the leg clenched in the trap. The wolf let out one rasping breath and then lay still, its sightless eyes reflecting the red moon.

"Hardly worth the walk up here," he looked down at the torn body of the small wolf and kicked at it with his boot. "May get a couple of dollars from some tourists looking to buy a lucky wolf's paw. Though they weren't too lucky for you."

Reed laughed at his joke, a harsh cackling sound ending in a smoker's cough. A cold wind blew through the clearing, and suddenly, he felt lightheaded. The world swayed, and Reed reached out a hand to steady himself but, failing to find purchase, tumbled to the ground. The last thing he saw was the blood moon shining down on him. Then all went black.

◆ ◆ ◆

Reed awoke lying on his side in total darkness; a cacophony of voices surrounded him. A roughhewn cloth rubbed against his face, and he realized a hood was over his head.

"Hey, what's going on?" He struggled to move, but someone had tied his hands behind his back and bound his feet together.

"Who's out there? Someone untie me!" An air of panic was creeping steadily into his voice. "This ain't funny!"

"Reed? Reed Culvers, is that you?" A vaguely familiar voice called out to him.

"Jimmy? Jimmy Dodge, I'll kick your ass if this is your idea of a joke." Reed had known Jimmy Dodge since high school and shared many a drunken night at Red's Tavern, but this kind of joke was taking things a little too far for his liking.

"It's not me, Reed. I'm tied up; I can't see anything," his voice sounded on the verge of outright hysterics.

"I'm tied up too!" A young man's voice called out to them. "My name is Danny Stern."

"Shut up, all of you," a harsh older man whispered at them. "I'm trying to listen to what they are saying around us."

Strong hands grabbed Reed by the shoulder and dragged him onto his knees. The rough cloth scraped over his face as the hood was removed, and the night air felt cool on his sweaty face. That bright red blood moon shone down on the four men as they knelt tied in a clearing.

A chorus of boos and hisses rang around them, and Reed's mind reeled at what he saw. Just outside the tree line encircling the clearing, he could make out the shape of hundreds of animals. Big antlered deer, snarling wolves, hulking black bears, and all manner of forest creatures, great and small, surrounded them. Birds filled the tree branches, and all the animals seemed to be…talking.

"What the…," Reed had to be hallucinating. The animals were yelling at them and shouting catcalls.

"Kill them!"

"Make them pay!"

"Filthy humans."

"Oh sweet Jesus," Jimmy's blonde head swung from side to side in terror. "Oh, sweet Jesus."

Reed noticed a dark-haired teen to the left of Jimmy; the kid hung his head low and cried as a stain of urine spread across the front of his blue jeans. He figured that must be the Stern kid. Between Jimmy and Reed knelt a stern-faced bald man; his deep-set beady eyes stared straight ahead, and a sneer formed on the man's lips.

Directly in front of them sat three figures on large boulders carved into the shape of crude thrones. The moonlight through the trees cast shadows on the figures, and Reed thought the light must be playing tricks on his eyes. On the center throne sat a creature that looked like a human tree, easily twelve feet tall. A square head that resembled an upside-down tree stump with green humanlike eyes studied the four men. Leaf-covered branches extended upwards and outwards from the head-like hair, and two large branch-like arms and legs extended from the creature's tree trunk torso. Dark green vines slithered around the creature's body and limbs like snakes, and a large midnight black crow sat on the creature's shoulder.

On the tree creature's right sat a lithe black-haired woman whose body and limbs seemed entirely comprised of an ever-blowing windstorm of leaves. Only her pale neck and face seemed of truly corporeal form, and a crown of rose thorns sat on her head with four red rose buds that sat at equidistant points on the crown. Her coal-black eyes filled her eye sockets as they stared malevolently at the four men.

The third throne sat to the tree creature's left, occupied by a woman-like form comprised entirely of churning water with a skirt of lily pads encircling her waist. Green grass-like hair hung down in long, lush strands and framed a face that contained a pair of blue-green eyes above two small nose holes and a wide slit of a mouth. Her face was otherwise featureless, defined only by the constant flow of water that gave her substance.

"Demons!" The man next to Reed hissed before his voice rose to a shout. "Hellfire will take all over you!

"I don't think you should make them mad, man." Jimmy's voice trembled with fear.

"Lord God cast away these evil spirits, cast them into the lake of fire for all eternity," white flecks of spittle flew from the man's mouth as he shrieked. "I am a God-fearing man; you cannot harm me, you devil!"

"Silence! Silence while the charges are read," a rotund beaver stepped into the clearing and stood before the man, pointing at him.

"What the hell," Jimmy stared at the creature in shock.

"Lord Jesus, send down your holy fire…" The man's yelling was cut short by a sizeable clawed fist that struck down the man's head like a hammer. The man's head dipped forward, and his shoulders slumped as his eyes tried to refocus. The assembled animals cheered raucously.

Reed glanced sideways and saw the giant form of a black bear standing on its hind legs directly behind them. The bear turned his massive head to look down at Reed, and the hunter quickly averted his eyes.

"Please restrain yourself," the tree creature extended his hand in a gesture of restraint. His voice was deep and rich with an echoing quality that made Reed feel like it was coming from within a cave.

"I am sorry; I meant no disrespect to the Lord of the Wood," the bear's growling voice responded as he bowed his head reverently towards the three thrones.

"May I continue now?" asked the beaver turning towards the Lord of the Wood, and the tree creature nodded in acquiescence.

"These four men are charged with murder in our woods," the animals renewed booing and shouting angrily, but the beaver waved his paws for calm.

"This man," the beaver pointed at the crying Danny Stern. "Shot six crows for sport this morning; their bodies still lay in the north fields. They were crows from one of the old families who flew down from Mount Baker to find mates."

The teen cried hysterically when the trees filled with the angry chirping of birds called for his blood; his shoulders shook with uncontrollable sobs.

"Mistress of the Wind, he should die!" The birds called out, and the dark-haired woman nodded in agreement.

"This man," the beaver stepped in front of Jimmy. "This man killed a doe today. After he wounded her, he followed her through the woods as she tried to get home to her family and delivered the killing shot as she tried to ease the pain of her wounds with a drink of water from the stream."

The animals angrily shouted and stamped their paws and hooves against the ground. A buck with a rack of antlers nearly three feet tall stepped into the clearing.

"I demand justice!" His nostrils flared as he bowed his head low to the Lord of the Woods.

"He slew three ducks that sought refuge from the Lady of the Waters in the Dawn Lake," the beaver pointed to the balding man as the assembled animals gasped at the affront.

The man raised his head in time to see the watery spirit on the throne turn to the Lord of the Woods, "It is true; I granted those ducks sanctuary from harm." Her voice was sweet and melodic, tinged with the sound of a babbling brook.

"Psalms fifty-eleven," the man shouted defiantly. "I know all the fowls of the mountains and the wild beasts of the field are mine."

He appeared ready to shout something else, but the brown bear behind him lunged forward and completely engulfed the man's head in its cavernous maw. There was a muffled scream and the sickening sound of crunching and tearing as the bear tore the man's head off at the shoulders.

A scream escaped Reed's throat as blood fountained from the decapitated body, showering the three kneeling men. Danny collapsed and curled up on the ground, and Jimmy almost toppled over him, trying to shuffle away from the spray of blood as the body fell forward, twitching.

"I'm sorry. I could not help myself," the blood-soaked bear apologized to the court.

"It's quite alright," the Lady of the Waters replied

before turning to the Lord of the Woods. "I accept the punishment as served."

The Lord of the Woods nodded and then turned his green eyes on Reed, "Continue with the charges."

"Ah yes," the beaver sidestepped a puddle of blood. "And this man slew the young wolf born on a midsummer night. He trapped him in a steel trap and then shot him as he lay helpless."

Reed felt his bowels turn watery as a chorus of snarls and howls from the assembled wolves echoed through the woods.

"No. No, it wasn't me," Reed's voice cracked as he denied the charge and looked desperately up at the three figures sitting impassively on their thrones.

"Hardly worth the walk up here," cawed the crow from atop the Lord of the Woods' shoulder, repeating Reed's words. "May get a couple of dollars from some tourists looking to buy a lucky wolf's paw. Though they weren't too lucky for you."

"It wasn't me. The wolf was dead when I found him."

"Quit your noisemaking," cawed the crow. "Baaaaam!" The bird's-dark eyes bored into him as they echoed the gunshot.

"Baaaam," the bird repeated, the noise so loud some of the animals encircling the clearing jumped. Even the black bear behind the men seemed cowed by the noise. "Baaaam, baaam."

The Lord of the Woods extended both arms, his long branch-like fingers outstretched in a gesture that brought silence to the clearing. Only Danny's whimpering cries broke the silence.

"The charges have been heard," his voice was a deep rumble. "What say you?"

"They are guilty," the Mistress of the Wind's harsh rasp sounded like a summer night windstorm.

"Guilty," the Lady of the Waters nodded to the center throne.

"It is decided," the Lord of the Wood looked over the three blood-spattered men. "You must leave my woods tonight. Until then, all the beasts of the woods are free to hunt you."

"We'll leave; we'll leave right away and never come back," Jimmy agreed readily, a tone of relief flooding his voice.

"For your crimes against those who dwell here," the Mistress of the Wind hissed. "You will bear the hurts you have caused."

"What does that mean?" Reed asked Jimmy as all the animals began to stomp the ground and bellow at the top of their lungs.

The Lord of the Woods raised his hand, and Reed's world went black again.

❖ ❖ ❖

An excruciating pain in his leg brought Reed

back to consciousness. He lay on his back in the clearing, staring up at that blood-red moon, and it took several disorienting moments for him to realize that the screams he was hearing were emanating from his mouth. Reed looked down at his right leg; it bent at an unnatural angle at the shin, and blood had soaked his pant leg and filled his boot.

"Reed, buddy, it's going to be ok," Jimmy's pale face appeared before him, his blue eyes filled with pain and his blonde hair soaked with sweat. Reed could see Jimmy was holding his hand over a wet bloodstain on his left side. "Let me take a look at your leg."

Reed screamed with pain as Jimmy touched his leg.

"Aw man, it's bad," he moved his hand away from Reed's leg. "I think your bone broke through the skin."

"What's happening?" Reed was trying to control the pain enough to talk.

"The animals are gone. And those things. The kid's gone, too, runoff. He had some wounds on his arms I couldn't make out. They got me too," he gestured to the blood oozing through his plaid shirt.

A howl rang out in the distance as the sounds of the forest began to come alive. They could hear raccoons and other forest creatures agitatedly chittering, and the treetops began to shed leaves as birds flittered about the upper branches.

"We need to get moving, Reed. Can you get up?"

"Not without help."

Jimmy winced from his wound as he tried to help Reed off the ground. Reed screamed as his broken leg flopped uselessly, and Jimmy set him back down.

"You stay here for a minute, Reed; I'm going to find some sticks to bind your leg up."

Reed lay there sweating from the pain and watched Jimmy disappear into the woods. He could see the shadowy form of some bird circling the clearing. Around him, the clearing was empty except for the decapitated body that lay motionless beside him in a pool of drying blood. Reed sat up, the movement caused pain to shoot up his ravaged leg and into his groin. He reached over and riffled through the dead man's pockets, smiling when his fingers found what they were seeking.

Reed had noticed the man had the stale smell of a cigarette smoker, and he still had a pack of cigarettes and a lighter in his pocket.

"One left," Reed looked into the red and white labeled cigarette pack. He brought the pack to his lips and slid out the last remaining cigarette. Flicking the lighter, Reed lit the cigarette and inhaled deeply, making the tip glow a bright red. He exhaled a lung full of smoke and crumpled up the empty pack of cigarettes.

"Add littering to the list," he tossed the crumbled package into the dark woods and looked at the burning tip of the cigarette. "I should burn this whole damn forest to the ground."

"I got a couple of good sticks," Jimmy walked out of the woods with a handful of thick branches in one hand, his other hand still pressed against the bloody wound under his shirt.

Jimmy looked right at Reed and did not see the movement in the woods off to his left, but Reed did. A large buck charged out of the woods, head lowered, and slammed into Jimmy's side. Reed saw the surprise and pain on Jimmy's face as the buck struck the rib-shattering blow. The sticks flew from his hand as his body slammed into a tree. Jimmy barely had time to look up before the buck slammed into his mid-section; a sickening cracking noise filled the clearing as the buck's head made contact with his breastbone.

Reed watched helplessly as Jimmy just slumped to the ground, and the buck slammed forward again, piercing his face and chest with its antlers. An antler sunk deep into Jimmy's left eye, exploding the soft white orb into an oozing mass. Jimmy's mouth moved soundlessly as the buck reared back one final time and rammed into Jimmy's head.

The large deer stepped back and watched Jimmy's lifeless body tumble over, his left leg twitching spastically before going still. It turned to face Reed, puffs of gray vapor coming from the deer's snorting nose. Blood and gore dripped from the creature's antlers.

The buck slowly walked towards Reed, its dark eyes filled with malice as it approached the wounded hunter. Halfway through the clearing, the buck reared up on its hind legs and thrust its head skyward, letting out a guttural grunting scream that chilled Reed to the bone. The buck then darted off to the left and leaped out of the clearing into the darkness of the forest,

Reed did not realize he was holding his breath until the cigarette began to burn his finger.

"Goddamn," he shook the burning cigarette out of his hand.

Jimmy lay dead, his one remaining eye pointed skyward, reflecting the glint of the blood moon. Reed decided he needed to get moving and rolled onto his belly. Agony shot through his destroyed leg as he began to use his hands and uninjured leg to crawl.

◆ ◆ ◆

Sweat poured down Reed's face as he crawled through the forest, his beer belly scrapping over rocks and twigs as he slowly inched forward. Every movement caused agonizing pain to shoot up his leg, and once the pain began to subside, Reed knew that shock was starting to set in. He would not last much longer before the blood loss killed him unless something in the woods got him first.

Reed knew his only chance was to get through the forest to the Skagit River and float downstream the few miles to the ranger station in Rockport, where he could receive medical attention. Around him, the forest was alive with activity. He could hear creatures large and small moving about him in the woods; they growled and snorted just outside his sight line. Reed thought the animals were tracking his movements, but nothing attacked or hindered him.

The crawl through the forest went agonizingly slow, and he felt like he could almost cry with relief as the ground began to slope downwards toward the river, and the sound of rushing water reached his ears. Reed dragged himself to the top of a rise and lay his face on the cold earth, his body exhausted, his fingertips raw and bleeding. Below the ridge lay the Skagit River and a chance at survival; he was so close if he could push on a little longer.

The sound of yelling filled the night. Too tired to raise his head, Reed's eyes moved toward the ridgeline on the other side of the river. Against the moonlit night, he could see the outline of a small man hurrying along the high ridge. Behind him, the dark form of a bear slowly stalked, herding the man forward.

"Leave me alone," the voice was that of Danny Stern. Reed could see him stumbling along the ridge, desperately throwing the occasional rock back at the bear.

The bear edged forward but made no move to charge the teen. Danny was trapped. Behind him waited the bear, and before him, the ridge ended in a long drop to the boulder-strewn riverbed. The sound of wings flapped over Reed's head as a flock of birds issued forth from the forest. Reed could see their dark wings flapping in the moonlight as they headed towards Danny, loud caws announcing the crows' night flight.

Reed watched as the crows swirled around Danny. The teen's hands beat at the air in futility as the crows swooped in, tearing at his head and face with sharp beaks and claws. Danny cried out in pain as the crows struck him repeatedly, then skirted out of his reach. He flailed at them until one crow hit him square in the face with its claws. The teen reared backward, lost his footing, and tumbled from the ridge with a terrified scream.

The dark screaming form pirouetted through the air, desperate to grab anything to stop his fall. Danny's scream was cut short by bone and flesh impacting the jagged rocks below. The crows circled once and then flew back towards the forest, their cawing filling the forest night. Reed could see the dark outline of the bear turn and slowly return to the darkened woods.

Fear cutting through his exhaustion, Reed resumed his agonizing crawl downwards toward the water. His breathing felt fast and labored. Behind him, his ravaged legged bounced on the rocks like a tin can tied behind a car, shock masking the pain of the wound.

As the earthen edge of the forest gave way to the river's rocks, the flesh on Reed's hands and chest shredded as he crawled over the jagged stones. The sweat on his face mingled with blood as a jutting rock tore into his cheek as he slid past.

The roar of the river grew louder, and Reed could see the rushing water just a few yards further. In his weakened state, he knew it would be a challenge not to drown in the river's cold water, but this time of year, there were always large branches and debris that he could hold onto and float. The ranger station at Rockport was four or five miles downriver; if he could stay afloat, the river could take him there in twenty minutes. Shock might take him before that, or hypothermia in the cold water, but anything would be better than what could happen to him in the forest.

"All of this over some mangy wolf cub. I will pay those Dalton boys to lay every trap I have in the forest. Let the wolves chew their legs off to get out and see how they like it," he left bloody streaks on the rocks as he edged closer to the river.

A cold icy feeling rushed over his raw fingers, and Reed realized that his hand had slid into the river.

He laughed with relief, "They'll be nothing but three-legged wolves in these woods after this."

Reed began to slide forward the last few inches into the water, but his body refused to move. No, not refused, could not move. Then something tugged him backward, the water slipping out of his reach. He looked behind him, and three wolves stalked him; their yellow eyes narrowed as they looked at him. Two wolves bared mouths full of razor-sharp teeth and snarled ferociously at him. The third wolf stared back at Reed, the booted foot of his mangled leg in its mouth. The wolf tugged on Reed's foot, and he slid further away from the river.

"No, no," he screamed as the wolf slowly dragged him back across the rocks toward the woods.

Reed's bloody hands reached out, seeking purchase, but the wolf dragged him faster. His eyes darted wildly as the clear night sky and blood-red moon were blotted out by the forest canopy as he was pulled back into the woods. More wolves stepped out of the forest and encircled him, the smell of his blood filling their nostrils and stoking their fury.

The one dragging him by his leg stopped, letting the booted foot fall to the ground with a dull thud. The wolf stepped onto Reed's back and snarled so close to his head that he could feel the beast's hot breath and saliva on his neck. The wolf threw back its head and howled at the moon, a deep, mournful sound. The other wolves surrounding Reed added their howl in a terrifying cacophony.

Then the howling stopped. The wolf on his back sunk its teeth deep into Reed's shoulder and shook its head, tearing muscle and sinew from the bone. Reed screamed a feral scream of pain, and the other wolves leaped on him, razor-sharp teeth biting and tearing.

◆ ◆ ◆

Seattle Daily Times

Life / Local News / Northwest / Outdoors

Search Paused For Four Men Missing In The Cascade Mountains

October 8, 2022. Twenty-eight days after four men vanished separately in the Cascade Mountains, the Skagit County Search and Rescue team has suspended their search. The four men, Reed Culvers, Daniel Stern, Jeremiah Kory, and James Dodge now join the over 1,600 people estimated to be currently missing in the wildlands of the United States...

THE FEAST OF ANGELS

Eleko sat cross-legged on the earthen floor; he held the one-foot length chain by its middle link and swung it gently over the large square of dark cloth lying flat on the ground. The thin chain consisted of four concave nuts from an Opele tree linked at equidistant intervals down each side. As the village's Babalawo, their shaman, the divination chain was Eleko's means of channeling Orunmila, the Yoruba god of wisdom and knowledge.

Across from him, Adagba, the leader of the village's hunter's guild, the *Egbe Ode*, sat cross-legged, watching the chain pendulum over the cloth. Sweat beaded along the forehead of the man's midnight-black skin, and his dark eyes gazed intermittently from the chain to Eleko, who chanted the sacred Odu of Ifa.

With a flick of his wrist, Eleko cast the string of nuts onto the cloth; it landed in a twisted, snake-like pattern as if a great serpent writhed on the floor. Both men leaned forward and peered intently at the configuration of the chain.

"What does the Opele tell you, Eleko?" the broad,

muscular shoulders of the hunter visibly knotted with tension.

Eleko stared at the divination chain; his lips pursed as he studied every twist and turn. The *Babalawo* blew out a deep breath and sat back, his eyes filled with regret when he finally looked up at the hunter. Adagba met his gaze, searching his face for meaning; his shoulders slumping in resignation.

"It is bad then," Adagba got slowly to his feet.

"Yes, it is bad," Eleko nodded as he looked at the larger man. "Orunmila sees that these Christians will bring grief upon us."

"Then we must fight," Adagba slammed his fist into his open palm as he began to pace the floor of Eleko's simple home.

"Adagba," Eleko spoke softly. "More villagers join the Christians on their hill outside the village daily. They are abandoning the ways of our ancestors by the lure of this nailed god."

"Have you seen the market?" Adagba pointed toward the front door, but Eleko knew he meant the village market beyond. "No one sells carvings of the gods anymore. There are no more charms or amulets. Just wooden crosses."

"All we can do is adhere to the old ways, be there for our people who still believe," Eleko forced a smile. "This will pass in time. These English holy men will tire of our little village and leave. Our people will return to the gods."

"No," Adagba's eyes blazed with defiance. "I will re-form

the *Egbe Aro*, and we will fight these Christians just like we fought the Oyos in my great grandfather's time. I will take the head of the Englishman and place it upon a spike alongside the heads of that traitor Ajayi and the twinnings, Yemisi and Bola."

"Adagba," Eleko got to his feet and placed a calming hand on the hunter's arm. "Do not do anything rash. Do not do anything to Ajayi or the twinnings; steer clear of the Englishman on the hill. I will speak to Ademola today; the chief will know what to do."

"It may already be too late," Adagba shook his head; his dark eyes held a hint of sorrow when they looked upon the shaman. "Most of my hunters have already gone to worship the nailed god, and Ajayi and the twinnings convert more of our people daily."

Adagba gave Eleko a resigned nod and reached for the door handle leading out into the courtyard when he stopped and cast a sidelong look toward the small wooden table beside Eleko's bed. The big man turned and stared at the skeleton of the small monkey perched on the table as if it sat on a tree branch.

"Is there something wrong, Adagba? Eleko raised an eyebrow and cocked his head at the man.

"The monkey," Adagba squinted at the skeleton and then looked at Eleko. "When I entered your home, I was sure the monkey's arms stood raised. Now they rest in the monkey's lap."

"Tunde is just a skeleton, bones held together with wire and twine. He could no more raise an arm than I could a heavy rock." Eleko gave a little laugh and looked at the skeleton.

Adagba shook his head and looked around the small dwelling. Amulets and charms of stone, branches, and bones hung on the walls alongside ornately carved images of the gods. "Of everything in your home, nothing disquiets me like that little monkey. Why don't you let me bring you a live monkey from the woods to keep you company."

"Thank you Adagba," Eleko smiled. "Tunde is good company and much quieter than a living monkey. I like to think of him as a messenger from Eshu."

"Well, if he is a messenger from Eshu, I hope the trickster god is watching over you," Adagba looked back at the house as he opened the door. "Ajayi and the twinnings are not just preaching to turn from our gods; they are telling people to destroy their graven images. Your home will not sit well in the minds of these Christians."

Eleko nodded in sad acknowledgment to Adagba as he closed the door behind the hunter. He leaned his bald head against the door and sighed deeply, troubled by the times in which he lived; then, he cast a sidelong look at the monkey skeleton on the bedside table.

"Why do you take such risks, Tunde?" Eleko turned to face the skeleton, folding his arms across his chest. "Adagba is a friend and a believer in the gods, but even he has limits."

Tunde hopped down from the table and skittered across the floor, his skeletal feet making tiny striations in the earthen floor. The creature leaped up, sailing through the air to land softly on Eleko's shoulder like a butterfly on a flower. Eleko chuckled as Tunde nuzzled his boney skull against the *Babalawo*'s smooth head, and the shaman stroked the creature's spine lovingly.

Eleko did not understand the magic that re-animated the dead monkey, and he had not lied to Adagba when he said he thought the monkey was a messenger from Eshu, the Yoruba trickster god. He had found the monkey abandoned in the forest, sick and near death.

The shaman had wrapped the frail monkey in a blanket and brought it home; he nursed it day and night with herbs and medicines. Eleko's heart would melt at the monkey's human-like eyes staring at him as he ministered to it; the look was the closest thing he had ever seen to pure love. When the monkey died in his arms two weeks later, the old shaman cried unabashedly, wetting the dead monkey's face with his tears.

Eleko buried Tunde, the name he once planned to name a son, in the courtyard of the house in a sunny spot the poor creature seemed to enjoy in its short life. When he awoke to find the skeletal form perched on his bedside table several days later, he felt no fear. Eleko recognized him as a gift from the gods. He welcomed Tunde home but kept his true nature secret from the villagers. To all who visited his home, the monkey skeleton was just another odd accouterment in the shaman's home of talismans and carvings.

Tunde cast the hollows of his eye sockets down to the divination chain sprawled on the cloth, and the monkey's clean white jawbone chittered its teeth together.

"Yes, Tunde," Eleko nodded and petted the tiny skeleton

again. "The Opele says death is coming to the village."

◆ ◆ ◆

As Eleko walked through the village streets to the market, he sensed an air of tension and hostility that he had never felt before. Once friendly faces, villagers he had known for a lifetime scowled at him or averted their eyes as they walked past. A few still smiled and called greetings, but the village where he spent his whole life seemed wholly unwelcoming.

"*The Englishman has sown much discord within the village,*" Eleko thought as a childhood friend stared at him with openly distrusting eyes.

Minister John Cotton had arrived outside the village over a month ago, accompanied by Ajayi, a Christian convert from Okeodan. The English minister set up a makeshift church on a hill beside the village, and Ajayi came among the people and preached the gospel of the nailed god.

At first, the man met with varying degrees of scorn and indifference from the villagers, who still worshipped the old gods of the Yoruba. Then the *Ibeji*, the twin brother and sister, Yemisi and Bola, converted to Christianity. They stopped wearing traditional Yoruba clothing made from handwoven Aso-Oke, in favor of clothing of a European style Minister John provided them. Soon, villagers converted in droves, leaving the village daily to worship their new god on the hill.

One morning Eleko stopped a family carrying wooden statues of the gods with them. Some were very old, likely handed down from several generations, and Elku asked where they were going.

"We are taking them up the hill," the father answered. "To burn as we ask forgiveness from the one true god for our sin of idol worship. You should do the same, Eleko; make yourself right with god before the Day of Judgment arrives, or you will burn for all eternity in the lake of fire."

Eleko had been aghast that they were burning such sacred objects, but he had seen many families repeating the journey up the hill with charms, talismans, and wooden figures.

As he entered the marketplace, Eleko was surprised to see most villagers were wearing European shirts and trousers or dresses and head coverings for the women. Only a few women wore the traditional wraparound skirt, loose-fitting blouse, and head tie. Fewer men wore *agbadas*, the customary Yoruba robe, and *fila* caps. Gone altogether were the colorful dyes, beadwork, and stitching that made Yoruba clothing so beautiful to behold. They were replaced now by the drab, dark, unadorned clothing of the Europeans.

Eleko saw a small crowd around a young man in a jacket and trousers, holding a leather-bound book high. The man appeared to be speaking animatedly, and Eleko recognized him as Ajayi, Minister John's envoy to the village. The shaman quickly turned away and approached a gray-haired man in a European jacket with various vegetables on a dark blanket.

"Good morning, Saburi," Eleko smiled as he looked over the vegetables, nodding with appreciation at the excellent selection. "I will take three of those delicious-looking yams and five of those plantains."

"They're not for sale," Saburi scowled as he waved a hand over the produce.

"Oh," the smile slipped from Eleko's. "Then I will take six eggs."

"Not for sale," Saburi's dark eyes were hard and cold as they stared at the shaman.

"Very well then, good day to you, Saburi," Eleko smiled and nodded at Saburi as he moved on to the next outstretched blanket.

However, as Eleko moved from blanket to blanket, the villagers were unwilling to sell him okra, rice, beans, or *moin moin* bean cake. In one case, immediately after refusing to sell Eleko *ponmo*, a delicacy made from cow skin, the man sold the piece to a young man in a white shirt and trousers.

"Good morning Eleko, how are you enjoying the market this day?" a soft voice behind Eleko called.

The shaman turned to see Ajayi with his broad, ever-present smile, flanked by the twins, Yemisi and Bola, approaching him.

"It seems like quite an unprofitable day for the market," Eleko forced a smile and gestured toward the table of meats. "They have carried all these fine foods to the market, yet none are for sale."

"That is because these foods are only for the chosen of god," Yemisi's eyes had the coldness of a crocodile when she spoke.

"They are for the children of god to prepare for the feast of angels," Bola, the older brother, by less than a minute, added as he brushed dirt from his black trousers.

"What is this feast of angels?" Eleko chose to ignore the twins and address Ajayi directly.

"Let me share with you the word of god, Eleko," the grinning Ajayi held the holy book before him. "I will teach about the god, his angels, and all his bountiful blessings."

"Thank you for the offer, Ajayi," Eleko smiled and dipped his head in thanks. "I have worshipped the *Orisa* for all my long life. I feel Ogun, Shango, Jakuta, and all the *Orisa* who serve the great Olorun around me all the time. My house would feel very empty with just one god in it."

"Then you will burn in the hell fires of damnation," Bola's eyes were wide and filled with a fanatical gleam.

"Bola," Ajayi grimaced momentarily, then the toothy smile returned.

Yemisi placed a restraining hand on her brother's chest, "What my brother means is that the one true god offers eternal life and happiness to those who believe; however, a far different fate awaits those who deny him."

Eleko studied the twins carefully and found Yemisi's calm coldness more frightening than Bola's stormy volatility. In the Yoruba culture, the second twin was the elder and wiser, having sent its sibling out into the world first to ensure all was well. The shaman felt this aptly applied to Yemisi and Bola. Yemisi was all calculation and cunning, while Bola was brash and hot-headed.

"Come read with me for a while, Eleko," Ajayi tapped the book. "Our god is a god of peace and love, and when you return to the market, you will find everything for sale again."

"Why would a god of peace and love turn neighbor against neighbor simply over a difference of beliefs?" Eleko looked into Ajayi's wide, welcoming eyes but noticed the corners of the man's mouth twitch slightly at his words. "The Yoruba have many gods, and it is no fault to favor one over the other."

Bola muttered but quickly quieted when he saw his sister shoot him a withering look.

"You are a holy man, and of course, you have many questions," Ajayi touched Eleko lightly upon the shoulder. "Come up the hill with me; we can discuss these things with Minister John."

"Why does your Minister John not come down to the village," Eleko sweepingly gestured to encompass the marketplace. "We can discuss these things in front of the whole village; I am sure many would be interested to hear."

"Minister John will be here for the feast of angels," Bola looked sidelong at his sister as if expecting a rebuke.

"What is this feast you speak of?" Eleko caught Ajayi's hint of annoyance again at Bola's words.

"The feast is a celebration in honor of the Lord's mighty host of angels," Ajayi raised his eyes toward the sky.

"The Lord of hosts will prepare a lavish banquet for all people on this mountain," Yemisi stares unwaveringly at Eleko. "It's from Isaiah, twenty-five, six."

A commotion drew their attention, and Eleko could see Adagba in a heated argument with one of the villagers selling vegetables. The tall hunter held a yam in one hand and pointed angrily at the villager, who adamantly shook his head, further enraging Adagba.

"It appears Adagba has just discovered that none of the food at today's market is for sale," Eleko watched the heated exchange a moment longer, then turned to Ajayi and the twins. "You may worship a god of peace and love, but Adagba worships Jakuta, the *Orisa* of thunder, lightning, and fire. Unless you are eager to meet your god this afternoon, I suggest you not cross paths with him when he is in such a foul mood."

"I wish you an enjoyable afternoon," the smiling Ajayi nodded to Eleko and gestured for Yemisi and Bola to follow him in the opposite direction of Adagba.

Yemisi gave Eleko a curt nod, and Bola eyed him warily as they trailed behind Ajayi. He turned back, sighed, and saw a small crowd forming around Adagba and the villager. This village was peaceful and harmonious only a few weeks ago.

"Eleko! Eleko!" a large, heavy-set man called to the shaman from a courtyard doorway across the market. The man's meaty, dark brown arm gestured for Eleko to join him.

Eleko smiled to see at least Chief Ademola still wore a traditional brown Yoruba robe and matching *fila* cap. They had been friends since childhood, and the village chieftain often sought Eleko's advice and divination abilities in resolving dilemmas. If anyone could navigate the village through this Minister John's business, it was Ademola.

"Eleko, my old friend, how are you?" the village

chieftain had a broad, welcoming face and a booming laugh that often became infectious.

"I am well, my friend," Eleko embraced his old friend in greeting. "Though my heart is troubled."

"Oh?" Ademola's face creased into a frown. "Come in, Eleko; let us talk."

"I am concerned about these Christians," Eleko followed Ademola into the courtyard. "I was just in the marketplace and had attempted to buy..."

Eleko's words trailed into a grave silence, and Ademola stared at the shaman with concern, "What is it, Eleko?"

"What is that, Ademola?" Eleko pointed toward the chieftain's home at the large wooden cross that hung beside the door.

Ademola followed Eleko's gaze and closed the courtyard door to give them privacy. When the chieftain turned to face Eleko, his face was a mask of shame.

"Ademola, have you become a Christian?" Eleko could not hide the sadness and disappointment in his voice.

"No, No," Ademola shook his head but did not meet Eleko's eyes. "You know me, Eleko; I believe in the gods."

"Then what is that doing here," Eleko gave Ademola a withering look as he pointed at the cross.

"Eleko, we must be able to change with the times," Ademola shrugged. "The English and their Christian god are here; we cannot ignore that. We can still believe in the gods in our hearts, but we must join with the others and their Minister John."

"The others?" Eleko searched his friend's face. "How

many others have gone up the hill to Minister John?"

"Almost everyone, Eleko, that's what I wanted to speak to you about," Ademola looked pained. "Most of the village has already joined Ajayi, and those damned twinnings, all of the elders except old Oluwole, have become Christians. If I am to be their chieftain, I must be a leader of the village, not an outsider like you, Adagba, and Oluwole."

"Then lead the people out of this darkness that turns friend into foe," Eleko grabbed the chieftain by the shoulders. "There is still time."

"No, Eleko, there is no more time," Eleko recoiled from the deep look of grief he saw in Ademola's eyes.

"What do you mean?" Eleko's voice came out hoarse as his throat dried with a horrible apprehension.

"Minister John refuses to come into the village as long as there are blaspheming idols here. Tomorrow on *Ojo-Aiku*, the day Minister John calls Sunday, they will hold their feast of angels here in the village. Ajayi and the others intend to remove all the offending items from the village before then. Starting with the wards placed around the village."

Eleko looked up in alarm, "Ademola, you are our chief, the *oba* of this village; you cannot let that happen. Those wards guard against evil spirits; they have existed since our ancestors came to this village to protect the Children of Oduduwa."

"Eleko, there is nothing I can do. The people will not listen to me and go against Ajayi and Minister John. They believe in all that has been promised them from this nailed god," a pained look crossed Ademola's pleasant face. "Listen to me. Leave this place right now, go up the hill, and join the Christians. I cannot protect you from what may come if you do not."

◆ ◆ ◆

Eleko dropped the long wooden locking bar into place as he closed his courtyard door, something he had not done in decades. The conversation with Ademola had badly shaken him, and he felt a fear unlike he had ever experienced before. He knew the Opele spoke the truth when the divination chain revealed that death was coming to the village; however, now Eleko wondered if it was coming for him too.

Tunde chittered noisily as Eleko stepped through the doorway, hopping from one skeletal foot to another.

Yes, Tunde, I feel it too," Eleko nodded. "Something bad is coming."

The monkey skeleton hopped onto the wooden table where Eleko ate his meals and watched the shaman with his dark, hollow eye sockets. Eleko removed several wooden images of the gods from their places on shelves. There was the image of Oshun that had once belonged to his mother, the images of Ogun and Eshu he had carved as a child, and the carved totem of Obatala covered in a sacred white cloth that had been in his family for generations. The shaman placed these lovingly on his bed.

Eleko added the Opele and several other precious talismans to the pile. They were irreplaceable and more beloved to Eleko than life itself. The shaman took a small bowl from the table, and Tunde cocked his head curiously as the shaman slid the wooden bed to the side and dug in the earthen floor, using the bowl as a makeshift shovel.

Tunde hopped onto the bed and stared into the hole, then over at Eleko's sweat-streaked bald head. The shaman sat back on his behind and let out a deep breath. He turned to the monkey and smiled, petting the creature's skull with a dirty hand. Tunde made a chattering noise with his teeth and glanced into the hole.

"No, Tunde, "Eleko smiled. "You are not going back into the hole."

Eleko wrapped the idols and talismans in his mother's old blue head tie and placed the bundle gently into the hole. He filled the hole with reverence, secreting away the precious items. The shaman put a small rug over the area to hide the disturbed dirt, then pushed the bed back into place. Satisfied he had done his best to hide the items, Eleko flopped onto the bed, tired from the stress and exertion of the day.

Tunde hopped onto the bedside table, his skeletal tail swaying slightly. The monkey leaned in close to Eleko, chittering quietly.

"I know Tunde," Eleko stroked the monkey's back. "I am afraid too."

❖ ❖ ❖

Eleko was awoken from a restless night's sleep by shouts and pounding on his courtyard door. He sat up, suddenly alert, the night air feeling stale and oppressive. There was an acrid smell of smoke in the air, and Tunde was hopping with alarm on the table.

A loud cracking noise accompanied the thumping on his courtyard door, and Eleko knew that the locking bar would fail shortly.

"Tunde, you must hide," Eleko's voice came out in a panicked hiss. "Now!"

The skeletal monkey scurried around the small dwelling, looking for a place to curl and secret away. Outside, the locking bar gave way with a loud crash, and Eleko heard angry voices rush into the courtyard. He was not violent; it was not in his nature; he would reason with them but not resist.

Eleko stood and flattened out the creases in his robe with sweaty hands. He looked and could not see Tunde; smiling, he said a silent prayer to Eshu to keep the mischievous monkey safe.

The shaman jumped as the door crashed open, and men rushed in the door. They were faces he recognized, knew, and laughed with, but tonight the men's dark, sweaty faces held nothing but malicious in wide, crazed eyes. They threw Eleko to the ground, strong hands pulling and punching him. Kicks rained down on his body, and he desperately tried to cover his head. The room became a cacophony as the men smashed and splinted all they could find; Eleko gasped and grunted as they kicked and punched him mercilessly. Then all became still.

Men still held his arms and legs, but the rest backed away. Eleko spit out a mouth full of blood and looked toward the doorway as Bola entered the room. The man's white shirt was soaked red with blood, and he carried a thick, two-foot wooden cross in his hands. Blood and gore darkened the cross's wood and dripped onto Eleko's floor.

Bola's eyes stared hatefully at Eleko as he slowly approached.

"This is the home of a blasphemer and idol worshipper," Bola addressed the mob of men. "Burn it all!"

The men cheered wildly, and Bola grinned at their adulation. He stood directly above Eleko and stared at the shaman, his eyes wide and nostrils flaring. Eleko met his gaze defiantly; he would not give Bola the satisfaction of seeing any fear in his eyes. Bola gave a feral scream as he raised the cross high above his head, bringing it crashing down on Eleko's skull.

Eleko felt the jarring blow echo through his head, and his vision swooned before all went black.

◆ ◆ ◆

Consciousness came slowly back to Eleko, his head throbbed, and his eyes failed to focus correctly. He could not move his arms or legs, and the shaman struggled to fill his lungs with air.

Eleko heard someone calling his name from far off and turned toward the sound. After blinking several times, the battered face of the elder Oluwole slowly came into focus. The man was mouthing something through bruised lips, and after several moments Eleko realized the man was saying his name. Incomprehensibly, Oluwole seemed to be flying, soaring like a bird with outstretched arms.

"Eleko, can you hear me?" Oluwole's voice was a desperate whisper

"Oluwole?" Eleko's voice sounded weak and faint in his ears.

"Yes, Eleko, it's me," the man's face was swollen and bruised. "Do you know what happened to Abagda?"

"Abagda? No." Eleko struggled to shake his head; then, he peered groggily at the elder. "Oluwole, am I flying too?"

"Flying? Eleko, wake up! They are crucifying us like their nailed god," Oluwole's words finally jarred Eleko back to full consciousness.

Eleko blinked and saw the sun was low in the sky, early evening by his account. He looked at Oluwole and realized the man was bound to a large wooden cross several feet off the ground. Thick ropes tied Oluwole's outstretched arms to the cross and his feet to the lower portion.

The shaman saw that his arms and feet were similarly affixed to a cross. With some effort, Eleko could lean his head forward far enough to see a dozen crosses standing before the marketplace, where villagers were busy placing large plates of food on a long wooden table. Some cast furtive glances toward the men and women on the crosses, and others sneered and laughed at the crucified figures, but most averted their eyes. Eleko saw Ademola, dressed in a European coat and trousers, glance toward Eleko and quickly look away.

Eleko's cross was closest to the woods at the end of the twelve crosses. Thoughts of escape quickly faded as he heard a mixture of laughs and cries emanate down the line of crucified villagers. He craned his neck, and he could see Bola, a long spear grasped in his hands, making his way down the line of crosses. Bola would thrust the spear into the crucified villager, and he would laugh cruelly as they cried out. Eleko watched the twin make his way down the line. Thrust. Laugh. Move.

"Bola, how could you do this to your own people?" Oluwole stared down at the man, shaking his head.

"Thou shall smite every male thereof with the edge of the sword," Bola spouted with fanatical zeal as he thrust the spear into Oluwole.

The gore-slick spear slipped in Bola's hands, the pointed tip grazing Oluwole's chest, leaving a bright red line and sliding into the elder's eye. Bola frowned as he pulled the spear free with a sickening sucking noise, and Oluwole's head lolled forward lifelessly.

"That was not supposed to happen," Bola shrugged and grinned at Eleko. "Our Lord and Savior was pierced as he suffered on the cross. Minister John wishes you heathens to feel that pain."

Bola thrust the spear upward, and Eleko grunted as he felt the tip slide into his left side, just below the ribs. Eleko gritted his teeth, waiting for the pain to subside into a mind-numbing throb.

"I had you placed here last Eleko," Bola's grin was broad and filled with malice. "I wanted you to have the perfect view of the feast."

Bola laughed as he joined the others around the large table. From the corner of his eye, Eleko saw Ademola watching the exchange and turned toward the chieftain. Their eyes met momentarily, and Ademola's mouth moved as if he was going to speak; then, he hung his head and turned away.

As his lifeblood leaked from the wound in his side, Eleko watched the villagers assemble around the table. Had it not been for their dark skin and black hair, Eleko imagined this was how European church gatherings likely looked — the men in their fine black jackets and pants, the women in long dark dresses.

A hush came over the villagers as Ajayi led a tall blonde man dressed in a white shirt, black trousers, and wide-brimmed black hat into the village. Eleko knew this must be Minister John; the man was tall and lean with beady blue eyes and a sharp, pointed nose.

"Praise the Lord, you his angels, you mighty ones who do his bidding, who obey his word!" Minister John raised his hands skyward as he greeted the assembled villagers. "For the Son of Man is going to come in his Father's glory with his angels, and then he will reward each person according to what they have done."

Many villagers raised their arms in imitation of the minister, while others knelt and clasped their hands together in prayer. Several shouted Hallelujah and other praises that Eleko could not hear clearly.

"Human beings ate the bread of angels; he sent them all the food they could eat," Minister John gestured to the bounty of food the villagers had assembled.

Ajayi and Yemisi stood behind Minister John as he extolled the goodness of the villagers, the bountifulness of their feast, and their devotion to the one true god.

"With the assistance of Brother Ajayi and Sister Yemisi," Minister John gestured to the two, who bowed their heads deferentially to the man. "I have chosen this village amongst all the Christians in the land to host the angel's feast."

Ajayi and Yemisi gave smiles that did not reach their eyes as the villagers cheered at the minister's words and sang the praises of their new god. The minister began to stomp his feet and flail his arms in a chaotic dance, shaking his body wildly as he chanted and called out to god and the angels. Eleko saw many of the villagers imitating the same mad, frenetic dancing.

"He will send his angels with a loud trumpet call, and they will gather his elect from the four winds, from one end of the heavens to the other," Minister John shouted above the din of the feast, and Ajayi raised an ivory horn to his lips and blew a loud clarion call.

A loud thunderclap overhead answered the horn call, and Eleko raised his head to see clouds swirling over the village, moving in a circular pattern unlike he had ever seen before. Many of the villagers looked skyward in awe.

Eleko felt something thump against his outstretched arm, and with great effort, he turned to look. Tunde's hollow eyes stared back at him as the creature chittered at him.

"Tunde," Eleko smiled through the pain of his injuries at the sight of the skeleton. "You are alive; I was so worried about you."

The monkey's head cocked this way, and that, as he surveyed the ropes binding Eleko; then he scampered down the length of the cross, and the shaman could feel the monkey's skeletal claws against his feet. With fierce determination, the small monkey sank its teeth into the rope binding and began to tear at the strands.

"But you have come to Mount Zion, to the city of the living God, the heavenly Jerusalem. You have come to thousands upon thousands of angels in joyful assembly," Minister John had stopped dancing and thrust his arms heavenward. "Then I looked and heard the voice of many angels, numbering thousands upon thousands, and ten thousand times ten thousand. They encircled the throne and the living creatures and the elders."

The villagers stood transfixed as the swirling cloud took on the shape of flying forms, dozens of human-like creatures; they were snow white with broad feathered wings and long, flowing hair of golden blonde. To Eleko, they circled the village like vultures over a carcass. Men and women fell to their knees praising the nailed god, some weeping uncontrollably.

"Then I saw another angel flying in midair, and he had the eternal gospel to proclaim to those who live on the earth — to every nation, tribe, language, and people," Minister John's voice sounded loud, shrill, and maniacal as he looked from the flying angels to the villagers. "It was time to feast."

Eleko saw the feral grin on Minister John's face as the first angel dove from the sky, the soft white skin of its face stretched wide as the creature crashed into Ademola, driving the chieftain to the ground, its mouth full of jagged teeth sinking into his face. The angel raked long, sharp talon's across Ademola body, spilling his innards onto the earth in a rush of hot blood.

Voices raised in praise and worship turned to screams of pain and terror as the angels swooped from the sky and tore into the villagers, feeding upon them in a blood frenzy.

Eleko felt the ropes around his feet slacken as Tunde climbed back up the cross and began working on the bindings around his right hand.

"Hurry, Tunde," Eleko looked from the monkey to the angels darting from the sky in terror.

Minister John surveyed the scene, grinning and laughing, as Ajayi and Yemisi smirked behind him as the villagers called out to save them.

"Eat my angels, eat," Minister John laughed and clapped his hands.

Eleko saw Yemisi watch impassively as one of the angels fell upon her brother, tearing his face from his skull before sinking its long teeth into his neck, Bola's red blood splatting the pure white wings.

Amid the carnage, a tall man stepped from the shadows, and Eleko quickly recognized Adagba. The hunter bore a long spear in each hand. Eleko did not know if he was more amazed that Adagba had survived the purge of non-Christians, or that the man had returned to aid those that had forsaken him.

Eleko watched as the Adagba reared back one mighty shoulder and let one of the spears fly. The long shaft sailed through the air and pierced the chest of one of the angels; the creature pirouetted out of the sky like skewered meat and crashed to the ground in a pile of broken wings and bones. The hunter raised his fist triumphantly and readied another spear just as three angels fell upon him, teeth and claws tearing at the valiant warrior. Eleko turned away from the grisly scene but could not block out the anguished sounds of Adagba's dying screams.

Tunde freed the shaman's right hand, and Eleko silently prayed to the gods that the monkey could free him before an angel spotted him. However, for the time being, the angels seemed fully occupied, feasting upon the villagers. The night carried the iron-like scent of blood and the terrified and pain-filled cries of the village converts as the feast of angels continued unabated.

◆ ◆ ◆

Eleko groaned as pain shot through his wounded side. The monkey freed the shaman's left hand from the bonds, and his body tumbled from the cross to land hard upon the earth. Tunde hopped down, landing beside the shaman, his skeletal face closely inspecting Eleko's dark features.

"I'm ok, Tunde," Eleko grimaced and placed a hand over his wound. "We need to get to Abeokuta; the city is fortified, they will be able to stand against these Christians and their angels."

Eleko got slowly to his feet, still numb from the bindings, and swooning, realized how significantly weakened he was by his wounds.

"We do not have much time, Tunde," Eleko pressed a hand firmly against his wounded side. "I fear my life force is draining from me like the sands of an hourglass."

Tunde hopped onto his shoulder, and the shaman ran

a loving hand over the creature. He half ran, half stumbled into the forest's darkness, leaving the dying cries of his village behind him.

◆ ◆ ◆

They stuck to the cover provided by the canopy of trees to hide from any angels searching the woods overhead for more victims. Beads of sweat dotted Eleko's forehead and bald scalp like glistening pearls when he finally stopped against a tree to catch his breath. Tunde hopped from his shoulder and scurried into the underbrush as Eleko stared after him. The shaman noted that the edges of his vision were black, a further sign that his body was quickly failing.

"Tunde, have you finally run back to Eshu?" Eleko called after the disappearing form of the skeletal monkey.

However, when Tunde returned moments later, the monkey gripped large handfuls of green leaves and bright red flowers in his boney fingers. Eleko watched the monkey shove the leaves and flowers between his bone-white jaws and teeth, grinding them into a mushy red-green ball that he spat back into his paws. The monkey's hollow eye socks gazed up at Eleko as he held out the ball to the shaman and placed it in his palm.

"What's this?" Eleko sniffed the ball and raised his eyebrows in surprise. "The flowers and leaves of a Roselle plant."

Tunde pointed to the wound on Eleko's side; the shaman nodded and winced as he packed the ground mixture into the wound. The wound was raw and painful, but the medicinal plant took some stinging away within a few minutes.

"I am ready," Eleko nodded to Tunde, and the little monkey hopped back onto his shoulder.

The two pushed on through the night, stopping only once more for Eleko to drink cool water from a stream. As the shaman knelt to drink, he spied two piercing yellow eyes staring at him through the darkness. He could smell the stink of the beast's breath on the night air and the guttural growl of the lion knotted Eleko's innards with fear.

"*To come all this way, only to be eaten by a lion,*" the thought almost made Eleko laugh.

Tunde stepped forward, placing himself between the lion and Elku. The small monkey silently stared at the lion, the dark hollows of his eye sockets meeting the lion's gaze until the beast receded further into the forest's darkness and troubled them no more.

Eleko rose and staggered into the night, with Tunde following behind.

◆ ◆ ◆

The night was giving way to sunrise as they approached Abeokuta, the horizon glowing a golden orange as the sun rose behind the fortified city. Eleko's steps had become labored from blood loss and exhaustion as he emerged from the forest. His body swayed precariously in the morning light as he peered at Abeokuta.

Eleko let out a deep breath that turned into a muling sob as he sank to his knees. The shaman's shoulders slumped as he gave in to despair. Tunde hopped onto

Eleko's shoulder, placing a boney paw on the man's head. The monkey turned his skull toward Abeokuta, and the creature's hollow eye sockets stared at the long dark shadow on the ground. Tunde followed the length of the shadow up the city walls to the large wooden cross that stood upon battlements in the morning sun.

AMONG THE WOLVES

Piotr Kowalczyk lived by a simple mantra, "Sweep and live." He was an old man, nearly sixty-five, in July 1943 when the Nazis had rounded up all two hundred and thirty-five people in his small village of Michniów and executed all but the two dozen or so who they sent to the camps. The Waffen SS soldiers had burned every structure in the Michniów and buried the bodies in the trenches the local partisan units and Polish Home Army groups had dug for defense.

Piotr did not know why the Germans spared him and executed the rest of his family, his two sons, his sweet grandchildren, and his beautiful Ania. Perhaps the Germans thought him too old to waste a bullet on, or he supposed they wanted a few cowed survivors to warn others of what happened to those who opposed the Third Reich. Regardless, he was sent to Special Camp 137 to be an orderly for the camp commandant, Major Horst Vetter.

Piotr swept Vetter's two-room office as an orderly, polished his boots, and occasionally made his coffee.

A task that Piotr was amazed the arrogant SS officer would allow a prisoner to do. How easy it would be for Piotr to poison the coffee and get some justice for his Ania and all of Michniów. While sweeping the office one day, Piotr had found a small ball of rat poison and slipped it into the lining of his grey prisoner's shirt. At night, he fantasized about dissolving the little white ball in Vetter's coffee and watching the Nazi turn blue as he clawed at his uniform collar with its precious SS lightning bolts, gasping for air like a fish out of water. But Piotr could never muster the courage to do it.

"One day," Piotr would always think to himself. "One day, Ania, I will avenge you."

Piotr and the other three camp orderlies slept in separate quarters from the other prisoners in Special Camp 137, mainly because Vetter and Doctor Grabner, who ran the medical research facility, did not want the orderlies contaminating their workspaces with the lice that infested the malnourished residents in the prison barracks. A special cell with four bunk beds was attached to Doctor Grabner's medical research building. The cell was at the end of the hall of a long corridor of cells that housed the objects of Doctor Grabner's research.

Piotr was always careful not to look at the occupants of the cells as he passed by, the living mutilations of Doctor Grabner's research. At night, Piotr and the other orderlies would try to block out those poor souls' screams and whimpering cries.

The other three orderlies, all Slovaks, worked in the medical research building next to Vetter's two-room headquarters. Vetter had selected Piotr as his orderly because, unlike the three Slovaks, Piotr had blue eyes, and Vetter found dark eyes distasteful to look upon.

Piotr was sweeping the outer office the night Sergeant Metz brought the stranger in. Metz was precisely the kind of man the Nazis liked to attract into their ranks. He was a burly blue-eyed brute with a blonde crew cut and an unfathomable penchant for cruelty and violence. Piotr had often seen Metz mercilessly beating prisoners for even the slightest infractions. The look of feral glee that filled the Sergeant's face as he doled out pain and suffering to the unfortunate souls of Special Camp 137 haunted Piotr's dreams. Once, Piotr heard guards joking that you could always tell a prisoner who had met Metz because they were missing teeth. The result of Metz's trademark kick in the teeth while a prisoner was down on the ground.

When Metz walked into the outer office, Piotr was careful to look down and avert his eyes, but he could still see the jackbooted Nazi kick the mud off his feet onto the floor.

"Clean this up." Metz sneered at Piotr as the two German guards with him chuckled.

Piotr nodded wordlessly and quickly began sweeping the dirt from the wood floor as Metz walked by him. He could see a fourth man with the Germans, a tall man in a dark suit with black hair and a thin mustache. Something about the man seemed very familiar to Piotr.

"Where have I seen that face before?" thought Piotr as Metz instructed the man to wait against the wall as the two guards took up a position by the door.

Metz knocked on Major Vetter's office door and then

quickly slipped in and shut it behind him when the commandant had given permission to enter.

The dark-haired man seemed to be studying Piotr closely as he swept up the mud and deposited it in a metal pail. The man's intense scrutiny made Piotr very uncomfortable. However, something about the man seemed familiar, and Piotr could not help but keep glancing at him.

To Piotr's horror, the man walked across the room and up to him. Something in the man's gait tickled a memory in Piotr's mind. Piotr nervously looked over at the two guards, who, curiously staring straight ahead, did not notice the man's movement.

"Do we know each other?" asked the man in perfectly accented Polish.

"I do not think so, Sir," Piotr looked down at his feet.

He was not supposed to talk to anyone but other prisoners and never in his native tongue; at any moment, Piotr expected the guards to walk over and begin beating him.

"Here now, good man, let me look at you."

"Sir, please, you will get me in trouble." Piotr pleaded with the stranger in a hushed tone.

"Nonsense, let me see you."

Piotr looked up, and the man seemed to study his face with his dark piercing eyes. The man brought his hand to his chin and made a much-exaggerated thinking gesture as he looked at Piotr. The orderly's eyes nervously darted to the guards, who seemed oblivious to the exchange.

The man squinted and pointed at Piotr. "It will come to me; I am certain we have met before. In the meantime, can I ask you a favor, my good man?"

"A favor?" Piotr's unease was growing steadily.

"I would like to leave something with you. Could I do that?"

"What is it?" Piotr's eyes continually darted to the guards to see if they noticed the conversation.

The man reached into the pocket of his dark suit and produced a gleaming silver dog whistle attached to a silver chain. Writing in a language that Piotr did not recognize covered the whistle. As the man reached out and handed the whistle to Piotr, a shock of recognition ran through the old Polish man's body.

"It couldn't be," thought Piotr. "It just couldn't be. And why is he speaking with a Polish accent now?"

The man placed the whistle in Piotr's hand and closed his fingers around it. Piotr stared into the man's face, a face he had not seen in a very long time, unable to speak.

"Now, if you hear a dog, I need you to blow that whistle. Can you do that?"

Piotr just nodded.

"Good. Good. You won't forget now, will you?"

Piotr shook his head. A big smile crossed the man's familiar face, and he walked across the room to where Metz had told him to wait. Piotr looked over at the guards, who continued to look straight ahead uncaringly as he slipped the dog whistle into his pocket.

❖ ❖ ❖

Major Vetter looked up from his desk at Sergeant Metz with disdain.

"Can you repeat what you just said, Sergeant," Vetter ensured he spoke in a tone that let the brutish Sergeant know that it was a command, not a request.

"An Englishman came to the camp gate this evening requesting to speak to you, Sir. He said it was a matter of great importance," Metz stared at his commanding officer with dull, slack eyes.

"And you checked this man for weapons?"

"Yes, Sir, two times, very thoroughly. He had no weapons."

"Where did he come from?"

"He did not say, Sir. But he must be a spy. Should I have him shot?" Metz failed to hide the hint of eagerness in his voice.

"Idiot, what kind of spy walks up to a gate and knocks?" Vetter shook his head, increasingly irritated by the Sergeant's ignorance. "Bring him in."

"Yes, Sir!" The Sergeant snapped to attention and then exited the room.

Major Vetter knew that the Third Reich needed men like Sergeant Metz, and he had to admit he was very effective at keeping the prisoners in line, but he was so limited when it came to thinking. Before the war, Horst Vetter had been an engineer and enjoyed creating order by solving complex problems and making things fit. That is one of the reasons he had joined the

Waffen SS, the armed wing of the *Saal-Shutz* or "SS"; the SS had solutions to problems. The SS created order. As commandant of Special Camp 137, he had secured a senior position in the *SS-Totenkopfverbande*, the SS-TV, or Death's Head Units. He played a leading role in solving the problems of Germany once and for all. Dealing with mindless brutes like Sergeant Metz was just a cost of doing business. Metz was just a cog in the machine that ground down the problems of the Third Reich into ash and dust.

Sergeant Metz returned to the room with a tall man in a dark suit. Vetter quietly studied the man with his ice-blue eyes, a look he knew made the prisoners cower with fear. He enjoyed watching the wretched creatures wither under his gaze. Major Vetter saw the Aryan race as a bright sun that scorched the undesirable weeds of humanity wherever they tried to grow among the flowers of Germany insidiously. To Vetter's surprise, not only did the man return his gaze with dark piercing eyes, but the man smiled. Not a cursory cordial smile, a genuine natural smile that reached up to the man's eyes.

"Major Vetter, I presume!" The man in English cheerfully extended his hand in greeting.

"I fear you have me at a disadvantage; you know my name, but I do not know yours." Vetter stared coldly, not shaking the man's hand.

"Oh yes, yes, of course. Do you mind?" The man gestured to the wooden chair on the other side of the SS Major's desk.

"By all means." Vetter nodded, but something about this Englishman's nonchalance was beginning to bother him.

The man sat down on the wooden chair, unbuttoned the front of his suit to make himself more comfortable, and looked around the room.

"Maybe this man is some kind of spy," thought Vetter agitated at the uncertainty.

"Well, look at that," the man leaned over to look out the office's window. "You even have a view of the night sky; what a beautiful full moon it is tonight too!"

"I believe you were about to tell me your name." Vetter's tone made it clear that he was not amused. He had seen even seasoned combat soldiers pale when he took this tone of voice with them, but this man seemed unperturbed.

"Yes, of course. My name is Janus Greystone," the man replied as if he had shown up for afternoon tea.

"You should wipe that smug look off your face, Englander," Metz hovered menacingly over Greystone.

Major Vetter raised a hand and cut off Metz with an annoyed look.

"You are aware that England and Germany are at war, are you not?"

"Oh, of course, dreadful business." Greystone shook his head and furrowed his brow.

"So you will understand our curiosity at an Englishman showing up on our doorstep in the middle of the night."

"While I do speak English that does not make me an Englishman." corrected Greystone.

"He's clearly an Englishman and a spy," started Metz but

was silenced by a stern look from Major Vetter.

"Wenn ich Deutsch sprechen würde, wäre ich Deutsch?" If I spoke German, would I be German? Greystone said in perfectly accented German.

"If you come here seeking to play games, Mr. Greystone, I think you will find I am in no mood for folly." Vetter leaned forward, his eyes cold and serpentine as he lost his patience.

"On the contrary, Major, I am here to take a problem off your hands." Greystone crossed his right leg over his left to make himself more comfortable.

"Mr. Greystone," Vetter's lip curled upwards in a half sneer. "Nobody takes anything from the Third Reich. The Reich takes what it wants from those that do not deserve what they have."

Major Vetter punctuated his words by moving his hand to his collar and rubbing his thumb over the SS Death's Head insignia on his collar. As he watched his commanding officer losing patience with the Englishman, Sergeant Metz let a wolfish grin cross his face. The Nazi sergeant sensed violence was about to unfold and would revel in the chance to break this Englishman.

"Let me clarify," Greystone raised his hand with his index finger extended to make a point as he spoke. "You have someone residing at your camp, three someone's actually, that I believe would be mutually beneficial if you turned them over to me."

Major Vetter laughed mirthlessly, and Sergeant Metz followed the officer's lead with a grunting laugh that sounded more like a boar searching for a forest truffle.

"Mr. Greystone, it is improbable you will be leaving this camp, let alone taking anyone from it!" Major Vetter's voice was thick with malice.

"I am speaking of three brothers, the Kovak brothers, identical triplets. Though one has a scar on his right eye," continued Greystone, unperturbed by Vetter's threats and moving his index finger across his right eye from brow to cheek to demonstrate the man's scar.

Sergeant Metz screwed his face into a look of puzzlement, "Doctor Grabner has three Serb twins in the research building."

"Triplets," corrected Greystone.

"I have grown tired of this game," Vetter laced his words with irritation. "Sergeant Metz, take our guest for questioning; I want to know where he is from and how he got here. Mr. Greystone, I think you will find Special Camp 137 far less hospitable than where ever you came from."

"I can assure you, Major Vetter, that by tomorrow morning, your career in the SS will come to an unceremonious end if I do not leave here with the Kovak brothers this evening," Greystone answered coolly.

Sergeant Metz appeared ready to throttle the Englishman, but Major Vetter stayed his hand. He studied the unusual man before him; Greystone was as calm as he had ever seen any man. Not even a bead of perspiration dotted his forehead despite Vetter having just assured him of certain torture and death. While in Berlin, he had heard rumors of the Gestapo training men to pass as Englishmen or Americans for special operations. Could this Greystone be a Gestapo agent? He had shown no credentials, but what other explanation for this bizarre visitor could there be? Greystone had spoken both English and German with equally impeccable accents.

"Sergeant Metz, go find Doctor Grabner," ordered the SS Major.

"Sir?" Metz appeared confused by the sudden change in orders.

"Go ask Doctor Grabner to join me. I want to hear what is so special about these Serbs."

The Sergeant snapped to attention and left the room. Greystone sat wordlessly, barely even paying attention to Major Vetter. He seemed more interested in craning his neck to peer up at the night sky.

"Who sent you?" Vetter hated the sound of uncertainty in his voice.

"I assure you, Major, I come of my own accord." Greystone gave a casual smile that Vetter found increasingly maddening.

"The man must be Gestapo," Vetter's thoughts turned ominous. "Probably someone high up in Himmler's circle to be this confident."

Major Vetter found himself racked with indecision. If this man was indeed a secret agent of the Gestapo, harming or hindering him in any way would be career suicide. It could even result in an assignment to the Eastern Front. But on the other hand, this was precisely the kind of ruse the English and their allies were capable of. If he let an English spy walk out of his camp with three important prisoners, he would surely face the firing squad. He needed to hear what Doctor Grabner had to say about the Serbs.

Greystone reached into his jacket and checked a pocket watch. Vetter watched as the dark-haired man frowned down at the timepiece and returned it to his coat.

"Do you have somewhere to be?" Vetter was starting to feel unnerved by this whole encounter.

"No," Greystone sighed. "But time is always of the essence."

Sergeant Metz returned to the room with a thin, bald man with small round spectacles and dressed in a white doctor's lab jacket with a swastika emblazoned on the left breast pocket. Vetter noticed the jacket had tiny pencil-tip-sized speckles of dried bloodstains on it.

"Sergeant, that will be all. You can wait in the outer office," commanded Vetter before gazing at the doctor. "Heinrich, thank you for coming."

The burly Sergeant saluted Major Vetter sharply with the stiff raised arm Nazi salute and turned sharply on his boot heels, exiting the room and closing the door behind him.

Heinrich Grabner was a senior Nazi party official and member of the Allgemeine SS, the branch of the SS responsible for enforcing the Third Reich's racial policies. His work at the camp consisted mainly of experiments on the prisoners to identify other genetic traits of undesirables and further highly classified research. Although Vetter was in charge of Special Camp 137, he primarily managed the camp's prisoners and maintained security. Grabner was senior to him within the Nazi party, and his medical research was the camp's priority. However, this did not cause friction between the two men as they shared mutual respect based on the same ideological beliefs and religious devotion to the Third Reich.

"Sergeant Metz told me this is about the Kovak triplets?" The bald doctor grabbed a chair and seated himself at the edge of the desk, eyeing Greystone suspiciously.

"Yes, it is." Vetter showed his annoyance at Metz for discussing the matter with the doctor and made a mental note to discipline the Sergeant later.

"I would like the boys turned over to me."

Doctor Grabner's raised his eyebrows, surprised at the unusual guest and his forthright request.

"And you are?"

"Janus Greystone." He gave a slight nod of greeting.

"He is here to take the Serbs; what are your thoughts on that?" asked Vetter.

The doctor looked at Vetter for several seconds with serious, studious eyes. Vetter knew the doctor was coming to the same conclusions as him; such a request only comes from the Gestapo secret police.

"The Kovak boys, teens really, are interesting specimens. They were captured in Serbia in the vicinity of a town called Zarozje. They are strong for their size and have a high tolerance to pain."

"Pain? I trust they have not been hurt," Greystone narrowed his eyes at the doctor.

"No, they have not been hurt. Though they may

have found some of my experiments and tests uncomfortable."

"What have your tests discovered?" Vetter leaned back and folded his arms across his chest.

"All three boys are uniformly strong; my guards must take special precautions when moving them. When they first got to the camp, we had several severe injuries due to them breaking loose from their bonds and attacking my staff. Their pain threshold is remarkable. When I conducted these same tests on other patients, I broke their will to resist in minutes, but these boys did not twitch. It's remarkable."

"Who has seen your reports, Doctor?" Vetter gave the man a withering look.

"My work gets reported to the most senior members of the Allgemeine SS. It's my understanding that my reports are received with great interest." A look of smug arrogance crossed his face.

This was all beginning to make sense to Vetter, senior members of the Third Reich would be very interested in genetics that made a soldier stronger and more pain resistant. Vetter suspected Himmler was aware of Doctor Grabner's findings, perhaps even the Fuhrer.

"Though their dietary habits are still a mystery," added the doctor.

"Dietary habits?" asked Vetter raising one eyebrow.

"Yes. At the time of their capture, the Kovak boys were eating the corpse of some of our recently killed soldiers. As a matter of fact, they appear unable to digest any food aside from fresh meat; they regurgitate anything else we have fed them."

Gunfire suddenly punctuated the quiet night, followed by shouts and screams. Major Vetter leaped up from his desk, his hand going to the pistol holstered on his hip. A look of concern crossed the Nazi doctor's face. They were deep within Reich-held territory; this was supposed to be a safe and secure area where he could conduct his research.

"Sergeant Metz, what's going on?" shouted Vetter.

"Gentleman, I am afraid I warned you that time was of the essence." Greystone shook his head, his face a mask of disappointment.

◆ ◆ ◆

"Sergeant Metz, what's going on?" called the Major from behind the closed office door.

The sounds of automatic gunfire and screams were escalating outside. When he recognized the tall, dark-haired man, Piotr knew something would happen tonight. A smile crossed Piotr's lips, perhaps the first he had smiled since that July morning in 1943.

The two German guards lay sprawled on the floor and motionless, their empty coffee cups broken and shattered alongside their bodies. Sergeant Metz, the monster in the nightmares of so many prisoners in Special Camp 137, lay on the floor, his legs kicking wildly as he clawed at his neck for air. Rivulets of blood seeped out of the scratches he tore into the skin of his neck as he gasped for air.

Piotr walked over to the struggling Sergeant, stepping

over the spilled remains of the poisoned coffee. He looked down and noticed with satisfaction that the brute had urinated on himself, soaking the front of his uniform pants as he struggled to breathe. The man looked up at Piotr, his blue eyes bulging and bloodshot; his face blued with the lack of oxygen from the poison attacking his respiratory system. Piotr smiled down at the Sergeant and kicked the flailing Sergeant in the mouth with all his might, sending a spray of blood and broken teeth across the floor. He watched the man's kicks slowly lessen to a light flutter, wrinkling his nose in disgust as the Sergeant's bowels vacated themselves.

"This is for you, Ania," thought Piotr with a smile as he stared down into the Nazi beast's lifeless eyes.

Outside, all chaos was breaking out, and he could see flashes of automatic rifle fire lighting the night. Though Piotr thought he detected more screaming and less gunfire than he had moments before. Then over the maelstrom unfolding outside, he heard a dog's clear and distinct howl.

The man reached into his pocket and withdrew the silver whistle. Putting it to his lips, Piotr began to blow.

❖ ❖ ❖

"What is this Greystone? What have you done?" demanded Vetter drawing his Luger pistol and pointing it at Greystone.

"I have done nothing." Greystone sat back calmly in the chair. "This was all within your power to avoid Major."

"Metz! Where the hell is Sergeant Metz?"

"Hell is probably an excellent guess." Greystone let a sardonic smile slip across his face.

"I'll go get him," offered Doctor Grabner running to the office door.

Just as Doctor Grabner turned the doorknob and swung the door open, a huge brown wolf-like beast leaped through the open door and onto the Nazi doctor. Major Vetter watched in horror as the beast dug its claws into the doctor's chest and clamped its large jaws down on the doctor's screaming face. It was the most enormous wolf Vetter had ever seen, at least twice the size of any of its species, with a coat of thick grey-brown fur. The creature's teeth were easily the size of a man's index finger.

Doctor Grabner's muffled screams snapped Major Vetter out of his momentary shock, and he pointed his Luger at the beast and fired several shots into its side. The creature swung its massive head to look at Vetter with eyes as dark as coal, taking the vast majority of Grabner's face with it. Lidless eyes bulged out of Grabner's skinless face, a gaping hole remained where the doctor's nose had been, and a lipless mouth screamed inhumanely as the doctor's limbs flailed in mindless agony.

The wolf snarled at Vetter; pieces of Grabner's face dangled from the creature's razor-sharp teeth like curtains of fluttering meat. The wolf seemed unfazed by the bullet wounds and rounded on Vetter. Malice filled the creature's dark burning eyes, and Vetter noticed the beast had a scar running down the right eye, from brow to cheek. He backed away, trying to put his desk between him and the beast. Out of the corner of his eye, he saw Greystone sitting as calmly in his chair as he was just moments before.

A second wolf of equal size to the first padded into the room and, as casually as someone would sniff a flower, sank its teeth into Doctor Grabner's writhing body and tore free a mouthful of flesh and stringy intestines, prompting an inhuman scream to burst forth from the Nazi doctor's ravaged mouth.

"You did this," the Major turned his weapon on the smiling Greystone.

Vetter pulled the trigger, and the gun let out a loud click. Empty. Greystone smiled that remarkably calm smile at him and shrugged. Then the beast was upon the SS Major, slamming him to the ground. Blood gushed from his neck, coating the Death's Head insignia on his collar as the wolf tore into Vetter's neck. His screams became choked gurgles as the beast tore through muscle and sinew.

◆ ◆ ◆

Piotr watched as the giant wolf waited in the doorway for the other two members of its pack. Shortly after he blew the whistle, the first of the enormous wolves had run past him and leaped into Major Vetter's office through the open door. A second wolf followed shortly after the first. The beast that sat patiently in the doorway looked at Piotr but showed no malice towards him. Piotr decided he would keep his distance nonetheless.

The sounds of fighting outside had died, and Piotr no longer heard gunshots. The two gore-covered wolves appeared from Vetter's office and calmly trotted by Piotr without so much as a sidelong glance. They joined their companion waiting by the door, and all three walked calmly outside and into the night.

Piotr leaned his head into the office and saw the faceless, disemboweled body of Doctor Grabner lying torn and mangled on the floor, and he smiled. In his mind, Piotr pictured all the townspeople of Michniów celebrating around a massive bonfire in the afterlife. His sons and grandchildren would be there running happily around the fire, and of course, his beautiful Ania would be there with the firelight reflected in her eyes.

"I think I will be seeing you again very soon, my beautiful Ania," thought Piotr with a wan smile.

To his surprise, the tall, dark-haired man appeared in the doorway of Major Vetter's office and smoothed out the wrinkles of his jacket with a calm hand. He looked up, surveyed the dead Nazi guards, rested his eyes on Piotr, and smiled. Piotr stepped forward and handed the silver whistle back to the man.

"Good job," said Greystone in perfect Polish, raising the whistle and putting it in his pocket. "Excellent job indeed."

"I...I know you," stammered Piotr failing to keep the nervousness from his voice.

"Oh?" Greystone cocked his head, interested.

"When I was a little boy, my grandfather took me to Prague. We went to a carnival to see the animal shows when we were there. It was called the World's Most Wondrous Traveling Carnival. You...you were there.

You were the ringmaster. You walked over to me, leaned down, and gave me a balloon, the same way you handed me the whistle earlier. That's when I recognized you. That's how I knew it was you; the movements were identical. The Germans called you Greystone, but you went by a different name then."

"You have an excellent memory. I have gone by many names," Greystone smiled. "Piotr, isn't it?"

"Yes, that's me. But how? That was over sixty-five years ago. You look exactly the same."

Greystone just smiled and shrugged. "I am a collector of oddities; some would even say I am an oddity myself."

He patted Piotr on the shoulder and started to walk out the door toward the wolves, then stopped and turned back towards Piotr.

"Did you like it?"

"Like what?" the question caught Piotr off guard.

"The show, when your grandfather took you to see the carnival, did you like it?"

"It was the most amazing thing I have ever seen," smiled Piotr, remembering that wondrous day so long ago.

"Piotr," Greystone had a curious look on his face. "Would you like to come with us?"

"Yes, I would like that very much." Piotr gave the man a broad smile that made him look almost childlike.

"Ania, it looks like we will have to wait a little longer to see each other again," thought Piotr as he walked alongside the ringmaster and the three wolves out into the darkness of the night.

THE EATER IS COMING

The full moon illuminated the Swaine farm as Reverend Smith hitched his horse to the wooden rail beside the cabin. The branches of the nearby forest cast long shadows along the ground, like thousands of clawed fingers reaching for the Puritan minister of Wethersfield.

The weather was unnaturally cold for late April in the Connecticut River Valley, bad for the spring planting and, indeed, the hand of the Devil as far as the Reverend was concerned.

One of the Swaine's hunting dogs sniffed intently at the floorboards of a nearby wagon, ignoring the tall, lanky minister as he passed by. The Reverend cast a sidelong look into the back of the cart, where a huddled form lay covered by burlap. Something dark and wet seeped through the burlap and pooled along the floorboards. He shoed the dog away with a kick of his foot, and the dog scampered off into the darkness.

Reverend Smith brushed the dust from the ride off

his dark doublet and breeches, noting with annoyance that mud hat splattered onto his stockings. He removed his wide-brimmed, black felt hat and opened the cabin door.

Inside, two men seated around the oak table stood expectantly. A white-haired man, heavy-set with a wide bulbous nose, rushed forward to meet him.

"Reverend Smith, thank you for coming so quickly," the man looked relieved to see the minister. "I am confident the Devil's work is afoot in the Great Meadow, and all the souls of Wethersfield may be in danger this night."

"Yes, Reverend," a dark-bearded man with red-rimmed eyes and a face tight with tension nervously tugged at the white cuffs of his doublet as he slowly stood. "God bless you for coming."

"If what you say is true, the Lord has called me here to be his vessel of salvation," the Reverend nodded to the bearded man before turning his attention to the other. "Clement, whose body is in the cart?"

"It's the body of the witch's consort," Clement spoke with evident distaste. "A Pequot sorcerer, he was killed when the men seized her this afternoon."

"I see, "Reverend Smith folded his arms across his chest and pursed his lips. "William Swaine, how did the witch come to infect a Christian household?"

"Reverend," the bearded man's voice quavered, and he looked at his feet. "It's all my fault."

A great wracking sob shook the man's body, and he collapsed back into the chair as he covered his face with shaking hands.

The Reverend and Clement exchanged glances; the heavy-set man placed his hand on Swaine's shoulder, "William, why don't you tell Reverend Smith everything from the beginning?"

"Five days ago," Swaine looked at them with tear-filled eyes, his face a mask of anguish. "Some Dutch fur trappers came out of the forest to barter for cattle. They had some spices and furs to trade for one of my cows."

The Reverend looked contemplative, then his face registered shock and disapproval, "William, five days ago was Sunday. Are you saying you conducted business on the Lord's Day?"

A fresh wave of sobs wracked Swaine's body, "I'm sorry, Reverend, I knew it was wrong. Now God is punishing me."

"Tell him about the witch, William," Clement gently urged.

William sniffed deeply and tried to wipe away his tears, "There was a woman with them, a Dutch woman. She gave my daughters, Mary and Rose, each a doll. I thought they were hideous things made of straw and leather ties, but the girls wanted them so badly, so I allowed it."

"She gave them to your daughters freely, without trade or barter?" Clement looked genuinely surprised as William nodded.

"The Devil gives away his gifts freely," Reverend Smith sighed and shook his head dourly.

"Everything seemed fine until last night. The girls had been playing out behind the barn," Swaine's eyes looked far off in memory, and he shook his head disbelievingly. "We sat down to dinner and our thanks to the Lord for his bounty, and that's when it happened."

"That's when what happened?" the Reverend eyed the man inquisitively.

"Mary's doll," Swaine looked at the men with sheer terror in his expression. "It…it spoke. We were sitting at the dinner table, and this small, high-pitched voice called from the girl's room."

"What did it say?"

"It said, 'The eater is coming,'" Swaine's voice broke with emotion as tears streamed down his cheeks. "Over and over again, it said, 'The eater is coming.'"

◆ ◆ ◆

Clement held the lantern high, leading the Reverend and Swaine behind the barn. Before them, torchlight burned around the large tree stump that Swaine used for chopping wood. The shadow of a man in the dark attire and wide-brimmed felt hat of the Puritan settlers stood guard with a long smooth-bored musket. The fire of the torches glinted off the large hunting knife belted to his waist.

As the men approached, they saw a small doll nailed to the top of the stump. It was a crude thing with a body and limbs of straw and branches bound together with thin leather strands. The head was rough-hewn fabric with dark sewn dots for eyes and a nose, a thin mouth, and similarly tied over the straw body with leather. It lay spread across the stump, held in place by an iron nail driven through each limb.

"It's hideous," Clement winced in disgust.

"Reverend," the man on guard nodded. "It's good to see you."

"The Lord is blessed to have men like you on guard against evil, John Finch," the Reverend nodded in return. "Which doll is this?"

"It's Rose's doll," Swaine answered quietly.

"And this is not the one that has spoken?" the Reverend inspected the doll closely, careful not to touch it.

"No, Reverend, only Mary's doll has spoken," Swaine averted his eyes from the doll.

"Has this doll been examined thoroughly?" Reverend Smith looked at Clement, who shook his head. "Brother Finch, please check the doll with your knife."

"What are you looking for?" Swaine peered over Clement's shoulder as Finch drew his hunting knife and moved guardedly toward the doll as if approaching a snared wolf.

"Witches are known to hide evil eyes within objects to spy on Christian homes for the Devil," Reverend Smith watched Finch intently as the man poked at the doll with the tip of his knife.

The blade sunk easily into the head of the doll and the limbs; however, the knife his some resistance in the center. Finch looked questioningly at the Reverend, who nodded for him to continue. The man picked at the center of the doll, cutting through the straw and thin branches. Finch stopped and peered closely at the doll before stepping back aghast. Clement gasped in horror as Finch moved backward, and the torchlight danced off a mass uncovered in the center of the doll. It was something dark and meaty, wrapped in tendon and ligament.

"What is that?" Clement stared in horror.

"I believe it's a chicken heart or maybe a rooster," Finch nodded with certainty as he resumed poking at the mass.

"What does this mean, Reverend?" Swaine's voice quivered. "What has it done to my daughters?"

"You have brought a great evil into your house William Swaine," the Reverend's eyes blazed in the torchlight as Swaine groaned miserably. "Where are the girls now?"

"They are with their mother and aunt at John Plumb's farm," Clement tore his eyes away from the mangled doll to look at the Reverend.

"Good, it's best to keep them away from here until we sort this out," the Reverend nodded contemplatively. "Where are the witch and the other doll?"

"They are in the barn," Finch re-sheathed his knife. "John Plumb and William's brother Abraham are guarding them."

"Take me to them," Reverend Smith looked sidelong at Clement and nodded. "You were correct in calling for me; this is surely the Devil's handiwork!"

❖ ❖ ❖

The Reverend stared intently at the woman as she sputtered and gasped into wakefulness, rivulets of water running down her face and long, unkempt blonde hair. Her hands were tied behind her to the thick center pole of the barn with a length of rope that chaffed and reddened her wrists. The woman wore no shoes, and her feet were similarly tied at the ankles.

"She's awake now," John Plumb placed the empty bucket beside his feet.

The shock of the cold water had startled the woman from her slumber; however, now she studied them warily as she struggled to catch her breath. One eye had swollen shut from a blow to the face, but her one good eye darted nervously from face to face. The Reverend noted fear in that blue eye, a sign he took that he had the Devil on the run. He looked disapprovingly at her dirty bare feet and homespun dress that revealed too much skin at the low neckline.

"Why have you done this to me?" the woman's thick Dutch accent slipped between purpled lips, split and swollen from a recent beating. "I have never done your people any harm."

"The witch speaks lies, Reverend," Abraham Swaine kept his musket pointed at the woman.

"Why is she in this condition?" the Reverend's voice was dispassionate as he eyed her bruised face, displaying little concern for her condition.

"She put up a struggle when we seized her," Plumb raised his musket. "I struck her with the butt of my musket before she could invoke the Devil against us."

"The witch and her Pequot demon cavorted in a wigwam in the woods," Abraham sneered. "No doubt rutting like pigs."

"We caught them both together," Plumb nodded.

"Conspiring with the Devil to cast their witchcraft on Wethersfield."

"No, Sassakusu and I are healers," the woman shook her head vehemently. "Where is he? What have you done with him?"

"Your demon lover will be dancing with the Devil under the moonlight no more," Abraham smiled maliciously as he patted the side of his musket.

The woman's shoulders slumped as tears ran done her cheeks, and a moan of grief escaped her lips. "Sassakusu was a healer among his people. He sought only to teach me of this land's healing herbs and remedies. He was no witch, nor am I."

"Then how do you explain that vile thing?" the Reverend pointed to the far end of the barn, where the other straw doll, a replica of the one on the stump, was tied around the waist to a support pole.

"You gave those Devil toys to my girls," Swaine pointed an accusatory finger at the woman. "It spoke with the voice of Hell."

"It spoke?" the woman became suddenly very still, her voice hushed. "What did it say?"

"Reverend, she admits her witchcraft on the child's toy," Clement took an involuntary step backward.

"We found your witch seed in the other doll," Finch slid his hunting knife from its sheath. "I am certain we will find one in this doll as well, witch."

"No, you don't understand. The dolls were given as wards against evil," the woman eyed the doll and then turned her bruised face to Swaine. "You say it spoke;

what did it say?"

"She admits her witchcraft, Reverend," Abraham raised his rifle and pointed it at the woman. "We should kill her now before she calls her Pequot demons to free her."

"You are all in great danger," the woman looked beseeching at each of her captors and then again at Swaine. "You must tell me what it said."

"We will not repeat the words of the Devil," the Reverend held up his hand to prevent Swaine from answering.

"Reverend," the woman stared at the minister's grim countenance. "What you found in the doll, Sassakusu gave me a protection charm to put in the dolls to protect the girls because I feared for their safety."

"To bewitch them and steal their souls," Plumb spat on the floor.

"Why? Why do this to my beautiful little angels," Swaine moaned as he raised his hand to hide his tears.

"Because they are the light of Christ," Reverend Smith put a consoling hand on Swaine's shoulder as the man sobbed. "We will save their souls, William."

"You don't understand," the woman shook her head sadly. "We sought only to help you, and you killed poor Sassakusu for his kindness."

"Hush your witch's mouth," Abraham slid his finger over the trigger of his musket.

"Your god cannot save you from what is in these woods," the woman stared at them remorsefully. "You will die. Your families will die. Your children will die."

"Our Lord is all-powerful," the Reverend's eyes blazed fervently as he took a menacing step toward the woman. "He will protect us from your witchery!"

"The Dutch fur trappers that found it were Christians, too," the woman laughed mirthlessly and shook her head. "Your god's protection did them no good."

"What is this evil she speaks of?" Clement's eyes opened wide with fear.

"I have hunted these woods since we came to the river valley," Finch shook his head and laughed. "There is nothing that walks these woods that a musket ball cannot kill."

"Then you are as big a fool as those fur trappers," the woman glared at Finch, then turned to the minister. "They encountered a cleft in an ancient oak that ran into the earth. The trappers thought it might be a rabbit warren or fox's den, but foul air blew up from it, and the men feared going into the dark. One among them laughed at their fear and climbed into the hole."

The men stared at her as she looked at each of them, her unswollen eye unflinching from their gaze. "When he came back up, he was changed."

"Changed how?" Clement swallowed hard.

"There was something inside him. Something ancient and evil," her eyes fell upon the stern face of Reverend Smith. "Something hungry. It fell upon the trappers, ripping and tearing them. The one that escaped and reached my home was holding his innards inside with his own hands. He lived long enough to tell me what I have told you. No longer."

Silence fell over the barn as the men looked at each other uneasily. Then the Reverend clapped his hands so hard that several men jumped. He clapped his hands and laughed as his dark eyes stared at the woman.

"The witch weaves a tale to deceive us and save her life," the Reverend's face became impassive, and his voice steely. "You have been judged. You have condemned yourself before the Lord and these god-fearing men. You will burn at the stake before this night is done."

The eater is coming.

The voice was high and shrill and spoke in a sing-song tune.

The eater is coming.

All eyes in the room turned toward the small straw doll tied to the pole. Its black sewn eyes stared sightlessly at the horrified faces of the assembled men.

"Lord protect us," Clement whispered in terror.

The eater is coming.

◆ ◆ ◆

The woman looked up into the night sky and she said a whispered prayer to the old gods of her ancestors to take her quickly from this world as the men stacked wood about her feet. The ropes binding her hands and feet to the six-foot length of wood pole driven upright into the ground was so tight she could not feel her fingers and toes. Beside her, the men stacked wood around a second pole that held fast the bound form of the small doll. William Swaine deposited the last of the wood at her feet, keeping his eyes averted from the woman.

As tears flowed down her bruised cheeks, the woman shook her head, "I was only trying to protect your girls."

When he met her gaze, hatred blazed in Swaine's eyes, and he spoke through gritted teeth, "You tried to consign their souls to hellfire for all eternity."

He turned his back on her and stalked back to the men waiting with their torches held high. The burning fires of the torches sent wisps of smoke into the night sky and illuminated the men's faces in an eerie glow. Three women and two young girls approached and joined the men as the Reverend stepped out from the assembled group.

"On this day, the twenty-third of April, in the year of our Lord sixteen hundred and thirty-seven, the good people of Wethersfield have found you guilty of witchcraft," Reverend Smith clutched his bible against his heart with one hand and raised his other arm skyward. "It is the law of God as written in Exodus twenty-two, eighteen, that though shalt not suffer a witch to live."

"You fear what you do not understand, and you have blinded yourselves to the world around you," the woman scanned the faces of the assembled men and women. "You should run from this place and seek the help of the Pequots; only they understand what roams these woods."

Only dispassionate faces and hateful stares looked back at her. She gave a joyless laugh, "but you won't do that. You are too ignorant and hateful of anyone not like you to accept help from the only people who could save you and your families."

"Burn her," Agatha Swaine, the girls' mother, shouted.

"Burn her!" Other voices among the assembled crowd joined until it became a chant on the night air. The Reverend nodded curtly, and Abraham Swaine and John Finch moved forward and lowered their torches to the pyres. The wood began to crackle and pop as the flame quickly spread through the kindling, billowing smoke as the men and women continued to chant and jeer.

Through the darkening smoke, the woman could see the two young girls; their faces contorted with malice, chanting to burn her. She could feel the heat of the fire growing in intensity as the smoke made her eyes sting. John Plumb rushed forward, the remains of the dissected doll impaled on a pitchfork. He tossed the straw doll into the fire, and the flames quickly consumed the dry straw and branches. The woman watched with morbid fascination as the cloth face of the doll burned to ember and the chicken heart sizzled to char.

The eater is here.

The woman looked over at the doll bound to the pole beside her as the small, high voice called out again.

The eater is here.

The doll began to smoke as the flames of the pyre reached the small straw form. As the fire quickly engulfed the doll and swirled around the pole, the woman heard the voice one last time.

The eater is here.

As the flames began to climb up her dress and lick at the skin beneath, the woman stared out at the chanting figures. Their eyes looked excited and expectant as the flames finally reached their victim. All eyes except that of Mary Swaine, the little girl backed away from her mother and sister to stand behind the crowd. Her eyes lay riveted on the woman, and a wicked grin crossed her face.

Through the dark smoke that made her eyes water and her throat burn, the woman saw the dark of Mary's eyes grow until it consumed the white of her eyes. Round black orbs, so dark they did not even reflect the firelight, stared back at the woman.

The little girl's grin grew wide, spreading from ear to ear to reveal a wide maw of jagged teeth. Her arms and legs lengthened into long limbs with patches of thick back hair. The woman could see Mary's hands elongate into sharp black claws as the girl grew to a size that towered over the men and women before her.

As the flames reached the woman, her screams mingled with those of the assembled men and women as the eater began to feed.

THE HEART OF THE ISLAND

"Nearly two hundred years ago, the Rasphuis was a convent before it became a prison for men in fifteen ninety-six," the white-haired Sergeant-of-the-guard looked over his shoulder at Daan Heppostall.

The Dutch lawyer followed the Sergeant-of-the-Guard up the torchlit stone stairway, his buckled shoe sending a small rat scampering down the stairs. Behind him, two men followed, carrying a short wooden stool and a small writing desk. Each man wore the black prison guard uniform of the Rasphuis, with white-frilled collars and long, thin rapiers.

"Our prisoners shave wood from Brazilwood trees and make a powder used in red pigment for paint in Amsterdam. It keeps the prisoners occupied, and it's very profitable for the prison," the Sergeant sounded disinterested, as if he was reciting the words from rote memorization.

"Mr. Van der Sloot does manual labor here?" Daan could

not hide the surprise in his voice.

The Sergeant stopped his ascent up the stairs and turned to face the young attorney. Pale blue eyes stared coldly at Daan as the man's white forked beard surrounded lips drawn tightly together.

"No," the Sergeant failed to contain the distaste in his tone. "That particular prisoner does not participate in work activities."

He grunted and placed a gnarled hand on his sword hilt as he returned to his trek up the stairs. They continued the rest of the climb in silence, their heavy footfalls echoing in the long, narrow stairway.

The stairs ended on a small landing containing a single thick wooden door with a barred window no larger than the palm of a man's hand. Daan watched as the Sergeant unlocked the room with a large iron key and swung open the door.

Daan followed the Sergeant into the dimly lit chamber, illuminated only by the light of a small barred window, ten or twelve feet off the floor. The air in the room smelled of damp, musty stone mingled with the odor of human waste that Daan surmised came from the chamber pot in one darkened corner.

A prisoner lay atop a straw-filled mattress on a wooden cot against the wall, the room's only furnishing, and he sat up as the small procession entered the room. The man's bare feet and hands were manacled together and connected with a short length of heavy chain that Daan imagined made it impossible to stand fully upright.

He wore a shirt and trousers that may have once been white but had grayed with the constant grime of the cell. The man's thinning blonde hair was greasy and clung close to his scalp as he studied them with deep-set blue eyes. He breathed deeply through a nose that was too large for his face and spat a wad of mucus into the corner of the room before turning to grin at the Sergeant with yelling teeth.

"I'd walk over and spit in the chamber pot," the man raised a manacled hand to a purplish bruise on his cheek as he glared at the white-haired guard. "But it seems I'm a bit clumsy when I try and walk."

The Sergeant glared at the prisoner as the two guards set the small writing table and chair down in the room.

"Mr. Heppostall is here to prepare your case for the magistrate," the Sergeant gestured to Daan and then turned to face him. "We will be outside on the landing if you require assistance."

"Don't worry, Sergeant, I'll be on my best behavior," the prisoner winked at the guards. "But I'll be sure to call you boys if I need any assistance wiping myself later."

The Sergeant only grunted as he left the room with the two guards, swinging the heavy wooden door closed behind them. Daan sat down on the stool and withdrew a piece of parchment, an inkwell, and a quill pen which he placed on the writing table. He felt the prisoner studying him, from the tips of his dark buckled shoes to the perfectly clean frill of his circular collar and the shoulder-length curls of the powder-white wig. Daan smiled awkwardly at the man as he shifted the inkwell and parchment on the desk.

"Mr. Van der Sloot, I am Daan Heppostall; the Dutch East India Company has sent me to...," Daan clasped his hands together to keep from nervously fidgeting.

"I know who you are," the prisoner leaned forward from his seat on the edge of the bed, letting the light streaming through the small window fall across his homely face. "I requested Mr. Von Drieberg send you specifically."

"So I have been informed. Mr. Van der Sloot, you are charged with a very heinous crime. The gruesome murder of a young woman, and if you are found guilty, you will hang from the neck until dead," Daan spoke slowly to be sure the man understood what he was saying. "We have far more experienced lawyers that may be better suited to make your case before the magistrate. I am still apprenticing with Mr. Von Drieberg; my responsibilities have largely consisted of drawing up routine contracts and wills."

"Mr. Heppostall, I don't give a rat's ass about the magistrate, and I think we both know that I am guilty of what I am accused," Van der Sloot stared fixedly at the young lawyer. "I asked for you because I want you to write down my tale, then I will give you something and ask something of you in return."

"I...I don't understand," Daan looked at the prisoner in confusion.

"You will," Van der Sloot sat back in the shadows and leaned against the wall. "To comprehend the reason for my rise and fall, you must understand the island of Lanka, where I have spent most of my adult life.

"I had seen you before, Mr. Heppostall when I was a man of some prominence with the Dutch East India Company. Underneath that wig and white powder, I recognized your features. You are a Dutch Burgher, half Dutch and half Sri Lankan. My guess is your mother was an island girl."

Daan opened his mouth to speak and then closed it. He studied Van der Sloot for a long moment before he spoke, "Yes, I am a Burgher, and you are correct; my mother is, was, Sri Lankan. She is deceased now. However, I do not see how this has any bearing on your murder of a young woman."

"Ahh, but it does, young Heppostall. It has everything to do with the murder," Daan could make out the faint lines of the man's face in the shadows. "It has everything to do with the murder; it has everything to do with the cause of her death."

"And why is that, Mr. Van der Sloot?"

Van der Sloot leaned forward, and the sunlight caught a gleam of madness in his eyes, "Because it has to do with the heart of the island."

❖ ❖ ❖

"I first set foot on Sri Lanka almost thirty years ago; I was just a lad in my twenties then, but I was already the second in command under Captain Andies Villiers, the Dutch East India Company's commandant of Mullaitivu," Van der Sloot's eyes took on a far off look. "It was a paradise. The Portuguese were gone, the women were beautiful, and we had peace with the island's Kandyan Kingdom. I was in charge of exports of cinnamon and betel; Captain Villiers and I could have grown rich on that alone. We even shipped elephants to Bengal and Golconda. For use in battle, of all things!"

Daan looked up from his writing and saw Van der Sloot's look had gone wistful. "However, Captain Villiers had higher aspirations than just riches; he wanted power. Villiers desired real power, and not just in Sri Lanka. He wanted power in Amsterdam.

"So he set his sights on the gemstone trade, and to his credit, we made an abundant trade in tourmaline. Labor was cheaper than harvesting cinnamon, and Europe could not get enough of it. We were making more money than we ever imagined, and the Dutch East India Company could not be more pleased."

"This won't last, Van der Sloot," he told me one night over drinks. "Sri Lanka is too profitable for those fatted calves in Amsterdam to let us keep running things."

"We have done well here. I told Villiers that if the company moves us, they will send us someplace even more profitable, like India or the Spice Islands. But he insisted that our days in Sri Lanka were numbered, and we would need to secure our financial futures before that day came."

Van der Sloot laughed mirthlessly and shook his head, "That is when Pieter Crozier came to us. May the Devil take that man for what he started."

"Who is Crozier?" Daan glanced up at Van der Sloot.

"Crozier was a Dutch Burgher, like you," Van der Sloot pointed at the young lawyer. "He worked within the Kandyans, in the central area of Sri Lanka. Crozier came to Villiers and me with a fantastic story."

"I'm sorry, Mr. Van der Sloot, I find this all very interesting," Daan laid the quill down on the writing desk. "But I fail to see how this has any bearing on the murder."

Van der Sloot's expression soured, and he leaned forward, placing his elbows on his knees. The chains affixed to the manacles rattled loudly as he moved. "Don't you worry, Heppostall; just keep writing."

Daan sighed, picking up his quill and dipping it in ink, "Very well, proceed."

"In four seventy-two AD, Kasyapa the First, the Sri Lankan king's son by a royal consort, usurped the throne and became ruler of the Moriyan Dynasty. There was a legend that Kasyapa was aided in the takeover by the discovery of an Alexandrite stone in one of the mines of Rathnapura. The stone was rumored to be as large as a plum and would turn a brilliant green in sunlight and violet-red in the torchlight. However, when Kasyapa held the gem in his hand, it would turn into a cat's eye, with a band of light running right through the middle of the stone."

"Kasyapa used this stone to finance the overthrow of his father?" Daan looked up at the disgraced merchant.

"No, son, this gemstone had a magic all its own. It was the heart of the island, and it saw into the soul of Kasyapa, learned what he desired most, and granted it to him. But it also carried a curse."

"A curse?" Daan eyed the prisoner curiously.

Van der Sloot nodded slowly, "Such powers are not to be trifled with. We are all fools to think we could control such power. The Heart of the Island betrayed Kasyapa, as it did to all who thought they had mastery over it.

"In four hundred and ninety-five, Moggallana, the

rightful heir to the throne, made war upon Kasyapa. The king rode into battle on a war elephant with the Heart of the Island embedded in a crown atop his head. The legends say that the cursed stone drove the elephant mad in the thick of the fight, and it fled the battlefield with Kasyapa still upon its back. Thinking their king was fleeing, Kasyapa's army deserted, and Mogallana seized the throne. Rather than be captured, Kasyapa committed suicide. However, before he did so, he entrusted a loyal servant to bring the stone back to its resting place in Rathnapura.

"The lure of the Heart of the Island was too great for the servant to part with, and he secreted it somewhere within the old fortress on top of the Sigiriya rock. The servant took its location to the grave, and its hiding place remained a mystery."

"Until Crozier?" Daan looked up, proud of his deduction.

"Until Crozier." Van der Sloot nodded appreciably. "The man was accompanying merchants to a Buddhist temple on Sigiriya when he stopped to draw water from an octagonal pool with a raised podium in its northeast corner. As he filled his water skin, the strap snared upon a stone at the podium's base, just below the water line. While freeing the water skin, Crozier dislodged the rock and found it intentionally hollowed out.

"Crozier reached into the hollowed space in the podium, and his fingers ran over something large and round but with facets, not smooth like a stone. When Crozier withdrew his hand, he saw through the water it was the largest Alexandrite gemstone he had ever seen. He feared taking it from the water lest one of the merchants or Buddhist monks spy what he discovered and seize it. So he replaced it in the hollow and covered it with the stone so that he could return for it."

"Did Crozier sell you the Heart of the Island?" Daan was reluctantly beginning to find himself caught up in the tale.

"Not exactly," Van der Sloot shook his head. "He wanted to partner with Villiers and me to use our company contacts to sell the stone in Europe, perhaps to one of the royal families. We would split the proceeds evenly amongst the three of us.

"But first, he needed our assistance in retrieving the gem. Sigiriya is deep within the lands of Sri Rajadhi Rajasinha, the Kandyan king. The way is long and fraught with many dangers; carrying the Heart of the Island such a distance would be perilous, even for one as skilled as Crozier. So he needed our assistance."

"The company allowed you to take soldiers into Kandy?" Daan could not contain his shock.

"Heavens no," Van der Sloot laughed bitterly. "To do so would violate every treaty we had with the Kandyans. They would be raiding our forts and burning our garrisons just like they did thirty years ago. The Governor would have had Villiers and I on the first ship back to Amsterdam if we even suggested such a thing."

"So what did you do?"

Van der Sloot gave him a wry smile and a shrug, "We did it anyway. Villiers selected a dozen of our best men, and we traveled to Sigiriya disguised as merchants. Kasyapa's palace lies in ruin now, maybe for a thousand years or more, but what a spectacle it must have been in the days. The frescos, the gardens, the Lion's Gate."

The prisoner sighed and fell silent for so long Daan began to wonder if he had fallen asleep. When Van der Sloot spoke again, he sounded contemplative.

"The Dutch, the English, the French, the Portuguese, all of us. We think the world is ripe for our taking; we go to lands we have no business in and claim them for our own. Our explorers *discover* lands inhabited by peoples since the dawn of time," Van der Sloot laughed mirthlessly. "How do you discover a land where people have lived for millennia?

"We trample upon their ancient cities and loot their sacred treasures. We think there will be no accounting for that. There will be no balancing of the books. Villiers, Crozier, and I should have left the Heart of the Island in its hiding place. We had no claim to such a treasure. In our arrogance, we brought about our ruination."

Daan studied Van der Sloot quietly and asked, "What happened?"

"We had almost made it back to Dutch territory when we encountered the Kandyan patrol. Villiers feared they would discover the Heart of the Island. A melee ensued as muskets were drawn and shots fired. I would tell you that I fought valiantly beside my comrades, but we are both well past believing I am the hero of any tale. I fell to my knees and hid among the brush until the shouts and firing stopped. When I emerged from my hiding place, I found all the Kandyans and our men slain. Crozier lay dead with a musket ball through the eye. Only Villiers remained alive, albeit just barely. He was shot in the leg and gutted with a sword; I discovered him sitting up against a tree, trying to keep his innards from spilling out — a horrible way to die, slow and painful. We were not the best of friends, but I liked the man, and I sat with him until he gasped his last breath. Then I pried the Heart of the Island from his bloody, clenched fist and left.

"The incident caused quite the uproar on the island. The Governor accused the Kandyans of attacking a merchant party, and the Kandyans accused us of a military incursion into their territory. It was quite the diplomatic row. I claimed ignorance of the incident and let the blame fall upon Villiers and Crozier as I traveled to the court of the Kandyan king to make amends. The company and the Governor were so happy with my handling of the situation that I received an appointment to handle all of the company's affairs on the island. In a very short time, I became the wealthiest merchant on the island."

"And what of the Heart of the Island?" Daan was enrapt in the merchant's tale as he dipped the quill's tip into the inkwell.

"I kept it locked away after the Villiers-Crozier Affair; possessing such a treasure would have raised too many questions at a sensitive time. However, I suspected that, like Kasyapa before me, my rise to power came from the stone's mysterious power. I was just too arrogant to believe that I, too, would fall under its curse." Van der Sloot stared down at his manacles and ran the thick iron chain through his fingers.

"What evidence do you have that the stone had anything to do with your success in Sri Lanka?" Daan set the quill pen down on the writing table and folded his arms across his chest. "It sounds very logical that someone in your position with the Dutch East India Company on an island such as Sri Lanka would enjoy rich financial rewards. Is it not conceivable that your rise and fall were wholly your own doing and this ancient legend surrounding the stone is a mere fable?"

Van der Sloot leaned forward, his blue eyes slit into a gaze that reminded Daan of a serpent preparing to strike, "I have been a merchant my whole life; you strike a deal when an arrangement is advantageous to both parties. Occasionally, you come across a fool agreeing to more profitable terms for you than for them. Once I came into possession of the Heart of the Island, people always agreed to terms that benefitted me disproportionately, and they did so with a smile on their faces. I do not profess to understand how the stone's power works, but I believe it is how Kasyapa was able to win the hearts and minds of his countrymen to overthrow a just and righteous king and place him on the throne."

"So you have no empirical evidence to support your claim. Will you not at least entertain the notion that you were responsible for your success and undoing?" Daan stared defiantly at Van der Sloot. "If you genuinely believed in the stone's power of persuasion, then why not use it to convince the magistrate to let you walk free? Why continue with this farce of laying the culpability for the murder of a young woman on an inanimate gemstone?"

"Let me be clear with you, young Heppostall," Van der Sloot's face contorted into a mask of contempt. "I have never assuaged my responsibility for the crimes committed, and I welcome the final justice of the gallows. It is what I deserve and desire."

"You said that you wished to ask something of me and, in turn, had something for me," Daan did not shrink from the man's withering gaze. "You can tell me what they are now, or I will burn this parchment and leave you alone with your stinking chamber pot."

Van der Sloot stared at Daan, his blue eyes icy cold. He then slid his hand along the sweat-stained sheet to a hole toward the foot of the bed. His fingers dug inside the hole and withdrew a small folded slip of parchment that he unceremoniously tossed onto the writing table.

"What is this?" Daan picked up the parchment, unfolded it, and scanned the scrawled writing inside.

"It's instructions on how to retrieve the Heart of the Island from its hiding place," Van der Sloot whispered, casting a wary eye toward the cell door to catch any guards eavesdropping. "You wanted to know what I would ask of you? Bring the stone back to Rathnapura."

"And do what with it?" Daan looked from the note to Van der Sloot. "Just hand it to the King of Kandy?"

Van der Sloot shrugged, "Bury it in the ground or throw it in a lake, I don't know. Just bring it back to Rathnapura before the curse spreads any further."

"Spreads to who?"

"I don't know. It could spread to the company, Amsterdam, or maybe the whole republic," Van der Sloot shook his head at the limitless possibilities and met his lawyer's gaze. "You wanted to know what I would ask of you; there it is. As to what I would give you, you will have to wait until the end of my tale. We're almost there."

Daan looked at the prisoner and saw him, really saw him for the first time. Van der Sloot was a sad, pathetic man -likely insane. At one time, Van der Sloot was one of the most powerful men in the Republic of the Seven United Netherlands; now, he stood accused of an unspeakable crime and faced certain death on the gallows. He picked up the quill pen, blew a deep breath, and then nodded for Van der Sloot to continue his tale.

"Her name was Priya," Van der Sloot gave a sad, wistful smile. "She was the daughter of a pearl diver in Colombo. I know I am not handsome, but I could have any woman I wanted with my wealth except for Priya. We met at the Governor's estate during a dinner party to celebrate the Christmas holiday; she was a serving girl in the palace and one of the favorites of the Governor's wife. Her hair was long and black, and her dark eyes peered from a face of perfect, tan skin. I was smitten from the first time I met her.

"I began to court Priya immediately, bestowing lavish gifts upon her and her family. Her father was thrilled at the prospects of a union so high above his family's station, but Priya only smiled politely and engaged in small talk. I arranged to have her moved from the Governor's home to work in my estate, which soured the Governor's wife toward me from that day forward. Priya initially protested until I offered to provide accommodations for her family on the estate, and even then, she only accepted to improve her family's life.

"One evening, she approached me and asked to speak with me after the evening meal. I acquiesced enthusiastically, thinking I had finally made progress with her affections. That evening I cleaned under my fingernails and ate dinner in my finest coat and trousers. I dismissed the servants early and awaited her by the fireplace with a bottle of wine and two goblets.

"Priya smiled tentatively when she approached me, looking nervously from the bottle of wine to her feet. When she met my eyes, I felt my soul swooning in the darkness of her pupils."

"Mr. Van der Sloot," She immediately corrected herself when she saw me open my mouth to protest. "Hendrik. You have been very kind to me and my family."

"I can do so much more for them…and you if you let me," I told her as I placed her hands in mine.

Priya smiled and looked away for a moment, staring into the fire. When she faced me again, there were tears in her eyes. "Hendrik, I believe you are a good and kind man, but I am sorry; I need you to understand that I will never love you in the way you desire. I am going to go to my room and pack my possessions. Tomorrow I will return to the Governor's home; the Governess will take care of all the arrangements."

"She squeezed my hand and gave me a sad smile as she turned and left me standing agape," Van der Sloot's eyes had a far-off look, lost in memories. "My heart was racing, and my mind spiraled as a final desperate thought took hold."

Daan looked up from his writing, studying Van der Sloot carefully as his voice hinted at madness.

"I grabbed Priya's arm to stop her from going, and I could see the alarm in her eyes. I asked her, begged her, to allow me one indulgence before she left."

"Hendrik," her deep brown eyes looked into my face, and I could see the discomfort this prolonged goodbye was causing her.

"Before you go, let me just show you something. I promise I will not hinder you further if you allow me this kindness." I let go of her arm and held my hands up in a non-threatening act of contrition.

"Priya sighed deeply and gave me a slight nod of capitulation. I saw her concern and hesitation when I told her what I wanted to show her was in my bedroom; however, I assured her my intentions were only honorable. Even so, she entered the bedroom just beyond the threshold and watched me apprehensively as I worked the lock on the ornate chest on my nightstand."

Van der Sloot looked at Daan with eyes alight with excitement, "I will never forget Priya's reaction when she first looked upon the Heart of the Island. She gasped as her breath caught in her chest and looked incredulously from the stone to me."

"May I touch it," Priya reached a trembling hand toward the gem, and I nodded slowly.

Van der Sloot laughed bitterly and shook his head, "In all the time the Heart of the Island was in my possession, I never witnessed the cat's eye effect in the gem. However, the second it lay in Priya's gentle hands, I saw that cat's eye right through the center of the stone. I should have given it to her right there and then and been done with it. We all would have been better off."

He fell silent after that, and Daan watched as he ran his tongue over his top teeth, lost in thought.

"Priya fell in love that evening. Not with me, of course,

with the Heart of the Island. It was no superficial affection like the women of Amsterdam feel toward their beautiful trinkets and bobbles; Priya detected some inner beauty in the stone that intoxicated and consumed her. When I withdrew it from her grasp, she had the desperate look of an opium fiend deprived of their smoke.

"I will admit to you that all manner of chivalry left me at that moment as I spied her desperation for the stone. I told her that if she stayed, if she came to my bed chamber in the evenings and indulged my carnal desires, I would allow her to hold the Heart of the Island until morning. She, of course, agreed."

Van der Sloot looked up and smiled at the look of distaste on Daan's face, "I see you think I am a cad, and I cannot say that I disagree with you. However, there was little joy in my victory. I shared my bed with a woman who held no interest or affection for me yet lovingly curled her body around that damn stone like a woman suckling a newborn.

"The arrangement caused me far greater trouble than joy. Her father disapproved, so I had to ship him and her mother off to Mullaitivu to work on one of my lesser holdings. The Governess was displeased that I had once again deprived her of Priya's services and company, and I fell out of favor with the Governor.

"Due to our nightly relations, Priya quickly became with child, and I had to arrange for a merchant acquaintance to take the wretched thing once it was born for fear she would neglect it unto death. She was like a wraith, haunting the halls of my home, devoid of all joy except when holding that damn stone. I soon became as disinterested in her as she was in me."

"On the night that I told Priya she would be leaving in the morning to join her parents in Mullaitivu, she clutched the Heart of the Island close to her breast and begged to take it. She said the stone belonged to her, and she to it. When I told Priya I intended to sell the stone, she flew into a rage. The woman was like a person possessed by a demon. Clawing. Biting."

Van der Sloot became suddenly quiet, his eyes downcast toward the floor.

"Sir?" Daan's voice was hushed as he prodded the man to continue.

"We struggled," Van der Sloot's eyes looked hollow and haunted when they met the young lawyer's gaze. "Priya fell. Her head struck the nightstand, and there was a loud snapping noise. Her neck, I think. She just lay there on the floor, hands locked around the stone. Priya's eyes were wide open, and she stared at me unblinkingly. Her mouth hung open, emitting a horrible keening, a constant wailing sound, with no changes in pitch or pauses for breath — just that ceaseless wail.

"I tried to get her to stop. I begged her to stop. The sound was maddening; I couldn't think straight. I just wanted her to stop making that terrible noise. I grabbed a pillow off the bed and put it over her face."

Daan stopped writing and looked at Van der Sloot in shock and horror. The man stared at the floor as if seeing Priya lying there, his arms outstretched, chains and manacles rattling. Then his shoulders slumped in resignation, and his hands collapsed into his lap as he exhaled a long breath.

"I just wanted her to stop. When she finally did, and I removed the pillow, she was gone. Priya's dark eyes stared sightlessly at the ceiling; her mouth hung open in an eternal scream."

"I told everyone it was an accident; I said Priya slipped and fell getting out of bed. The incident would have passed quietly with my connections and money. However, the Governess would not let it rest and insisted action be taken. My money and influence put me beyond even her reach; however, in the end, the company decided re-assigning me was in the best interest of everyone involved. I spent ten years in Bengal and another twelve in Golconda afterward.

"I had opportunities to sell the Heart of the Island a hundred times for incredible prices, but in the end, I could not. Maybe it was guilt over Priya's death or a sense of the wrongness I committed by taking the gem from the island. I don't know." Van der Sloot's voice trailed off.

"Mr. Van der Sloot," Daan chose his words carefully. "This written account could be construed as your confession to the murder of the young lady."

"I know," Van der Sloot nodded. "I see her almost every night in my dreams. Sometimes I dream that she is in the room with me, or I spot her from very far off, but she is always staring at me with those unblinking eyes, that open mouth, and making that horrible keening noise. Often I wake screaming and covered in sweat. An Irish merchant said they call such a thing a Banshee in his country.

"I finally returned to Amsterdam last year for the first

time in almost four decades, a very wealthy and eligible bachelor. Some friends introduced me to the dowager daughter of the Marquise van Eeden, a delightful creature. Emma was a kind and beautiful woman whose only misfortune in life was marrying a Dutch Officer who got himself killed in the Transvaal.

"Our courtship became quite the topic of conversation among the nobility, even in the court of William the Fifth. The wealthy bachelor from the Far East and the even wealthier widow from one of the most powerful families in the Republic of the Seven United Netherlands, we had all the gossiping tongues wagging."

Van der Sloot pursed his lips and looked at Daans with an expression that the young lawyer took for genuine earnestness, "I loved Emma; I loved her very much. With all I have accomplished across the empire, winning her hand was my most outstanding achievement. She made my waking hours pure paradise."

"However, once I was alone in the dark," Van der Sloot's face was a tumult of storming emotions that Daan could not read. "My nightmares had gotten worse since I arrived back in Amsterdam. It was as if the further I traveled from Sri Lanka, the more my dreams intensified. Priya haunted my dreams every night, making that continuous horrific wailing noise as she clawed at my sheets, chased me through the corridors of my home, or ransacked my room, searching for the Heart of the Island, I presume. I would awaken in the night shrieking so loud that my throat became sore and hoarse the next morning. I feared explaining my constant night terrors to Emma once we married and shared a bed."

Van der Sloot sighed and looked sidelong at Daan, "When the day came, our wedding was a spectacle to behold. I spared no expense to ensure that Emma's every wish was satisfied. It cost a small fortune, but it was worth it to see her radiant smile. The Netherlands had never seen a bride so beautiful, nor will it ever again.

"She delighted at the gasps and envy of the ladies of the court when I presented her with my gift at the reception- the Heart of the Island embedded as the center stone on a necklace of flawless Sri Lankan diamonds. The stone glowed a vibrant violet in the lights of the ballroom as we danced the night away.

"That night, as we slept in our marital bed, I had a terrifying nightmare of Priya's hands, ice cold and boney, clasped around my ankles, pulling me down into the grave. My hands sought purchase but found only loose dirt, which ran through my fingers as she pulled me inexorably downward.

"I awoke with an overwhelming feeling of dread. As my beloved slumbered next to me, my eyes searched the room in vain for the source of my unease.

"Priya, I know you are here," I called out. *"Leave me be; go back to whatever dark hell births you every night and trouble my dreams no more."*

"My shouting awoke Emma, who sat up in our bed. I turned to comfort her but found myself staring into the milk-white eyes of Priya, her mouth wide open, clutching the Heart of the Island necklace to her breast.

She began that terrible keening noise.

"I screamed in terror and covered my ears with my hands, but nothing diminished that horrible sound. I begged Priya to stop; however, when I opened my mouth to speak, I heard that horrendous wailing noise coming from my mouth as well. We sat there in bed, mouths open, wailing-the sound was maddening.

"I forced my mouth closed, grabbed Priya by the shoulders, and began shaking her. She fell back onto the bed, and I climbed atop her and grasped her jaw in my hands to force that fiendish mouth closed. The wailing continued unabated as I felt the bones of her jaws crack and shatter, her teeth tearing the flesh of my fingers as the broken jaw slammed shut. However, that horrible sound rose from her throat like a howl deep within a well. I clamped my fingers around her neck and squeezed with all my might until I felt her windpipe crush inward. The keening turned into a gasping hiss, and I pressed my fingers to her throat until Priya lay deathly still. Exhausted from the nightmare, I collapsed onto the bed and remembered no more.

"The following day, I awoke to a woman's screams and sat bolt upright in bed to see our chambermaid run shrieking from the room. I looked in shock at my beloved and found my scream joined with the chambermaid's. Emma lay there with sightless eyes staring at the ceiling, her sweet lips blue, her jaw broken and misshapen. Dark purple bruises ringed her neck where my hands squeezed her breath from her body, and dried streaks of tears ran down her face."

Van der Sloot fell silent, his tale complete. Daan stared at the words on the page in horrified disbelief. It was a tale of madness.

"You believe this was the doing of the stone's curse?" Daan did not look up from the parchment.

"I believe it does not matter if it was the stone's curse or my insanity," Van der Sloot's voice came out as a harsh whisper. "I have killed them both, poor Priya and my beautiful Emma; for that, I welcome the gallow."

"Why me?" Daan looked up at the man. "Why have you chosen me to record this terrible tale?

"I desire for you to be the one who confesses my guilt to the magistrate," Van der Sloot smiled faintly. "I wanted to give you that satisfaction."

Daan's face was a mask of confusion as he stared at the disgraced nobleman.

"Come now, Heppostall, do you truly not know?" Van der Sloot narrowed his eyes at the lawyer. "You are the child I gave away. I gave you to Lars Heppostall and paid him handsomely for his discretion."

"No," Daan shook his head. "My mother died giving birth to me. Lars Heppostall is my father; you are a monster and a murderer."

"I am that," Van der Sloot nodded. "And in truth, Lars is more your father than I ever was or would have been. However, Priya was truly your mother, and it is only fitting that I give you the gift of seeing her killer brought to the gallows."

"What you ask of me…" Daan began, but Van der Sloot cut him off.

"What I ask of you is for you to write up my confession to both the murder of Priya and Emma, I will sign it, and you will bring it to the magistrate. Make no mention of the Heart of the Island. When the deed is done, and my neck is stretched on the gallows, bring the stone back to Rathnapura and bury it deep so the curse may end before it brings even greater ruin."

❖ ❖ ❖

The rain fell steadily on the cobblestones as Daan watched the guards walk Van der Sloot up the wooden steps of the gallows and place a black hood over the man's head. A horse-drawn carriage containing the Marquise van Eeden and his wife sat as the only other witness to the execution. Daan caught only glimpses of the grieving parents through the carriage's curtained windows as the hangman slipped the thick rope noose over Van der Sloot's neck.

The hangman drew back the lever, and a trap door beneath Van der Sloot's feet fell away, and the man dropped two feet to dangle in the air. Whether by incompetence or intent, the noose was not sufficiently tight to break Van Der Sloot's neck when the weight of his body pulled the rope taunt. He dangled in mid-air, manacled feet kicking, as a gruesome gurgling noise called forth from beneath the black hood. The man's bladder and bowels emptied as his body gyrated, the gurgling lessening and kicks slowing until he hung still.

One of the guards casually released the rope, and Van der Sloot's body crashed unceremoniously to the ground as the coachman slowly guided the Van Eeden's carriage from the courtyard. Daan watched as the guards loaded the body onto a gurney and carried it back into the Rasphuis.

He knew that in the days to come, they would bury the body in a potter's field in an unmarked grave and without the final sacraments of the church, as was befitting a murderer. Daan's hand ran over the inside pocket of his coat, reassuring himself that the plum-sized gem remained secreted within as he left the courtyard and the prison behind.

◆ ◆ ◆

Excerpt of a letter from Daan Heppostall to Lars Heppostall, 1795

Father, having now witnessed the unmatched beauty of Sri Lanka, I am certain Van der Sloot was wrong about the nature of the gemstone. He thought the stone possessed great power but bore a curse of equal strength with it.

The very nature of the stone is intertwined with the island of Sri Lanka. It is, in fact, the Heart of the Island and the magical wellspring of this land's beauty and majesty. The stone freely bestows great fortune upon all who encounter it. However, the stone expects reciprocity for its gifts, asking only to be restored to the earth to continue its nurturing of Sri Lanka.

Like Kasyapa before him, Van der Sloot became enriched by the stone but reneged in his sacred duty to return it to the land and thus brought about his ruin. If they had freely given the stone back to Sri Lanka, they would have lived out a lifetime of prosperity.

I will endeavor to right the wrongs of these men and restore balance and harmony to the magic that makes this land so unique.

◆ ◆ ◆

Author's note:

According to historical records, Daan Heppostall died in Mullaitivu in 1795; there is no accounting of whether this was by misfortune or misdeed. He likely traveled to Mullaitivu to bury the Heart of the Island with Priya rather than in the mines of Rathnapura. Did he succeed before his untimely demise? I offer two bits of circumstantial evidence that he did not.

Firstly, Van der Sloot believed great misfortune lay ahead if the stone was not returned to its resting place within the Sri Lankan earth. Shortly after Heppostall's death and the disappearance of the Heart of the Island from history, the Batavian Revolution overthrew the Republic of the Seven United Netherlands, the British replaced Dutch rule of Sri Lanka, and the Dutch East India Company, which stood as the most successful company in the world for over two hundred years, went bankrupt, and was dissolved. Curse or coincidence?

The second piece of circumstantial evidence surrounds Lieutenant Friedrich von Drieberg, Commandant of Mullaitivu. Heppostall was apprenticed to Von Drieberg's father at the time of his encounter with Van der Sloot and his subsequent travels to Sri Lanka.

Nothing suggests that Von Drieberg hand any responsibility for Heppostall's demise; however, he may have come, at least temporarily, into possession of the Heart of the Island. After a rise in fortunes, Von Drieberg suffered a series of crushing defeats at the hands of the famed Tamil chieftain, Pandara Vanniyan.

Even after the British took control of Sri Lanka from the Dutch, Von Drieberg stayed and continued his pursuit of Pandara Vanniyan. Is it possible that Von Drieberg came into possession of the Heart of the Island, only to have it liberated and secreted away by Pandara Vanniyan? The only existing clue may lie in a line written to Von Drieberg's paramour in Amsterdam upon his decision to remain under British rule.

"My love, I promise you will remain only so long until I have recaptured the heart of the island."

Is Von Drieberg speaking of strategic matters or something more? I'll let you decide.

NO MAN'S LAND

"Sarge, what are we going to do?" McCauley's eyes were darting around wildly with panic.

"Hold it together, McCauley," Sergeant Buchinsky grabbed McCauley by the front of his uniform and pulled him so close the steel brim of their M-1917 helmets almost collided. "I'm going to get us all out of here."

He released McCauley's uniform, and the smaller man leaned back against the earthen wall of the giant bomb crater that the squad was using as a trench. Buchinsky figured only a shell fired from one of the German "Big Bertha" howitzers could have created a crater large enough to hide the six soldiers from the American 91st Infantry Division, the "Wild West Division" from Washington State. He had seen combat engineers dig up one of the unexploded German artillery rounds when they first arrived at the frontline in Belgium three months after the Battle of Poelcappelle in October 1917. The artillery shell was almost as tall as a man, eighteen inches wide, and weighed over a thousand pounds.

Sergeant Charlie "Duke" Buchinsky looked at the men huddled in the crater alongside him; three of the men had been with him since the unit left Camp Lewis in Tacoma, Washington, that summer. Private Michael McCauley was a small redheaded twenty-year-old with a face full of freckles from California. McCauley had a smart mouth and quick wit that gave people the impression he was a streetwise kid. However, the truth was that Army boot camp had been the first time McCauley had ever been further away from home than family vacations to the beach. Duke was beginning to worry that three months of constant combat in Flanders, the meat grinder of the Great War, was starting to push the kid's nerves to the brink.

Duke was the only child of Lithuanian immigrants, so he felt some natural kinship with Private Johannes "Dutch" Fourie, the burley son of Dutch immigrants who settled on Whidbey Island to open a bakery in 1905. Back at Camp Lewis, Dutch had a reputation as an imposing boxer with a quick temper that made even the toughest guys in the Wild West Division look away when his pale blue eyes stared them down. He did not talk much unless he was talking about the best ways to bake bread, which seemed to be an unrivaled passion of the man. The worse things got on the frontlines, the more Dutch talked about bread, but Duke figured there were worse ways to deal with the daily horrors of war.

When Duke left Camp Lewis, Lieutenant Morris placed twelve soldiers under his command. Morris died in a hail of German machine gun fire their first week in Flanders. Nine of Duke's men lay dead somewhere in No Man's Land, the wasteland of barbed wire, bodies, and bomb craters that divided the German line of trenches from those of the American, French, and British allies.

After only three months, McCauley, Dutch, and Private Joey Bucca were all the only survivors of the original twelve. Bucca was a tough-talking Italian kid from Brooklyn, New York, with an innate resentment for authority. Duke heard from one of the other sergeants that Bucca fled to Oregon after getting into trouble in New York. Then he joined the Army to escape some situation he found in Oregon. Remarkably, Bucca seemed relatively unphased by the fighting in Flanders and took each day as it came.

"When I go over the trench wall," Duke had heard Bucca telling the other guys during the voyage across the Atlantic. "Either I come back, or I don't. End of story."

At first, Duke thought Bucca was putting on a good show in front of the other soldiers, trying to look tough, but after seeing him in combat for three months, he believed the kid's Devil may care attitude was for real. Moreover, Duke admitted that Bucca's clear thinking had saved them all this morning.

Just before dawn, the squad had charged across No Man's Land with the 362nd Infantry Regiment to soften the German lines for a larger British offensive scheduled for that morning. The Germans fired flares that illuminated the battlefield as they slowly drifted to the ground on parachutes and rained machine gun fire and a constant artillery barrage down upon the American soldiers. Duke led his men to a thirty-foot dugout to get them some cover. He crested the edge of the dugout and raised his rifle to shoot any Germans hiding in the trench but froze at what his eyes beheld. The men inside, Germans from the remains of their uniforms, had all been torn apart. As bullets whizzed by him, Duke stood immobilized with horror at the sight; he had seen a lot of death in the past three months, but nothing like this. The soldiers had been torn limb from limb; scattered arms, legs, torsos, and heads lay strewn throughout the trench amid tattered uniforms and discarded weapons. The Germans must have taken a direct hit from an artillery round and been blown apart, but there were no scorch marks, and incredibly, there was very little blood amidst the carnage.

The sound of his men yelling at him for guidance snapped him out of his daze. Machine gun fire was sending up sprays of dirt all around them, and exploding artillery rounds were tossing soldiers of the 362nd hurtling through the air like rag dolls. Bucca spotted the large crater and got the squad safely into it as the relentless German weapons fire butchered the men of the 362nd all around them.

They found two other soldiers already seeking shelter in the crater, Corporal Don Glantz, an American medic from the 362nd, and a semi-comatose Australian soldier with a nametag that read Anders. Glantz had spotted Anders in the crater, huddled and rambling gibberish as the Americans advanced across the battlefield. When the German barrage began, he had been trying to give the man medical attention.

"Alright, everyone listen up," Duke made sure to look each man in the eye, except for Anders, who curled into a fetal position and stared skyward. "The 362nd has retreated to the American lines. The sun is up, so for now, we are stuck in No Man's Land."

McCauley opened his mouth to speak; however, a sudden burst of machine gun fire in the distance, punctuated by a scream, cut him off.

"That is why we're going to sit tight and wait for nightfall," Duke gestured over his shoulder with a thumb. "When it gets dark, we'll slip out of this hole and return to our lines. Until then, we will keep our heads down and not attract any attention from the Germans. Any questions?"

Duke looked at the mud-smeared faces of the men in the trench and stared hard at McCauley, who looked ready to protest, then decided to sit quietly.

"Good," the sergeant tried to give his most confident smile. "We'll enjoy this Belgian sunshine, then get home in time for supper."

◆ ◆ ◆

"What the deal with the Aussie?" Duke watched the thin, dark-haired soldier murmur to himself as his face twitched uncontrollably and his eyes blinked rapidly.

"He's got shellshock," Glantz took off his helmet and ran his hand through his short, curly hair. "When I found him, he told me I had to hide, that there were monsters in the mists. That they killed all the men in his unit."

"The damn Germans are monsters, all right," McCauley shook his head and looked weary beyond his years as he tried to wipe mud from his rifle. "This whole country is a nightmare."

"I don't think he was talking about the Germans," Glantz looked sadly at the murmuring soldier. "He said that they were creatures that looked like a man but were pale white and walked on their hands and feet like spiders. He claims they sucked the blood from his buddies."

"My father used to call such creatures *kludde*, demons," Dutch made a chomping motion with his teeth at McCauley. "They would eat little boys like you."

"The man's lost his mind," Duke squinted at the blue sky and wondered if the Germans were getting ready to lob more of those giant artillery shells into No Man's Land to keep everyone on their toes.

"Probably, but you know what's strange?" Glantz pointed at Anders, who had gone from chittering nervously to wrapping his arms around himself and quietly rocking back and forth. "You see that patch on his shoulder, the square with the purple over the blue."

"Yeah, what of it?" Duke was watching Bucca affix a small tin mirror to the tip of his bayonet with bubble gum and then slowly raise the bayonet above the lip of the crater to surveil the surrounding area without risking a bullet in the brain case. "Bucca, don't let the sun reflect off that mirror. You'll let every German in Flanders know we're here."

Bucca just dismissed the warning with a thumbs up that irritated Duke. Though he had to admit, it was a bright idea.

"I did some training with some of the ANZAC medics. That patch is The Fighting 10th, the tenth battalion. They were part of the third brigade of the Australian 1st Division."

"I didn't think we had any Australian soldiers fighting in this part of the line," Duke reflected on the briefings he had attended with Lieutenant Morris. "Just British and French on either side of us."

"Exactly," Glantz was about to say more when McCauley nearly jumped up, then remembered the German machine gunners scanning the battlefield.

"The tenth is the unit that disappeared during the Battle of Poelcappelle. Right before we got here," McCauley eyed the Australian soldier nervously. "All the guys were talking about it; they disappeared in the fog near Passchendaele. None of them returned."

"That would mean he's been living out here for three months," Duke eyed Glantz skeptically. "Doc, that's not possible."

"Maybe he escaped from the Germans," Glantz shrugged his shoulders.

"How are we going to sneak quietly out of here tonight without that cracked egg giving us away," McCauley pointed toward Anders. Duke had been thinking the same thing moments earlier and could see Dutch nodding in agreement. "We can't bring him with us; he'll get us all killed."

"Sergeant, we have someone coming," Bucca pulled the bayonet down and slipped the mirror off the knife.

"German?" Duke grabbed his rifle and saw the others doing the same.

"He's wearing a British uniform and low crawling right for us across the battlefield from this direction," Bucca pointed over his head as he readied his knife.

"Everyone lower your guns," Duke waved his hand down. "It's probably another doughboy like us stuck out here. I don't need any itchy trigger fingers advertising our positions to the Germans."

"It's broad daylight; how the hell are the German machine guns not Swiss cheesing this guy?" McCauley shook his head incredulously.

"Maybe they don't see him. Maybe he's small like you," Dutch nodded his head toward McCauley.

"Hell, Dutch, I'll thank my short Irish mother every day if I am too short to be shot."

"Both of you quiet," Duke hissed as the sound of something scurrying across the ground got closer.

Bucca crouched low as a head and shoulders of a small blonde-haired man appeared over the lip of the crater. He reached up, grabbed the front of the man's khaki uniform, and pulled him down into the trench. The man hit the ground and rolled onto his back with a low grunt as Bucca touched the tip of his bayonet to the man's neck and brought a finger to his lip, gesturing to be quiet as he shook his head slowly.

"Ok, ok," the man held his palms out and kept his voice low. "I'm a British officer."

"Let him up, Bucca," Duke and the others visibly relaxed as the man sat up slowly.

"Thanks for letting the Germans know where we are," McCauley spit angrily onto the ground.

"I'm sorry, I didn't know anyone was here," the man's eyes darted nervously from face to face. "My name is Waters, Major Paul Waters. I was trying to get back to our lines and was hoping to find a place to lay low until nighttime."

Duke eyed the man in the mud-stained khaki British

officer uniform. Waters was a small, pale-skinned man with short, stringy blonde hair. He had deep-set green eyes and a wide mouth surrounded by thick rosy lips that he constantly licked in what Duke took for a nervous habit. A small gash across his thigh oozed dark blood through the torn leg of his khaki uniform.

"Sir, sorry for the less than neighborly welcome; where the hell did you come from?" Duke leaned over and shook the man's hand, which was cold and clammy.

"I'm with XVIII Corps, Headquarters Company," Waters nodded in greeting. "I was delivering a message when all the shooting started this morning."

"For the British offensive?" Duke nodded thoughtfully.

"Yes," Waters nodded eagerly. "That's right."

"We're going to stay here until it gets dark, then try and make our way back to the American lines," Duke waved over the medic. "Glantz, come take a look at the cut on his leg."

"Thank you, ole' chap, that would be wonderful! If I could ask a favor," Waters' eyes suddenly lit up with almost feverish excitement. "I don't suppose one of you has a cigarette? I could really use a smoke."

"There's no smoking in No Man's Land, Sir," Bucca gave the man a withering look.

"Oh yes, of course," Waters looked down dejectedly. "How foolish of me to forget. I just so love a good cigarette."

◆ ◆ ◆

"Hey, Sarge," Bucca crawled over to sit by Duke as the

sun's last light began to disappear over the horizon. The men all seemed alone in their thoughts as the time to leave the safety of the crater drew closer. Bucca nodded toward Waters, who sat quietly, his eyes scanning the sky. "What do you make of this guy?"

"Just another doughboy stuck in this mess like us," Duke looked sidelong at Bucca. "Why do you ask?"

"Something about the guy just doesn't feel right to me."

"You think he's a German?" Duke appraised the British soldier suspiciously.

"Can't put my finger on it," Bucca shook his head, his dark eyes studying the British officer. "Something about the guy feels wrong. Look at his boots."

"His boots?" Duke looked at Waters' worn brown leather boots and saw nothing remarkable.

"Back in Brooklyn, my old man was a shoemaker, so he always told me to look at a man's shoes. A real working man always has worn shoes, stuff like that. So, it became second nature to me to look at people's shoes. So I looked at the Major's boots while the Doc was working on his leg, and the sole is all wrong."

Duke stared at the British officer's boots but could not see anything unusual.

"You know how our boots have steel rivets on the bottom to help in the mud, right?" Bucca pointed to the rows of raised steel rivets on the sole of his boot as Duke nodded. "But American and British boots have an iron heel plate with hobnails; French boots use rivets on the heel. The Major's boots have rivets on the heel; they are French boots, not British."

Duke could see now what Bucca was talking about; there were rivets in a half-moon pattern on the heel of the Major's boots. "So you think he's a Frenchmen impersonating a British officer?"

"I'm just saying it's strange, is all," Bucca shrugged his shoulders but still looked troubled.

"It's just the jitters, Bucca; we're all feeling it," Duke put a reassuring hand on the younger man's shoulder. "Couple of hours from now, we'll be sipping coffee and eating some hot chow."

"Hey, why do you keep looking up like that?" McCauley stared irritably at the British soldier.

"I'm just watching for bombs," Waters grinned a mouth full of uneven teeth at the red-haired soldier.

"Well, stop doing it. Its bad luck," McCauley shook his head in annoyance. "You don't have to look for them; you'll hear them if they come."

"Booooooom," Waters mouthed and then chuckled as he made an exploding gesture with his hands.

"What's with this guy?" McCauley pointed at Waters and looked over at Dutch, who just shook his head.

"Ok, everyone gather round," Duke was dreading this conversation but knew he could not put it off any longer. The men crouched in a circle around the sergeant; he could read the nervousness on all their faces.

"Guys, we have a tough decision to make," Duke pointed over at the sleeping Australian soldier. "We can't take Anders with us; there's too much of a chance he'll give us away. So the question is, do we leave him out here for the Germans or...."

The words hung in the air as each man looked down or at their hands; only Waters stared at him with those deep-set green eyes.

"Or do we do him a kindness," Bucca finished his sentence. Duke thought the man put it eloquently and appreciated that Bucca did not make him say the words himself. He gave Bucca a small, grateful smile, and Bucca returned a quick nod of acknowledgment.

"He let me give him a morphine injection earlier. I think he will do so again," Glantz looked at his hands as he spoke. "I can give him an overdose; he won't feel any pain."

"I think he would appreciate that, Corporal Glantz," Duke offered the man a reassuring glance and could see the medic had tears in his eyes.

"You know you work so hard to keep the boys alive," Glantz's voice cracked with emotion, and he shook his head to keep the tears from coming. "But you're right; this is a kindness."

"Or I could stay with him," Waters offered with a weak smile.

"What?" Duke voiced the shock that all the others felt.

"With my leg wound, it would be hard for me to keep up anyway," Waters gave a casual shrug of indifference.

"Sir, it's little more than a deep scratch," Glantz looked at the man incredulously.

"I'll be fine," the Major's green eyes trailed over to look at the sleeping Anders. "When you chaps get back to headquarters, send a stretcher team back for us."

"Sir, why are you doing this?" Duke thought the Major was making the most incredibly brave or idiotic decision he had ever seen.

The Major opened his mouth to reply, but Dutch cut him off. "Major, who would win a boxing match, Ruby Rob Fitzsimmons or Gentleman Jim Corbett?"

Dutch's awkwardly timed question stunned everyone, and Duke squinted in the dim dusk light to get a good look at Dutch to see if the man had become unhinged under the tension. Dutch stared back at the British officer with the same disinterested look he always bore, though his jaw muscles looked tighter than usual.

"I'm sorry, I don't share your Yanks' love of pugilism," Major Waters gave a nervous smile.

"Dutch, I don't think this is the time…," Dutch raised a hand to pause McCauley mid-sentence.

"C'mon, Major," Dutch slid his rifle across his knees to level it at Waters, his cold blue eyes unreadable. "Who do you think would win? Fitzsimmons or Corbett?"

"Private Fourie," Duke leaned over to grab Dutch's shoulder. "Put your rifle down."

"Fitzsimmons knocked Corbett out in the fourteenth round to become the world's heavyweight champion. It was a punch to the solar plexus that finished off Gentleman Jim; the punch was legendary," Dutch stared unwaveringly at Waters.

"Yeah, I remember my old man telling me about that," Bucca nodded his head slowly, and then he, too, looked suddenly at Waters and brought his rifle to point at the British officer. "It was a big deal in all the papers because

Corbett was the American champion, and Fitzsimmons was an Englishman."

"That's right," Dutch nodded his head and smiled wryly. "I have never met a Brit that did not know Ruby Rob Fitzsimmons or take pride in the fact that he put the Yank champ down on his ass."

Waters' face twitched nervously as all eyes turned to stare at him. Suddenly, an ear-piercing shriek of pure terror shattered the hushed sounds of No Man's Land that startled even the ordinarily unflappable Bucca. The men turned to see Anders sitting up, staring at them, a look of abject fear contorting his face. The man's eyes were open so wide the whites nearly glowed in the darkness; his body shook and trembled like a leaf in a windstorm.

"Grab him," Duke recognized the look of a trapped animal in Anders' eyes and knew the man was going to run.

Glantz leaped forward and wrapped his arms around the Australian soldier's waist as the man began to scramble frantically over the side of the crater. Anders had dragged the medic halfway out of the crater when Duke heard the sound of the German machine guns open fire.

"Get down," Duke pressed himself low to the ground as German machine gun fire raked the lip of the crater.

Anders screamed as bullets peppered his torso, spinning him out of Glantz's grasp. The Australian soldier's body jerked as the large bore machine gun rounds struck and exited his body with small geysers of blood as he tumbled lifelessly over the side of the crater and out of sight. Glantz slumped motionless over the lip of the crater, a wet red stain growing on his back where a bullet had struck him.

"Leave him; he's gone," Bucca grabbed Dutch's arm and pulled him back as he reached for the lower half of Glantz's body which still dangled inside the crater.

"Anders was looking at you," MacCauley pointed an accusatory finger at Waters, who sat grinning madly in the crater. "He was terrified of you!"

The pop of German flare guns filled the night as they fired star shells into the air. The shells exploded high in the sky, releasing flares that blazed brightly as they descended by parachute, illuminating the area around the crater like the midday sun.

As the flares lit up the crater, Duke could see Waters clearly, sitting calmly with a wide grin on his face. The grin stretched wide across his face, making his mouth look too elongated to be human. Waters' teeth looked unnaturally long and jagged, and his green eyes appeared to have sunk deeper into his round, pale face.

"Why the hell is he smiling like that?" McCauley was sliding as far back from Waters as the crater would allow.

Duke stared transfixed at Waters as the flares began to burn out, casting the battlefield back into darkness. It took a moment for his eyes to adjust to the sudden darkness, but as the acuity of his vision returned, he saw Waters open his mouth into a gaping maw. A loud keening noise escaped from deep within the man's body; the wail turned into a series of high-pitched giggles that reminded Duke of how hyenas called each other at the zoo back home.

"What the hell?" Bucca stared in horror at Waters.

"Stop that noise," Dutch jumped on top of Waters, pushing the man onto his back in the crater. He pinned the British officer down with his knees and punched Waters repeatedly in the face. "Stop making that noise."

Waters' lips split, coating his jagged teeth with blood, but he continued smiling and making that chilling noise unabated as Dutch rained blows down upon his face. Popping noises from the German lines telegraphed another volley of star shells arcing high into the sky. The flares exploded overhead, illuminating the battlefield as German machine gun fire swept the area with a hail of bullets.

"Glantz is still alive," McCauley pointed at the medic's body sprawled across the top of the crater.

Duke could see by the light of the flares the medic's eyes rolling in their sockets as he struggled to extend his finger to point at something beyond the crater. He held his trembling finger out for a moment, then his arm went limp and dropped to the dirt as he expelled his final breath.

Dutch had wrapped his hands around the neck of the bloodied Waters and squeezed and shook the man violently to make him stop making that horrendous noise. Affixing his small mirror to his bayonet, Bucca slid the mirror over the lip of the trench to surveil in the direction Glantz had pointed.

Bucca pulled the knife back down and pulled it close to his chest as he pressed his back hard against the wall of the crater. His face had gone deathly pale, and his eyes held a look of terror and panic that Duke had never seen in the young soldier.

"There are hundreds of them," Bucca's hands trembled as he affixed his bayonet to the end of his rifle. "Pale white monsters, scurrying towards us on their hands and feet. I could see their eyes flashing in the light of the flare. I think Waters is calling them."

Boom. Boom. Boom. The sound of German artillery firing echoed across the battlefield. The night filled with the sound of explosive shells whistling overhead and the air vibrating with the concussive blast of their impact as they began to fall around the crater. Dirt and debris showered down on the men as each explosion fell nearer the crater.

"They are walking the shells in on us," Duke pressed himself against the back of the crater and gripped his rifle with knuckles white with terror.

"Hail Mary, full of grace," McCauley pulled his knees in tight against his body and rocked back and forth, his eyes squeezed shut. "Hail Mary, full of grace, hail Mary, full of grace…."

❖ ❖ ❖

Oberfeldwebel Hiram Maxim scanned the battlefield through the metal sight of his Bergmann MG 15 machine gun. The December air was freezing, and he was careful not to let his bare skin touch the cold metal of the machine gun. He had seen too many soldiers lose the skin off their cheek that way in these temperatures.

Maxim clenched and unclenched his fingers to keep the blood flowing to them and cursed Oberleutnant

Hauptmann for putting him on duty Christmas Eve for the hundredth time that night. At this moment, every squad member was sitting warm in the bunker, their bellies full of special holiday rations. Everyone except him and the new guy, Maxim, spit on the floor in disgust.

"*Haben sie eine zigarette?*" the soldier tapped him on the shoulder.

"*Nein,*" Maxim shot the man an angry look and then felt a pang of guilt at the man's dejected countenance.

It is Christmas Eve, he thought to himself. *It is not the new guy's fault that Hauptmann stuck me on machine gun detail. Hell, the guy is stuck out here, too, tonight.*

Maxim reached into the pocket of the heavy woolen jacket and slid out a cigarette. He tapped the soldier on the shoulder and offered the cigarette to him. The man's deep-set green eyes lit with excitement as he slipped the cigarette from Maxim's outstretched hand. A grin crossed the soldier's wide mouth as he slipped the cigarette between the thick rosy lips that he constantly licked in what Maxim took for a nervous habit.

"*Danke schön,*" the soldier nodded his head gratefully.

"*Bitte schön,*" Maxim smiled and turned back to surveil the battlefield. *Maybe tonight won't be so bad after all.*

WILSON

Wilson's eyes snapped open. Light streamed in the narrow opening along the door flap of his small tent, casting the sun's rays on his thin body as he lay on the sweat-stained cot. His ragged blanket had slipped off during the night, and the sunlight cast a line across his body, from his dirty white underwear up across his hairless sunken chest to glint off the small iron key he wore on a thin wire around his neck.

The hot sticky air bore the scent of stale popcorn and cotton candy. Judging from the number of voices passing his tent, the carnival had opened for the day. He must have slept late; how unlike him. Hamish would surely be furious with him if he did not have the photo booth open soon with the carnival so newly arrived in whatever Oklahoma Panhandle town this was.

As he got up and stretched, though only in his thirties, Wilson's thin arms and legs crackled and popped as he shook off his slumber. He surveyed the very few possessions in the tent; it contained all Wilson owned in this world. The old cot, a standing coat rack with the rumpled black suit and ragged top hat hanging from its lone hook, a vertical mirror, a small table with a pitcher of water and chipped glass, a rusty lantern that hung on the tent pole, and of course, the locked wooden trunk that contained his treasures.

He glanced sidelong at the elongated oval cheval mirror, its dark wooden frame seated between two posts that allowed it to tilt for a full-body reflection. The mirror's curved bracketed feet dug snuggly into the dusty Midwestern earth.

"Can't blame a man for sleeping," Wilson mumbled as he grabbed the black suit from the coat rack and threw it on his bed.

Wilson buttoned up the white shirt; its collar, yellowing from use, loosely circled his thin neck. He pulled on the baggy, rumpled black pants and jacket. Reaching into the jacket's pocket, Wilson produced a red clip-on bow tie and secured it to the collar of his shirt. He reached up and swiped the few remaining greasy wisps of dark hair across his balding head before placing the well-worn top hat on his head. He knelt before the wooden trunk and ran his bony hands over the cherrywood top. The trunk was worn, scratched, and dinged, but it held all his treasures. His eyes darted around the room, looking for any prying eyes before reaching into his shirt and producing the small metal key. He leaned down and unlocked the trunk's ancient lock without removing the wire around his neck.

Wilson opened the lid and peered down into the trunk. A dark blanket secreted all his treasures from view, all except the old Polaroid Land Camera Model 95. He lovingly picked up the camera, his eyes taking in the rectangular leather box of the camera, the black accordion-style extension, and the shiny chrome end plate with its circular lens eye. Wilson could see his reflection in the camera lens, his dark sunken eyes and thin, pointed nose. He smiled with a mouth full of stained teeth and cradled the device in the crook of his arm as he locked the trunk back up.

The noise of the carnival was growing outside as he walked over to stand in front of the mirror. In the reflection were his beloved camera, black suit and top hat, and red bow tie at his neck. He looked at his stooped form with his sunken cheekbones and hollow eyes. The black suit seemed too big for his small frame, the collar too loose for his thin neck, and his top hat constantly threatened to sink over his eyes.

"Don't we look fine today?" Wilson grinned into the mirror. "Yes, yes, we do."

◆ ◆ ◆

The Grand Ole Traveling Carnival was a veritable traveling city of tents that made its way through the dustbowl of the American Midwest, setting up in a new city for two weeks each month.

The north side of the carnival was home to the big tents where the animal shows, the performers, and all carnival spectacles took place. All manner of food could be found there, from savory meats to sweet cotton candy.

But the south side of the carnival was a different world. The tents of the south side were smaller and more intriguing places where only the more adventurous townsfolk would come seeking freak shows, tattoos parlors, or to watch private fighting matches between men or animals. Some came seeking drugs or the services of some of the ladies of ill repute that traveled with the carnival.

Wilson squinted as he stepped out of his tent into the bright daylight; the sights and sounds of the carnival assailed his senses. He never went to the north side of the carnival; too many people bumping and jostling; they would break his camera if they got too close with their pushing and shoving. But on the south side, people moved more slowly, talking in hushed tones, peering in open tents, or talking with the hawkers who tried to lure passersby into their tents.

He skulked about the fringes of the line of tents; Wilson needed to get to his photo booth before Hamish White, the carnival's proprietor, and ringmaster, saw him.

"Running late again, Wilson?" called a man with a thick Chinese accent.

"Hamish will feed you to the bears if you're late, Wilson!" laughed a deep male voice.

"What could a bear eat? He's just skin and bones!" said the Chinese-accented voice.

"I never see you eat Wilson; you need to put some meat on those bones," the other voice said.

Wilson cringed at the sound of the two familiar voices and turned to sneer at their source, two of the south side's more popular attractions. The Chinese voice belonged to Long Li, a tall, thin Chinese man with a neck that was over two feet long and gave the man the appearance of a human giraffe. Wilson often thought that the man's head looked so precariously perched atop his long neck that it could come tumbling off at any moment. He would amaze carnival goers by swallowing oddly shaped objects they would watch travel down his long neck. Then they would be delighted to watch the objects travel back up his neck and out his mouth. The carnival goers loved it, but Wilson thought it was quite disgusting.

The other man was The Human Walrus. Wilson knew that was different from the name his parents gave him at birth, but he never really bothered long enough with the man to learn his real name. The Human Walrus was a heavy-set man with dark bushy hair and a large mustache. But his most startling features were his two obscenely long canine teeth extending past his chin. At the carnival, the man earned his keep by popping balloons, skewering fruit, and poking holes in cans with his two large teeth. He was always very popular with teenage boys who seemed to delight in throwing fruit at the large man and watching him spear it midair. Wilson supposed one day, those long canines would snap off on some hard can or unripe watermelon, and the man would no longer be useful to Hamish.

Hamish had brought both men back from a trip to San Francisco last summer, and now the two shared a tent on the edge of the south side. Wilson knew they were constant gossipers, and if they saw that he was late setting up his booth, half the carnival would know shortly. He hurried past the two men and headed into the space that divided the north side of the carnival from the south side. His little booth sat in the middle of the open space.

As Wilson approached the small booth, he felt someone come up alongside him, a teenage boy scampering on all fours. The boy wore overalls with a lion-like tail sewn onto the back. He looked up at Wilson with light blue eyes that peered out of an adolescent face ringed with a mane of dirty brown hair that ran from the top of his head around his face. The black paint darkened his nose to make it look more lion-like. "Wilson," the Lion Boy said as he ran alongside him on his hands and feet. "Hamish has been looking for you."

"Thank you, Henry." Wilson winced, noticing several young children pointing at the Lion Boy, loping alongside him. Wilson did not need any added attention this morning.

"He's very annoyed, Wilson; he's been looking for you all morning."

"Thank you, Henry. You should run along." Wilson gestured with his hands for the boy to hurry off.

Henry gave Wilson a hurt look. It was not so much that Wilson disliked Henry; in truth, he had no opinion of the boy whatsoever. The boy was billed as half boy, half lion, and would perform for the crowd before the real lions came out in the big tent. Wilson had watched the boy act once; he jumped through a flaming hoop and caught raw pieces of meat out of the air.

"Have it your way," the Lion Boy veered off from Wilson to head towards a group of men and women. Wilson saw the boy stop and roar like a lion at the group, which made the women yell in surprise and then clap in appreciation as they watched him scamper off to the next crowd.

When Wilson reached his little booth, he noted the morning crowds were still relatively sparse, and it would be at least another hour or so before the carnival would start to fill with the day's customers. The sign over the booth read "Hamish White's Phantasmagorical Photos!" with a small round placard that read ".25 cents" just below the counter where Wilson sat on his uncomfortable wooden stool. The sign, however, irked Wilson to no end.

"It should read Wilson's Phantasmagorical Photos," he often thought. It was his camera, and he took the pictures after all.

He was thankful that at least the booth had a wooden ceiling that kept the hot Oklahoma sun from beating down on him. Wilson took his place on the wooden stool and withdrew a handkerchief from his pocket, lovingly wiping down the camera. He swirled the soft cloth over the delicate glass lens, the shiny chrome face, and the leather accordion frame. Wilson was always careful not to press the black bottom that sat atop the camera and never the red button next to it.

"Hello there, we'd like to have our picture taken," a smiling bald man walked up to the booth with a young boy.

Wilson looked up at the pair; the man was tall and lean with a drab shirt and pants that seemed so typical to Wilson of the people in these towns. But the boy with him wore a bright white sailor suit and sported an unruly head of dark curly hair.

"Of course. That will be twenty-five cents, please," Wilson gave the man a wide smile that he had practiced in the mirror.

The man handed Wilson several small coins, which he

slipped through an open slit carved in the top of the counter and made a loud clinking noise as they dropped into the locked tin box beneath. Wilson stepped out of the booth and positioned the two so that one of the carnival's large red tents stood behind them.

Wilson raised the camera to his eye. "Now, just give me a nice smile."

As Wilson looked through the viewing hole of the camera, the man placed his arm on the boy's shoulder and grinned widely. However, Wilson's attention went to the figure in the top hat that he spied over the man's shoulder. Hamish headed straight for Wilson's booth with his unmistakable red pants and jacket, bright white shirt, and black top hat. Alongside him was a thin, stiffly walking woman in a dark gray dress running from her neck to her ankles.

"Did you take the picture?" the bald man's question snapping Wilson out of his momentary distraction.

"Just one more moment," Wilson ensured the smiling man and his son stood framed correctly in the shot.

Wilson lightly depressed the black button, and the camera made a loud click and then began making a whirring noise. A black square slid out of the picture slot, and the man and his son gathered around Wilson to take a look. As Wilson stared at the black picture, the image of the man and his son slowly began to take shape, the large carnival tent silhouetted against the sun behind them. Wilson's eyes kept darting to the side, watching the approaching form of Hamish and the woman.

"Hmph," the bald man frowned, looking down at the

picture.

Wilson looked back down at the picture; the details were much clearer now, and he could see that the man had closed his eyes as the camera snapped the picture. The boy, too, had glanced up as if looking at a bird just as the camera captured his image.

"What a fine pair you make." Wilson offered as he handed the man the photograph.

"Let me see, Father," the boy plucked the picture out of Wilson's hand.

The man continued to frown and appeared ready to ask Wilson for another picture when the boy laughed loudly.

"Father, you look so funny!" the boy laughed delightedly.

Seeing his son's pleasure, the man's expression softened, and he nodded thanks to Wilson. They turned to leave just as Hamish and the woman approached. Hamish was a tall man, further accentuated by his high black top hat. The man's pale white complexion contrasted with his jet-black hair and the thin mustache that perfectly traced his upper lip. Wilson never liked looking anyone directly in the eye, and he found Hamish's dark beady eyes to be particularly unsettling, and he avoided holding the man's gaze at any cost.

"Wilson, so good to finally find you!" Hamish gave a toothy smile.

"Good to see you too, Hamish," Wilson took out his handkerchief and pretending to clean the camera's lens again.

Hamish gestured to the woman standing beside him. "Wilson, I wanted to introduce you to our guest."

Wilson looked at the woman glancing around the carnival with a look of distaste on her face. Her grey hair sat in a tight bun, and she appeared to have a face turned into a permanent scowl as if she constantly sucked on a sour lemon. She had small cold, dispassionate blue eyes that looked to be judging the world harshly from behind the round spectacles perched on her pointed nose. The woman clutched a bible against her black handbag with both hands as if expecting a purse snatcher to come running out of the crowd at any moment.

"Wilson, this is Misses Stammerall from the Council on Family..." started Hamish before appearing to search his memory for a word.

"From the Council on the Protection of Family Values and Proper Behavior," Mrs. Stammerall gave Hamish a withering stare.

"Yes, yes, that's it," Hamish clapped his hands together and grinned..

"Nice to meet you," Wilson felt as uncomfortable with the woman's stern gaze as he was with Hamish's.

"Wilson, Mrs. Stammerall has some concerns about our good carnival," Hamish feigned a hurt tone.

"To be exact," Mrs. Stammerall straightened her already stiff posture, "the C.P.F.V.P.B. has concerns that your carnival does not conform to the standards of decency that we have set for the good people of our town. We have heard reports of drunkenness, lewd acts, fighting, and all manner of immorality taking place here, Mr.

White. Not to mention your carnival is open on Sunday, which is the Lord's Day, Mr. White; it is not a day for the people of this town to be tempted by your traveling den of debauchery."

Hamish gasped and placed his hand over his heart in faux pain. "I assure you the Grand Ole Traveling Carnival is no such place, Mrs. Stammerall. If the P.V.C.S.B..."

"The C.P.F.V.P.B.," corrected Mrs. Stammerall. "As President of the Ladies Committee of the C.P.F.V.P.B., I will meet with Mayor Anders to demand he shut your carnival down immediately."

"Mrs. Stammerall," Hamish's tone was soothing, "that is why I brought you to meet Wilson here."

"Me?" Wilson failed to hide his astonishment.

"Let me at least make a peace offering," offered Hamish, extending his hands in a humble gesture.

"Hmphf," snorted Mrs. Stammerall. "I need nothing from the wages of sin."

"Oh, of course not, Mrs. Stammerall; Wilson is just a photographer. I wanted to offer you a picture to remember your day at the carnival."

Wilson held up the camera to show her, and he saw her cold blue eyes study the leather and chrome camera for a moment. Then he detected the faintest hint of a smile on her face. Wilson knew that in her mind, she saw the C.P.F.V.P.B. using the picture in a local paper under a headline that would read something along the lines of "C.P.F.V.P.B. Defends Town's Morals and Closes Carnival."

"Well, a picture would be nice, Mr. White," her voice

took on a conciliatory tone.

"I am happy you agree!" grinned Hamish

Mrs. Stammerall smoothed out the wrinkles on her gray dress and touched her tight hair bun to ensure it was firmly in place. She stood ramrod straight and offered a tight-lipped smile of determination as Wilson raised the camera to his eye. He angled it to center Mrs. Stammerall in the camera's viewport and then moved his finger to the black button.

"Wilson," Hamish hissed through his smile, "I think you meant to press the red button."

"The red button?" Wilson looked at him questioningly, his cheeks twitching as he felt a feral joy course through his veins. He caught sight of the look in Hamish's eyes and brought the camera back to his eye as a wolfish grin crossed his face. "Yes, of course, the red button."

Wilson stared through the viewport at the sour-faced woman, rigidly holding her bible and slowly depressed the red button. Just as it had done earlier, the camera made a loud click and then began making a whirring noise. A darkened square slid out of the picture slot, and Wilson handed it to Mrs. Stammerall.

"Free of charge, of course," added Hamish.

Mrs. Stammerall peered at the picture dispassionately as the blackness slowly gave way to greater detail. She gasped out loud and clutched her bible to her chest as she looked at the picture.

"Is there something wrong, Mrs. Stammerall?" Hamish peeked over at the picture. "Why, Mrs. Stammerall, you look positively radiant!"

"How? How is this possible?" Mrs. Stammerall stared from the photo to hamish.

She held out the picture. Standing amidst the tents and crowds of the carnival stood Mrs. Stammerall, but not as she looked today. The Mrs. Stammerall in the photo was a young, blonde woman with a short bobbed haircut in a revealing, short red flapper dress of the 1920s. She touched an aged finger to the picture and ran it along the contour line of the dress.

"That was my favorite dress," she whispered, more to herself than to Wilson and Hamish.

"It's a beautiful dress," Hamish put his arm around the woman.

"But how...?" she looked up at Wilson with bewildered eyes, but he, too, was staring intently at the picture, a dark glint in his eyes.

"You've been out in the sun all day, Mrs. Stammerall; maybe we need to get you home," Hamish soothed as he started to walk the woman towards the carnival exit. "Yes, I think I need to lay down for a bit," Mrs. Stammerall nodded as Hamish led her away.

Hamish had his arm around the older woman and spoke quietly to her as he walked with her. He looked over his shoulder at Wilson and gave Wilson a little nod, and then they disappeared into the crowd of carnival goers. Wilson watched until Hamish's tall top hat was out of sight.

His stomach growled with a rumble of hunger. Wilson ran his boney hand over his belly and looked up at the morning sun; it was early in the day, still many hours before he could eat.

◆ ◆ ◆

As the day wore on, storm clouds rolled in over the Midwestern plains, and a light rain quickly gave way to a steady downpour keeping away all but the most determined carnival customers. Wilson tucked his camera inside his jacket to keep it safe from the rain and stepped out of his booth.

The rain ran off the rim of his top hot in small rivers as he sloshed through the muddy earth back towards his tent. As he walked, he noticed the other booths and tents closing up to shelter from the rain.

His route back to his tent always took him by the faded red tent that belonged to Bella. If he had any friends in the Grand Ole Traveling Carnival, it was surely Bella. She always talked kindly to him, smiled, and waved if she saw him passing by. Some afternoons he would tell her stories of how the camera saw people. He remembered a judge had his picture taken in one town, and the camera saw him dressed as a big baby with a great white cloth diaper. The judge was simultaneously embarrassed and furious, but Bella laughed at the story. She laughed until tears rolled down her eyes, which was one of the happiest moments of Wilson's life.

She would always ask him what he thought the camera would see if he took her picture, but Wilson would never do that. Wilson would never take a special photo of her. He would tell her he could not spare the film, and she would pout. Wilson liked when she pouted almost as much as when she smiled. He liked her pretty green eyes and her long red hair. She wore very revealing dresses that would make Wilson blush, but he knew that was her costume, just like the black suit was his.

When her tent flap was closed, he knew she was in there with men. He could hear them sometimes, and that would make Wilson angry. But then he would find someone to take a special picture of, and things would feel better again.

Bella's tent flap was closed as he walked by, but Wilson guessed that was likely due to the rain, like almost all other tents on the south side. That was ok; Wilson did not feel like talking today. He just wanted to get his camera out of the rain, and he wanted to eat. The hunger gnawed at him ceaselessly, rising from a dull pang to an insatiable craving.

The rain beat a steady rhythm against the canvas top of his tent as he slipped through the flap and secured it closed behind him. With great care, Wilson placed the camera down on the wooden chest and hung his top hat on the coat rack before lighting the rusty lantern. The flickering light came to life as the kerosene-soaked wick caught fire, casting the room in a dancing light.

Wilson quickly stripped off his wet clothes and hung them on the coat rack, leaving them to drip muddy puddles on the tent's dirt floor. He avoided looking at his reflection in the large oval mirror. The sight of his spindly limbs and boney ribs disgusted him, and he knew the wet strands of his hair would only accentuate the baldness of his round head. Wilson lay down on the bed and pulled his raggedy blanket over his thin naked body, enjoying the protection the blanket afforded against the chill air of the rainstorm.

He turned his head and stared at the camera, and it

seemed to stare back at Wilson with its glass lens. Wilson was so hungry that his stomach ached with searing pain. He wrapped his arms around his belly and curled his knees into a fetal position.

Across the room, the camera began to give off a humming sound, and a beam of bright light sprang forth from the leans to shine directly into Wilson's right eye. His eyes opened wide, welcoming the light, then rolled back in his head as his body tingled. In the darkness of his mind, he felt a sensation of plummeting as if on a rollercoaster encased in blackness. The first few times he had felt this, he had screamed in terror, but now Wilson embraced the feeling. He took the ride.

Wilson was in total darkness when he opened his eyes, illuminated only by a small round window. Looking through the window, he saw his body curled on the dirty bed, staring sightlessly toward the window. Wilson turned away from the window and held up his hands; thick, strong fingers tipped by sharp nails appeared before his face. He clenched his fists and felt the power in his grip. He felt his long, flowing hair brush his shoulders when he looked down at his muscular body.

"*This is the real me,*" thought Wilson.

He knew he was in the in-between place now; Wilson opened his mouth and let out a primal roar into the darkness as he waited. Wilson knew that the camera saw people as they desired to be seen, as they saw themselves in their dreams and fantasies. Some dreamed of being younger or more desired. Others fantasized about different lives. The camera watched the movies in their minds and knew the roles they yearned to play. The camera saw it all and put it on film. It also carved a secret pathway into their mind, and Wilson just had to wait for that pathway to reveal itself.

There it was, a tiny pinprick of light in the distance. Wilson started to walk quickly towards the light. Wilson's gait quickened to a run, his powerful legs taking long loping strides, propelling him towards the light.

He felt a hunger building inside him as he rapidly approached the light. Wilson stopped just outside the perimeter of the light and peered in. This was the threshold into Mrs. Stammerall's mind, a place where she was the star of the movie.

He entered the light and found himself in a moonlit alleyway lined with refuse and garbage cans. Something skittered in the darkness, and Wilson sniffed its scent in the air.

"Rat," Wilson growled in a deep guttural voice.

Wilson's foot splashed through a puddle, and he looked down at his reflection. Long red hair flowed down to his shoulder and framed a wide brutish face with a flat nose and deep-set blue eyes that looked out from a heavy brow. The sight of his broad, powerful shoulders and muscled chest made the wide mouth full of jagged teeth open into a grin.

"*This is the real me,*" thought Wilson swelling with pride. "*This is who I was always meant to be.*"

His taloned hand rubbed at the pain in his side; the hunger ached deep into his muscles.

"*Need to feed,*" the thought cut through the pain.

Wilson edged to the end of the alley and looked out. A man with dark hair in a black suit with white pinstripes and a matching vest and tie walked down the street with the blonde woman in the red flapper dress. They walked arm and arm with a slight stagger to their steps. Wilson sniffed the air and smelled the alcohol on them. He could hear the woman giggling as they talked in hushed tones. If he recalled correctly, the man looked familiar to Wilson, an actor in an old movie. The thought made him snort derisively; the prudish Mrs. Stammerall's fantasy of a night out in the arms of a Hollywood star was playing out before him. He imagined she had dreamt of being wined and dined by the star and smiled at the thought that whatever else her dream held would not come to pass.

As the couple walked past the open alley, Wilson's clawed hand shot out and grabbed the young Mrs. Stammerall by the arm. The woman screamed in terror as he swung her hard into the alley wall with a sickening cracking of bone. The man in the pinstripe suit dissipated into the air as the tendril of imagination that dreamed him into being was severed.

The blonde woman lay crumpled on the alley floor sobbing, her left arm and leg bent into a misshapen angle. Wilson's heart pumped wildly as he loomed over the fallen woman. He grabbed her by the throat, lifting her off the ground. Mrs. Stammerall clutched at his arm with her unbroken hand, and her legs kicked wildly against the wall. Her blue eyes opened wide in terror as Wilson opened his mouth wide to reveal his maw of sharp teeth and breathed his hot breath into her face. She tried to scream, but the pressure on her throat only allowed a squeaking noise to emanate. Wilson did not care about this woman. He did not care about her hopes and dreams or the people that loved her and would mourn her. Wilson felt her terror warm his body like sunshine against his skin and watched dispassionately as a tear rolled down her cheek and over his hand, clutching her throat. He breathed in her fear like a sweet aroma, the scent exhilarating him. Wilson enjoyed this part most of all, the way their bodies trembled in trepidation, the feral sound of their screams, the look of anguish as he tore their flesh, and finally, the deep sadness in their eyes as he extinguished the light within them.

The hunger inside Wilson pulsed, and he sank his sharp teeth into her neck, enjoying the gush of warm blood that filled his mouth. Her blood tasted salty, and Wilson drank deeply as her slowing heart pulsed the warm liquid into his mouth, his lips sealing around the open wounds until the blood drained from her body. Wilson continued to drink from the woman's limp form, drinking deeper, draining her body of an essence and vitality beyond the physical. Some would call this the soul, but to Wilson, it was a sweet nectar that satiated his hunger and sustained him. He drank until all that was once Edith Stammerall was no more.

◆ ◆ ◆

Wilson awoke the following day feeling full and content. Feeding upon Mrs. Stammerall would keep him nourished for weeks, but he felt a pang of regret at the thought that he would not feel the exhilaration of a kill again until the next town. There were rules, no more than one per town. Not ever. But whose rule was that? Not his rule, certainly. Not the camera's rule. He was positive. It was Hamish's rule. The carnival's rule. How he yearned to take a picture of Hamish. Sink his claws into the man's beady eyes and hear him scream. The thought made Wilson smile as he glanced at the camera seated on the wooden chest.

"*One day,*" Wilson thought to himself as he looked at his reflection in the chrome faceplate of the camera.

He sat up and swung his feet onto the floor, curling his toes in the dusty Oklahoma dirt. Wilson glanced over at his pillow and frowned; a stringy clump of long black greasy hair lay deposited as always when he fed. But then a thought crossed Wilson's mind, and he smiled wickedly; he lifted his clenched right fist before his face and slowly opened his hand. Two blood-speckled teeth lay in his palm alongside little red indentations where the pointed roots had dug into his flesh as he clasped them tight. He did not fully understand how he could bring them back with him, but Wilson did not care; all he cared about was that he did.

Crawling over to the scuffed wooden chest, he slipped the metal key around his neck into the lock and clicked the mechanism open. He placed the camera in his lap, lifted the wooden lid, and removed the dark black cloth, which was soft between his fingers. Underneath were his treasures scattered over the bottom of the chest. Dozens of teeth stared back up at him, and Wilson ran his hands reverently over them, his eyes gleaming with the rush of savory memories that assailed him. He stared down at the teeth and felt his mouth salivating, a stirring feeling more of desire than hunger. Wilson did not always feed on them immediately like Mrs. Stammerall; he often enjoyed playing with them and relished their final screams as he sank his teeth into their neck. Sometimes they broke and just whimpered as he fed.

Wilson held the two new teeth between his right hand's thumb and index finger and held them up to his eye to appraise them proudly. Then he leaned forward and ran his tongue over the teeth. He closed his eyes and smiled at the sweet memory the taste brought back to him. Wilson then carefully deposited the teeth among the other tiny white treasures he had gathered and replaced the black fabric over them as if he was tucking them into bed for the night. He closed the lid and locked the chest, patting it with his boney hand. One day the trunk would be filled to the top with treasures.

◆ ◆ ◆

Wilson sat in his booth, watching the steady pattern of raindrops like little bomblets all over the open field. The previous day's rain had continued unabated and kept away the summer crowds that would usually be packing the carnival. That would undoubtedly put Hamish in a foul mood. The handful of visitors with their brightly colored umbrellas stuck mainly to the north side of the carnival, moving from one big tent to another. Nobody would want a picture of their rain-sodden day at the carnival today.

He sat on his uncomfortable wooden stool, hand supporting his chin as he leaned against the counter, daydreaming, replaying the night's events with a wicked smile. The more he daydreamed, the more he thought of the treasures in his wooden chest. Wilson felt as if the pearly, bloodstained treasures were calling to him. He wanted to return to his tent and run his tongue over them. Let the flesh of his tongue run over the rounded edges and the pointy tips of the roots, taste the blood. He would suck the teeth clean.

The thoughts began to build into a temptation he could not resist. Wilson glanced around, seeing Hamish nowhere.

Nobody will notice if I pop back to my tent for a few minutes, thought Wilson.

Then he spied the tall, lanky form of Long Li at one of the food booths across the way. The man wore a traditional black Chinese shirt and pants that Wilson thought looked like pajamas. His shaved head was topped with a black skullcap from which a long thin braid of hair emanated and ran down the tall Chinaman's back. If Li spotted Wilson leaving his booth or saw it empty, he would surely spread the word.

"Meddling busybody," Wilson mumbled as he watched Li buy a spitted kebab of chicken meat from the booth.

Wilson watched as Li paid and nodded his thanks to the man in the booth before heading back towards the meandering city of tents on the south side with his noonday meal. He pulled off large chunks of the chicken as he walked, barely chewing the roasted meat before swallowing it. The man's long braid swung from side to side like a pendulum as he walked, oblivious to the rain.

To Wilson's chagrin, the rain lessened and stopped when he felt Long Li was safely ensconced among the tents and out of view. He sat there glumly as he spotted the first ray of sunshine poking through the thinning clouds. It would not be long before he would spot the first headlights of cars coming from town, making their way to the carnival, and disgorging their eager occupants. His treasures would have to wait.

◆ ◆ ◆

As darkness descended on the carnival that evening, the city of tents became a maelstrom of sparkling lights. The big tents on the north side looked like small mountain peaks illuminated against the darkness. The night was also the time of day when the south side came alive. With most of the more respectable townsfolk home for the night, the town's more adventurous spirits would come seeking pleasures that the withered crones at the C.P.F.V.P.B. would find quite objectionable.

Wilson prodded the coin box underneath the counter with his foot, and it made an appreciable jingle. Hamish would be very happy with the day's take, so Wilson decided to return to his tent.

As he tried to do each night, Wilson walked by Bella's tent. He strolled past the myriad of tents, stopping to watch for a moment as a large bald man with a thick black mustache sat in his tent, tattooing a bright red heart on the forearm of a man seated with his back to Wilson. Several other tents had scantily clad women walking back and forth or smoking cigarettes on stools. They would often call him "cutie" and beckon him toward their tent or call him to take their picture, but he would keep his head down and walk past them.

As Wilson walked towards Bella's tent, he could see that

her door flap was open, making him smile. He could sit and talk with her for a bit. That would make him happy. But Wilson's smile quickly faded as he spied the man in the black bowler hat. The rolled-up sleeves of the man's white shirt revealed tattooed forearms, and a pair of suspenders trailed up from his pants to run over broad, muscular shoulders- Karl, the hawker for all the girls on the south side of the carnival.

Karl was talking to a man and pointing toward Bella's tent. He saw the man put some dollar bills in Karl's hand, and the hawker quickly slid the bills into his pocket. Wilson could see Karl patting the man on the shoulder and heading back into the crowd as the man started walking towards Bella's tent.

He was a large bald, heavy-set man with a thick blonde mustache. The man wore a grey epaulet shirt and dark slacks, a policeman's gold stripe down the side, and a deputy sheriff's shiny star on his chest. A large pistol sat snuggly in a holster on the man's right hip with a thick black nightstick dangling from his left hip. The deputy sheriff was looking into Bella's tent when he caught sight of Wilson peering. When his eyes settled on the camera in Wilson's hand, his eyes narrowed in suspicion.

"Here now, what are you doing?" the deputy spoke sharply to Wilson as he unhooked the nightstick from his belt.

Wilson looked down at his feet, not wanting to meet the man's eyes.

"Are you taking my picture?" the deputy poked Wilson hard in the chest with the round tip of the nightstick.

"I...I'm sorry, Sir," Wilson apologized, but inside he felt a rage boiling. He hated getting poked, and he especially hated to be poked in the chest.

"Oh, don't mind him, Sir," Bella stepped out of her tent. "That's just Wilson."

Bella was wearing a short, black silky robe that revealed the bottom curve of her pale buttocks and made Wilson blush.

"I don't need people taking my picture," the deputy angrily poked Wilson again in the chest with the nightstick so hard his top hat nearly tumbled off. "I was told this carnival was discreet."

"Wilson meant no harm; he has a special camera," Bella placed her hand on the man's shoulder.

"Special how?" the deputy sheriff squinted his eyes suspiciously.

"It sees things," Wilson held up the camera. "Special things. I could take a special picture of you."

"What does that even mean?" the deputy's anger gave way to guarded curiosity.

Wilson grew up with men like this deputy sheriff; they had poked him and pushed him around his whole life. He could see that the deputy was looking at him with thinly veiled disgust, and he self-consciously tried to adjust his old, ill-fitting suit.

"Never mind, Wilson," cooed Bella. "Why don't we go into my tent for a bit?"

"First, I want to know what's so special about this camera," the deputy eyed Wilson before turning his gaze to the revealing neckline of Bella's robe. "Then we go in your tent."

Wilson did not like how the man looked at Bella and did not like his thoughts of the two of them in Bella's tent. He wanted to take this man's picture very badly.

"Look, I'll show you," Wilson raised the Polaroid to his eye and clicked the red button.

The deputy sheriff had tried to raise his hand to protest as the flash went off, and Wilson had to step back to avoid having the man swat the camera away. The Polaroid whirred as the picture slot spit out a palm-sized black photograph.

"I normally charge twenty-five cents for pictures..." began Wilson.

"I'll not pay you for the picture!" the deputy held the tip of the nightstick against Wilson's chest and snatched the photograph from his hand. "I never agreed to that."

Only the faint outline of the big man, his hand outstretched, could be seen. The picture slowly sharpened as Bella and the deputy sheriff looked down. Wilson saw that Bella had slipped an arm around the deputy sheriff and had her face pressed against his shoulder, looking down at the picture. He could see the outline of her breast beneath the thin robe pressed against the man's arm, and he felt a sneer cross his face. He did not wait for the picture to finish developing before turning to go.

"You can keep the picture as a present," Wilson grinned as his eyes blazed with malice. "I must be on my way."

Behind him, Wilson heard Bella let out an excited gasp. "See, I told you his camera was special!"

"But how?" the deputy stared at the photo in complete bewilderment.

The deputy sheriff held the Polaroid picture in his hand, clearly showing him with his hand outstretched. The surroundings were just as they were in real life, and so were all the features of his face, but the man's uniform had changed to the dark blue coat with the gold branded sleeves and bright golden star of the Sheriff.

◆ ◆ ◆

Wilson cradled the camera protectively as he quickly navigated back to his tent. A look of malicious delight filled his face. He seldom took pictures of men; he preferred the camera's photos of women. Young or old, he did not care; he hungered for them all the same. Wilson loved the way the camera saw them.

"Move!" Wilson hissed as he pushed through a throng of men and women.

Wilson felt a pang of desperation. He needed to get to the mirror. Even now, the deputy sheriff was in Bella's tent. The thought of the man looking at her, touching her soft white skin, filled him with anger. He felt beads of anxious sweat run down his forehead.

Poke me in the chest, thought Wilson seething with rage.

Wilson pushed through the flap and into his tent, quickly tying it closed behind him. He gently placed the camera on the wooden crate facing him and lay on his sweat-stained bed, not even bothering to take off his black suit and top hat. He stared into the camera's lens and smiled wickedly as the beam of light sprang forth from the camera into his eyes. Wilson laughed maliciously as he felt his body tingle and his eyes roll in his head. He closed his eyes and let the darkness overtake him.

◆ ◆ ◆

Sheriff Bo Hayes strode through the corridor of the police station as a god among mortals. Blue-clad police officers snapped to attention as he passed.

He approached the frosted glass door that read "Detective Bureau" and turned the knob. The brightly lit room smelled of coffee and gun leather, and a large picture of him smiling as he shook hands with the governor hung on the wall.

As he walked down the middle of the row of desks, his chest swelled with pride at how the detectives did not feel worthy to meet his gaze. Detective Tom Childs was the man who had beaten him out of the starting running back position on the high school football team, his brow covered in sweat at the thought of disappointing the Sheriff. A large-bellied policeman with the three stripes of a sergeant stepped into Sheriff Hayes' way and then, realizing his mistake, apologized profusely.

Sheriff Hayes remembered the sergeant's snide face when the policeman had told him he failed to pass the detectives exam. Now the man groveled for his approval like a redbone coonhound. Hayes extended his arm and shoved the sergeant away with a dismissive glance.

The Sheriff's eyes fixed on the large-breasted blonde secretary with the very short skirt. She beamed at him as he walked towards her.

"Good morning, Sheriff!" her eyes stared at him adoringly.

There was a time when Sally Mae had rejected him whenever he asked her to dinner. The unapprovingly way she had always looked at him made him feel small. But now, Sallie Mae was at his beck and call, happy to meet his every need.

"In my office now, Sallie Mae," Sheriff Hays slapped her hard on the backside, eliciting a delighted squeal from the woman.

He strode into his office, adorned with many awards for bravery and heroism, and sat behind his large oaken desk. The Sheriff pushed his chair back from the desk, leaving enough room for Sallie Mae.

"Shut the door behind you, Sallie Mae," the Sheriff ordered as the beaming secretary entered his office.

As Sallie Mae shut the door, a large shape sprang forward, causing the image of Sallie Mae to dissipate into the air. The creature was large and muscular, with long red hair and blue eyes that burned hot with malice. Hayes saw the creature's mouthful of jagged teeth as it moved impossibly fast across the room.

All Sheriff Hayes could do was get his hands up to protect his face as the creature bounded up over the desk and into the space between him and the desk. The beast only grabbed him by the wrists and snapped the Sheriff's arms like old, decayed branches. The loud snapping noise mixed with Hayes' screams of pain and terror.

Hayes stared helplessly at the creature as his broken arms hung uselessly at his side. He watched in horror as the beast extended one long finger tipped with a sharp black talon and held it before his face. Then the creature poked Hayes hard in the chest with the outstretched finger, causing the Sheriff's chair to slide backward with each blow. Once, twice, and then the third time, the creature reared its arm back, and Hayes screamed and felt his bladder and bowels empty as the creature twisted the taloned finger inside his chest.

With a sickening sucking sound, the creature withdrew the gore-soaked digit from the Sheriff's chest and smeared it across the screaming man's face, leaving bloody streaks. The beast grabbed Hayes and dug his fingers into the man's head and shoulder. Hayes screamed, cried, and beat futile fists against the creature's muscular chest as it bent his head to expose the pulsing arteries of his neck.

Then Wilson began to feed.

❖ ❖ ❖

Wilson awoke smiling. He sat up and brushed the greasy clump of dark hair from his pillow with a boney hand. A troubling thought momentarily crossed his mind: he had broken the rules but shrugged it off.

Wilson added the man's teeth to his collection of treasures and reluctantly covered them with the black fabric. A sudden uproar outside caught his attention, causing his eyes to look sidelong at the tent entrance. Wilson slammed down the lid of the chest and locked it. A cacophony of voices rose outside, far more commotion than was usual for the south side, even on carnival days.

He ran a boney hand over the wrinkles in the suit, trying to smooth them out before donning the top hat. He grabbed his camera, carefully cradling the precious device in his arm as he stepped out of his tent.

The bright Midwestern moon was high in the sky, and the post-rain mugginess made him sweat instantly inside his suit. People were quickly walking past, gathering further down the row of tents. With a feeling of apprehension, he realized they were congregating over by Bella's tent.

Wilson tried to move through the press of people, arms wrapped around the camera to protect it from the jostling crowd. He grunted as a man elbowed him in the eye, nearly dislodging his top hat with the force of the blow as Wilson tried to move past. He glared at the man, a large freckle-faced farm hand in overalls who looked dismissively back at him.

Wilson saw Karl talking to a short deputy sheriff, feigning a look of naiveté at the officer's questions. Then he saw Bella, she looked distraught, and Wilson noticed how her usually happy face was contorted into a look of horror. Tears streamed down her face as she held a thick red blanket around her; two other carnival women from nearby tents had their arms around her consolingly.

A murmur suddenly ran through the crowd, and Wilson saw Bella gasp and hide her face in one of the women's shoulders. Two carnival hands walked out of Bella's red tent with a stretcher held between them, a large form wholly covered by a coarse woolen blanket lying on the stretcher.

The carnival hand in front stumbled momentarily before regaining his footing. Nevertheless, the awkward movement was enough to cause the woolen blanket to shift, revealing a blonde head beneath. A cry went up from the gathered crowd as the Midwestern moon shone down brightly on Deputy Sheriff Hayes' face, his mouth stretched impossibly wide, frozen into a rigor of terror; peering out from a pale, sunken face was bloodshot eyes that stared lifelessly at the sky.

◆ ◆ ◆

Wilson lay in bed that night, untroubled by the night's events. The flickering light of his kerosene lamp illuminated the small tent. His eyes drifted to his wooden chest, the camera sitting atop it. The look on the deputy sheriff's face was vivid in his mind, and he kept wondering what the women whose pictures he took looked like when people discovered their bodies.

He smiled to himself, thinking of the looks on their faces when he took their picture. The way they looked down on him. How different they must have looked in the end. The terror, his terror, forever on their faces. They must have all had funerals with closed caskets, which made him chuckle.

Wilson looked over at the camera and frowned. He always locked it away in the chest at night, but the thought of opening it with all the police officers made him pause. What if some nosy police officer stuck his head in the tent and saw his treasures? He could not have that; oh no, he could not.

A soft taping at his tent flap caused his eyes to dart nervously towards the opening. Could this be one of those policemen now?

"*Why would they need to speak to him?*" Wilson thought to himself. "*Could they have found the picture on the deputy's body?*"

"Wilson?" called a soft female voice.

A woman at his tent? That was very unusual indeed. Wilson stood up and wrapped his blanket around himself.

"Wilson? It's Bella. Are you awake?" called the voice.

He made his way to the tent flap and peered outside. Bella's tear-streaked face stared back at him, her eyes red-rimmed from crying. She still had the red blanket wrapped around her. A weak smile crossed her pale face when she saw him looking back at her.

"Wilson, could I come in?"

"Come in?" He chaffed at the surprise in his voice.

"If I'm bothering you…" she started, but he quickly cut her off.

"Oh, it's no bother; please come in," Wilson excitedly untied the tent flap.

She smiled at him as she walked in. Wilson saw her take in the meager surroundings of his tent as she walked in.

"Is it ok if I sit down?"

"Yes, of course!" Wilson tried to hide the nervousness in his voice.

He felt self-conscious of the dirtiness of his sweat-stained bed as she sat down on the edge. As far as he could remember, he never had a visitor in his tent. Wilson crossed the tent and leaned up against the wooden chest. She smiled weakly at him, and he smiled back.

"I'm sorry for coming over so late, Wilson. It's just that I have had such a terrible day, and I....I just wanted to be around a friend. You have always been so kind to me, Wilson."

He stared at her; her eyes looked so big and beautiful in the lantern light.

"Is it ok if I just sit here for a while, Wilson?"

"What? Oh yes, of course." Wilson picked up the camera and leaned against the wooden chest.

"May I have some water?" she pointed to the water pitcher and chipped glass on the little table. "I have been talking to policemen all night about what happened and am just parched."

"Yes, please. Have all you like."

Bella took the glass of water and drained the contents. She held the empty glass in her lap and stared down at it. Her shoulders began shaking, and Wilson realized she was sobbing again. He felt awkward and did not know what to do, so he reached out one boney hand and put it on her shoulder reassuringly.

"Oh, Wilson, it was just horrible. That policeman just began to scream and scream. And then his face...." Bella's voice trailed off as her crying resumed.

Suddenly the tent flap flew open with a loud snap, and Wilson jumped up in surprise. Bella gasped as Karl angrily strode into the tent. Wilson could smell the pungent stench of whiskey around the man before he even spoke.

"What is this?" Karl snarled ferociously.

"Karl, please," Bella stood up from the bed. "I was just talking with Wilson."

Karl looked past Bella at Wilson's scrawny form, his hands clenching into fists. The carnival hawker turned to look furiously at Bella, grabbing her roughly by the arm.

"You beg me for the night off because a man dies between your legs, and you turn around and give it away for free?" A vein in Karl's forehead pulsed as he yelled at her.

Bella began to sob, and Wilson's eyes darted nervously around the room like a trapped animal. In Karl's agitated state, Wilson feared the man would lash out and smash the camera.

"Please, I was just talking," sobbed Bella, her shoulders shaking.

"If this wretch wants you, he pays like the others!" Karl point at Wilson. "There are no freebies."

Karl shook her arm roughly, causing her to cry out, and his elbow struck the mirror's frame, causing it to rock back and forth.

"I...I have no money," Wilson barely got the words out before Karl brought one booted foot up to kick him hard in the chest.

The blow caused Wilson to fly backward into the chest, dislodging the camera from his hand. Wilson frantically reached for the camera, trying to catch his breath as it tumbled. He snatched it from the air in the nick of time, his finger inadvertently depressing the red photo button and filling the room with a bright flash.

"No money, no whore!" snarled Karl. "Maybe the lion trainer will let you stick one of the goats before he feeds it for dinner."

Karl turned and pulled Bella out of the tent. Wilson caught sight of her sad eyes as she turned to look at him one last time before disappearing out of the tent. The camera whirred and spat out a black square onto the floor.

Wilson quickly unlocked the wooden chest and safely stored the camera before further mishaps occurred. He sat sprawled on the floor, his back against the wooden chest, breathing hard. His ribs ached from the kick, and he ran his hands over what he was sure was a reddening boot print on his chest.

He looked over at the mirror, relieved it had survived the encounter. The blow from Karl's elbow had swiveled it down slightly to reflect more of the floor. Wilson looked at the reflection in the smooth glass and groaned. The mirror reflected the image of the picture. The camera snapped when he caught it as it fell. In the lantern's flickering light, the picture slowly developed to reveal Bella clad in comfortable-looking pajamas adorned with strawberries.

◆ ◆ ◆

Wilson wanted to return to the thin crumpled form with the bruised chest that lay curled on the bed. But the hunger turned him towards the light. As if the limbs were not his own, the legs started to move towards the light, accelerating. His heart pounded in his chest as he ran. The hunger in his body filled him. His tongue flicked over his sharpened teeth as he moved toward the light.

He came upon the light and stared into that sacred place in Bella's mind. There was Bella; she lay in a large bed clutching a cloth doll with bright red yarn hair. She wore white pajamas with red strawberries embroidered on them. A tall mustached man and woman with the same long red hair and green eyes that Bella possessed stood over her. The woman bent over and kissed Bella on the forehead, and Bella beamed with delight.

"Good night, kiddo," tall man patted her on the leg.

"We love you, dear," the woman smiled lovingly at Bella.

Bella returned a smile that reached from ear to ear, "I love you too!"

The man put his arm around the red-haired woman, and they walked to the door, looking back one last time at Bella with big smiles before turning out the light and closing the door.

Bella had never told Wilson much about her life before the carnival, and for a moment, he wondered if what he was seeing was a desire to return to life in the past or a passion for a life that never was.

Wilson felt his hands clenching and unclenching. The thought of having Bella in his wooden chest full of treasures made him smile wolfishly. She would be all his and only his evermore.

Wilson lowered himself to lay flat on the floor and

slithered across the soft carpet like a snake. While alongside her bed, he quietly rolled onto his back and slid underneath until his upper body was sticking out the other side. He raised one strong hand, sunk his talons into the soft blanket, and tugged lightly.

He waited. No response. He tugged again and could hear the bed creaking as Bella moved atop it. Bella's familiar face, the face of his only friend, with her green eyes and red hair, peaked over the edge of the bed. The little doll still clutched in her arm. Wilson stared up at her.

"Boo!" he opened his eyes wide and bared his teeth menacingly.

Her face became transfixed in abject terror, and she screamed as Wilson pulled her from the bed, his teeth sinking into her neck.

❖ ❖ ❖

Wilson stayed in his tent when they found Bella's body the following day. In the end, he had enjoyed Bella's fear and suffering as he did with all the others, but he had no desire to see what he had wrought upon his one-time friend. However, he did go out when he heard shouting later that morning as a group of policemen had taken away a struggling Karl.

As he stood in the crowd of onlookers, Wilson had overheard Long Li saying a Federal Bureau of Investigation man was looking into murders that seemed to follow the Grand Ole Traveling Carnival. Karl had done bad things to women when he was with the army in Korea, and they seemed to suspect he was up to his old ways. With the death of the deputy sheriff and

Bella, the police knew they had their man. One of the carnival hands that Wilson did not know said that Karl was sure to get the electric chair, which made Wilson smile.

But Wilson had more significant problems than the police right now. He sat in his booth on the wooden stool, and although he stared down at his feet, he could feel Hamish's piercing gaze upon him. The carnival's proprietor stood in the booth window and tapped his index finger against the coarse wood. Unlike the mask of contorted anger, Wilson expected to see, Hamish's face was unsettlingly calm.

"Do you remember where I found you, Wilson?" Hamish gave Wilson a withering look.

"In Texas."

"Yes, but where in Texas?" Hamish raised his eyes upwards as if trying to remember.

"In the street," Wilson hunched his shoulders meekly.

"Oh yes, that's right. In the street. Do you remember what I told you?"

"You told me I was special," Wilson looked up at the carnival owner.

"And do you remember why I said you were special?" Hamish leaned into the booth's window so close that Wilson could feel the man's hot breath against his face.

"Because of my camera."

"Oh yes, because of your camera!" Hamish stood up and pounded a hand on the counter. "And what would have happened if I did not take you in?"

"Someone would have broken my camera," Wilson looked up at Hamish.

"Someone would have broken your camera."

Hamish reached into the booth, put his hand under Wilson's chin, and raised his head to face him. "And what would you be without your camera?" he asked.

"Nothing," Wilson's voice was quiet, almost child-like.

"You'd be nothing," Hamish's voice filled with menace. "We have rules, Wilson. You must follow the rules, or you will be back on the street, and you understand what that means, yes?"

"Yes."

"Good." Hamish's face broke into a malicious smile. "You have yourself a good day Wilson."

Hamish straightened his red coat, tipped his hat back, and turned away from the booth as if nothing had happened. Wilson seethed with rage. He hated the carnival owner with a passion. He hated groveling before the man and following his rules. Who was Hamish anyway?

Wilson watched the man striding away and felt himself filled with hatred. With a sneer, Wilson raised the camera to his eye; the image of the carnival owner with his red coat and pants and tall black top hat filled the viewport.

A grin of pure hatred crossed Wilson's mouth as his finger slid onto the top of the red button.

"I'll be seeing you soon, Hamish."

He pressed the red button downward. And nothing.

No flash. No whir. Nothing. Wilson pressed the button again, and still nothing. In front of him, Hamish had stopped walking, and Wilson felt his blood run cold with terror. He returned the camera to his lap, and the carnival owner started walking again.

Over the din of the carnival crowd, Wilson could hear Hamish laughing.

◆ ◆ ◆

The hot sun had given way to evening, and the lights of the Grand Ole Traveling Carnival illuminated the night sky like a small city. Wilson saw the Ferris wheel lights slowly turning on the carnival's north end. The air carried the scent of popcorn, cotton candy, and roasted meats of questionable origin as he walked through the tents of the south side.

The din of the carnival's north side belied the popularity of the rides, shows, and spectacles, with townspeople looking for a distraction from their everyday lives. The dark attractions of the south side always gathered a more subdued crowd, but the heightened police attention brought on by the two deaths of the past week had kept away many of those that sought out the dark corners of the carnival.

Those that came to the south side tonight were mostly men either walking alone in the shadows hoping not to be recognized by their neighbors or more rowdy groups of teens looking for some of the thrills found on the south side of the carnival.

Wilson ran his fingers lovingly over the leather and chrome of the camera as he walked; the night air was cool and a pleasant respite from the sun of this dust bowl state. He walked past Bella's faded red tent, it was dark inside now, and he was sure the other carnival residents had already picked through her few positions and taken anything of value. Wilson stuck his head inside the tent's opening and breathed in deeply. The scent of Bella's perfume still lingered in the air, and the smell of it brought back a flood of memories. Wilson felt a stirring in his loins at the mental images of Bella's last moments. Adrenaline coursed through his veins as he recalled the feeling of his raw strength overpowering the small woman. He swayed a little on his feet, lost in the moment, his tongue flicking over his yellowed teeth, remembering her taste. The little man raised a thin hand to his neck and lightly touched his skin, recalling the panicked panting of her last breaths upon his neck. The feeling made him groan quietly with pleasure.

"Excuse me," said a soft-spoken woman's voice, shaking Wilson out of his reverie.

He felt a momentary panic at his discovery as he turned around. But when Wilson set eyes on the woman, his mouth opened in utter surprise. She was perhaps the most beautiful woman he had ever seen. Her skin was a porcelain white, and she had soft full lips and large doe-like dark eyes framed by jet-black hair tied with a red ribbon that fluttered lightly in the cool night breeze. She wore a plain blue dress and held her hands nervously in front of her. The woman immediately reminded Wilson of sitting at the cinema as a child and watching Snow White and the Seven Dwarfs.

"I'm sorry I did not mean to startle you," the woman

wrung her petite hands nervously.

"Oh, it's no bother." Wilson gave her his most reassuring smile. "How may I help you?"

"I seem to have gotten all turned around out here; I cannot find my way back to the entrance. Would you be able to point me in the right direction?" Her voice was a sweet melodic tone.

Wilson felt a hunger for this beautiful woman unlike anything he had ever experienced. She seemed so sweet and young and innocent. His eyes lit up with thoughts of what he would do with her. Her skin seemed so white and flawless that Wilson felt himself salivating at the thought of her taste.

"I could do better than that," Wilson tried to hide the eagerness in his voice. "I can take you to the entrance if you like."

"I hate to put you in any trouble." She protested though Wilson could see the relief in her eyes.

"It's no trouble at all."

She blushed. "You must think me a very silly girl."

"No, no, not all."

This seemed to delight her greatly, and Wilson felt his face beaming with a wide smile. He then gestured to his camera.

"I can even take a picture of you," Wilson quickly added, "Free of charge!"

Hamish had warned him not to violate the rules again. One town, one feeding. But how could he allow this beautiful creature to slip away? She needed to be a part of his treasures. He would deal with the ramifications later, even if Hamish kicked him out of the carnival. He wanted this woman in his collection.

"That is very kind of you, but it's too dark over here; the picture would come out dreadful." Her gaze cast about, looking at the shadows. "How about by the entrance? It's very bright over there."

"That would be wonderful!" Wilson felt exhilarated. "This camera takes very special pictures." Wilson patted the camera lovingly.

"Wow!" Her eyes alighted with excitement. "I'm so happy I met you, Mr...."

Extending his hand forward to her, "My name is Wilson."

"My name is Dahlia," she shook his hand.

Wilson felt his heartbeat quicken at her touch. Her hand was soft and warm, and he could feel the gentle thrum of her pulse when he held her hand.

Wilson was usually a slow walker, but this evening he walked quickly, eager to make their way to the entrance. Dahlia did not seem to mind and could keep stride with him easily. She explained to him that her mother had not wanted her to go to the carnival, but she had snuck out and come alone because she wanted to see the animals. A deep frown crossed her beautiful face as she told Wilson how sad it was to see the animals in cages, so she decided to leave and lost her way. She wanted to get home before her mother realized she had gone out.

As she talked, Wilson felt himself staring at her. Dahlia was perhaps the most perfect creature he had ever seen. Her features were delicate and unblemished. Her simple blue dress hinted at what Wilson was sure was a perfectly formed body beneath. Her large dark eyes exuded a childlike innocence, and Wilson could barely contain his excitement at the thought of those eyes filling with pain and terror. Wilson smiled to himself; he would take his time with little Dahlia.

"Here we are!" Wilson grinned, pointing to the large white sign with red letters that read "Welcome to the Grand Ole Traveling Carnival" and underneath in smaller black letters, "J. Hamish White, Proprietor."

"Oh, Wilson, thank you so much!" Dahlia clapped her hands and bobbed delightedly.

"It was my pleasure! Now for that picture."

"Oh yes! Where should I stand?"

"Just right there under the sign is perfect." He stepped back and raised the camera to his eye.

Wilson could see Dahlia standing perfectly under the sign through the viewing hole. Her hands were on her hips, and she had a perfect smile. He depressed the red picture button, and the flashbulb briefly illuminated them, making Dahlia giggle and blink rapidly. The camera whirred, and the black photograph slid out from the camera. Dahlia eagerly crowded over to look and frowned deeply at the black squares.

"It didn't come out," she pouted with genuine disappointment.

"Just give it a moment," Wilson reassured her, "The film has to develop, and when it does, you will be amazed!"

The two of them looked down at the developing

film. Dahlia made excited little noises as her outline became visible, and the carnival sign became clearer with every passing moment. As Dahlia's image became more visible, she became even more excited, but Wilson began to frown. He felt his mouth turning down and his brows furrowing as the picture became fully developed.

He stared at the picture; Dahlia looked exactly like she did when standing under the sign. There was absolutely nothing different about the photo.

"You don't like it?" she frowned, seeing the disappointed look on his face.

"It's just that I think I could do better," Wilson tried to cover up his confusion.

"I don't know, Wilson, it's getting late, and I need to get home. I think the picture looks just grand."

"Just let me take one more," Wilson slipped the photo into his jacket pocket.

"Well, ok. Just one more, and then I have to go," she smiled and nodded.

Dahlia took up her pose beneath the sign, and Wilson raised the camera, pressed the red button, and took another picture. The camera whirred and produced a black square. Wilson and Dahlia stared down as the pictures developed. The outline of the sign and Dahlia became visible, and just like before, Dahlia looked precisely the same.

"Oh, Wilson, you were right; I like this one even better." Dahlia plucked one of the pictures from his hand and pressed it against her heart. "I love it, Wilson, thank you."

Wilson just stared from the picture in his hand to Dahlia and back again. Something like this had never happened before.

"I am so happy I met you, Wilson." She beamed as she patted him on the shoulder. "I hope to see you again one day. Take care!"

Wilson watched as she turned and walked quickly out of the carnival, turning one last time to wave at him before disappearing into the darkness. He stood there dumbfounded for a moment, perplexed at what had happened. Then he looked down at the picture; Dahlia's beautiful face smiled up at him.

A wicked smile slowly crossed Wilson's lips as a deep malicious hunger burned away the last of his perplexing thoughts.

"Oh, you will see me again, Dahlia," he grinned evilly.

◆ ◆ ◆

Wilson lay naked in his bed. The flickering light from the tent's lantern reflected off the camera's lens seated on the wooden chest. He glanced over at the camera and then at the three pictures of Dahlia he held in his hand like playing cards, staring at her fine features. He looked longingly into her large dark eyes, picturing how they would look when he came to her that night. The surprise. The terror. The pain.

Then Wilson frowned at the pictures, troubled that they seemed to capture her exactly as she was. He looked back over at the camera. Was it broken? Had whatever magic that gave it its power run out? No, that did not seem right. It still functioned the way it always did.

Was it Dahlia? Then he wondered to himself. Wilson knew the camera captured how and what people desired to be. Was it possible that Dahlia was so perfect that she was exactly how she had wanted to be? He could understand how other women could want to look like Dahlia; she was perfection. But did Dahlia really not desire more than to live the life she lived? He studied the picture and was utterly amazed that there was absolutely no difference. She did not desire to be taller or shorter, for her hair to be longer, or even her breasts to be larger.

Wilson could feel his eagerness to see his prey again, his hunger to feed upon her soul and render its life from the fabric of the world. Wilson smiled to himself, enjoying the building anticipation. He replayed the night's events, savoring his memory of her every movement. The sound of her laugh. The feel of her hand. He ran his tongue over his lips as he recalled every feature of her face.

When the camera whirred to life and the beam of light sprang into his eye, he felt a wolfish grin cross his face, hands clenching and unclenching in anticipation. Wilson closed his eyes and felt the blackness begin to overtake him. He welcomed the rollercoaster sensation, knowing that he would soon be gorging himself on Dahlia's terror and pain, and he felt a wicked laugh leave his lips as the blackness took him.

When Wilson opened his eyes again, he delighted at the feel of raw strength flowing through his limbs. Wilson smiled when he looked at the strong hands with their black-tipped talons, hands made to rend and tear.

His shoulder muscles bunched as he turned his head towards the light, enjoying the feel of his long red hair brushing along his naked back.

He started for the light at a run. In his mouth, his tongue flicked over sharp teeth, teeth that would bite and taste Dahlia's sweet flesh soon. He salivated at the thought and felt the rush of power pulsing in his veins.

The light drew closer until it filled his vision. Wilson stopped just outside the perimeter of the glow and ran his rough hand over the outer edge. Just one more step and he would be inside Dahlia's mind, within the place where she held her deepest secrets and desires.

He peered into the light; it was a bedroom with a plush pink blanketed bed. It had four large posts with a lace canopy that hung like a silken spider web over a bed adorned with soft round pillows. Wilson stepped into the light. The bedroom had a thick carpet that felt softer than grass against his clawed toes. He smirked evilly at the Snow White and the Seven Dwarfs movie poster on one wall; there would be no Prince Charming for Dahlia. The sightless eyes of a myriad of finely dressed dolls filled the other wall of the room, and watched as Wilson stalked into the light.

An open door leading outside was on the far wall, and Wilson could smell the fresh scent of the outdoors blowing through. He stepped into the doorway and looked out. It was a panoramic scene of a wooded glade. Tall mountains rose in the distance beneath a sun-filled cloudless sky. A gentle breeze blew across a green grass field, and wildflowers stretched from the door into the wooded glade. He could see where Dahlia's footsteps had crushed down the soft grass, and he began to follow her trail.

Wilson followed the trail into a forest of tall oaks and pines, branches and pine needles crushing under his mighty feet. He heard rushing water and could see a hint of blue up ahead; his heart began to beat faster, anticipating his hunt would end.

The trees changed from oaks and pines to white-trunked aspen trees, whose fallen branches left scars on the trunks of the trees that looked like so many eyes. Wilson could hear Dahlia humming over the rushing din of the river, the sweet innocence of the sound feeding his animalistic hunger.

At last, he came upon her, still dressed in her blue dress with the red ribbon in her black hair. Dahlia was humming a Disney tune he did not know by name, and she had one outstretched hand running her fingers through the river's water. Wilson saw his shadow fall over the young girl and noticed with delight that her humming had stopped, and she had frozen in place. He panted, expecting what would come next, her turning and seeing him, her terror, and, best of all, her screams.

Dahlia turned her soft white face to Wilson, and to his great dismay, she smiled.

"Wilson!" her eyes danced with excitement. "I knew we would see each other again!"

Wilson felt the wolfish grin slip from his face, and for the first time, he felt a shock of apprehension slice through his muscular body. He stepped closer to the river and looked down at his reflection. Wilson half expected to see his scrawny form looking back at him but was relieved to see his reflection's muscular chest and shoulders, piercing blue eyes, and long red hair.

"See, Wilson, I have a mirror, too," Dahlia cooed happily as she brushed her hand over the water's surface, and the river stopped.

Wilson's reflection stared back at him from the calm water and then began to change. The reflection changed to the image of a thin, dark-haired teen seated on the floor amid the old boxes and crates of what looked like an old dusty attic. In his hand, the boy held an old Polaroid camera that he had taken from one of the attic boxes, and in front of him, an old sheet lay over something tall and thin. Wilson watched as the boy looked around him to make sure he was alone and then reached up and tugged on the sheet. It slid away to reveal the familiar oval wooded frame of the mirror. Wilson stared at the image transfixed.

A light appeared behind the boy, and Wilson saw the teen turn around in alarm. A tall bald man charged into the image, and Wilson knew the man was the boy's uncle, who had taken him in when his parents had died in a car accident. The uncle was upset with the boy for going where he was not allowed to go and touching things he was never supposed to touch. The boy stood with the camera behind his back as the uncle poked him in the chest to accentuate each word as he scolded him. The boy put the camera on a box and stood protectively in front of it as the uncle picked up a hammer from one of the crates. The uncle raised an arm to smash the camera, but the boy grabbed his arm, they struggled, and the boy pulled the hammer free of his uncle's grasp as the older man fell to the ground. Then the boy was on the uncle bringing the hammer down repeatedly.

Dahlia moved her hand, and the image faded, again replaced by the rushing river. She looked at Wilson with her large, dark, doe-like eyes that seemed filled with sadness.

"You were not a good boy Wilson. Mother told me you were not a good boy."

Wilson felt rooted to the ground, a tremble rippling through his mighty limbs. Dahlia reached her hand into the pocket of her dress and withdrew the photograph Wilson had taken of her. She looked down at the picture and smiled.

"I love the picture you took of me, Wilson," she beamed as she looked down at the picture. "I look so pretty in it."

Then her face clouded with darkness, and she looked back at Wilson.

"Mother said you like me the way I want to be. But you would not like me the way I really am. Is that true, Wilson?"

As he stared at her, the dark pupils of her eyes began to grow until they consumed the whites of her eyes.

"Is that true, Wilson?" Her voice became hoarser.

She stood up, and Wilson watched in horror as her arms lengthened until the skin split and thick black hairy limbs tore through the skin. He took an involuntary step backward as the beautiful features of her face began to lose shape, and the skin of her face began to split as mandibles and gaping maw began to tear through, a large mouth with rows of wicked-looking teeth. Two more long black hairy legs burst forth from Dahlia's chest, and another pair tore through her back.

The creature's mouth opened, screaming at him shrilly, "Am I still beautiful, Wilson?!"

Wilson watched the creature shake off the last of Dahlia's skin and stand erect on now eight legs that protruded from a large round black hairy body. The black eyes stared darkly at him from atop a mouth full of jagged fangs.

The giant spider began to move towards Wilson, and he turned and began to run. Fear filled the beast as it ran through the forest, the sounds of Dahlia scurrying after him not far behind. He saw now that the scars on the aspen trees seemed to blink like so many thousand eyes watching him.

"I used to live in a movie house, Wilson. I watched all the movies over and over again. I loved the princesses the most!" he heard Dahlia saying in a hoarse-sounding roar, and Wilson felt a scream leave his lips.

Wilson ran over the green field, trampling the wildflowers under his taloned feet. His heart beat not with excitement but with terror for the first time, and he felt fear inhabit every fiber of his body. The powerful legs took him through the door and into Dahlia's bedroom.

He caught sight of the Snow White poster again and, with growing horror, realized his mistake. The camera had seen Dahlia exactly how she desired to be. The creature that pursued him now had dreamed in the deepest reaches of its heart to be like a Disney princess, and that is precisely what the camera had seen.

Wilson ran out of the light of the room and into the darkness. Before him, he could see the light coming through the mirror from his tent, and he ran towards it with desperation. A whimpering noise was coming from his mouth, and he felt the cold sting of tears streaming down his cheek. He could hear Dahlia close behind him, but she, too, was now in the darkness, and he could not see her.

The light streaming in from the camera's lens was growing closer. Wilson just needed a few seconds more and would be back in his tent. He just needed to place his hand on the window, and Wilson would return to his body on the other side of the lens. He felt sheer terror inhabiting his very being and knew his only chance was to hurl himself through the window onto the other side.

The mirror was so close now Wilson pushed off from strong trunk-like legs and leaped for the mirror. He could see his sweat-stained bed with his scrawny naked form writhing on it, mouth moving in a soundless scream. The powerful muscles of his body rippled as he dove for the mirror.

A cry escaped his lips as the thin strands of a silken web tangled his limbs. Unseen in the darkness, he could now see the flickering light from his tent shining through the window of the thin strands. He hung suspended in the dark as he frantically kicked and swung his legs, trying to break free. The silken threads tangled in his long hair, and he felt a reverberation ripple through the web. The thoughts in his head were frantic with terror as he looked up and saw the spider's large, bloated black body inching its way down the web. Wilson felt the hot flush of urine run down his legs as terror emptied his bladder.

As the spider edged closer, he redoubled his frantic effort to free himself and reach the mirror. His massive body began to swing closer toward the mirror. He screamed again as he felt the giant spider's hot exhalation washed down upon him.

With a last desperate effort, Wilson thrust his arm out towards the mirror and felt his mighty hand strike the cold glass and punch a hole through to the other side. The jagged edges of the broken mirror tore through the flesh of his arms, tearing muscle and sinew. He felt the strong hand brush the night air of his tent, and then he was swinging back into the darkness of the web.

◆ ◆ ◆

Wilson's body hung enshrouded in a silken cocoon up to the nose. His eyes were wide with terror, and tears flowed unbidden down his cheeks. He moved his mouth beneath the silken shroud in an unintelligible whimper. Wilson's eyes cast upwards and opened even wider, the silk covering his mouth barely containing a blood-curdling scream. He bobbed momentarily on the silken chords and then jerked upwards. The sounds of his terrified shrieking filled the darkness.

Wilson came to a sudden stop in the darkness. Sobbing in terror, his powerful body immobilized by fear. Then Wilson felt his blood run cold.

"Wilssssoooon," came Dahlia's voice out of the darkness.

He leaned his head and saw two dark shiny orbs staring back at him, seeming to glow in the darkness.

"Wilson, I am going to drink your soul," Spider's voice

was hoarse and vaguely feminine. "I am going to suck all the sorrow from your bones, and I am going to make it last a very long time."

◆ ◆ ◆

Hamish covered his nose and mouth with a handkerchief as he entered the little tent. The stench was overpowering, and the carnival owner wrinkled his nose in disgust. He gazed around Wilson's tent at his few paltry possessions until his eyes found the camera.

He walked over and looked down at the old Polaroid camera; its shattered lens cast tiny slivers of glass that glinted in the light of the flickering lantern.

"Pity." Hamish looked down at the ruined camera with a frown.

He turned to look dispassionately at Wilson; his limbs curled in upon themselves. His neck stretched upwards, and his mouth froze open in a silent scream. Wilson's eyes remained rolled back in his head, and the skin around the bottom of his eyes drooped downward, the rims red and raw. He had bitten off his tongue, and the chunk of flesh lay covered in flies on his pillow. Hamish could see maggots wriggling in the cavities of Wilson's nose.

"Is he dead, boss?" called Long Li from outside the tent.

"Oh, he's quite dead," Hamish nodded without a touch of emotion in his voice.

"I'll tell the boys to start digging a hole," called back Long Li.

"Here now, what's this?" Hamish's eyebrows rose in

surprise.

He reached over to the little table, grabbed the glass of water, and unceremoniously poured out the contents. Leaning over Wilson's body, rigid with rigor mortis, Hamish scooped the glass against Wilson's taught neck.

"What have we here?" Hamish held the chipped glass up to the lantern's light.

Inside the glass, a small black spider peered back at Hamish, and a broad smile crossed the carnival owner's face.

THE LAST REAPING

There was little warmth in the October wind of Roanoke Island despite the sun shining brightly in the cloudless sky.

"The winter is going to come early this year," Thomas Stevens pulled his dark cloak tightly around himself.

"Thomas, that is why we have to meet with these savages," Ananias Dare crossed his arms across the leather jerkin covering his broad chest and stared at the shorter man.

"Maybe we should not speak so freely," Thomas glanced nervously at the Secotan warrior dressed in a wide-brimmed hat and dark linen shirt and breeches that were so common among the colonists of Roanoke.

"Matthew is now our Christian brother," Reverend Archard looked heavenward. "He was the first soul I brought out of the darkness of this heathen land."

"He was running half-naked with the rest of them two months ago," Thomas stared down at plain leather shoes and kicked the dirt. "It is like we have come across a new land filled with the wild Irish."

"Thomas, you should remember the Irish were ignorant

of God until the intervention of Christian men to guide them to learn the true meaning of religion." Reverend Archard took off his wide-brimmed hat and ran his fingers through his thinning blonde hair.

Ananias thought he detected the slightest tilt of Matthew's head toward their conversation but the approach of the leader of the colony's militia, Captain Vaughan, in his heavy leather corselet drew his attention.

"Sir, they are here," the burly captain of the guard was holding the long musket so tightly in his hand that his knuckles had gone white.

"Very well, Captain Borden, let them in," Ananias nodded to the guardsman.

The man turned and waved to two of his fellow guards standing at the wooden stockade fence gate. The two men waved back in acknowledgment and lifted the long piece of wood that secured the door to admit three Secotan warriors.

A short Secotan warrior with a clean-shaven head and wearing a buckskin shirt with a fringed leather apron and leggings walked through the open gate flanked by two taller warriors. The two warriors had their hair shorn into Mohawks and sported tomahawks tucked into their leather belts. Their muskets held at ready, the two guards fell in behind the Secotans trio as they strode defiantly toward the awaiting men.

"Chief Kocoum," Ananias smiled and dipped his head in greeting the bald warrior. "We are honored by your presence here today."

The man nodded back at Ananias but did not return the

smile. Ananias noticed that one of the warriors behind the Secotan Chief was eyeing Matthew with unveiled scorn.

"Sasawpen, do the Englishmen keep you like a pet and dress you up like a doll, little brother," the warrior called to Matthew in the language of the Secotans and spat on the floor. "Our mother would weep if she saw you."

"Our mother would be proud to see the way I make a place for myself among the English for the good of our people," the Secotan words felt awkward in Matthew's mouth.

"I am happy that English musket ball freed her spirit rather than see you this way," the warrior appeared ready to say more, but Kocoum halted him with a gesture.

"Matthew, I thought we discussed the sin of speaking in the Devil's tongue" a disappointed look crossed Reverend Archard's face.

"I am sorry, Reverend Archard, my older brother Necotowance was passing along well wishes from my family."

"He will need to learn how to do so in proper English," Reverend Archard's blue eyes looked disapprovingly over Necotowance before he turned to the shorter man. "Chief Kocoum, have you thought any more on my offer of bringing your people to our church service?"

"My people worship the spirits of this land, just as they have done for generations," Chief Kocoum's eyes narrowed suspiciously. "Your English god has nothing to offer us."

"He can offer you everlasting salvation," Revered Archard's face took on a hardened expression. "But also be warned that no Christian man will tolerate the worship of false gods or the devil in this colony."

"Let us turn to what we need to discuss presently," Ananias interrupted the Reverend before he could further antagonize the Secotans. "We need to talk about meat for the winter."

"My people can provide all the deer and fowl you will need for the winter," Chief Kocoum let his intense stare linger on the Reverend for a moment longer before turning his gaze to Ananias. "We will trade at the same price we have for summer and fall, even though the deer and geese are less numerous."

"Chief Kocoum," Ananias gave the Secotan Chief a mirthless smile. "We do not wish to trade; my men will hunt for their own throughout Roanoke Island."

The three guardsmen anxiously shifted the grips on their muskets as Chief Kocoum glared from man to man.

"That is not what has been agreed upon," the Secotan warriors tensed at their Chief's angry tone. "English do not hunt on Secotan lands; they will trade for the game we provide. We have always been fair in what we ask in return."

A sneer crossed Ananias' face, "Chief Kocoum, it is fifteen eighty-seven; these lands belong to Queen Elizabeth and England, not to the Secotan."

Chief Kokcoum's face reddened with rage, and he took an angry step toward Ananias, which caused Thomas and Reverend Archard to step back in fear even as

Ananias stood his ground. Captain Borden struck at the Secotan Chief from his blindside, striking him in the face with the butt of his musket. Blood sprayed out of the Secotan Chief's mouth, and nose as the diminutive man crumpled to the floor. The two Secotan warriors surged toward their fallen Chief as they reached for their tomahawks. Matthew grabbed the tomahawk in Necotowance's hand and kicked his legs out from under him, bringing Necotowance to his knees in the dirt.

"Don't be a fool, brother," Matthew struggled to pull the tomahawk from Necotowance's grip.

The booming report of one of the guardsmen's muskets echoed through the stockade as the other Secotan warrior arched his back and fell face-first into the dirt, a bloody hole blackened from the proximity of the musket gaped behind his left shoulder. The other guardsman placed his finger on the trigger and pointed his musket directly into Necotowance's face but held his fire as Ananias tried to restore order.

"Everyone calm down," Ananias noticed that the musket shot had begun to draw a crowd of onlookers among the other colonists. "Chief Kokcoum, please tell your man to stop struggling before there is more bloodshed."

Blood flowed freely from the Secotan Chief's nose and mouth as he glared hatefully up at Ananias and Captain Borden, who pointed his rifle at Kokcoum's chest. Chief Kokcoum narrowed his eyes at Ananias, spit a mouthful of blood onto the dirt, and spoke something to Necotowance in their native language. Ananias did not know what the Chief said to his warrior, but the man stopped struggling and let Matthew take the tomahawk out of his hand.

"Good. Good, now we're all friends again," Ananias crossed his arms and looked down at Kokcoum. "Chief Kokcoum, tell your man that you will stay with us as our hostage this winter. He should go back and inform your people that we will be sending out hunting parties, and if your people care to keep their chief alive, they will not interfere with them. In addition, they will provide us a ransom of two deer and four geese every week."

"And what if my people would rather kill English than keep me alive," Kokcoum sneered up at the man through bloodied lips.

"Then, when the English ships return in the spring, they will fire their canons on your village until there is not a Secotan left on this island."

Chief Kokcoum looked ready to respond angrily when Matthew began speaking in the Secotan language, looking from the Chief to his brother. Ananias did not understand the words; however, he noticed that Kokcoum and Necotowance listened intently to the man's impassioned words.

"Matthew, what are you doing?" Reverend Archard looked aghast. "Why are you speaking in that heathen tongue?"

Matthew ignored the Reverend and continued speaking forcefully to his former tribesmen. Chief Kokcoum looked thoughtful and nodded as Matthew spoke while Necotowance eyed his brother suspiciously. When Matthew finished speaking, the Secotan Chief turned to Ananias, the look of hostility replaced by an almost bemused look.

"We will comply with your terms," Chief Kokcoum bowed his head in acceptance.

Ananias noticed a crowd of nearly forty colonists had gathered to watch the altercation with the Secotans, so he sent Thomas and Reverend Archard to assure everyone that everything was in order. Captain Borden and one of his guardsmen roughly shoved Chief Kokcoum to his feet. They escorted him to the colony's makeshift jail as two other guardsmen escorted Necotowance back out the gate. Matthew watched his brother leave, an indecipherable expression etched across his tan face.

"What exactly did you say to them?" Ananias roughly grabbed Matthew by the arm.

"I explained to them how things must be for the Secotan to survive."

◆ ◆ ◆

"Mr. Dare, there was a problem with the Secotan's ransom," the burly Captain Borden had a smirk on his face as he stood in front of Ananias' writing desk.

"Don't tell me they did not bring what we asked," Ananias set down his writing quill in disgust and rubbed his fingers across his eyes. "I hoped we would make it a week before we had to hang their chief."

"No, Sir. They brought us more than we asked for," a wide grin crossed Borden's bearded face. "The savages brought us twice as much. They brought us four deer and eight geese. Maybe they can't count."

"No, they can count. I traded with them all summer.

There's something else going on here," a dawning realization suddenly crossed his face. "Captain Borden, have one of the geese cooked up and brought to me immediately."

"Yes, Mr. Dare. I'll have it done right away."

◆ ◆ ◆

Ananias stood flanked by Captain Borden and two guards as he placed the platter with the roasted goose in front of Chief Kokcoum. The Secotan Chief sat on the straw floor of the jail, his hands and feet manacled together to prevent escape. His nose and lips were still purple and swollen from the earlier altercation, but he still smiled at the sight of the freshly cooked goose.

"Your people made their first ransom payment today," Ananias dropped the platter of roasted goose onto the straw beside the Secotan Chief. "I want you to be the first to sample their offering."

"Such hospitality from the English," Chief Kokcoum smiled ruefully up at Ananias as he tore a leg off the roasted goose.

"Let's just say that if your people decided to poison the meat, you would be the first to know."

Chief Kokcoum let out a rough laugh before sinking his teeth into the greasy meat.

"You do not understand the Secotan," he bit off a large piece of meat from the leg. "Only the English would poison meat."

◆ ◆ ◆

Ananias pushed the empty plate away from him and leaned back in his chair. With the hearth fire warm against his back and his belly full, Ananias felt sleep quickly calling him. He rubbed his hand across his full stomach and adjusted his belt, noting that it might be time to add another notch to loosen the belt.

Across from him, Thomas and Reverend Archard were engaged in a heated conversation while they downed the last pieces of goose and venison on their plates. Both men had lost the gauntness caused by the voyage from England and the first harsh months of establishing the colony on Roanoke; now, they looked as robust as they did before the journey began. If not, more so.

He smiled to himself; the Secotans continued to provide at least double the ransom amount each week, which far surpassed the meager amount of food the colony's hunters had been able to provide. Many colonists were eating far better than they had in England; he even noticed his wife's rump had gotten fuller and rounder in recent weeks.

"What are your thoughts?" Reverend Archard looked expectantly at Ananias.

"I'm sorry, Reverend; I was lost in my thoughts for a moment."

"I was telling Thomas that our winter has been so prosperous we wanted to hold a feast to thank the Lord for his bounty this Thursday. A glorious celebration for the entire colony!"

"I think that's an excellent idea, Reverend Archard, Christmas is still over a month away, and the people could use something to break the monotony of the early

November snows."

"Tell him about the Indians," Thomas rested his hands on his paunchy midsection and looked sidelong at the Reverend.

"The Secotans?" Ananias' good feelings were beginning to turn into misgivings over this idea.

"Well, yes, but only the Christian ones."

"Your tame Indian Matthew is the only Christian Indian I have seen," Thomas shook his head disapprovingly. "To the degree that he is even a Christian."

"I assure you Matthew is washed in the blood of the Lamb," Reverend Archard threw Thomas an irritated glance before turning to Ananias. "I would like to roast the venison and fowl outside so it will fill the air with the scent. Then I will go to the Secotans, with some of Captain Borden's men, and offer that any who accept Christ can join in our feast. I have seen the Secotans who bring the weekly ransom; their faces look long and drawn from hunger. Christ will feed their empty souls, and I will feed their empty bellies."

"Has Captain Borden agreed to this?"

"Captain Borden said that the more Secotans that become Christians today, the less heathen savages there will be to fight in the spring."

"Well, gentlemen," Ananias leaned back and smiled wolfishly. "It is hard to argue with that logic."

◆ ◆ ◆

The smell of roasting venison filled the air as the colonists turned four deer carcasses on spits over open fires. The women cooked corn and other vegetables in large iron pots and smiled at Ananias and Thomas as they walked by. The sun shone warm and bright on the late November afternoon, heating the day enough that the snow underfoot was wet and sticky. Several children and younger colonists were fully engaged in a snowball fight as the younger boys sent a barrage of snowballs sailing through the air.

"Everyone is certainly in good spirits," Ananias breathed in deeply as they walked past one of the roasting deer spits. "I think the Reverend's celebrations of giving thanks to the Lord is turning into a splendid idea."

"Until he shows up at the stockade gate with a horde of hungry savages," Thomas shook his head disdainfully.

"Oh, come now, Thomas, they will be Christians."

"These savages dance with the devil under the moon and commit all kinds of acts of witchery in the name of their heathen gods, and we're just going to let them roam among the Christian women of the colony?"

"What's this?" A commotion at the stockade gate caught Ananias' attention, and the two men quickly diverted their path toward the small gathering of men.

As they got closer, they saw two guards holding up Reverend Archand, who looked battered and bruised. A trickle of blood ran out one nostril, and his right eye quickly swelled shut. Four other guards were being helped toward a fire; all limped heavily.

"Reverend Archand, what's happened?" Ananias began to get a sinking feeling in his stomach as the minister looked up at him dazedly.

"It was the Secotans, Mr. Dare," Captain Borden walked over after seeing his injured men. "They set upon the Reverend and the men I sent with him. The savages beat them and took their weapons."

"Was anyone badly hurt?" Ananias looked at the bloody footprints in the snow and the darkening pool of red around the Reverend's feet.

"They stuck spear points into our right feet," pain filled the Reverend's blue eyes. "They beat and stabbed each of us in the right foot."

Ananias stared at the trail of bloody footprints that led through the gate and into the forest beyond. Captain Borden shouted orders for his men to secure the gate as the two heavy wooden doors swung closed.

"Mr. Dare, what does this mean?" William Farthowe, the colony's blacksmith, looked over at the beaten guards and bloody snow.

"It means there will not be any Indians coming to our feast tonight," Thomas tried to hide the wry smile that crossed his lips.

◆ ◆ ◆

In the time before time, the Native Americans referred to them as "Mound Builders," giants who strode the land like conquering heroes. Some legends say the gods punished them for some horrible affront. Other stories say a trickster god turned them into monstrous beasts in exchange for immortality. Whatever the truth, the Wendigoes stirred beneath their mounds, awakened from slumber by the drums and dances of the Secotan.

Claw-like nails dug through the earth of the mounds, clawing inch by torturous inch until long, boney fingers broke through to the surface. Skeletal arms slid up from the earth, spreading along the ground and straining to pull themselves up from the holes. Thin desiccated bodies emerged from the ground into the night air, ashen gray skin looking pale and ghostly in the moonlight. Lips, tattered and bloody, gasped in the forest air, filling lungs that lay dormant during the creatures' hibernation. The Wendigoes' deep-set, coal-black eyes blinked from the moon's brightness on their gaunt faces, and they shook their heads to free the dirt from their long, stringy hair. Their breath came in deep hisses as they gnashed jagged teeth to loosen the muscles of long-stilled jaws.

The Wendigoes freed themselves from their mounds until nearly fifty of their kind cast long shadows under the moonlight. A Wendigo with beads made from bird bones interwoven into its long hair stood to its full height, over nine feet tall, as it tilted its head to sniff at the air, the scent of human blood carried on the wind, fueling an insatiable hungering. Its tribe let out long hissing breaths as they breathed in the fragrant aroma of human blood. Then all as one, they began to run.

Like a pack of monstrous wolves, they followed the scent until they picked up the bloody trail in the forest. Some stooped down to lick the red snow as they ran; others scooped handfuls of bloody snow into their mouth. They burst forth from the forest, driven by blood craze as they ran toward the stockade fence and the scent of human flesh.

◆ ◆ ◆

Thomas Gramme and William Browne leaned against the log wall of the stockade fence with their muskets by their side as they enjoyed the roasted goose legs Elizabeth Glane brought to them as they stood their watch. The men, often considered Captain Borden's best militiamen, were not a match for the distraction of Ms. Glane, both strikingly beautiful and one of the colony's few unmarried women. Therefore, when she showed up with a plate of food for each of them, they gave her their full attention.

Both men were fully engrossed in their roasted goose legs and missed the moment when Elizabeth Glane's expression changed from a flirtatious smile to eyes and mouth opened wide in abject terror. The large gray-skinned form hurdled over the stockade wall and crushed Elizabeth to the ground.

The men were too stunned to move as the Wendigo, perched on Elizabeth's crumpled body like a feral nightmare, turned its skeletal head to look at them. Blood ran over its tattered lips and down the gray skin of its chin as it chewed noisily on a large chunk of the girl's flesh. Elizabeth's blank eyes stared at the night sky as the grotesque wound in her neck pumped her lifeblood onto the November snow.

More Wendigoes streamed over the wall ripping and tearing at the two guardsmen before they could even scream. The putrid smell of rotting flesh filled William Browne's nostrils as the Wendigo furiously chewed a hole into his chest. The last thing William saw before his eyes went forever dark were scores of the creatures rushing towards the doomed colonists as they gave thanks for their bountiful feast.

❖ ❖ ❖

Before Thomas Stevens could sit down to enjoy the celebration, he had to satisfy his misgivings about the Secotans. The incident with Reverend Archand earlier in the day had deeply shaken him, and visions of the heathen savages storming the colony during the celebration to free their Chief and make off with the colony's women haunted him all day. He nodded in greeting as Edward and Wenefrid Powell passed him, eagerly making their way to the celebration.

Thomas turned the corner alongside Henry Rufoote's horse stable when he noticed Richard Darige was not at his guard post in front of the small cabin that served as the colony's jail. His feet trudged along through the snow, the sounds of the starting celebration fading into the distance as he approached the cabin.

The chair where Darige usually sat his guard lay overturned, and his drink spilled into the snow.

"I need to have words with Captain Borden about the delinquency of his men…" the thought froze in Thomas' mind as he realized the spilled liquid that stained the snow crimson was blood.

A figure stepped from the darkness beside the cabin; it was the Reverend's tamed Secotan, Matthew. However, the man was dressed all wrong; he wore no hat, his tunic shirt was unbuttoned, and his hair was wild in the style of the Secotans.

"Matthew, what are you doing?" Thomas stepped back as the Secotan warrior moved out of the shadows.

"My name is Sasawpen," Matthew's arm swung out of

the darkness, a war club with a ball-like head in his hand.

A surprised gasp of air escaped Thomas' lips as the rounded head of the club struck him at the base of the skull with a loud cracking noise that seemed to resonate inside his head. He fell backward into the snow like a felled tree to lay face up, looking at the bright November moon. Thomas felt no pain; he felt nothing at all below his beck. He struggled to speak, but his lips could not form the words.

Matthew looked down at him; his face a mask of scorn and hatred. A second face appeared next to Matthew, peering down at Thomas. It was Chief Kokcoum, whose bald head had sprouted thick stubble from his weeks of captivity.

"The Wendigo are awakened from their slumber. Every winter, they rise from their mounds and hunt the Secotan," Chief Kokcoum's face bore a look of defiance. "This year, they will feast upon the fatted English."

"Your Bible says a man reaps what he sows," Matthew shook his head angrily. "Tonight, you English will reap what you have sown in our land."

◆ ◆ ◆

The colonists had arranged five long wooden tables in the center of a ring of fires that warmed the nearly one hundred celebrants. Platters of corn, venison, and fowl adorned the tables, as did many pies and baked goods.

The laughter and happy chatter of the men and women hushed as Reverend Archand stood. His face looked swollen and bruised from his beating at the hands of the Secotans, and he struggled to stand on his injured foot as he waved his hands for silence.

"Will Eleanor be joining us for the celebration?" Margery Harvie leaned over and whispered to Ananias, her aged face bearing its ever-present kind smile.

"I'm afraid not," Ananias gestured to the large fires surrounding the celebration tables. "Even with the fires, we thought it would still be too cold for little Virginia."

"Very wise of you, Ananias; you don't want a three-month-old getting a chill so early in the winter." Margery pulled her shawl closer around her shoulders to accentuate the point.

"Look at this bounty the Lord has provided us," Reverend Archand spread his hands wide and smiled broadly through his bruised lips. "We have suffered many hardships. We have weathered trials and tribulations as we wrestle this land from the hands of devils and heathens."

The assembled men and women nodded enthusiastically, looking from one to another.

"The Lord promised us in Psalms, for every beast of the forest is mine, and the cattle on a thousand hills. I know every bird of the mountains, and everything that moves in the field is mine. For the world and all it contains are mine."

A murmur of approval rippled through the crowd, and Ananias felt himself nodding along with the others.

"Outside the walls of this settlement, the Secotan and their heathen allies attempt to deny us what the Lord has already given to us as our birthright as free

Englishmen and Christians. But we will not let them prevail against us."

A rousing chorus of angry agreement rose from the colonists, many shaking their fists defiantly.

"Thomas is certainly missing a good sermon," Ananias thought to himself as he looked over at his friend's empty chair.

"For our struggle is not against blood and flesh," Reverend Archand quoted more scripture. "But against principalities, against authorities, against the universal lords of this darkness!"

The Revered threw his hands up heavenward to emphasize his words and then inexplicably flopped face forward onto the table. Stunned silence and confusion came over the colonists as the Reverend looked up dazedly; a fresh trickle of blood dripped from where his nose slammed into the wooden table. Young Ambrose Viccars snickered, and his mother quickly slapped his hand, silencing the boy. Richard Berry and his brother Henry rushed over to help the Reverend, but before they could reach his side, something pulled the stricken man away from the table and into the darkness beyond the firelight.

The Berry brothers jumped back in shock, looking at each other in bewilderment, and Audry Tappan let out a little shriek that she followed with a fit of nervous laughter. The Reverend's wife, Joyce, walked to the firelight's edge and looked out into the darkness.

"Arnold?" Her voice shook as she peered into the darkness. "Arnold, are you ok?"

A large gray shape leaped out of the darkness and

landed on the table in front of Audry Tappan. The Wendigo crouched low, though, was twice as tall as a man was. Its knobby spine protruded against the thin skin of its back as it leered down at Audry. The creature whipped its head back and forth, making the tiny seashells braided into its hair click wildly. Then it grabbed the shrieking woman's face in its long boney fingers and pulled her forward out of her seat as it sank its jagged teeth into her soft face. Blood sprayed out from both sides of its mouth, dousing horrified colonists with flecks of red as Audry's limbs flailed wildly.

Suddenly, more of the creatures began leaping out of the darkness, and Ananias saw the Berry brothers fall to the ground under three of the monsters. One of the Wendigoes rushed out of the night, decapitating Joyce Archand as it ran past and cracking her dismembered head in its mouth like a large walnut.

Screams filled the night as some of the colonists died where they sat, seated in front of the plates of steaming celebratory meats, as the Wendigoes devoured them. A few men and women fled into the darkness only to be chased down by the creatures and torn asunder. The carpenter, John Gibbes, escaped the carnage at the tables only to run into the waiting arms of one of the Wendigoes in the darkness, his last sound being a horrible gurgling noise as jagged teeth tore into his neck.

Ananias began to run and crashed into Margery Harvie, knocking the woman sprawling to the ground. Two creatures pounced on her as she screamed for him to help her, tearing at her flesh with their claws until they separated her upper body from the lower half in a bloody gush of end trails.

He ran into the darkness heading for his cabin as the screams and cries of the dying colony filled the night.

◆ ◆ ◆

Thomas felt no sensation, just jerking and pulling at his body. His head lolled back and forth as the Wendigoes tore handfuls of stringy red meat from his body.

Through the darkness, his pale gray eyes watched the shadowy forms of Matthew and Chief Kokcoum climb over the wall of the stockade fence and escape into the forest beyond. The image of the two escaping Secotans jerked away as one of the Wendigoes turned his head violently. Coal-black eyes stared down at him as nose holes in the creature's desiccated, skeletal face pulsed in and out with excited breaths. The Wendigo smelled of decayed meat and rotted earth as it hissed and opened its cavernous maw. Slabs of Thomas' flesh hung from its bloody teeth as it bit down on his throat, tearing through muscle and cartilage as the colonist's warm blood filled its mouth.

◆ ◆ ◆

Ananias burst through the half-opened door of his cabin, his chest burning with the exertion of his terrified dash through the night. His eyes opened wide in shock and horror as he witnessed little Virginia's legs and feet slipping down into the Wendigo's mouth and out of sight. The bulge moved down the monster's throat like a python swallowing its prey. Eleanor's unseeing eyes stared at him as she sat in her rocking chair, her midsection torn wide open; one of the Wendigoes sat at her feet, feeding her intestines into its mouth hand over hand. Another of the creatures stood behind the rocking chair, its black eyes staring at Ananias as its powerful jaws and jagged teeth bit into Eleanor's skull as easily as eating an apple.

Ananias began to scream. It was a feral sound of rage and terror that shook his body as his bladder vacated itself. The Wendigo that had only moments earlier consumed Virginia swung its skeletal hand at him. The creature's boney, clawed hand struck him on the jaw and severed the mandible from his face, spraying the cabin's wall with blood.

Ananias Dare staggered backward out the door, his scream turning into a strangled gurgle of blood in his throat. A large Wendigo with beads of bird bone in its long greasy hair stepped from the darkness and thrust its clawed hands into Ananias' chest. The creature pulled open his chest, tearing through muscle and shattering bone as it fileted open his rib cage. Ananias' eyes rolled back in his head as the Wendigo slid its head into his chest cavity and crushed its teeth upon his beating heart.

◆ ◆ ◆

As the morning sun rose over the Roanoke colony, Necotowance looked down from the hill into the empty settlement. Crows hopped among the plates of untouched food on the wooden tables, pulling off pieces of meat with their sharp beaks. All that remained of the one hundred and fifteen men, women, and children were large swaths of snow stained crimson with blood. There was no sign of the Wendigos, with their bellies full and hunger satiated by the plump colonists; they had returned to their mounds, slipping back into their long winter's sleep.

Sasawpen stepped back from the tree and studied his work; the word "Croatan" was carved deep into the tree's trunk with his deer bone knife.

"In the spring, the English will come looking for their colony," Sasawpen spoke in the ancient Secotan tongue when he saw his brother's quizzical look. "When they see this, they will think our enemies, the Croatans, were responsible."

"Come, brother," Necotowance smiled broadly at his brother. "Let us go hunt together again."

THE VINEYARD

"*Vacations never go how you plan them.*"

It was supposed to be an idyllic summer weekend in Oregon's Willamette Valley wine country. We would leave our busy work lives behind us in Tacoma, Washington, and celebrate our third anniversary in style. Our plan called for a weekend of good food, great wine, and even better sex at the Tungsford Family Winery's bed and breakfast. Driving down Interstate 5 Friday night, we looked apprehensively at the orange glow to the east. Summer is forest fire season in the Pacific Northwest. Mary fanatically searched the AM dial for the latest reports, worried our weekend would get derailed by a fire spreading through the Tillamook State Forest. I thought Willamette Valley seemed safe enough away from the current series of blazing fires that an evacuation would not affect us, but

"That's enough of that," Lil Jon intoned everyone to go to the window, to the wall, after I reached over and switched the radio back to FM. "This is our weekend away. Everything will be fine."

"But the wildfire in Tillamook is only 30 miles from the winery."

"Thirty miles is pretty far, babe. The fire crews will keep it far away."

"What if Portland Electric shuts off power in areas adjacent to the fires? I hear they do that to decrease the chance that downed power lines could further spread the wildfire."

"Then we stay curled up in bed all weekend," I smiled slyly at her.

"But all the restaurants will be closed."

"That's ok; I could use to lose a few pounds," I patted a midsection that was softer at thirty-five than it was at twenty-five when we met.

She smiled playfully at me and turned the radio up.

Get low, get low, get low, get low,

To the window, to the wall…

We drove through the wrought iron gates with the winery's "TW" logo and up the long winding road to the bed and breakfast. It was a large converted farmhouse set atop a hill on the 50-acre Tungsford vineyards; the moonlight illuminated hundreds of rows of grape vines that stood like a silent army surrounding the winery. The hill was the highest point in Willamette Valley, and guests at the B&B could enjoy their breakfast while enjoying a scenic overlook of the estate and surrounding forest.

As I unpacked our luggage from the trunk, a strong wind blew the smell of smoke from the northwest, where the fire in Tillamook continued to blaze on the horizon.

I knew we were not the only guests this weekend, primarily because, to my great disappointment, someone booked the deluxe room with the Jacuzzi tub. Several other cars were already in the small grass field next to the B&B, serving as a makeshift parking lot. The parking lot solar lights dimly illuminated a beat-up red Chevy pickup filled with empty wooden wine barrels, a big black Ford F-150 pickup with Texas plates, a white Tesla with personalized local plates that read WineGRL, and a red Honda Accord with "Just Married" sprayed in white across the back window. Well, damn, I guess I know who got the Jacuzzi room.

I smiled as I followed Mary up the porch steps; she was just as beautiful as the day we met. Her dark hair blew wildly in the wind, and she giggled as she struggled to keep her blue sundress from catching the wind and fluttering upwards.

As we walked to the door, an old grey-muzzled hound lay sprawled on the porch and lazily lifted its head to look at us.

"I can't wait to see this place in the daylight," Mary took in the surrounding view from the porch. "Even at night, it's breathtaking. It feels like we are alone at the top of the world."

The door to the B&B was an old heavy oak door ornately carved with grape vines that creaked like a horror movie prop when we opened it. The reception area was cozy and looked like a living room with two antique plush couches and an old writing desk with a gold plate inscribed "Reception." Mary loved the quaintness;

I thought it reminded me of my grandmother's house sans plastic couch coverings. A lamp made out of a sizeable Tungsford wine bottle illuminated the room.

"At least they left a light on for us. Everyone seems to have gone to bed already," I looked around the empty reception area. "I guess these family-run places don't staff the place late."

"Did you tell them we were checking in late?" Mary perused the framed pictures of the vineyard that decorated the wall over the desk.

"Yeah, I told them we'd drive down from Tacoma after work. The lady said they'd leave us a welcome package."

"Ah, here it is." Mary waved a crisp white envelope with "John and Mary Murphy" scrawled on the front. "Should we check out the room?"

"Oh yes," I smiled mischievously at her.

◆ ◆ ◆

The following day we walked hand in hand down the stairs, images of last night's and then this morning's sexy time still dancing through my head.

The smell of fresh bread and cooking bacon assailed our senses as we walked into the dining room, where a long wooden table with ten place settings sat empty. The space opened up into a working kitchen where a woman in her mid-sixties with her gray hair in a bun and an apron adorned with grapes worked a pair of tongs in one hand, flipping bacon on a large skillet and poked at a skillet full of scrambled eggs with a spatula in her other.

"Good morning!" Mary called cheerfully over the sound

of sizzling bacon.

"Good morning! You must be the Murphys," the woman gave us a warm smile and waved a greeting with her greasy tongs.

"I guess we're early for breakfast," the smell of the cooking bacon made my stomach rumble like a freight train.

"Oh no, you're right on time," she waved an egg-splatted spatula down the hall. "Everyone else is in the sitting room watching all the hubbub on the television."

Mary looked quizzically at me, and I shrugged my shoulders. We left the woman to her cooking and headed down the hall to the sitting room. The corridor opened into a vast windowed room that led onto the wrap-around porch and looked out over the vineyards, hazy in the morning sunlight. A wine bar with an ornate hand-carved "TW" on its wooden base lined one side of the room.

Someone had turned several comfortable-looking red couches that I supposed typically face the windows toward a sizeable flat-screen television hanging on the wall and draped with fake grapevines. A group of anxious-looking people sat on the couches while others stood, intently watching the television.

On the couch closest to us, a young Hispanic couple sat close together holding hands, the owners of the newlywed vehicle, I surmised. Her young tan face looked distraught, and her large dark eyes seemed on the verge of tears as the man reassuringly patted her leg.

Across from them sat a squat, bald man in a crisp

white dress shirt and tan slacks. Beside him was a mid-aged blonde woman dressed in a green pants suit that I recognized from the cover of Mary's Anne Taylor catalog. She wore an excessive, no doubt genuine, diamond ring and matching earrings, and both bore an unmistakable look of annoyance.

"This is going to impact our reservations. I know it. We have wine tastings all over the valley this weekend," the woman shook her head with exaggerated displeasure.

"They will have to find a way to accommodate us; we have had this planned for over six months," the man's face was pinched with displeasure as he folded his arms across his chest.

"I think people have more to worry about than your reservations," a man with a thick graying mustache in a red plaid button-down and jeans quipped in a slow Texas drawl as he leaned against the wall, causing the woman to let out an annoyed huff of indignation.

A heavy-set white-haired man in overalls talked quietly with a similarly dressed black man in his thirties; both men kept their eyes on the television.

"Oh, John," Mary's voice was concerned as she stared at the unfolding scene on the TV.

The TV showed a mass of people swinging and clawing at each other, and my first thought was it was a riot at a European soccer game. Then I saw the blood, and my brows knotted in confusion at what I saw, as a group of people seemed to be tearing others apart. The word caption in the corner read "McMinnville, Oregon."

The screen switched to a newsroom where a reporter with Ken doll perfect looks narrated, "The governor has reportedly called out the National Guard as violence spreads in the wake of the Tillamook fires. FEMA representatives are recommending people stay indoors and avoid...."

"Welcome to the party," the man with the Texas drawl looked right at Mary and me.

"What the hell is going on?" My mind was racing, struggling to process the images on the television.

"It's the fires," the black man answered, shaking his head unbelievingly.

"The smoke from the fires is driving people crazy. Making them attack each other," the Texan walked over to the older man and put a hand on his shoulder. "Jake, what do you say we close up that big iron gate at the end of the road."

The older man appeared deep in thought but nodded at the suggestion.

"I'll take care of it, Mr. Tungsford," the black man added.

"Thank you, Timothy," the older man patted the black man on the elbow.

"Absolutely not," the bald man on the couch objected. "We have places to be; we did not pay good money to get locked in here."

The young Hispanic woman buried her face in her husband's shoulder and began to sob as the room seemed about to erupt in open confrontation.

"Breakfast is served!" the older woman, her grape apron dotted with fresh grease stains, blissfully entered the room, utterly unperturbed by the events unfolding. "Everyone in the dining room before the eggs get cold."

◆ ◆ ◆

To keep the peace, Jake Tungsford agreed that Timothy, the groundskeeper, would lock the gate after the couple, which I learned were Mr. and Mrs. Alfords from Portland, left for their wine tastings shortly after breakfast. The Alfords promptly ate breakfast and departed to pack without a word to the others at the table.

The older woman, Mrs. Tungsford, spent much of the meal regaling about the sights in the valley to Mary and the new bride, Tilda, who seemed to teeter on the verge of hysterics. I caught several sideways looks from Mary in my direction, questioning the sanity of the exuberantly happy host in the face of crisis. The other newlywed, David, sat to my right and listened intently to Mr. Tungsford, Timothy, and the Texan, Alex Daley, theorize over the cause of the unfolding events.

"Something burning in those woods is getting into the air and making people crazy," Daley slid a forkful of bacon and eggs into his mouth.

"Like a zombie apocalypse?" David's wide eyes seemed like a window to the images of World War Z running through his head.

"More like a rabies outbreak, is my guess," Jake Tungsford stroked his bushy white beard thoughtfully. "The way those people attacked each other was more like madness. I've seen some rabid coyotes turn on each other like that when I was a kid."

"I bet it's the chemicals they spray on those trees," Timothy pursed his lip. "You can't trust the government to tell you what it puts in those sprays."

"So what do we do?" I had barely picked at my meal despite my earlier hunger.

"Way I see it, we have two problems. The first is those crazy people out there," Daley pointed his fork at the window while he spoke. "The thirty miles between them and us can get small, fast."

"And the second problem?" David asked nervously.

"The second problem," Daley's face looked grim. "Is the wind. Whatever is making those people crazy is in the smoke. I can tell from how those trees are swaying that the wind is blowing strongly in our direction. Maybe that bad smoke can travel this far, and maybe it can't. We don't know."

We have to sit tight until the National Guard arrives," Mr. Tungsford sopped up the greasy remains on his plate with a last corner of bread.

"All depends on where they set up their cordon," I added. "If Mr. Daley is right about the wind, then the National Guard may not be too keen to get too close any time soon."

"Don't they have gas masks and those yellow hazmat suits?" David was leaning heavily on his zombie pop culture knowledge for comfort.

"We are ready to leave now," Mr. and Mrs. Alford stood impatiently at the entrance to the dining room.

"I'll take care of it, Mr. Tungsford," Timothy took the last sip of his coffee and followed the Alfords out of the room.

Mary and Tilda helped Mrs. Tungsford clear the table,

the woman's cheerful tone explaining the house's history and vineyard. We watched through the window as the couple loaded their luggage into the Tesla and headed down the road. Timothy casually walked behind the car as it drove off, and Mr. Daley's warnings about the wind echoed in my mind as I watched how strongly the wind made the legs of his overalls flap in the breeze.

The Alfords sped out through the gate, and Timothy gave them an unreturned wave of farewell as he started to push one of the heavy iron gates closed.

"Anyone cares for another cup of coffee?" Mr. Tungsford picked up the coffee pot and gestured toward us. "I've got some Starbucks Christmas blend in the kitchen I could whip up."

"I never pass up an opportunity to pee or have a cup of coffee," Daley gave a crooked grin that made the corner of his bushy mustache rise on one side.

"Can't argue with that logic," I laughed, feeling the tension break momentarily.

"Hey, what's that?" David had continued to peer out the window.

I felt a pit growing in my stomach as we joined him at the window. David pointed, and our eyes tracked to where Alford's car had stopped halfway down the winding road from the farm. The Tesla just sat in the middle of the dirt road, idling. Without warning, the vehicle quickly began to reverse up the dirt road. I heard a sharp breath intake from Daley or Tungsford; I could not tell as a mass of perhaps thirty people appeared before the Tesla, charging down the road towards them.

The Tesla missed the first curve in the road and put its

back end into a ditch. Within moments, the mass of people surged over the vehicle, pounding at the glass and pulling on the doors. The car rocked back and forth as Alford tried to free it from the ditch.

Timothy must have known what was happening because I could see that he was rapidly pushing the second gate closed. David gasped as the Tesla's glass roof shattered inward, and the grabbing hands of the mob lifted a screaming Mr. Alford out of the car, limbs flailing as a crab plucked from the water. Bloody streaks ran across the roof of the Tesla as he quickly disappeared into the ditch, the mob swarming him like ants. Mrs. Alford had opened her door to run, but the group overwhelmed her. I saw blood-soaked shreds of that green Anne Taylor suit amidst the crowd.

Timothy, the gates secured and locked behind him, came running back up the road to the house. As the black man approached us, I followed Mr. Tungsford onto the porch with David and Daley.

"Mr. Tungsford," Timothy was breathing hard and trying to catch his breath.

"We saw Timothy," the older man said softly.

"Oh my god," David's fear-filled cry caught my attention.

"Forget the Alfords; It looks like we've got some problems of our own," Daley looked out at the dozen people standing outside the locked iron gates. Their eyes were wide and crazed as their bloody hands reached through the iron rails and pulled at the sturdy gates.

❖ ❖ ❖

Daley sat on the porch in an old rocking chair, his eyes intently watching the growing number of people at the gate. The iron gates swayed slightly against their agitated pulls and pushes but held firm otherwise. Running out from either side of the gate was an electrified fence with thick wooden posts securing it every eight feet. According to Tungsford, the fence keeps out deer and other wildlife that could salvage his grape vines, but so far, it seemed a fair deterrent against the "crazies," as we had begun to call them.

I had watched Daley go to his pickup truck earlier and unlock an area beneath the truck bed from which he drew a scoped hunting rifle and a large-bore revolver that looked like it could take down a bear. He sat with the pistol in his lap, watching the crazies through the rifle scope. Alongside him was a blue ceramic vase that took me a moment to realize was an urn.

"Who's that?" I gestured to the urn.

"It's my wife," Daley glanced sidelong at the urn, then back to the scope. "I proposed to her on the banks of the Columbia River thirty years ago. Cancer took her a month ago. I was planning to scatter her ashes there this weekend."

"I bet she would have been good in these situations."

"Nah, she would have shit her pants," he gave me a smile that reached right up to his eyes.

"What are they doing out there?" I looked out at the growing group of crazies gathering at the iron gates of the vineyard.

"Our new friends are pretty interesting," Daley peered through the scope. "Do you see how they keep looking at that blonde guy in the black shirt?"

I squinted but struggled to find anything in the churning melee of bodies.

"Here, try this," Daley handed me the rifle so I could peer through the scope.

The scope magnified my vision and gave me a close-up look at the mob; feral faces with bloodshot eyes stared back as if they could see me. Their clothes hung torn in places, paced, and swayed like tigers in a zoo. They did not exhibit any of the mindless hungry for brains characteristics of movie land zombies, which made the sight of them all the more chilling. Some nipped or clawed at each other, but mostly they searched for a way inside the gates. A few lingered hesitantly around the electrified fence. I spied the man in the black shirt; deep scratches ran down his face as if long nails had raked him.

Then I saw what Daley meant, the mob would pace, and several would constantly turn their head to look at him repeatedly.

"What are they doing?" The crazies' behavior transfixed me.

"It's pack behavior. They are looking to the alpha. Whatever is happening in their scrambled brains, animal intelligence is still there."

"Wow, it's cloudy out." David had stepped out onto the porch.

"It's ash," Daley corrected. "Blown up into the atmosphere from the fires."

"Is that what's making them act like this?" David

pointed at the assemblage outside the gate.

"Could be; who knows," Daley glanced sidelong at the rosebushes that lined the front of the porch. The tall green stems with their brightly colored red, orange, pink, and white roses bent towards us in the wind. I suspected that Daley was thinking that whatever was in the air was blowing our way.

"Tungsford wants to speak to us all inside." David turned and headed back into the house.

❖ ❖ ❖

"I recognize some of those people out there," Tungsford looked at the group assembled in the sitting room with a pained look. "They're from McMinnville, less than ten miles from us."

"Are we going to get like them?" Tilda's dark brown eyes opened wide, and her voice was shaky.

"I know we're all worried about what's on the wind from those fires," Tungsford spoke calmly and reassuringly. "McMinnville sits at the opening of the Van Duzer corridor, a geographic anomaly that channelizes winds from the Pacific Ocean and blows cooling air into the Willamette Valley. It is what makes this a good wine country. The strong ocean winds blow into the valley every evening, and the Van Duzer corridor funnels that wind and increases its velocity. McMinnville gets the brunt of that wind; our winery only gets the indirect effects. That's why I believe those people have been affected, and we're not."

"Or not yet, at least," added Mary, more a question than a statement.

"Or not yet, at least," agreed Tungsford. "I may be wrong, but I think the valley's geography protects us."

"Wine time," Mrs. Tungsford had continued her disconcertingly good cheer all morning. Now she stood behind the room's wine bar pulling the cork on a bottle of one of the winery's reds. "I think a tasting will get everyone back in the mood."

"Thank you, Suz," Tungsford spoke soothingly to his wife. "We'll all be over for some wine shortly."

"I think she's lost it." Mary leaned over and whispered to me. I quietly nodded my head in agreement.

"We've got plenty of food and supplies here, so we should be fine until this blows over," Tungsford gestured to Timothy, who leaned against the wall. "Last night, I had Tim put some extra supplies up on the second story of our barn out behind the house. Food and water. If those people get through the gate, we'll head to the barn's second story and pull the ladder. Nothing will be able to get up there."

"But the fence is electrified. They can't get through, right?" Tilda seemed to be gripping David's hand so hard I expected to hear the cracking of bone any minute.

"What about the power cuts? Will the fences go down if Portland Electric shuts off power to contain the fire?" Mary's knowledge of forest fire containment procedures has always impressed me.

"We're on our own power here, so that won't affect us."

"Besides, I'll wager no one is left trying to contain that fire. The fire crews would have gotten a full dose of whatever is causing this." Daley leaned against the wall and stroked his mustache thoughtfully.

"You know that's really not helpful right now." David put a reassuring arm around Tilda.

"What can we do to help?" I tried to refocus the conversation away from this direction of doom.

"We should be all set until this blows over or help arrives," Tungsford glanced at Timothy. "Tim and I just have to button up a little hole in the fence…."

"A hole in the fence?" Mary voiced the ripple of alarm we all felt.

"It's ok; it's up the hill behind the vineyard. It is not anywhere near where those people have gathered. I have kept an eye on it all morning, and no one is even close to it." Timothy spoke in a calm, measured tone.

"Tim and I will take the tractor up there now and patch it up; I should have done it weeks ago. We'll ride up there, fix and ride back down."

"I think we'll all start with a nice pinot noir," Mrs. Tungsford began pouring glasses of wine. I caught the look that passed between Jake Tungsford and Timothy, and Mary was not the only one doubting the sanity of the lady of the house.

❖ ❖ ❖

Mary and I stood on the back porch with Mr. Daley, watching Tungsford slowly climb the hill on his old John Deer tractor. Timothy rode in the little cart attached to the tractor, holding a shotgun. I could see his head turn to watch the trees, alert for movement.

Daley had left David and Tilda to keep an eye on

the front gate so that he could provide overwatch of Tungsford's repair operation with his hunting rifle.

"So far, so good," I squeezed Mary's arm reassuringly.

She smiled at me, and I felt my heart melt. I loved this woman so much.

"Hey," I turned to face her and hugged her. "I'm sorry about this."

"Stop; it's not your fault."

"You wanted to go to that cabin in Montana; I'm the one who wanted to come here."

"We both loved the idea of wine country for our anniversary. Next year we'll do the Caribbean, something tropical, with no trees to burn."

"Deal," I kissed her gently on the lips. "I love you, babe."

"I love you too."

"Mr. Daley," David ran to the porch's back end. "Something is going on at the gate."

"What is it?" concern roiled the Texan's weathered face.

"That man in black and three others ran off fast."

"In which direction did they go?" I felt like I knew the answer even as I asked the question. David just pointed toward the hill Tungsford's tractor slowly crested.

Daley scanned the top of the hill through the riflescope.

"Hey now," Daley seemed to be pressing the scope harder against his eye, willing it to see through the hill.

"What is it?" I had the urge to grab the rifle and look for myself.

"Tungsford is coming back over the hill."

I saw the old tractor returning over the rise to head toward the house. The older man appeared to be raising his arm and gesturing.

"He's giving us a thumbs up," Daley reported as he watched through the scope.

"They must have fixed the fence," I could hear the relief in Mary's voice.

"Oh shit," the Texan cursed as three figures burst out of the tree line, sprinting towards the tractor.

I could barely distinguish the figures in their blur of motion, but one was the man in black. They were running at the tractor's side, and neither Tungsford nor Timothy had seen them. Mary screamed as Daley's rifle boomed a loud report, and I saw one of the figures running at the tractor drop lifeless in the field. He was quickly working the rifle bolt to get another shot in place.

The shot had alerted Tungsford and Timothy, who seemed to be trying to retrieve the shotgun from where he had set it down in the cart. The man in black leaped through the air at the cart as Daley's rifle fired, missing its mark as the Texan cursed.

The man in black caught Timothy in the chest, and they tumbled from the cart in a grapple of hands and legs. Daley fired again, and the third figure in the field, a woman in a tattered blue dress, fell as a plume of red burst forth from the side of her head.

The man in black was on top of Timothy, tearing at him with his bare hands. Tungsford tried to turn the tractor, but the turn was too hard and the incline too steep. The tractor and cart tipped and rolled as Tungsford desperately worked the wheel to steady it. I saw the older man's body go beneath the tractor as it rolled sideways down the hill. His body lay sprawled at an odd angle as the tractor and cart rolled to the bottom of the hill. Daley's rifle fired once more, and the black man jerked and fell off of Timothy.

We watched with hopeful, expectant eyes, but neither Timothy nor the sprawled body of Tungsford moved again.

"They must have got inside before they fixed the fence," Daley lowered the rifle. "Waited for them to cross back and hit them in a blind spot."

"John," Mary grabbed my arm, and I turned to see her looking behind us.

In the doorway stood Mrs. Tungsford, her smile gone and her distraught face staring out into the carnage in the field. Her pale eyes were searching, her left cheek twitching slightly.

◆ ◆ ◆

"I don't think this is a good idea," I watched Mrs. Tungsford drink deeply from her third glass of wine. Her tight gray hair bun had given way to several strands that ran out unbidden from the mass. Tilda sat beside her, rubbing her back, saying something in a low voice.

"She just lost her whole world," Mary looked sadly at the old woman.

"There's no one else out there," Daley returned from his vigil on the back porch. "My guess is just those three made it through."

"Should we just leave them out there?" David looked pained at the thought, though I suspected the idea of retrieving the bodies did not sit well with him either.

"For now, we'll have to leave them there. Can you keep an eye on things here for a bit? I want to check out the barn situation," Daley said to David, who nodded quietly.

"Do you mind if I come too?" I wanted to see our fallback position if things got bad.

"I'm coming too," Mary added as Daley nodded.

We walked out into the cool, windy late afternoon air. All of us avoided looking at the hillside where Tungsford and Timothy lay. The barn was a sturdy two-story structure with two large wooden double doors wide open. Daley and I pulled them closed, leaving only enough room for a person to pass through.

"If things go south, we can pull it closed fast and drop that latching bar down to lock it," Daley pointed at a thick two-by-four that would slide into two brackets and hold the doors closed.

A few scattered light bulbs lit the barn, housing various barrels and winemaking or farming equipment. We walked to the back, where we found an old wooden ladder leading up to the second floor. The wood creaked as we went up the old worn rungs, Daley first, Mary, and me.

A single flickering bulb in the middle of the room lit the second-floor loft, hanging from a long wire from the barn's high ceiling. The wind howled through the room's single window, windowpanes long gone or broken. Outside, the strong winds began their nightly run through the Van Duzer corridor and into the valley.

In one corner, Timothy had stacked several cases of bottled water and wine and several crates of canned and jarred goods that garnered an appreciative nod from Daley. Daley walked back to the ladder and knelt to expect it.

"See these four nails holding the ladder in place," he pointed to where the ladder attached to the ledge. "We need to pull these up. If we have to flee up here, we can pull the ladder behind us, and no one should be able to get up here."

"But we'd be trapped." Mary looked skeptically around the loft.

"If we run up here, they'll be nowhere else to go anyway." His tone was somber and resolute.

"It'll be ok; this is a good spot to hold up," I assured her half-heartedly.

We searched around the first floor and found two old claw hammers that we brought upstairs and, with no easy effort, worked free the four nails.

By the time we left the barn, confident that it was as secure as possible, the winds had stepped up considerably, and the sun was halfway below the horizon. The air felt cold and smoky as we walked outside. The porchlights were on, and David was standing outside. When he saw us, he gestured wildly to us.

"I'm sorry, Mr. Daley, I tried to watch her," David's voice was frantic. "I only left for a moment to get Tilda settled upstairs."

"Oh no," Mary was the first to see what happened. A drunken Mrs. Tungsford was staggering her way toward the iron gates.

"Shit." Cursed Daley and broke into a run after her.

"I'm so sorry," David's voice was pleading and near tears.

Above the din of the wind, I could hear Mrs. Tungsford's voice calling to the agitated mob of crazies. "Welcome to Tungsford Wines; we are one of the oldest vineyards in the valley. Our pinot noir is the talk of the town."

She staggered and shuffled towards the gate, the crazies jumping and howling as she neared — her voice called in welcome to them. Daley was about halfway down the path to the entrance and breathing hard when he stopped. There was no way to reach her before she got to the gate. He looked down resignedly, and at that moment, he looked like a defeated man to me.

I heard Mary gasp as he raised the rifle to his shoulder and sighted the older woman. We both jumped as the gun fired, but an oblivious Mrs. Tungsford continued on her way as the shot went wide, and a crazed Asian woman flew back from the gate, mortally wounded. Daley feverishly worked the bolt and brought the rifle back up as the older woman reached the gate. Bloody, clawing hands came for her as she extended the key toward the gate lock.

Click.

The rifle's hammer fell forward on the empty chamber. Mrs. Tungsford twisted the key in the lock, and the gates flung up with the force of the crazies' rush; the heavy iron gate slammed into the older woman and swatted her like a badminton racket hitting a birdie. Her body rolled and crumpled beside the wide-flung gates, and I saw two young boys leap upon her still body, ripping and tearing.

"Get to the barn," Daley yelled up at us. He was too far down the road and too winded from the chase to make it back to us.

"I'm going to get Tilda," David called as he ran back into the house.

The surge of crazies was closing on him fast, and I watched as he drew that big-bore revolver and fired into the crowd. He struck the ones running in front, their falling bodies tangling with the runners behind them, momentarily causing the surging mass the falter. They were almost upon him when he fired his sixth and final shot. Mary and I stood transfixed as the Texan picked up his rifle and swung it at the oncoming horde; the heavy wooden stock cracked against the skull of a large bald man with a gaping maw, and then they were on him. Daley disappeared into the mass of bodies.

Mary grabbed my hand and started running for the barn. The wind howled about us as we slipped inside the open doorway, and we peered out, waiting for David and Tilda.

The door to the house opened, and I saw the honeymooners silhouetted there in the house's light. They looked towards the oncoming rush of crazies and stepped back into the house.

"No, come on. You can make it," we shouted at them. "Don't go back into the house."

I saw the terrified looks in their eyes as they looked at the onrushing crazies and the distance to the barn. I felt

Mary's body slacken next to me, and she shuddered a sob at the realization that they would not come.

David slammed the door closed as the crazies reached the porch. Some slammed into the ornately carved door, but others leaped through the windows, shattering the panes as they hurled their bodies inside. We heard the blood-curdling screams from inside the house, and I slammed the barn door closed and locked the latching bar in place. Mary flicked off the lights, hoping the darkness would dampen any chance at detection, and we stumbled to the back of the barn towards the ladder.

I made Mary go up first as the sounds of hundreds of hands pounding on the barn doors mixed with the howling wind. The ladder rocked dangerously as Mary climbed up, and I stayed at the bottom, holding it steady until I saw her safely scramble over the ledge into the loft.

"C'mon, John," Mary implored as she looked down at me, her hair blowing wildly from the open window above.

The ladder rocked and swayed as I scrambled up it, free of its restraining nails. The bottom of the ladder slid out, and the ladder tumbled downward. I heard Mary scream as I fell; my last vision was of her terrified face as my hands reached out to her while I fell. The air rushed out of my body as I hit the floor, my head struck the ground, and all went black.

❖ ❖ ❖

The first thing I realized was that my body hurt. Bad. My back and head did not feel right, but my limbs seemed to respond as I sat up. Dried blood crusted the back of my head, and my fingers found a sticky gash beneath my hair. A wave of nausea hit me, and a distant voice in my head remembered this was a concussion symptom. The barn was quiet, and I could see hazy daylight above in the loft.

I wanted to call Mary, but who knew if the crazies were still outside? I struggled to my feet, my head swooning. We a great deal of effort, I struggled to lift the heavy wooden ladder and slide it back up into the opening of the loft.

With an effort that almost made me vomit, I slid a few cinderblocks I found to secure the bottom of the ladder from slipping. Carefully I moved up the ladder, rung by rung, so as not to overly jostle the ladder and cause it to fall. I felt confident that a second fall would shatter my body into a million pieces.

A smoky haze filled the loft, stinging my eyes and burning my nose even before getting through the opening. I popped my head through the opening and looked around for Mary.

"Mary," My voice was little more than a rasping whisper.

I heard the scrambling of hands and feet and turned to look behind me. Mary was on her hands and feet, her bloodshot eyes wide as her fingers grabbed my hair and tore into my scalp. She jerked my head back as her mouth clamped down on my neck and tore out a fist-sized clump of flesh. I tried to scream, but no sound emanated from my throat except a harsh gurgling sound.

I lost my grip on the ladder, and we both tumbled downwards, her hands and teeth tearing at me until she struck the floor below with a sickening crack and lay still. I landed on my back, pain shooting up and out my limbs, before all sensations ceased. I lay there gurgling and choking as my last breaths left my body.

"Vacations never go how you plan them."

THEIR ROOTS RUN DEEP: OCTOBER 1404

Tomah's eyes scanned the dense morning fog looking for signs as they approached the island. Metanegwis was a short trip by canoe from the mainland; however, he knew his six tribesmen in the other two canoes would spread the word among all the Allanaki that Chief Socomotah's eldest son had gotten lost in the fog.

Behind him sat his childhood friend, Satquin, who paddled the canoe and watched expectantly as a loon dove steeply from the sky into the cold water. He gave a little cheer and happily pointed as the bird resurfaced with a small fish in his mouth; it was a rare moment that Tomah did not see a smile on his friend's face. The two men were like brothers; Tomah could not remember a time before they played together as children and hunted together as men. He looked back and smiled at the simple joy his friend found in the loon; then his eyes met those Squando who sat brooding at the back of the canoe. The short

Squando was the son of Neqtaq, the Allanaki's medicine man. Neqtaq expressed misgivings to Chief Socomotah about Tomah leading this expedition to Metanegwis, calling the chief's son too headstrong and impulsive to lead the party. However, Tomah's father dismissed Neqtaq's concern and sent Squando to accompany them, saying the young man's skills as a medicine man would keep the party from harm.

"Squando, how can you look so unhappy on such a beautiful day," Tomah lifted his muscular arms toward the blue sky.

"It's this fog," the small man looked about with his dark eyes. "It's a bad sign."

"Everything is a bad sign to you, Squando," Satquin rolled his eyes and laughed. "If a plump bass jumped into the canoe ready to be cooked for dinner, you would say that was a bad sign!"

"That would be a bad sign," Squando's eyebrows furrowed. "It is not in a fish's nature to jump into a canoe."

"Metanegwis!" one of the men in the canoe alongside them shouted and pointed.

As the three canoes broke through the fog enshrouding the island, the men of the Allanaki tribe looked upon the sandy beach and the sprawling forest of fir trees and spruce that covered the island. Tomah beamed with pride as the small party paddled toward the beach; he had easily found the island, even in the dense morning fog.

His father believed Metanegwis would play a role in providing food for the tribe, and the success of this party would be integral to achieving that. On the mainland, the Allanaki contended with the other Algonquian-speaking tribes, the Passamaquoddy, Abenaki, Penobscot, Mi'kmaq, and Maliseet, in the hunt for white-tailed deer, moose, and caribou. While the competition rarely resulted in hostilities, access to the abundant game would provide food for the tribe, animal skins for clothing, and bone for tools and weapons. Such abundance could see the Allanaki grow in power and prestige amongst their brothers. For Tomah, the success of this expedition would build his reputation and solidify his place as his father's successor.

Early scouting parties that paddled around the island found it uninhabited but rich in deer, raccoon, beaver, and moose. The island's sandy beaches had ample populations of seals and shellfish as well. Chief Socomotah had directed his son to take a party to the island and conduct a sacrificial burning of a small area of the forest, a practice they had perfected on the mainland. In the spring, new plants and saplings would grow in the fertile ground of the burned area and draw out animals hungry from the long winter. The tribe's hunters would lay in wait and return with canoes full of game.

"It's beautiful," breathed Satquin, the eyes on his broad, friendly face filled with wonder at the sight of the island.

◆ ◆ ◆

The tribesmen left the beach and walked through the forest thick with fir, birch, maple, and oak trees. Their moccasins left soft footprints on the ground, not trod by the Allanaki or any of the Wabanaki tribes since time remembered. Their breechcloths and leather leggings blended with the earth tones of the forest and made them look like ethereal shadows passing through the woods.

Chegwalis and Olamon brought down a turkey and three squirrels with their bow and arrows that they all ate with wild mushrooms as they talked about the deer and elk they had spotted in the distance.

"There is no question that He Who Walks the Woods created this island and filled it with such a bounty to feed the Allanaki," Squando raised his arms to the heavens in praise of their creator.

"I do believe you have finally said something I agree with," Satquin sharpened the blade of his knife with a stone and grinned at the young medicine man.

"Satquin, if you paid enough attention to your woman as that knife," Tomah stepped out of the woods into their camp. "Your wigwam would not need a fire to keep warm in the winter."

The men all chuckled at Tomah's gest, none more so than Satquin, who welcomed his old friend by the fire.

"You were gone in the woods so long we thought you finally found a woman of your own," Satquin passed Tomah a roasted slab of squirrel meat as another round of laughter passed through the assembled men.

"I have found the perfect clearing for our burning tomorrow," Tomah tore voraciously into the squirrel meat and skewered a mushroom with his deer bone knife. "A stream bounds it on one side and the most incredible birch trees I have ever seen on the other."

"By a stream is a wise choice," Satquin nodded approvingly. "It will contain the fire on one side and draw animals to the new growth and water in the spring."

"My brother," Tomah stared intensely at his oldest friend. "You must see these birch trees; they have bark that is unblemished and white as snow. If it were not for the leaves, I would never have thought they were even birch trees."

"These trees sound unnatural," Squando frowned at the men around the fire. "There is great evil when the Night Hunter changes the creations of He Who Walks the Woods; we should stay far away from the trees."

"You see the Night Hunter's hand everywhere, Squando," Satquin waved dismissively at the medicine man. "There is no evil on this island; it is a paradise."

Squando stared into the fire as the other men continued to talk amongst themselves. Suddenly, nothing on this island felt right to him.

◆ ◆ ◆

As the new sun rose over the horizon, the men stood in a wide semicircle so far apart that each man looked no taller than a man's thumb. Each bore a burning torch aloft in each hand as Squando walked into the clearing.

"Mighty He Who Walks the Woods," Squando reached his hands up to the sun. "Smile upon the Children of the Sunrise, given us guidance and wisdom, provide the deer and the moose, make the grass grow, and the rivers run swiftly, let our actions today make our grandfathers' spirits smile and bless us."

Squando, his blessing completed, stepped back into the large semicircle as his tribesman began lowering the torches to the dry grassland. The men moved quickly, lighting the fires whiles beating down and stamping out any fire that strayed towards the woodland.

The fire spread quickly towards the stream, consuming the small green saplings and dry brush. The men's faces became smoke-darkened, and sweat streaked as the billowing smoke rose into the sky amid the crackling flames of the consumed vegetation. The few larger trees in the clearing remained largely unscathed from the fast-burning flames, aside from the evidence of black scorching left along their trunks.

"The new growth in the spring will draw herds of elk, caribou, and deer out of the woods," Satquin's smoke-blackened face made his teeth look unnaturally white as he smiled broadly as he watched the fire burn towards the stream where it would die out.

However, Tomah was not listening to his friend as he wandered back into the woods. He heard Satquin and the others following behind him as he walked toward the grove of white-barked birches. The numerous birds on the island were silent in the grove and absented from the trees' branches.

"Are they not magnificent?" Tomah placed a hand on the smooth bark as he stared up into the branches of one of the birch trees. "The bark is completely unblemished."

"I have never seen anything like them," Satquin knelt and picked up a fallen leaf. "These are most certainly birch leaves, but the trees look like no birch tree I have ever seen."

"Imagine the canoe we could make from this tree," Tomah's eyes sparkled with excitement.

"How many trees are there?" Satquin stared in wonderment at the trees as the other men ran their hands over the smooth white bark of the trees.

"There are twenty-seven," Tomah smiled at his old friend. "Enough to build smooth white canoes and wigwams for all of us."

"We should leave these trees alone," Squando waved his arms emphatically. "This is not a good place; this is a place of the Night Hunter."

"Squando, you bark like a seal in the harbor," Satquin imitated the barking sound of the seals sunning on the granite rocks in the harbor.

"No," the diminutive medicine man pointed to the ground. "Their roots run deep. They reach into dark places in the earth. We should leave these trees and go. Tomah, you have fulfilled Chief Socomotah's wishes; it is time for us to return."

"You are right, Squando. My father will be pleased with the work we have done here today," Tomah stepped close to the smaller man and slipped his axe from his deerskin belt. "We will return home."

"Thank you, Tomah," Squando visibly relaxed but eyed the axe in the man's hand warily.

"But we will return with one of these trees," Tomah whirled away from the medicine man and buried his axe deep into the trunk of the birch tree.

As Tomah pulled the axe free, a splatter of crimson red tree sap dotted his arms and chest. Squando backed away, his face a mask of horror, at the blood-like liquid. The assembled men exchanged concerned glances at the sight of the unusual-looking sap.

"It tastes sweet," Tomah touched a spot of sap on his hand to his lips.

Tomah swung his axe again and cut into the trunk of the tree. The other men just stood and watched as he cut deep into the birch tree. Satquin drew his axe and stepped alongside his friend; Tomah stopped his chopping and looked at him.

"It tastes like maple syrup," Satquin touched a finger to Tomah's sap-splattered face and tasted it.

The two men smiled and then laughed heartily before taking turns chopping at the tree. The others, who eagerly added their axes to the effort, soon joined them in laughter. However, Squando fled the clearing and ran off into the woods, the sounds of chopping wood fading behind him.

◆ ◆ ◆

It was evening when the men returned to camp on the beach with a section of the tree the size of a long canoe. Exhausted, they washed the dirt, smoky soot, and dried tree sap from their bodies in the surf.

"It stains like berries," Satquin rubbed at the dark

splotches left behind from the sap.

"Good, I hope it takes a long time to fade," Tomah splashed water onto his face and through his dark hair. "Let all the Allanaki see the men who made this trip."

The men smiled with pride at the day's work as they gathered shellfish for their evening meal.

"It will make a beautiful canoe," Satquin wiped the salty remnant of the shellfish from his knife.

"Every tribe will recognize this canoe on the waters," Tomah lovingly ran a hand over the felled tree's bark. "We will build our wigwams out of those trees on this beach, Satquin."

"Build them here, not in the village?" Satquin could not contain his surprise. "Do you think your father will allow this?"

"This island is too abundant with game to leave unattended," Tomah's expression hardened in determination. "Other tribes will want to come here to hunt and for these trees. He Who Walks the Woods created this island as a gift for the Allanaki."

"Squando would disagree with you," Satquin smirked at his old friend. "He is still in the woods gathering herbs for a protection blessing."

◆ ◆ ◆

Darkness stirred in the woods as the Allanaki tribesmen slept on the beach. The Ancient One, like a wisp of inky smoke, a thin line of blackness rose from the stump of the felled birch tree. It swirled like a small, black tornado above the stump comprised of impenetrable darkness. Then the swirling mass began solidifying into a thick, black viscous mass that coated the stump and slid down to the ground. It seeped into the earth, sinking deep and seeking out the forest's subterranean network of thread-like mycelium that connected all the things that grew. The black mass coursed along the network, gathering knowledge as it went. It was finding the path the men took back to their camp, where they trampled the grass and broke branches in their passing.

The Ancient One burst forth from the sandy ground of the beach and circled the sleeping men before launching itself downward at the man like an arrow. The blackness filled the man's mind and body, consuming it in darkness.

◆ ◆ ◆

Satquin's eyes opened slowly, milky white and devoid of pupils. He sat up slowly and looked at the sleeping men around him, the firelight causing shadows to dance on their slumbering faces. With the stealth of a panther, he moved on hands and feet across the camp, drawing his knife as he came to the first two sleeping men.

Satquin slit their throats with quick slices of his knife; the two tribesmen died silently as their blood soaked the sand beneath them. He crawled to the next man, and as the sound of the sea's waves breaking against the shore filled the night, Satquin brought his axe down on the man's neck. The man's body twitched as his severed head rolled from his body and a spurt of blood sprayed the man sleeping beside him; the Ancient One knew this was the one called Chegwalis.

Chegwalis' eyes opened in surprise at the dampness, bringing his hand to his face. He strained to see the wetness on his hand in the darkness and stared confusedly up at Satquin. Satquin buried the axe deep into Chegwalis' forehead, and the man's eyes rolled upwards as if staring at the weapon as he fell back to the ground.

His feet reddened with blood as Satquin stepped over Chegwalis' body and picked up the man's bow and arrow. Satquin nocked an arrow, pulled the bowstring back to his milky white eye, and let the arrow fly. It thudded into the eye of one of the sleeping men, killing him before he could even draw another breath.

Satquin drew another arrow and sent an arrow into the last sleeping man's side. The man groaned on impact and let out a shuddering breath that turned into a wet gurgle as he slowly died. Emotionlessly, Satquin walked passed the dead and dying men, drawing another arrow as he approached Tomah's sleeping form.

In the distance, a seal barked somewhere in the darkness as Satquin let fly an arrow as he approached the sleeping man. Tomah awoke screaming as the arrow entered his left knee. Pain etched the man's face as his hand reached disbelievingly for the arrow, blood streaming down his leg. A second arrow flew through the air and buried itself in his right knee.

Tomah howled in pain, grabbing his knees and casting his eyes about for his unseen attacker. His eyes widened in shock at the sight of Satquin with the bow in his hand.

"Satquin, what are you doing?" Tomah stared in

disbelief at his oldest friend and the bloody bodies around the campfire. "What is wrong with your eyes?"

Without uttering a word, Satquin launched another arrow into Tomah's right elbow. The wooden shaft cracked bone and tore sinew as Tomah screamed again. His arm and legs were useless; Tomah held up a hand to stave off Satquin as the big man approached.

Satquin stared down at Tomah with seemingly sightless white eyes and brought Chegwalis' bow down on the man's left arm, breaking the bone as the wooden bow cracked. Tomah moaned and fell back onto the sand.

"Satquin, why are you doing this?" Tomah moaned as Satquin grabbed his breechcloth and began to drag him across the sand. "Where are you taking me?"

Tomah bit his tongue to keep from crying out as his injured armed and legs jostled along the sand. He beseeched Satquin to stop this madness and talk to him, but his oldest friend just stared ahead with those otherworldly white eyes. A gasp escaped Tomah's lips as Satquin effortlessly lifted him into the air by the scruff of his breechcloth and dropped him down on something rigid and curved. It took a moment for his pain-addled brain to realize he was lying on the birch tree, his arms and legs dangling agonizingly down the sides. Tomah's breaths were coming in ragged gasps as he stared at the night sky, uncomprehending the night's events.

Satquin looked down at him, his once familiar face made alien by those white eyes. Tomah's opened wide as he watched his old friend's arms swing wide and bring the axe racing down through the night.

"Satquin!" Squando gasped in horror as he watched Tomah's head roll off the blood-streaked birch log and thud onto the sand. The handful of protective herbs slipped from the medicine man's hand.

Satquin left the axe buried in the log by Tomah's lifeless body and turned to face the medicine man. Squando recoiled from the white eyes staring out from Satquin's bloody face and tripped over Chegwalis' corpse, causing him to fall back into the sand.

"No, no, don't," Squando pleaded as Satquin drew his hunting knife and walked over to him.

The tall, muscular form of Satquin loomed over the diminutive medicine man, and tears of fear began to flow unbidden down Squando's cheeks. Satquin raised the razor-sharp bone knife to his scalp and slid the blade slowly down his head and face. Blood poured down Satquin's body from the deep gash, and Squado felt his whole body trembling with terror.

He dropped the bloody knife to the sand and stared expressionlessly down at Squando for a long moment. The medicine man watched in horror as Satquin reached up with both hands and dug his fingers deep into the gash on his scalp. With a violent yank, Satquin tore the skin off his head and face as if peeling a fruit. Squando screamed in terror and vacated his bowels as Satquin sank to his knees, white eyes staring at him from a skinless head of pulsing blood and twitching muscles. Then, Satquin's body toppled to the ground, and he let out a lone shuddering breath before going still.

Squando got to his feet and began to run, his moccasins kicking up sand on the corpses of his tribesmen. He fell sprawling in the sand and crawled the rest of the way to the canoe, crying with relief as his hands touched the birch bark hull. The blackness of the bay lay before him as he pushed the canoe into the water, fighting the surf to get it clear of the beach.

The medicine man paddled against the incoming tide until his arms were sore, turning back to look at the island only once he was far out into the bay. He would tell his people what he had seen on the island; that it was a place of the Night Hunter. Squando mourned the loss of Tomah, Satquin, and the others and would ensure that none of the Allanaki or neighboring tribes would ever set foot on Metanegwis again. He would tell all that cursed trees cover the island, and their roots run deep into evil lands.

THEIR ROOTS RUN DEEP: OCTOBER 1604

"Isn't it beautiful, Minister Duqua," Samuel Dupont grinned as they watched the boats bringing supplies ashore from the three large sailing ships anchored in Passamaquoddy Bay.

Henry IV of France had granted Samuel exclusive rights to the island for conducting the fur trade for ten years. The charter had forbidden any fur trading in the area where he held his monopoly.

"Yes, Samuel," the Huguenot minister watched the scores of men bringing ashore the supplies of bricks and pre-fabricated frame buildings they brought with them from France. "The Isle Sainte Croix will be the perfect location to summon the natives to a knowledge of Christ. I hear they are barbarous people, atheists without faith or religion. This work will be my greatest challenge and most remarkable achievement. "

"We are all his servants," Samuel nodded to the Minister

appreciably, though he did not share the Minister's convictions. As far as Samuel was concerned, the natives were his only competition, and he would sooner see them filled with musket balls than the Holy Spirit.

"What is it the natives called this place?" the Minister's beady eyes followed the flight of a loon through the air as it dove into the water.

"I believe the Allataki call it Metanegwis," Samuel searched the beach until he found the blonde-haired of his wife Elyna; the slender woman was trying to corral his twin daughters off the beach. The eleven-year-olds were reveling in the barking noise a cluster of seals were making on the seaweed-coated outcroppings of granite in the makeshift harbor.

"Metangewis," the Minister's face looked like the words felt distasteful in his mouth. "I think Isle Sainte Croix is far more fitting, don't you agree?"

"Yes, of course," Samuel was thankful for the arrival of Pierre Dupont, his second in command. Behind the short, heavy-set man strode the expedition's military commander, Major Gabriel Anawan, with his bevy of weaponry. A large musket slung across the man's back, the bone handle of a large hunting knife poked out of a sheath on the man's hip, and he wore a flintlock pistol holstered on the other hip, a second slid into the front of his belt. Anawan had served alongside Henri IV during the Wars of Religion, though to Samuel's knowledge, the man had never seen combat.

"Samuel," Dupont was sweating and breathing heavily from the short walk up the beach; he held a leather-bound ledger in his hand. "All thirty-five men, thirty women, and fourteen children are accounted for, and the supplies will be finished coming ashore before nightfall."

"Thank you, Pierre."

"Sir," Anawan stroked his long dark mustache in a manner so self-important that Samuel despised talking to the man. "I would like to get the men working on fortifying the islet overlooking the harbor. I require work parties to cut trees for the barricade and three men to move the canon into a position to fire upon the harbor if necessary."

"As I explained, Major Anawan," Dupont moped the sweat off his forehead with a handkerchief. "Several men suffer from severe swelling from mosquito bites, and I have already selected others for their turn in The Order of Good Cheer."

"The Order of Good Cheer?" Samuel believed wholeheartedly that of all the men he recruited for this expedition back in Havre de Grâce, no two men were more unlike than the good-natured Dupont and the battle-seeking Anawan.

"Oh yes, the Order of Good Cheer is what I call the men who have volunteered to hunt for food for the good of the whole company each day," Dupont smiled broadly as he explained but cast a scornful look at Anawan. "And as I explained, they are not available for military responsibilities."

"If I may offer a suggestion," Minister Duqua stepped into the middle of the three men. "I fancy myself quite the huntsman. I will take my two sons, and we will bring back a bounty. After all, we all know Philippians

4:19."

The three men looked uncomfortably amongst themselves as the Minister stared expectantly at them.

"And my God will meet all your needs according to the riches of his glory in Christ Jesus." Duqua gave them a disdainful look at their continued silence.

"It is settled then," Samuel grabbed the leather-bound ledger from Dupont and headed down the beach toward his family. "Minister Duqua will handle the hunting until the barricade is built, and then the Order of Good Cheer will take over the responsibilities."

❖ ❖ ❖

Three weeks into his business venture on St Croix, Samuel had to admit it was going better than expected. Isabelle, the oldest of his twins by a full minute, stood by his side as he ran his hand over the large and growing piles of beaver and raccoon pelts. At this rate, his only concern would be running out of animals before he could get King Henry to expand his charter to the mainland. Even at twelve, Isabelle developed an interest in the business and had a good head for numbers, unlike her sister Fleur, who only delighted in cooking and housekeeping.

"Minister Duqua told us that Psalm fifty says, 'For every beast of the forest is mine, I know every bird of the mountains, and everything that moves in the field is mine,'" Isabelle's ice blue eyes studied the furs as she ran her hand over the soft hairs.

"For once, I agree with the Minister," Samuel smiled to himself; he would have to remember that Psalm could come in useful one day.

"Does the Psalm apply to the trees too?"

"Even more so to the trees than the animals," He brushed his daughter's long blonde hair from her shoulder and smiled at her inquisitive nature. "Trees have no souls; they are merely here so we could build our barricade for defense and our homes for shelter. To heat our fires for warmth and cooking."

She thought on this for a moment with an expression on her face that made Samuel think of someone mentally doing a math problem.

"Mr. Dupont and Major Anawan and their men cut down so many trees each day," Her face was solemn as she met his gaze. "If it takes so long for trees to grow, what will we do if we run out of trees?"

"If we cut down all the trees on St Croix," Samuel chuckled at her concern and smiled down at her. "Then we'll just move someplace with more trees."

That seemed to appease her concern, and she smiled back at him. She was correct; Dupont and Major Anawan had made excellent progress clearing the forest to have enough timber to complete the fortifications and construct a meeting hall and this storehouse for his furs. Dupont's foresight in bringing pre-constructed walling and roofing enabled them to raise the blacksmith's barn and several dwellings rapidly. He, of course, had his cabin with his wife and the twins, but most of the others were still living three families to a cabin as construction continued. Keeping the men busy felling trees and building homes had an added benefit; it meant Minister Duqua and his sons stayed occupied with hunting and out of the camp and his business. The tall, lanky Minister proved an adept and prolific hunter, and the trio provided ample deer meat for the whole company to eat well every night. They had even brought him back three thick, dark black bear furs from animals they had shot and skinned in the woods.

Much to Major Anawan's chagrin, even the natives had largely steered clear of the island. Their only encounter had been when three natives approached in a canoe and shouted at them from the bay. One of Anawan's men who spoke the Allanaki tongue said one of the men was a medicine man, and he was shouting for them to leave the island. A warning shot from the camp's canon had sent the natives rowing back to the mainland, with much cheering from the men and women of the camp.

"Samuel," Dupont stood in the doorway of the storehouse, his plump cheeks red from exertion. "I need you to come quickly; there's a problem with Minister Duqua."

So much for the Minister staying out of his business.

◆ ◆ ◆

The Minister's sons had their father's tall, lean frame and dark hair, and Samuel felt they would grow into near exact replicas of the man someday. The young men addressed a large crowd of families outside the meeting house. Nearly the whole community seemed to be present. Samuel could see a very agitated Major Anawan tugging at his long mustache as he spoke heatedly with the Minister's oldest son, Jebediah.

"The Lord has guided my father to the very spot where

the trees that will be made into our church grow," the Minister's younger son was addressing the crowd. "I have seen them, and they are tall and majestic."

Excitement rippled through the crowd as the men and women listened to the young man's words.

"Jebediah, Job, what news is this?" Samuel greeted both men as he pushed his way to the center of the crowd.

"My father has located the spot where the Lord has planted the trees for our church," Jebediah's brown eyes gleamed fervently as he spoke, and Samuel thought he heard a few "Praise God" ripple through the crowd.

"Well, that's excellent news," Samuel patted Jebediah on the shoulder. "We'll all be delighted to have our church built."

"Therein lays the problem," Major Anawan crossed his arms across his chest. "Minister Duqua is asking that we send everyone to fell the trees and bring them back to camp."

"Everyone?" Samuel felt his left cheek twitch slightly.

"Everyone," the military commander glared at the Minister's sons. "All the men. All the axes. All the horses and carts."

"Certainly, there is no more important work than to see the Lord's will be done," Job spoke to the crowd more than to the Major.

"The Bible tells us," Jebediah extended his arm and thrust a finger skyward. "'He shall build for me a house, and I will establish his throne forever."

Samuel heard the Amens; he saw the nodding heads in the crowd and the smiling exuberant faces and knew the Minister had already won the camp.

"Well, let us not tarry any longer; we have a house to build," Samuel gave the crowd his best fake smile, though his mind was calculating how much this lost productivity would cost him.

◆ ◆ ◆

Major Anawan and his five men stayed behind to protect the camp, while the remaining seventy-four camp members traveled by foot and cart to the Minister's sacred grove of trees. Led by Jebediah and Job, the men, women, and children sang church hymns as they trekked the two hours to the spot. Samuel was confident that many would turn back instead of crossing a stream that lay in their path, but the whole procession happily splashed across the cold water.

Samuel saw Duqua sitting on a tree stump, arms across his chest, and serenely gazing up at an unusual copse of birch trees. At least, he thought they were birch trees; the leaves certainly had the egg-shaped triangular-tipped leaves with serrated edges that grew on birch trees. However, the trunks and branches of the trees looked so light to be almost white and smooth in appearance.

"Aren't they magnificent?" Duqua raised his arms heavenward towards the trees as the procession approached. "They are like the trees in Genesis. 'Then Jacob took fresh rods of poplar and almond and plane trees, and peeled white stripes in them, exposing the white which was in the rods.'"

The people streamed among the trees; there were

twenty-six of the unusual trees in all, touching their bright white bark reverently. Some remarked at the remarkable straightness of the tall trees, and others commented about the smooth, unblemished bark.

"Minister Duqua, how many trees will the church require?" Dupont stared at the impressive trees.

"All twenty-six of them," Duqua's face beamed with delight. "We shall take all of the trees for our church."

"Father, where is this tree?" Isabelle pointed to the stump.

"It must have fallen, Izzie," Samuel looked at the stump, mesmerized by the sheer number of rings in it. They were so thin and tightly grouped from the center to the bark that they seemed too infinite to count.

"But then, where is the tree?" Isabelle looked around the stump. "And shouldn't the top look jagged and broken?"

Samuel was about to answer her when the sound of the first axe blade striking one of the trees rang out as the crowd cheered. An inexplicable cold chill ran down his spine at the sound of the axe cleaving the tree.

The cheering ended abruptly, replaced by a wave of anxious murmuring through the crowd. Samuel followed closely behind Duqua as he pushed his way through the crowd. The men and women stared at the tree and whispered silent prayers.

Jebediah stood before the tree, axe in hand; the blade dripped a red viscous liquid so dark it was almost black. The place on the tree where the axe struck oozed the dark sap, which ran in rivulets down the white trunk. He looked at his father as the Minister walked up and placed a hand on the axe mark. Duqua looked at the red sap that coated his hand with sheer reverence and turned to the assembled men and women who stared expectantly at him.

"The blood of our Lord and Savior," Duqua held his hand up to the crowd and looked heavenward with tears. "God ordains our work here."

The crowds' shouts of "Amen" and "Praise the Lord" echoed through the trees as the men eagerly took up their axes and set upon felling the majestic trees.

❖ ❖ ❖

"It will be a magnificent church," Minister Duqua smiled broadly as he surveyed the twenty-six tree logs. "We should declare tomorrow a day of rest to reward everyone for their toils doing the Lord's work today."

"I'm not sure anyone will be capable of working tomorrow," Dupont frowned at the lost productivity the camp was facing after the tremendous effort it took to fell the trees and bring them to the camp. "The men are exhausted, and the strain of dragging that timber to the camp nearly killed the horses."

"Mr. Dupont, surely, there is no reward like seeing God's will be done," Jebediah stared defiantly at Dupont with his hands folded across his chest.

"Of course not," Dupont swatted at a mosquito buzzing around his ear. "Jebediah, you still have some tree sap on your hands."

Samuel looked down at his hands, dotted with the unusual dark red tree sap from his turn with the axe.

"All the men bear the mark of the Lord's work this day," Jebediah looked at his hands and smiled. "The sap washed off, but some staining remained; I'm sure it will fade like blueberry stains. But for now, everyone is wearing the stains as badges of honor in the eyes of the Lord. Even the women have dipped their hands into it."

Samuel had watched Elyna dip her finger into the dark crimson sap and smear a little mark on each cheek; several others, including the Minister's wife, had spread the sap into a cross on their foreheads. The efforts to out-piety one another continued, with some men smearing large crimson crosses on their bare torsos. He noted with hidden amusement that only the fastidiously clean and notoriously squeamish Dupont remained free of sap stains.

"Looks like blood to me," Dupont failed to keep the disapproval from his voice as he continued his battle with the mosquito.

"Revelations teaches us that the righteous triumph by the blood of the Lamb," Minster Duqua turned to gaze reverently at the felled trees. "And what could be more righteous than what we have done today?"

◆ ◆ ◆

The ground was soaked with the fallen trees' crimson sap as a primal rage surged through the clearing where the twenty-seven birches had once stood. Not since the desecration of one of their number two hundred years ago had the Ancient Ones been awakened from their slumber.

Ethereal forms darker than the night rose from the

stumps of the violated trees; even the moonlight overhead failed to illuminate their shapeless forms. They congealed into a black, impenetrable cloud over the clearing as they raged in their ancient tongue.

The cloud separated into shapeless forms as they descended into the stumps. Filled with malice, the blackness coursed through the roots of the felled trees and into the earth saturated with their crimson sap. It joined with the forest's subterranean network of thread-like mycelium that shared water and nutrients among all the forest's trees and rode it like a highway, racing for the encampment of those who desecrated the sacred grove.

The forms seeped back to the surface amidst the scattered dwellings of the camp and swirled in the air like sharks circling prey. Had they not been sleeping, anyone that looked up at the night sky would have seen the dark shapes obscure the stars and moonlight as they passed overhead. Then as one, the shapes dove for the camp, passing effortlessly through the wooden roof and walls of the dwelling and into the sleeping forms of the fourteen children who slumbered in the camp.

The children awoke simultaneously, their eyes wholly white and absent of pupils as they sat silently up in their beds. Wordlessly, in every home, the children crept from their beds and quietly retrieved their father's axe, still stained crimson with the sap of the trees.

❖ ❖ ❖

"Grenier! Tremblay!" rage roiled up in Major Anawan's chest as he approached the two sleeping guards. He was tired of these unprofessional colonial guards and regretted not requesting King Henry have him assigned to a command on the continent. The native threat had not materialized, which provided him endless frustration; however, it was still inexcusable to sleep while on guard duty.

The two guards sat, legs outstretched on either side of the barred wooden gate that led to the beach, heads lolled in deep slumber. Anawan had reared a leg to kick Grenier awake when his boot stepped in something wet. His eyes opened wide, and his intestines gurgled when he realized it was a pool of blood. He knelt beside the guard and could make out the deep gash that nearly severed Grenier's neck from his shoulders. Tremblay bore a similar wound to the side of his head; both men were dead.

"The natives are attacking," Anawan heard the sound of terror in his voice as he reached for the pistol in his belt.

Major Anawan turned to raise the alarm, but a searing pain in his stomach caused the breath the rush from his lungs. His hand went to his midsection, and he gaped in disbelief at the blood that coated his hand, then at the blacksmith's nine-year-old son who stood in front of him with a bloody axe clutched in his small hands. There was something wrong with the boy's eyes; they were as white as snow. Anawan sank to his knees, mouth still trying to form words as the boy cleaved his skull with the axe.

◆ ◆ ◆

The terrified screams of his wife awoke Minister Duqua

from a deep sleep. He sat in his bed as moonlight streamed in from the open doorway. Duqua reached for her, but she seemed to fall away from him as something thudded into his lap. By the moonlight, he could see the face he had come to know so well staring back at him. Her eyes rolled back in her severed head as her mouth still tried to form words.

His mind was uncomprehending what he saw as he looked around the room. Both of his sons lay sprawled and bloodied outside the door. Beside him, his wife's headless body spurted blood soaking her grandmother's knitted quilt. Duqua turned to Pierre Peltier's boy, who stood beside the bed, soaked in blood and with sightless white eyes. Nothing made sense to Duqua.

Then the Peltier boy's axe struck him in the chest, propelling him backward into the bed. Duqua gasped for air as his chest gurgled with air bubbles from his exposed lung. Then the Peltier boy brought the axe down again.

❖ ❖ ❖

"Isabelle," Samuel tried to rub the sleep from his eyes. "What are you doing up?"

The girl looked odd to him as she stood by the foot of his bed staring at him, and she seemed to be holding something in her hand. A rhythmic thudding sound filled the cabin as he searched for his wife in the darkness.

"Elyna," his eyes tried to pierce the darkness. "Where are you? I think there's something wrong with Isab...."

A forceful blow to the side of his head that knocked him from his bed and onto the floor cut short his words mid-sentence. His body felt strangely detached, and he could not feel his arms or legs. Samuel cast about the cabin with his eyes, the only part of his body he could move. He blinked as something wet and metallic tasting ran into his eyes and mouth. Somewhere in the back of his mind, he knew it was blood. But whose?

The rhythmic thudding continued, and he finally made out the still form of his Elyna on the floor, her face a bloody ruin as Fleur struck her repeatedly with an axe. His wife's body reverberated with each blow of the small girl's axe. He watched in detached fascination until two legs stepped in front of him, obscuring his view.

Unable to move his head, Samuel looked upwards with his eyes into Isabelle's blank, expressionless face; her eyes looked like two white eggs as she cleaved her axe down into his face.

◆ ◆ ◆

Moonlight filled the deathly quiet encampment as the children slowly walked out of the cabins, dropping their axes as they entered the night air. They moved into single file behind Suzanne Rochefort, the oldest of the camp's children at thirteen, and walked to the gate.

Although the thick piece of wood that barred the gate typically took two adult men to put into place, Suzanne lifted and tossed it aside effortlessly. She swung the doors open, and the fourteen blood-soaked children followed her into the night. They walked in a line out to the beach and turned to face the cold waters of Passamaquoddy Bay.

One by one, each of them laid down face up in the cold surf. The children lay there motionless, sightless eyes staring unseeing at the moon as the incoming tide slowly rose around them. The waters steadily covered their arms and legs with every passing moment. Their chests disappeared below the cold dark waters and then their faces, leaving only faint trails of bubbles that lessened and then ceased.

THE TALL MAN'S DISCIPLE

The Tall Man's booted feet made no sound as he stepped to the edge of the forest and stared at the two men seated on the break wall of the bay. The moonlight showed down on the wide flat brim of his black Planter hat, casting his unearthly pale face in shadow. A light Pacific breeze blew off Commencement Bay and rustled the branches of the pines against his black frock coat and dark trousers. As he watched the two men lean in close as they talked, he flexed his long boney fingers and then balled them into fists so tight his long nails cut grooves in his thin, bloodless flesh. He exhaled a breath colder than the night's fall air as he moved out of the shadows of the forest and into the dim lighting of the deserted parking lot behind the men.

The two young men were engrossed in conversation as he approached soundlessly. A raccoon hunting among the rocks of the bay recoiled as the deathly pale man passed, its dark eyes wide and glinting in the moonlight.

❖ ❖ ❖

The man's light blue eyes narrowed as he watched the dark-haired man touch the blonde man's shoulder in a gesture of tenderness. The night air carried their voices to his ears as he closed the distance between them.

"It's beautiful out here at night. It's my favorite place in Tacoma," David let his Columbian accent come through heavily as he said Tacoma. People always liked the exoticness of his accent, so he laid it on thick when he was trying to catch someone's attention, and he most definitely wanted to hold the young blonde man's attention.

"That's Vashon Island, right?" Jeremy pointed across the bay to the sparse lights of the darkened island.

"Yes, that's Vashon Island," David smiled as he pointed to the island and then gestured over his shoulder at the forest. "That's Point Defiance, and right in between is us."

"Seeing the water reminds me of home," Jeremy brushed a strand of hair away from his blue eyes.

"From that twang in your voice, I'd say you're from the South," David let his desire for the man show in his eyes.

"Alabama, born and bred," Jeremy smiled sheepishly. "Have you ever heard of the local stories about the Tall Man?"

"Oh, that urban legend," David waved a dismissive hand. "That's for the Nickelodeon crowd."

"They say he's the ghost of a dead minister that walks the shores of Commencement Bay looking for sinners.

"I've heard the stories. Tacoma is a sketchy enough place for people to disappear without some undead Bible thumper being the reason."

"No, really, I've researched it," Jeremy stared over at the shadowy tree line of Vashon Island. "He was a Baptist Minister named Gideon Hayes that came here from Mississippi in April 1855 during the Puget Sound War. Hayes believed the Second Coming of Christ would only occur after all the world's sinners either became Christians or were put to death. He saw the Native Americans as heathens that needed to convert to Christianity. Any Native Americans that did not convert or settlers that did not repent of their sins he put to the test."

"What kind of test?" David slid closer, enjoying listening to Jeremy speak.

"He would throw them off the cliff Point Defiance. He believed God would make them float safely down like a feather if they were innocent, but if they were sinners, their bodies would break upon the rocks."

David grimaced at the thought of the agonizing fall and bone-shattering impact of bodies upon the rocks.

"He was instrumental in relocating the local tribes from Vashon Island to Fox Island in January 1856. However, one night some of the savages escaped from Fox Island and chased Hayes through the forest at Point Defiance. When they caught him, they tied him to a tree, sliced him open, and filled his body with straw so that his spirit could not pass into the otherworld."

"Sounds to me like that man got what he deserved," David brushed some dirt from the leg of his dark blue skinny jeans.

"Hayes was described as unusually tall for the time,

just like the Tall Man. The description of the clothing the Tall Man wears matches what a frontier Minister would have worn in the 1850s. I believe there are so many disappearances between April and January along Commencement Bay because that is the timeframe Hayes arrived in the area and was subsequently murdered on Point Defiance. The cycle repeats yearly, and there are never Tall Man sightings between January and April."

"Well, if that's true," David put his hand tenderly on Jeremy's shoulder and gave the young man his most mischievous smile. "You will need to protect me because a sinner like me would break like glass if he threw me down on the rocks."

"I was thinking that too," a coldness filled Jeremy's voice and eyes as he swung his arm and brought the fist-sized rock crashing into the side of David's head.

David opened his mouth, but no sound emerged as he snapped forward and then back at the force of the blow. Blood poured down the side of his tan face from the devastating wound on his temple as his eyes rolled back in his head. Jeremy shrugged the man's hand off his shoulder and pushed the man forward over the break wall.

David's body striking the ground below reminded Jeremy of the sound a slaughtered sow made when it dropped from the meat hook on the farm back home. He stared down at the body; the young Latin man's head and leg lay at an odd angle as the tide began to dislodge him from the rocks. Soon David would be dragged beneath Commencement Bay, food for the five-gill sharks.

As David's body slipped beneath the waves, a wicked smile crossed Jeremy's face. Beside him, the long shadow of a man in a wide-brimmed hat stretched along the floor.

❖ ❖ ❖

"It's done; he's been judged," Jeremy smiled like a child awaiting his parent's approval as he looked into the pale face of the Tall Man.

The slightest hint of a smile touched the thin, colorless lips of the thing which had once been Gideon Hayes. The figure nodded his head in approval.

"He was a gay. I knew he would break on the rocks," Jeremy slid the deer bone pocketknife out of his pants and flicked open the short, sharp blade.

He pulled down the neck of his shirt to reveal three red, raw-looking cross-like cuts on his chest in various states of healing. Jeremy gritted his teeth into a sneer of half pain and half ecstasy as he slowly drew the tip of the knife against his pale chest, adding a fourth cross-like wound. The blood felt warm on his skin, juxtaposed against the chill of the night air. He let go of the neck of his shirt and followed the Tall Man as the dark figure turned back toward the woods.

Jeremy first heard of the Tall Man from a classmate back in Cullman, Alabama. That night he spent hours on the internet reading stories of Tall Man sightings and his supposed victims. Prostitutes who serviced men in their cars, teens fornicating on the rocks, homosexuals, and drug addicts. As far as Jeremy was concerned, the Tall Man was no evil specter; he was an avenging angel doing God's work. The Tall Man was doing the kinds of things Jeremy only dreamed of doing.

When he came across the story of Gideon Hayes, a righteous man slaughtered by heathen savages, it all became clear in Jeremy's mind what he needed to do. He worked all summer and saved his money, then one September morning, he got in his beat-up red Ford pickup and drove the forty hours from Cullman to Tacoma, Washington.

Jeremy slept in his truck during the day and wandered along the shores of Commencement Bay at night. Sometimes he sat in the forest watching men and women sneak down by the beach to do drugs or have sex, and he waited for the Tall Man to come and deliver the Lord's justice, but he never did. He was ready to give up and go back to Cullman the night he spied the tall figure, barely visibly in the shadow of the Silver Cloud Hotel, as he stared out over the waters of Commencement Bay.

The Tall Man paid little attention to Jeremy as he walked past him, trying to get up the nerve to speak to him, though he could see the pale blue eyes in the shadows following him as he walked by.

"Gideon Hayes," Jeremy turned back to the shadowy figure. "You're Gideon Hayes, right?"

At the sound of the name, the Tall Man's head slowly turned to look at Jeremy. The Tall Man's face was translucently white beneath the wide-brimmed hat, and his eyes were beady and pale icy blue. Jeremy felt his insides tighten as the figure stepped towards him out of the shadows. Boney hands with long white fingers protruded from the sleeves of the black frock coat as the figure reached toward Jeremy.

"I think what those heathen savages did to you was terrible," Jeremy's knees felt weak as the Tall Man closed the distance between them. "You are the Lord's servant on earth. You bring God's wrath on the wicked. I came here to help you."

The Tall Man grabbed Jeremy by the front of his jacket and pulled him close so that his face was inches from his own. Jeremy felt his body shake with fear as the Tall Man's eyes seemed to study his face. The figure's breath was icy cold and stank of rotted leaves and wet straw.

"I...I can help you. And I can continue your work when you leave in January until you come back in April.

The Tall Man let go of Jeremy's jacket and took a step back, his eyes running over Jeremy appraisingly.

"I can help you," Jeremy tried to force some strength back into his voice. "I can be your disciple."

A tight-lipped smile crossed the Tall Man's pale face that reached nearly his high cheekbones.

◆ ◆ ◆

Jeremy looked down at the body of the red-haired prostitute, her eyes were vacant, but her mouth still moved as if she was trying to speak as she lay broken on the rocks below Point Defiance. Some of her blood speckled his cheek, and he resisted the urge to wipe it off with his thumb and taste it.

He slid the pocketknife from his pants and unzipped his heavy winter coat, eager to carve the ninth cross into his skin. The Tall Man stepped from the woods into the clearing, illuminated by January's full moon.

"Put up a bit of a fight at the end," Jeremy smiled at the ethereal form.

The Tall Man froze as a high-pitched animal cry sounded in the distance. The cry was almost dog or wolf-like, but the pitch sounded way off to Jeremy. A second cry echoed in the distance, and then a third, much closer than the first.

"What is that?" Puffs of warm vapor rapidly escaped Jeremy's mouth into the cold night air as he felt his breathing quicken.

Sounds of strange cries and running feet filled the forest. Jeremy gripped the pocketknife tightly in his hand, his eyes darting left and right, trying to see what was happening in the darkened woods. The Tall Man seemed to be backing away from him, moving to the far side of the clearing.

"Gideon, what's happening?"

Suddenly, the forest went deathly quiet. Jeremy could only hear the pounding of his own pulse in his ears. The Tall Man slowly turned his head to the forest as ethereal forms materialized out of the darkness.

The forms of twelve buckskin-clad Native American tribesmen began to step out of the forest, each gripping a tomahawk or deer bone knife in near-gaunt hands. Jeremy gasped as he looked into their faces. Their desiccated skin pulled tightly over their skeletal heads so that their lips pulled back from their teeth. Their noses were sunken holes in their face, and coal-black orbs sat where their eyes should have been, so dark not even the moonlight reflected off them.

"Is this why you disappear every January," a horrible dawning filled Jeremy. "Do they kill you again every year?"

The tribesmen looked from the Tall Man to Jeremy as they spread out, blocking any escape into the forest.

"Gideon, we can fight them." Jeremy held his pocketknife towards the tribesmen and balled his other hand into a fist.

One of the tribesmen looked down at the body sprawled on the rocks below. His skeletal face was expressionless as he looked back at the Tall Man and shifted the grip on his tomahawk.

The Tall Man looked at the skeletal tribesman and raised his arm, extending a pale boney finger toward Jeremy. The tribesman turned those black eyes toward Jeremy and slowly pointed his tomahawk at him.

"Gideon, what are you doing? Help me," Jeremy raised his pocketknife as two of the tribesmen rushed toward him.

One of the skeletal tribesmen easily batted the small knife out of Jeremy's hand as the other landed a stunning blow to his forehead with the flat side of his tomahawk. Jeremy reeled from the blow as blood flowed down from the gash in his forehead into his eyes. Skeletal hands gripped his arms with vice-like strength, holding him fast.

Jeremy tried to struggle free of their hands, but they only tightened their grip until he fell to his knees and cried out in pain. Blinking blood and tears from his eyes,

Jeremy saw the Tall Man starting to walk toward the woods.

"Gideon!" his voice sounded hoarse as he called out, but the Tall Man never even looked back as he moved toward the woods.

It suddenly became clear to Jeremy that Gideon Hayes had only accepted him so he could take the Tall Man's place on this fated January night. He, not Gideon, would be tied to the tree, gutted, and filled with straw this night.

"Gideon, don't leave me," tears of pain, fear, and betrayal ran down Jeremy's cheeks as he cried out to his mentor in futility.

Jeremy watched through the blood and tears as two tribesmen blocked the Tall Man's path to the woods. The wide-brimmed hat moved back and forth as if he was shaking his head, and the tribesmen grabbed him. The Tall Man tried to pull back, but the two tribesmen forced him to the ground.

His hat tumbled away as the tribesmen began to drag him towards a tree, a third following behind with a length of rope. The Tall Man violently shook his pale, bald head as they pulled him across the cold ground. His mouth contorted into a moan and a sound like "no" escaped his lips, the first sound Jeremy had ever heard him make in the three months they had spent together.

The tribesmen dragged the Tall Man up to a standing position with his back to a tree, yanking his arms roughly behind him as they bound him to the tree. The moonlight illuminated his pale face, now a mask of terror, as a long strand of drool dripped from the corner of his mouth.

A tribesman with a long-bladed deer bone knife stepped in front of the Tall Man as one of the others tore open his frock coat and shirt to reveal a pale, sunken chest. His icy, blue eyes followed the blade as the tribesman raised it high up into the air and then sliced the knife down the Tall Man's body from neck to crotch in a deep cutting motion.

The Tall Man screamed and howled in pain as the blade cut him wide open, and the tribesmen reached into the wound and pulled it open wide with a sickening tearing sound. Jeremy vomited as foul-smelling black blood, and rotten innards poured forth from the Tall Man and sloshed to the ground. A long blackened string of intestines hung from his open bowels to the rotted pile of organs and blood. The Tall Man's head bobbed lifelessly as a tribesman stepped forward and shoved handfuls of straw into the empty husk of the Tall Man.

Relief flooded Jeremy at the thought that Gideon's plan to trade places with him had failed. He would get in his pickup truck and drive straight back to Cullman this very night.

Globs of bile and vomit hung to his lips as he looked up at the tribesmen holding him. They stared back down at him with those blackened orbs and then looked up at their leader, who was studying the Tall Man's corpse.

He poked his tomahawk at the Tall Man's head, making it loll from side to side. Then he cast his black eyes toward Jeremy and the two tribesmen and jerked his head. With remarkable strength for such skeletal limbs, the two tribesmen effortlessly heaved Jeremy upwards into the air and off the cliff.

Jeremy screamed as he fell backward through the air, the cold wind rushing past his body as he hurdled toward the jagged rocks below. The impact was jarring as his back splintered against the rocks, the agonizing pain of his shattering limbs suddenly replaced by a lack of sensation.

His broken body lay strewn and unmoving amidst the rocks, the black eyes of the tribesmen staring down at him from the cliff above. The waters of Commencement Bay rushed over him, filling his mouth and lungs. Jeremy gagged and spat, expelling the water and gasping for air as the water receded. A second wave broke over him, filling his mouth.

Jeremy's eyes opened wide with fear as his lungs burned with the effort to gasp for air as wave after wave broke over him as the waters slowly rose above his face, stinging his eyes. He stared at the bubbles coming from his mouth, breaking the water's surface as a skeletal hand brushed his cheek and closed around his chin.

Kelp and seaweed swayed from the hand as it turned Jeremy's head to the side. The rotted face of David, his eyes white and milky; his gray skin pockmarked from the bites of sea creatures, stared back at him. A final rush of water surged into Jeremy's mouth as he tried to scream. David's rotted fingers closed about Jeremy and pulled him down into the depths of the bay.

VESUVIAN'S DAY

Consus Livius Marius stood on the balcony and smoothed the creases of the bright red toga that sat atop his white tunic as he watched the Roman centurion guide the cart full of women into the courtyard. He glanced sidelong at the small bald man that ambled up alongside him. The man's red toga stretched across his expansive belly.

"Tell me about our guests Marcellus."

"Yes, Domus. Centurion Valerius has brought us six non-citizens for the Vesuvians Day celebration. Strong women, accustomed to a life of struggle and hardship."

Consus watched the women step off the cart in their plain homespun woolen tunics and wonder at the meticulously cultivated garden surrounding the courtyard's inner wall. They milled about, wide-eyed and hesitant.

"Looks more like five and a half." He stared disapprovingly at a small raven-haired girl kneeling to pick up a crow's feather from the courtyard.

"That one is a Dacian from the Carpathian Mountains. She's young, but Valerius assured me she's very suitable."

"Dacians! Trajan should have exterminated their lot when he conquered that god-forsaken land. They are stubborn and troublesome people. What of the others?"

"The red-haired one and the tall, dark-haired girl are local girls from insignificant farming families. Those two are sisters from Gaul; Valerius tells me they have quite the reputation throughout Mogontiacum as thieves." The bald man pointed to two women walking closely together and talking amongst themselves."

"And that one?" Consus pointed to a tall thin, dark-skinned woman.

"Ahh her. Valerius acquired her from a trader that recently returned from Byzantium."

Consus appraised the woman with a warrior's eye; she was all muscle and sinew with the poised gait of a lioness. Her hair was close-cropped on top and shaved to the skin around the sides and back.

"I knew I would find you two gawking at our guests." A tall, dark-haired woman with a cup of wine strode onto the balcony and placed her hand on Consus' shoulder.

"Flavia, my darling." Consus smiled at his wife.

"Shall we begin?" She took a long sip of the wine, and Consus' bowed his head in acquiescence as he extended a hand toward the end of the balcony.

Flavia handed her cup of wine to a male servant, who grabbed the bronze cup and hurried away. She stepped to the edge of the stone balcony and stared down at the six women.

"Ladies. Greetings!" Her melodious voice filled the

courtyard, and six sets of eyes turned expectantly towards her. "I am Flavia, and I expect most of you know my husband Consus, Domus of our fair city of Mogontiacum."

Flavia smiled broadly at the six women and extended her arms wide. "Welcome to our home; we are delighted to have you as our honored guests."

"Each year on Vesuvian's Day, we honor all those Roman citizens who lost their lives when Mount Vesuvius erupted fifty-three years ago with a great celebration. To replace the rich texture of lives lost to the Roman Empire on that sad day, our Domus selects a handful of women and bestows upon them the rights and honors of a Roman citizen. You are those worthy women. You are the future of Rome. Tonight will be a night you will remember for the rest of your lives!"

She surveyed the six women; the two Gauls whispered amongst themselves, and the dark-skinned women stared stoically at her, faces unreadable. The two local girls positively beamed as their smiling faces stared at her.

"Every little girl dreams of being Roman," Flavia thought, smirking at the unmistakable excitement on the tall, dark-haired local girl's face. Then the smile faded from her lips as she spied the Dacian girl preoccupied with stroking the crow's feather in her hand.

"My darling, can I interest you in some figs?" Consus hooked his arm out towards his wife. "Marcellus tells me they are very fresh today."

"That sounds delicious, my love," her gaze lingered on

the Dacian girl a moment longer before she turned and slid her arm into Consus'. Something about the girl disquieted her, but her smile returned as she looked at Consus' proud, handsome face.

❖ ❖ ❖

"Rhea, we are going to be Roman citizens," Messalina grasped her hands together in excitement. "Do you know what that means? We won't be farmer's wives with dirt under our nails. We will marry wealthy merchants or soldiers, like that centurion Valerius. Maybe even a senator."

Rhea smiled at her friend. They had known each other for 18 years, all their lives, and Messalina had always dreamed of being wealthy and important. She always pointed out to Rhea the women in the market with their fine clothing or ornate jewelry and told her that one day that would be them. Now here they were.

The six women sat in the bathhouse as servant girls tended to each of them, pouring scented water over their shoulders and brushed their hair. Rhea noted that while a servant girl easily brushed Messalina's long dark hair, the girl tending to her struggled to run the brush through her unruly red mane.

"We will be ladies of Rome," Messalina ran her hands through the bath water.

"Why would you want such a thing?" asked the dark-skinned woman in her exotic accent.

"Rome is the center of the world. To be Roman is to be special." Messalina answered indignantly.

"Bah, there is nothing special about Rome." The water glistened off her dark skin as she waved dismissively.

"Then why are you here if you do not wish to be a citizen?"

"I am here for the same reason you are; that centurion showed up at my door and ordered me to come with him."

"It is an honor to be chosen on Vesuvians Day; you should show more gratitude to the domus and his wife."

"A Roman conquered my land. A Roman made my family slaves. A Roman took me from my home and brought me here. I would rather be thrown into Mount Vesuvius than be Roman."

"I am sorry for what has happened to you," a softness filled Messalina's voice. She looked over to the two Gauls, Sedata and Ricina, who talked to each other in their guttural language as the servant girls scrubbed at patches of dirt on the women's necks and then back at the dark-skinned woman. "But to be a citizen means a life of comfort and purpose. You will be part of something bigger than yourself. Something that will endure forever."

The woman snorted derisively and turned away from Messalina. "Nothing is given freely in this life, and Rome never gives; it only takes."

Rhea turned from the two women and looked over at the Dacian girl. The servant woman struggled to get the brush through the girl's knotted black hair and knocked the crow feather from the young girl's hand. The Dacian girl intently watched the feather float on the water, looking eager to extricate herself from the servant's clutches and retrieve it.

"Here you go," Rhea scooped up the feather and handed it to the girl. The Dacian girl's coal-dark eyes lit up with joy, and a smile split her lips as she took the feather. "I'm Rhea."

"Dava." She pointed a thin finger at her chest; her accent was thick and alien to Rhea.

"It's very nice to meet you, Dava. That is a beautiful feather."

The girl smiled back and clutched the feather to herself.

◆ ◆ ◆

The women exited the bath, cleaned and perfumed, as the servants clothed them in tunics of a soft, delicate material. Each woman wore a tunic of a different color. The Sedata and Ricina wore gray and orange. Dava wore a white tunic which seemed almost too large for her petite body, and the dark-skinned woman, who Rhea learned was called Dido, wore a light blue accentuating her solid and sinewy arms. Messalina was given a brilliant red tunic and Rhea a dark forest green.

"Have you ever felt anything so soft?" Messalina ran her hands over the tunic. "And they gave me one the same color as Flavia's. Oh, Rhea, do you ever think I could be as beautiful as Flavia?"

"You are more beautiful than Flavia, just don't ever tell her I said so," said a male voice.

The women turned as Valerius strode into the room. A bronze breastplate hung over his white tunic, with a short sword belted around his waist. His hair was close-cropped in the style typical to Roman soldiers, and he had a broad, pleasant face with an easy smile.

"Centurion Valerius," Messalina blushed and smiled. "Will you be at the celebration?"

"But of course, I handpicked each of you for the honors of Vesuvians Day. Flavia demands a special kind of woman be selected, and in all of Mogontiacum, there are none better than you."

"Flavia, not the domus?" asked Rhea.

"True, the Domus is the only one who can confer citizenship in Mogontiacum. But he leaves the Vesuvian Day celebration to Flavia."

"And this is Flavia's vision of the flower of Rome?" Dido gestured towards the women. "Farm girls, foreigners, and a dumbstruck child?"

"Dido does not understand what an honor Rome bestows upon us." Messalina placed her hand on Valerius' arm. "She is not as appreciative as some of us."

Valerius smiled at her, and a hunger flashed in his eyes. "I look forward to seeing you at tonight's celebration."

◆ ◆ ◆

Rhea heard Messalina gasp as they walked along the white marble floors into the main hall of the Domus' house. Three of the walls bore murals dedicated to Roman military conquests, but the fourth wall contained a larger-than-life tile mosaic of a nude Flavia with such intricate detail that Rhea almost blushed looking at it. Sculptures of Roman gods and goddesses dotted the room, their muscles chiseled in smooth marble.

The elite of Mogontiacum lounged on couches around the room as servants hurriedly refilled goblets of wine and served plates of delicate cheese and meats. Servant girls ran up to the six honored guests and handed them tied bouquets of fragrant flowers. Messalina's smile exuded pure joy, but Rhea noticed Dido and the Gauls eyed the room suspiciously. Dava clutched the crow feather in her tiny hand, and her dark eyes looked wide and frightened. Rhea smiled at the girl reassuringly, and Dava returned a meek smile.

"It'll be ok, Dava; stay close to me."

Flavia was seated on a couch with Consus and Valerius and rose to her feet as the girls entered the room.

"Future women of Rome!" Her smile was wide, and her voice loud. "Welcome to your Versuvian Day celebration! Bring them wine!"

Servants quickly handed the girls full goblets of deep red wine as guests rose from their couches and surrounded the girls. Rhea felt Dava's hand grip hers as the Roman nobility surrounded them. Smiling faces offering congratulations, making introductions, asking questions. She tried to stay close to Messalina, but the tall girl had already become encircled by the men and women of Mogontiacum's nobility. She was basking in the glow of their attention.

Dava looked ready to make a run for one of the room's four large doors, and Rhea wondered what the two Roman soldiers stationed at each door, with their golden armor and long spears, would do if the girl tried such a thing. Rhea navigated the girl through the crowd to a place along the wall by one of the incredible murals. A few of the nobles came over to greet them and exchange pleasantries. Many asked about her work on her father's farm. Did she have to lift heavy things? Did she ever slaughter any of the farm animals? But in time, the nobles and their wives left Rhea and Dava alone, choosing instead to congregate around the other girls.

Messalina looked to Rhea like the goddess Venus, surrounded by her adoring worshipers, smiling and laughing as she entered Roman society. Valerius was by her side, his hand often on her arm or against the small of her back, and Rhea caught the two exchanging flirtatious glances several times.

"Are you enjoying yourselves?" Flavia strode up to them with Consus dutifully by her side.

"Oh yes, thank you very much." Rhea nervously averted her eyes and took a long sip from her wine goblet.

"I try and personally speak to all our honored guests before the main festivities. And don't you have the most beautiful red hair!" She brushed her hand through Rhea's long hair.

Consus turned his attention towards Dava, who fixedly stared at the mural. "Do you like it? I had an artisan come from Rome to make it."

The girl just turned expressionless dark eyes toward the domus. Consus stared back at her momentarily, and then a flicker of understanding crossed his face.

"Ah yes, of course, you find it interesting. It depicts Trajan's defeat of your people in Dacia." Consus pointed to a depiction of Roman soldiers attacked by men with dark claws and long sharp teeth on the mural. "During the First Battle of Tapae, priests of the Dacian god Zalmoxis called forth beasts from the underworld that killed to a man the Fifth Legion of the Lark, the Gallica Legion created by Gaius Julius Caesar himself."

"But see here," he pointed to a later section of the mural depicting Roman soldiers killing dozens of bald men in white tunics. The Roman swords and spears were red-tipped with the blood of the men. "Before the Second Battle of Tapae, my father led men of the Tenth Legion, the Gemina Legion, and slew all Zalmoxis' priests. Without their monsters, the Dacian warriors could not stand against the might of Rome."

The man's smile reminded Rhea of a wolf sizing up prey. "The Dacians were fierce fighters; I hope that same blood flows through your veins as now we will all be citizens of Rome together."

Dava raised her small hand to the mural and ran a finger over the images of the slaughtered priests.

"Marcellus, it is time." Flavia called to a heavyset bald man who sat lazily on a couch.

"Yes, Flavia."

The bald man stood and walked over to a flat, circular metal disc suspended from the ceiling near the center of the room. He picked up a small mallet and struck the metal disc, causing a loud gong to emanate through the room. Almost instantly, all the conversation in the room died. Rhea saw the questioning look on Messalina's face as the smiles on the noble's lips turned to vulpine-looking grins.

The bald man struck the disc again, and the Roman soldiers closed the doors. Rhea almost cried out as

Consus gripped her arm and started to usher her toward the center of the room, where the soldiers began forming a circle. She looked frantically around and saw hands started to push Dido and the Gauls towards the center of the room. Flauvia shoved Dava alongside her, laughing as the girl stumbled and fell.

"What's happening?" Rhea tried to keep the rising terror out of her voice, but Consus' face was as expressionless as stone.

Dava scrambled along the floor as men and women kicked her towards the circle. Rhea saw only malevolent stares as she scanned the crowd of faces laughing and smiling only moments before. She caught sight of Messalina, looking pleadingly at Valerius as he roughly pushed her into the middle of the circle.

Consus pushed Rhea past a Roman soldier, her elbow banging painfully against his breastplate and into the circle's center. She turned back towards him and saw the Domus reach down and lift Dava by her hair. The terrified girl looked like a cat held by its scruff as he tossed her into the circle. Rhea saw the crow feather slip from Dava's hand and flutter to the ground as the girl landed hard against the marble tiles and sprawled on the floor.

"Wha..what is happening?" Messalina's eyes filled with tears of shock and bewilderment. "Valerius?"

A woman in the crowd took a deep drink from his goblet of wine and spit the mouthful at Messalina. She let out a strangled cry as the bright red liquid showered her fine, soft tunic, and the assembled guests roared with laughter. Tears began to flow unbidden down her face.

"But I am going to be a citizen of Rome." She whimpered, and the crowd roared with laughter again.

"Messalina." Rhea tried calling her through vocal cords tight with fear, but the gong sounded again, and the room fell silent.

The crowd turned as Flavia stepped onto a dais alongside the metal disc. Consus and the bald man, Marcellus, flanked her. Only the Roman soldiers stood unmoving, a wall of red tunics and golden armor facing the six young women. Dido paced the circle like a tiger, and Sedata and Ricina crouched back-to-back like cornered animals. Rhea looked at Messalina, who stood pitifully, still holding her bouquet, crying and whimpering to herself. Somewhere to her left, Dava lay sprawled on the floor, unmoving.

The gong sounded again, and Flavia held up her arms.

"Men and women of Mogontiacum, fifty-three years ago, Mount Vesuvius extinguished the lives of our friends and fellow citizens in a storm of fire and ash. Pompeii had grown weak in the eyes of Jupiter, no longer worthy to be children of Rome. So Jupiter commanded Vulcan, the great god of fire, to vanquish Pompeii before its weakness could infect the whole empire."

"We must always guard against such weakness so that our city and empire shall never lose the gods' favor. Each year on this day, we select six women, non-citizens all, to represent the six great houses of Pompeii. The strongest among them will have the honor of giving birth to a new citizen of Rome, fathered by our brave Centurion Valerius and raised in the home of Quintus

Petillus."

The crowd cheered loudly as Flavia gestured towards a gray-haired man and woman in gold-trimmed white togas over red tunics.

"Messalina, what is happening?" Rhea saw her friend staring numbly at the floor and trembling. Droplets of wine dripped from the tip of Messalina's nose, and her lips moved as if she was mumbling to herself.

"The Romans are being Romans." Sneered Dido as she paced the ring of stoic-faced Roman soldiers.

Dava rose to her feet, her dark hair covering her face, as Sedata and Ricina couched like coiled snakes prepared to strike.

"Honored guests," the crowd turned to face the six encircled women as Flavia began to speak again, her voice rising to a fever pitch. "You have been bathed like citizens of Rome, dressed like citizens of Rome, and fed like citizens of Rome. Now you will fight like citizens of Rome!"

The metallic disc sounded three times, and with each gong, the Roman soldiers surrounding the women took one step backward, enlarging the circle. A man reached past the ring of soldiers and tossed a rock larger than a fist into the circle. The woman watched as the large rock struck the white marble floor and came to rest in front of Dido. Another man stepped forward and tossed a large bronze serving spoon into the circle of women. Others threw an arm's length of rope, a silver water pitcher, and a thick, smooth branch nearly two feet long. Finally, a woman in the crowd reached out and threw a large clay pitcher into the ring that struck the floor and shattered into large jagged pieces.

The women stood unmoving and stared at the array of items scattered around the circle as Flavia's voice rose above the crowd's murmuring. "Only one of you can leave the circle."

A feral scream of rage rose above the room's noise as Sedata jumped up and ran at the Roman soldiers. The crowd roared approval as the soldier effortlessly batted her to the ground with the haft of his spear. She landed on her knees and looked up at the soldier with hatred in her eyes. Behind her, Dido grabbed the large rock as she stepped forward and brought the rock down hard on the Gaul's head.

Rhea screamed as the Sedata's face went slack. Dido brought the rock down on the Gaul's head twice quickly, the last time with a sickening crack that echoed through the room. Sedata toppled to the floor, blood pouring from her shattered skull like spilled wine. The crowd cheered exuberantly.

Regina picked up the silver water pitcher and swung it wildly at Dido, who countered by trying to land a blow with the bloodied stone. The heavy stone proved cumbersome, and Ricina brought the pitcher down hard on Dido's bloody hand, causing her to cry out and drop the rock.

The Roman soldiers began to beat the hafts of their spears against their golden breastplates as the two women grappled with each other and fell to the floor in a tangle. The crowd pushed forward for a better view as Dido and Ricina punched and clawed at each other. The Gaul raked a hand across Dido's face, leaving a path of bloody lines and torn skin. Dido roared in pain and wrapped her legs around Ricina, managing to twist her way behind the Gaul. Ricina tore bloody tracks in the dark-skinned woman's sinewy legs in an attempt to extricate herself as Dido reached out and grasped the length of the rope.

Dido looped the rope around the Ricina's neck and pulled it taunt. The Gaul clawed at the rope, tearing bloody lines in her skin as she tried to get her fingers between the cord and her neck. Dido leaned back with all her weight, her muscled arms shaking from the strain as she pulled the rope tighter. Ricina's eyes bulged as she struggled, her face reddening.

Tears flowed down Rhea's face as she watched the Ricina's body go limp and lifeless. The crowd roared and cheered with savagery as Dido finally released her grip on the rope and sat breathing heavily.

Messalina surveyed the carnage in the circle with a bewildered gaze and then looked at Rhea with wild, crazed eyes.

"Messalina!" Rhea reached out to her.

Messalina ran towards Rhea and sprawled across the floor at her feet. Rhea thought her friend had fallen until a searing pain cut across the bottom of her leg and caused her to collapse to the cold marble floor. She screamed in pain and looked down at her ruined leg. A gaping wound poured blood from her severed Achilles tendon. Messalina rose above her, a bloody shard of pottery gripped in her hand.

"This is my night!" Messalina's voice was a wild shriek. "I am supposed to be a citizen!"

A movement across the circle caught Messalina's attention, and Rhea saw through tear-filled eyes that Dido had gotten to her feet and gripped the smooth wooden club in her hand. Blood and sweat streamed down the dark woman's face and neck in thick rivulets.

"Messalina!" Valerius' arm jutted out from behind a Roman soldier; his dagger extended hilt first toward Messalina.

A smile crossed Messalina's face as she reached for the dagger and heard him say, "Do it for Rome."

"For Rome," she repeated, and the crowd cheered.

"For Rome. For Rome." Flavia led the crowd in a savage cheer.

Dido let out a roar of primal rage and charged Messalina swinging the smooth club at her head. Rhea saw the women collide and heard the loud knocking as the wooden club struck Messalina's head. Both women collapsed to their knees, and a sudden hush settled over the crowd.

Messalina raised a shaking hand to her head and touched a bloody flap of skin over her left eye. Hot sticky blood ran down her face, and she looked disbelievingly at her bloody hand. Across from her, Dido let out ragged breaths through clenched teeth, her hands resting on her knees. Blood flecked her lips with each breath, and Valerius' knife sat buried to the hilt in the middle of her chest. Dido looked skyward for a moment, and then her eyes rolled back in her head, and she toppled lifelessly to the ground.

The crowd cheered wildly and began to chant, "Messalina!"

"Messalina! Messalina!"

"Finish them!" called one voice from the crowd.

Messalina looked around, and a broad smile crossed her blood-streaked face. She basked in the adoration of the crowd. A hand reached out from the crowd, and Messalina looked up to see Valerius' smiling down at her. She took his hand and rose unsteadily as the crowd roared approvingly.

"Messalina, please," pleaded Rhea as she watched her friend pull the knife from Dido's body with a sickening wet sound.

Messalina's eyes blazed with fervor as she looked from Rhea to Dava, who stood unmoving. She fixed her gaze on the small Dacian girl and began walking towards her, Valerius' blade clutched in her hand and still dripping Dido's blood. A murmur of excitement rolled through the crowd as she closed on the small girl.

Dava looked up at Messalina, the first movement Rhea had seen her make since the killing started. Her dark hair hung in loose strands among her face, and her coal black eyes watched emotionlessly as Messalina stalked towards her.

The Dacian girl opened her mouth wide and screamed. It was a scream unlike any Rhea had ever heard; it sounded like a high wind in the mountaintops. The scream stopped Messalina in her tracks and hushed the crowd.

Dava's scream continued unabated, rising in volume and tone. Her mouth opened impossibly wider, beyond what her small jaw should have allowed. The Roman soldiers held their spears at ready and took up defensive crouches.

From where she lay sprawled on the floor, Rhea could see Dava's feet lift off the floor as the small girl rose into the air until only the tip of her big toes touched the marble floor. Dava's eyes darkened and grew in size until the blackness filled her whole eye socket with a complete darkness that no longer reflected any light.

Her scream suddenly rose in pitch, and all the doors in the room slammed closed. Terrified guests tried to force the doors back open in vain. Dava's scream rose in pitch again, and Messalina's body bent completely backward, shattering her spine and leaving her suspended in an upside-down "U" shape. The golden breastplates worn by the Roman soldiers crumpled inward like discarded parchment crushing their chests and turning the circle into a ring of corpses.

Rhea stared into Messalina's face, suspended upside-down in front of her. The dying girl's lips trembled, and her lifeless eyes held an expression of shock; then, her limp body crashed to the floor and bent at an unnatural angle.

Valerius drew his short sword and charged at Dava, who slowly closed her mouth and stared at him intently with those coal-dark eyes. The centurion froze mid-stride, a look of strain crossing his face as he tried to will his limbs to move. Then the hand holding his sword began to slowly move towards his face. Valerius's eyes opened wide as he watched his hand slowly inch the swordpoint towards his face. Sweat poured from his brow, and he gritted his teeth as he tried to force the approaching sword away.

Valerius' let out a strangled cry as his hand, guided by Dava's will, pushed the sword threw his clenched teeth, tearing the skin and shattering bone as it buried itself in his throat with a gurgling thrust. The centurion fell dead at the Dacian girl's feet.

The crowd descended into a terrified mob, shoving and pushing each other desperately to escape the malevolent force unleashed in their midst. Rhea saw the aged Quintus Petillus and his wife lying motionless among other bodies crushed underfoot by the frantic mob.

Dava stood motionless except to raise her arms to shoulder level. As she did, the bodies of the dead men and women scattered around her began to twitch slightly at first and then more violently. Rhea watched in sheer terror as the bodies began to rise. Messalina, Dido, the Gauls, Valerius, and the Roman soldiers all rose like puppets on a string, moving in jerking twitching movements.

She saw Quintus Petillus, his left eye dangling from the socket of his partially crushed skull, suddenly pull down a woman in the crowd and tear into her with hands and teeth. His aged fingers dug into the woman's throat and tore free a mass of skin and cartilage. Shrieks of terror filled the room as those dead only moments before clawed and tore at the crowd.

Messalina dragged her broken body across the floor and grabbed the hem of a man's toga, tearing at his legs with her teeth. As Sedata and Ricina tore out a servant's innards, Gore splashed the murals. A man beat futilely at the breastplate of one of the Roman soldiers as he bit into his shoulder.

As the crowd succumbed to the onslaught, they, too, rose and began to attack the living. Rending and tearing former friends and family members. Rhea saw Consus pull the metallic disc from its mounting and batter it against the wall of undead that surged over him.

Flavia pushed a flailing Marcellus into the tearing arms of the crowd in a bid to buy herself a few more moments of life as they tore open his rib cage and disgorged his beating heart. A dark-skinned arm surged from the crowd and grasped Flavia's neck, pinning her to the mural of Trajan's victory. Flavia's eyes widened in terror as Dido shambled forward from the crowd and clamped her teeth on the Roman noblewoman's cheek. Dido bit off a chunk of flesh from the screaming woman's face and, in a frenzy of violence, tore at Flavia with her teeth until only a faceless corpse remained to slide down the blood-spattered wall.

Rhea watched the carnage unfolding in the room, unable to move or flee. Tears streamed down her face as she glimpsed the last of the pocket of the guests, trying to fend off the clawing hands and gnashing teeth. Her hand brushed something on the floor, and her fingers closed around it. In a last act of desperation, she thrust her arm up towards Dava.

Dava saw the red-haired woman sprawled on the floor beside her grab an object, and thrust her hand up towards her. Instinctively, Dava made the woman's arm snap back, shattering the forearm and twisting her head back at an angle that crushed vertebrae and broke her neck. As the woman crumpled lifelessly to the floor, her hand released the object, and the crow feather fluttered slowly to the ground.

As Dava bent to pick up the jet-black feather, a smile crossed her face, and she stroked its soft bristles. She trailed it against her cheek, delighting at the ticklish feeling. The doors to the room slowly opened, and the undead shambled out of the room, leaving bloodstained footprints across the white marble floor.

The small Dacian girl followed behind them, trailed by a red-haired corpse, its head at an unnatural angle, arm dangling uselessly, and leg dragging.

Cries and screams began to fill the night as they descended upon the doomed city of Mogontiacum.

BY THE LIGHT OF DAY

A calm, salty breeze blew off the Black Sea and rustled the trees. The brisk night air barely moved a single finely groomed blonde hair on Tomas' head as he walked around the hotel pool. Behind him, the lights of the ten-story luxury hotel blazed into the night; however, he sat in an area illuminated only by the green glow of the pool lights.

In the shadows, he could hear Bulgarian businessmen chatting with scantily clad women in hushed tones as they snorted cocaine and exchanged room keys. To his right, bikini-clad women frolicked in the pool, laughing and giggling as men hungrily watched them from the darkness. None of these things interested Tomas; he focused all his attention on the dark-haired man in the midnight blue button-down sipping a martini at one of the poolside tables. Twins, two hulking bald men in black suits and matching turtlenecks that seemed to strain to contain the sinews of their thick, muscular necks, flanked the man.

The twins watched Tomas with deep-set beady eyes as

he approached, taking in the expensive cut of his dark burgundy suit. He wondered what these men would have thought had they seen him in the days when he had dirt under his nails from working in the fields all day. However, that was long ago.

Tomas walked up to the table and gestured to a nearby white-clad waiter for a double espresso, and the without seeking permission, slid out the iron chair across from the man and sat down. In unison, the twins rose a little in their seats, tree-branch thick arms resting on the table as they emotionlessly prepared to pounce on the newcomer if necessary.

"Do I know you?" the man raised an eyebrow and casually took a sip from his martini, the skewered olive barely moving as the man drank.

"You acquire things Mr. Pistorius," Tomas was proud of how his practiced urban accent vanquished the harsher Bulgarian farm boy lilt he had grown up speaking. "I procure things for men who need to acquire something special."

"Special is hard to come by."

"Special is why I charge the fees that I do."

"Interesting, "the man crossed his legs and leaned back in the chair. The gesture appeared to make the twins visibly relax their posture a bit. "Do you know who I work for?"

"You work for the Bish...," Tomas began, but the man raised his hand dismissively, and Tomas bristled at making such a foolish faux pas.

"There's no need for names. A simple yes will suffice."

"Yes, I know who you work for." Tomas thanked the waiter as the man placed the small cup of espresso before him.

He could feel Pistorius' appraising gaze as he sipped the hot beverage. Tomas took his time tasting the bitter drink and then placed the ceramic mug back on the table to regain a little control of the conversation.

"What I have will be more to the liking of your employer," Tomas gestured dismissively towards the pool. "Then what the current availability offers."

Pistorius seemed to think on this for a moment. "You do understand that my employer purchases. He does not rent. There is no return."

"I am well aware of your employer's requirements."

"And how is that?" Pistorius' gaze turned hawkish. "How do you know so much about what is secret?"

"Because I am very good at what I do. Because all of my clients' value my...." Tomas paused as if searching for the correct phrase. "My discretion."

Pistorius nodded appreciatively, never taking his eyes from Tomas.

"Show me what you have."

Tomas reached into the inner pocket of his suit and slid an envelope into the middle of the table. One of the twins picked it up and handed it to Pistorius. He gave Tomas one last gaze before opening the envelope and glancing at the picture. Tomas smirked as Pistorius raised an eyebrow in surprise.

"Young. Pretty," Pistorius closed the envelope and handed it to one of the twins who secreted it inside his black jacket. "She is clean, I presume?"

"Yes, she has been tested."

"We will do our tests as well. My employer insists."

"But of course," Tomas took a long sip of expresso.

"Where is she from? Roma women are not acceptable."

"She comes from a small farming village. She is Bulgarian. Her people will not ask after her or look for her."

"Good. Good," Pistorius nodded thoughtfully. "The number in the envelope is the price?"

"Yes. It is non-negotiable."

"You understand that the price pays for her silence and yours."

"As I said," Tomas finished the espresso and put the cup down. "My clients trust and value my discretion."

"Let us hope for your sake that that trust is not misplaced."

"My number is in the envelope," Tomas stood up and deposited a large bill on the table, enough to cover the espresso and several rounds of drinks. "Have one of your people arrange payment and delivery location."

Pistorius nodded, and Tomas walked casually back toward the hotel. His gait implied a confident man without a care in the world, but internally Tomas felt his insides finally begin to unknot.

◆ ◆ ◆

Katerina stood alongside Tomas in the parking lot

and self-consciously ran a hand down her short, olive-colored dress to smooth out unseen wrinkles.

"Stop fidgeting; you look fine," Tomas was watching a pair of approaching headlights with quiet intensity.

"The dress is too short," Katerina felt goosebumps run down her thigh to her knee. "My legs are cold."

"It's fine. This is them," Tomas put a hand on her arm as the long dark limousine rolled to a halt in front of them.

Katerina looked at her reflection in the dark, opaque windows of the limo. Her blonde hair was cut short into a bob that she felt made her look even younger than her eighteen years. Tomas had told her they would like her better this way as he took the pictures of her. She wore little makeup, just some eyeliner to accentuate her dark eyes. Tomas had warned her that makeup would make her look older, which they did not want.

The rear passenger window of the limo rolled slowly downwards, and Pistorius leaned forward to glance up at them. His dark hair was slicked back, and he wore a blue suit and matching tie. He nodded up at Tomas and then looked Katerina up and down.

"You do good work, Tomas," Pistorius' face looked smug with the wicked smirk he bore. "If the rest of the deal goes as well, then we may be doing a lot of business in the future."

"I look forward to seeing you again, Mr. Pistorius," Tomas smiled down at the man and eased Katerina forward as one of the twins exited the front passenger seat and opened the rear door. The bald man gestured for Katerina to enter and placed a meaty hand on her arm. Katerina hesitated for a moment, but Tomas gave her a reassuring smile.

She stepped towards the limousine and bent over to peer inside. The backseat had two rows of seats that faced each other: Pistorius and a thin, bald be-speckled man with a satchel on the floor between his legs. The man had a pinched, unpleasant face, and his gray suit looked of a cheaper material than Pistorius' finery.

Katerina slid into the row of seats facing the men, and the door closed behind her. As the limo turned and sped out of the parking lot, she glanced a last look at Tomas as he watched them leave. His face was resolute but expressionless.

"Katerina," Pistorius inhaled as he lit a cigarette, exhaled a plume of smoke in her direction, and gestured to the man alongside him. "This is Doctor Radev; he is going to check you."

The bald doctor reached into the satchel and withdrew an electric thermometer. Katerina did not like how Radev put his hand on her leg as he leaned forward to swipe the thermometer across her forehead. Nevertheless, Tomas warned her about this part, and she knew it would worsen.

The doctor leaned back, looked at the reading, and then nodded to Pistorius.

"Good," Pistorius gave Katerina a lupine grin. "The doctor has one more test to perform, though this will be more...invasive. We need to make sure you are not carrying any diseases."

The doctor withdrew a long thin wooden handled Q-tip and indicated for her to open her mouth. Again, his hand slid onto her leg as he leaned forward and swabbed the inside of her cheek. The man stared intently at her as he ran the Q-tip end over her gums and cheek, but she could see Pistorius' eyes running up and down her body lasciviously.

The doctor withdrew the Q-Tip from her mouth, leaving her gums dry and cottony, and dipped it into a small vial. The clear solution in the vial turned a light pink as he swirled the Q-tip around.

"She is clean," the doctor again nodded to Pistorius before sealing the vial and returning everything to his satchel.

"What did Tomas tell you about this evening?" Pistorius' tone was cold and inquisitive.

"He just told me I would be spending time with an important and powerful man," Katerina infused her voice with a humility that was not commonplace for her.

"You will spend time with Bishop Grigori; he maintains a summer home in Golden Sands. The Black Sea air is good for his joints; he has arthritis."

"Arthritis," Katerina's eyes opened wide. "Is he a very old man?"

"No, he is barely older than me," Pistorius chuckled mirthlessly. "He fought many battles in his youth; the arthritis is just a symptom of the toll it took on his body."

"Is he a war hero?"

"In a manner of speaking," Pistorius took another long drag of his cigarette. "He is one of the Church's most successful vampire hunters in Bulgaria."

"Vampires?" Katerina let out a girlish laugh. "Now I know you're teasing me."

"It is no gest, girl," the doctor said harshly in a thick Bulgarian accent. "Bishop Grigori has scourged the land of vampires. He is a great man. You should feel honored to be here tonight."

"I'm sorry," Katerina cast her eyes down to her feet, staring at the red nail polish on her toes. "I meant no disrespect."

"Forgive Doctor Radev," Pistorius placed a warm hand on the exposed skin of her knee. "Those of us who work with the Bishop are very passionate about our work. You must understand when you work so close to true evil, the toll can be very heavy upon even great men. The strain the Lord's work requires of us magnifies even the basest desires and appetites."

"I...I think I understand," Katerina's voice sounded small and distant in her ears.

"Our work requires us to sacrifice a part of our humanity to carry out the mission God has called us to fulfill. In return, we require sacrifice from others to provide us relief from the constant storm of waging holy war."

Bedside him, the doctor was nodding his head emphatically. Katerina did not like the look of hunger and fanaticism in their eyes. They looked like lions watching a gazelle.

◆ ◆ ◆

When the limousine finally stopped, they all exited

into the circular driveway of a two-story mansion in a remote area north of Golden Sands, overlooking the crashing waves of the Black Sea. A full moon hung high in the sky and elongated their shadows to the peaks of the house. Pistorius and the doctor entered the house in front of her through an ornate wooden door carved with the likeness of innocent pudgy-faced cherubs. Behind her, the two bald twins stalked like lumbering giants.

The mansion's inside was immense, with high cathedral ceilings decorated with intricately painted Biblical scenes. Pictures of various Bulgarian saints hung on the walls, some she recognized from books she read as a child. A massive crystal chandelier that hung in the center of the ceiling lighted the room; Katerina gaped at its size. The chandelier was easily the size of a small car with hundreds of crystals that hung down like rain and reflected the light.

A winding staircase wound up to the second floor, and the high sheen of the polished wooden stairs, spindles, and banister reflected the chandelier's light. With a wave of his hand, Pistorius gestured for Katerina to head up the stairs.

"The bishop's study is the first door on the right."

The four men watched her walk to the staircase, the echoes of her footfalls the only sound in the house.

"Is there anyone else here?" She turned back to look at them.

"All the servants have been sent away for the night," Pistorius' lupine smile had returned, and Katerina felt disquieted by the feral stares of the others as she slowly walked up the long winding staircase. She watched as the men's gaze followed her as the stairway wound its way upward.

"You don't want to keep the bishop waiting," Pistorius made a move-along gesture with his hands to encourage her to increase her pace. "We'll be right here."

Katerina did not like how a malevolent smile crossed the twins' faces at Pistorius' words.

◆ ◆ ◆

At the top of the stairs was a thick wooden door of rich dark color. It was at least ten feet tall and bore a detailed carving of St Michael with his wings outstretched, plunging his sword into the Devil. Katerina had seen depictions of dragon-shaped Devils, but in this carving, the Devil bore the form of a horned man. She leaned her face closer and could see that the mouth of the Devil was open to reveal two large fangs.

She hesitated a moment before knocking on the door, then a creaking on the stairs caught her attention, and she turned. Pistorius and the others had stopped on the staircase and peered at her, a carnal hunger in their eyes. Katerina turned back and knocked twice on the door.

"Come in," the voice on the other side of the door was deep and calm.

She opened the door and slipped into the warmly lit room, glancing back one last time at the four men on the stairs before closing the door behind her. The space inside was a large study with three plush red antique Victorian-style couches around a sizeable fireplace. The thick blazing logs, each as long as a man's arm, crackled and burned, casting a warm glow throughout the room. Two windowed French doors led out to an expansive balcony; in the moonlight, she could make out the shape of a tall wooden structure. Bookcases lined the back wall of the study, filled with expensive-looking old tomes that covered the wall except for a wooden door with a golden doorknob that caught the light of the fireplace and reflected shards of light onto the high ceiling. Directly in front of the door was a large teakwood desk with sprawling tree limbs carved into the front.

A heavyset man sat at the desk in an expensive red robe with gold stitching. He ran a hand through his thinning dark hair and looked up from his reading as she entered. A wide, friendly smile crossed his face.

"My child, so good to see you," he opened one of the lower desk drawers and withdrew a bottle of wine and two glasses.

"Uh, hello, I'm Katerina."

"Of course you are; I am Bishop Grigori," he poured the deep red wine into both glasses. "Please come closer."

Katerina walked hesitantly towards the desk as he stood and picked up the glasses of wine, extending his hand with one for her.

"Thank you," she took the glass but looked away from his intense, appraising stare.

"You are such a pretty little thing," he raised his hand and brushed some of her blonde hair from her face. She flinched and stepped back. "Oh, there's no need for that; we're all friends here. Come try your wine."

She brought the glass up to her lips and then hesitated. He looked at her and chuckled, a deep rumbling sound, and sipped his wine. "I'll drink first; see nothing in it but wine."

Katerina smiled weakly at him and took a sip; the wine had a smooth berry flavor that she had to admit was excellent. She glanced at the desk and caught sight of the book the Bishop was reading, and the page was open to a detailed drawing of a mouth with elongated fangs. He noticed her eyes looking towards the book and cocked his head with mild interest.

"Is it true that you kill vampires?" Katerina returned her gaze to him.

"Oh yes," he beamed with pride and placed a hand on his ample belly. "I have hunted vampires since I was a parish priest in the countryside. They seemed to like Bulgaria for a time, and you know they'd love to take a sweet little thing like you and do terrible things to you before you died."

"It must be terrifying work," She opened her eyes wide in wonder. "Are they hard to kill?"

"Oh yes, they put up a terrible fight. You must fight past their claws and fangs to drive a stake into their black hearts. It is very dangerous work. Only through the light of our Lord and Savior do we prevail."

"It sounds like a horrible nightmare," Katerina shuddered and took another sip of the wine, which brought a smile to the Bishop's lips.

"It is for the good of humanity that we take on this burden," he ran a hand up her arm to her shoulder. "Blessed be those who bring us comfort."

Katerina took another step back and slid her shoulder away from his touch. He only smiled at her and took a deep drink of his wine, finishing the contents and then pouring himself another glass.

"Can I show you something?" the Bishop walked over to the French doors and beckoned her to follow.

She hesitated momentarily and followed him out the doors onto the moonlit balcony. The air was chill, and she could hear the lapping shores of the Black Sea. The balcony was square-shaped and large enough to accommodate at least thirty people comfortably. She could see now that the wooden structure was an inverted cross, perhaps ten feet high.

"If we are lucky enough to capture a vampire alive," Bishop Grigori gestured to the inverted cross. "We crucify them upside down in the late hours of the evening. When the first light of the Lord's sunrise strikes them, they hiss and burn. Their skin burns away, then their flesh until their bones turn to ash. Their screams are music to the Lord's ears."

"That must be a terrible way to die," a look of horror crossed Katerina's face.

The Bishop laughed heartily, "I certainly hope so."

"Why do you hate them so much?"

"Child, they are an abomination to God," a look of fervor filled the Bishop's eyes. "Even the young ones are spawns of Satan himself."

"Young ones?" She looked aghast. "You do this to children?"

"Girl, I have driven a stake through the heart of a

vampiress as its baby suckled at its chest and then threw the screaming whelp into the sunlight to burn like a dried leaf."

"That's monstrous! Where does it say in the Bible to do such things?"

"You speak of them as if they are people. They are the offspring of the Devil. That which is not of Christ is the enemy of Christ."

She shook her head in disbelief at the Bishop's cruelty and backed away from him.

"You blaspheme by questioning my methods," a sneer crossed his face as he stepped closer to her and grabbed her roughly by the arm. "I'm tired of these niceties."

"You're hurting me!" Katerina tried to wriggle free of his grip, dropping the glass of wine that shattered on the stone balcony, but his hands only closed tighter around her arm.

He threw his glass of wine to smash against the inverted cross and pulled her close to his face. "You don't know what pain is. Not yet."

The Bishop dragged her back into the study just as Pistorius and the others entered the room, closing the door behind them. They smiled wickedly as the Bishop pulled her across the room; her struggles to free herself from his grasp elicited malicious laughter from them.

"Get the door," the Bishop ordered, and one of the twins opened the door behind the desk.

Katerina banged into the desk, spilling the bottle of wine onto the books sprawled on the desktop. The Bishop cursed as the red liquid spilled over the priceless books, and he barked at the hulking twin to clean it up before the wine ruined the pages.

Bishop Grigori roughly tossed Katerina through the open door, causing her to stumble and sprawl on the cold tiled floor. He stepped into the room behind her and slammed the door closed. He was breathing heavily from the exertion and looked at her angrily as he locked the door.

Katerina realized this was the Bishop's bedroom, and a sizeable four-post bed faced four large, heavily curtained windows that looked out over the Black Sea. He saw her look towards the windows and smiled evilly.

"It's a straight drop down," he laughed.

"How can you do this? You're a bishop" She looked at him as he approached her.

"I can do this precisely because I am a bishop."

"It's a sin."

"Matthew 15:11, Not that which goeth into the mouth defileth a man," the Bishop stepped in front of her and dropped his robe, revealing the soft naked rolls of his body.

The Bishop leaned his head back and smiled as he felt her hands on his bare legs. His eyes opened wide, and he screamed as a sharp burning pain shot up his legs and roiled his insides. He staggered back and fell onto the bed as blood poured down his leg in long streaks. The Bishop's hand went to the wound and looked at Katerina in horror as he felt two round holes against his femoral artery, pumping out his lifeblood.

Katerina stood up and wiped her mouth as her eyes

blazed and blood dripped from her two fangs. The Bishop's screams became a strangled cry as he began to shiver and shake.

"Bishop, I remember the day you broke into my house and killed my family. You dragged their bodies outside to burn in the sun. You were just a village priest then."

The Bishop looked towards the door as a heavy banging began, but Katerina shrugged indifferently.

"You were the monster we all feared. All the children knew that Father Grigori could come and kill them in their sleep. I would be terrified to go to sleep at night. I had sleepless nights worrying that you would come to kill me, kill my family. And then you did."

The Bishop began to shake violently, eyes becoming bloodshot.

"That's the vampirism taking hold in your system," Katerina glanced toward the banging on the door as the frame began to crack and laughed. "What will your friends do when they find you like this? A vampire."

"We hunted you for a long time. All those young girls you made disappear and blamed on vampires were like breadcrumbs right to your door."

The Bishop reached toward the door as the frame gave way, and the door swung open with a crash.

"Help me," his voice was a harsh croak, and his body shook violently as a slow transformation process crept through his body.

"Hello, Kat," blood and gore spattered Tomas' face and suit as he strode through the broken doorway. In his hand, he dragged a bleeding Pistorius by the collar.

The man shook and spasmed as he, too, underwent his transformation into a vampire.

"My sister was Tomas' betrothed," Katerina smiled at Tomas, his fangs dripping with blood.

"Shall we get started?" Tomas sent the writhing Pistorius sprawling across the floor.

"Oh, yes." Katerina gave a feral grin.

◆ ◆ ◆

Gorgi arrived early at the Bishop's house, the cook was grateful for the previous night off, but he knew Bishop Grigori would expect his breakfast ready on time. The first rays of the morning sun were breaking over the Black Sea as he unlocked the door and stepped into the darkened house. That is when he heard the screaming begin.

"Bishop Grigori?" Gorgi called up the staircase as the screaming increased in volume and duration.

The cook, a veteran of the Bulgarian Army, began to run up the stairs as the shrill screams filled the house. He did not hesitate to run through the study's open door, stopping only when he saw the carnage inside.

The twins lay broken in the center of the room; their heads twisted at an odd angle. Their matching, unseeing eyes stared up at the ceiling. He gasped when he saw the body of Doctor Radev seated up against the wall, his throat torn out, and two long wooden Q-tips thrust deep into his eyes. Above his head, the word "unclean" was scrawled in blood.

The smell of burning flesh wafted in from the open

balcony doors and filled the room. Gorgi cautiously peered around the corner of the French door and recoiled in horror. Pistorius hung crucified upside down on the balcony, his body writhing as the skin of his face burned away, the flesh beneath glowing red like a hot coal.

Gorgi tugged on one of the curtains, putting all his strength into it until the thick wooden curtain rod snapped, and the thick fabric fell to the floor. Pistorius' screaming faded to a thrumming noise from his throat as the cook ran over and draped the body in the curtain, his hands feverishly beating at the curtain to extinguish the flames beneath.

Once he thought he got the fire out, Gorgi pulled the curtain off of Pistorius, and a puff of dark sooty ash exploded outward, Pistorius' body wholly incinerated.

The cook's mind struggled to comprehend what had happened in the house overnight when he heard a faint whimpering noise. He stopped and strained his ears to listen.

"Bishop Grigori?" the cook cautiously returned to the room, pausing every few steps to listen for the sound.

Stepping over one of the fallen twins, Gorgi was sure he heard the noise from the Bishop's bedroom.

"Bishop Grigori, I am coming," the cook leaped over the other twin and ran for Bishop's door.

The door hung broken, but there was some resistance when the cook tried to open it. Grigori lowered his shoulder and slammed into the hardwood door. The door gave way, and he burst into the room. Almost immediately, the screaming began.

The first thing he noticed was that someone had affixed rope from the inside of the door to the curtains; when the cook had burst through, the rope had torn down the curtains in the room, filling the space with the morning sun's light.

The Bishop lay naked on his bed, hands, and feet tied to the bed's four posts. As the rays of the risen sun struck his body, Bishop Grigori began to burn by the light of day.

ABOUT THE AUTHOR

Jack Finn

Jack Finn is a folk horror & fantasy author living in the wilds of the Pacific Northwest. He is a life long believer that the Tooth Fairy is proof that body parts can be traded for cold hard cash.

His previous novel, The Seven Deaths of Prince Vlad, provides an unexpected twist on the history and lore that gave rise to Bram Stoker's Dracula.

Jack can be found on Threads, Twitter, and Instagram @TheRealJackFinn

BOOKS BY THIS AUTHOR

The Seven Deaths Of Prince Vlad

"An unexpected twist on the history and lore that gave rise to Bram Stoker's Dracula."

Printed in Great Britain
by Amazon